Danger City has been ruled by the bloody iron fists of the Winters crime family for decades.

When the Summers family waged war on the Winters in an attempt to take their power, violence reigned with no mercy on both sides of the conflict. The Summerses were eventually defeated, and as a result Max Summers lost everything.

Sixteen years later, Max is a new man, no longer a gangster, just a simple primary school teacher still grieving the loss of his first love and trying his best to raise his children as a single father.

Then his old rival Sam Winters re-enters his life when their oldest sons meet at school and become best friends.

During their time apart, Sam continued on the path laid out for him, climbing the organisation's ranks, right to the top. He has become every inch the mighty and lethal crime boss he was born to be.

After their unplanned reunification, both men are forced to confront the nightmares of their joint past and the burgeoning desire developing between them.

Can Max allow himself to fall in love with anyone again, let alone the man who was once his greatest enemy?

SUIMMERS POWER

Danger City, Book One

BL Jones

A NineStar Press Publication
www.ninestarpress.com

Summers Power

First Edition, November 2024

ISBN: 978-1-64890-816-3

Also available in eBook, ISBN: 978-1-64890-815-6

CONTENT WARNING:

This book contains sexually explicit content, which may only be suitable for mature readers. Depictions of violence, torture, animal attack (recounted), and abuse of a child by a parent.

To everyone who took a second chance at love with the last person they expected to find it with.

Chapter One

I NEVER ASKED for this life.

In all honesty, if someone had told me when I was a child that one day I would be working as a primary school teacher, then I would have been horrified. I would have said my father—my *father*—wouldn't allow that to happen.

When I was a boy, I thought my father was the strongest, bravest, most important man in the world. I don't think that's particularly odd within itself; many sons look to their fathers.

It was just unfortunate for me that mine was a violent criminal. Worse, he was a violent criminal who failed to be the *best* violent criminal in Danger City. When he tried to take down the behemoth that is the Winters family, they ground out my father's rebellion like King Arthur and his knights ferociously beat down the Saxons.

I often used to wonder what would have been different if I'd just tried harder to fight my fate. At the time it had seemed inescapable. But now I look back on my choices and realise all the times when I could have been stronger, taken more control of my own life. I have to tell myself over and over again that I was young and scared, and I just wanted to please my father. To please him and survive him, a task many before me had failed to accomplish.

I've learned the hard way that people can do strange and terrible things out of desperation. I don't believe anyone who hasn't grown up as I did could understand what it's like to live a life surrounded by different doors, yet still know you'll only ever have the key to one of them.

My father trapped me with his choices, his mistakes. I felt like I couldn't be anyone other than who he wanted me to be. Of course, now I know that wasn't true. But hindsight is, as ever, mostly useless.

I've tried very hard not to trap my children in the same way. I want them to have every choice. I want them to feel free to be themselves, even if the world disagrees. I want them to fight back when someone tries to force them into a corner.

My son, Rory, started secondary school this year, and he's made some interesting new friends. A best friend in particular who has caused me a great deal of anxiety.

When Rory asked if he could go over to his new best friend's house after school on the last day of term before the Christmas holidays, I couldn't think of a reason to say no. Not that I would particularly want to. But the thought of facing the father of my son's new best mate is somewhat daunting.

When Rory first told me he'd made a friend named Elijah Winters, I was only mildly alarmed. I told myself that Danger is a large city. There could be plenty of people running around with that surname. It didn't mean anything. Elijah could very well not be *his* son.

But another part of me knew. As soon as Rory said that name. Part of me knew there was no chance he could be anyone else's son. I'd already accepted the fact, had let the sense of inevitability take over and the resignation sink in.

It made sense to me in a strange way that another one of the changes in my life had been invaded or influenced by Sam Winters.

I saw Sam at the school when I dropped Rory off last week. It was the first time I'd clapped eyes on the bastard in years.

It seemed mad to me that so much time had passed, yet I still felt a rush of defensive anger hit me when I looked at him. Sam always pissed me off simply by existing. I don't know how he does it, and I probably never will. Being angry at Sam felt easy, like slipping on an old, well-worn coat. I was genuinely tempted to start hating him all over again, on principle.

But then I remembered I'm supposed to be an adult, and adults aren't supposed to hate their childhood rivals.

Intellectually, I know I shouldn't still let him get to me. I should have moved beyond the point where he was capable of it. But it would be a lie to say I felt nothing at the sight of him. Something about him just sets me on edge, and always has. I can't explain it rationally. He *affects* me like no one else I've met in my life.

Growing up, my father worked for the Winters. Our families had been tied together for generations.

Then my father tried to take over, dragging me and my mother along with him. He started a war he was ill-equipped to finish.

The Winters family are the largest and most influential crime syndicate in Danger City, one of the most powerful in the whole of Europe. It seemed inevitable to me that they would win the war. They were just too strong. Too clever. Too bloody *vicious*. They are wolves, unscrupulous killers.

The Winters family holds a brutal dominance over Danger. Unlike other criminal organisations, theirs isn't just a well-maintained business. They don't deal, they rule.

Even standing there outside his son's school, doing nothing at all,

Sam all but vibrated with a kind of undeniable power. It was practically elemental.

Why my father ever thought he could take them on, I will never understand.

I was so lost after everything went down. My mother was dead. My father was in prison and would likely stay there for the rest of his life. I had everything taken away from me. Not just my money and my home and my dignity; they took my future.

It was decided when I was a teen that my crimes against the family showed me underserving of being part of the Winters organisation. They did the equivalent of banishing me, making sure I would never be allowed to become what I had been raised and groomed to be all my life.

I didn't feel shame over this. I know they wanted me to. They wanted me to feel sorry. And I was sorry. I was sorry I couldn't protect anything I cared about. I was sorry I'd hurt people under my father's instruction in a vain attempt to keep my family alive. I was sorry my mum died, in the process laying waste to all the sacrifices and moral concessions I made to save her.

But I would never be sorry for not turning my back on my family and joining the Winters's side. As far as I was concerned, they could all go jump off a cliff. I didn't give a shit about what was right or wrong. I don't think I ever really did. I don't think I even thought about it that much back then.

It wasn't about being a good or bad person for me. I did what I had to do to survive.

Some things simply are what they are, choices that can never be unmade. I've known that since I was a child, and it's one of the few absolutes I haven't let go of.

I was free to go after they stripped everything away. They just…told me to leave. To leave and not come back. Well, why would I?

What would be the point? I was nothing and no one. They ground out my existence in their world. Threw me out into another one I had no idea how to navigate.

I was alone. Alone and scared and so bloody tired. I thought about curling up in a corner somewhere and just waiting to die. But I'd survived the war and the police and the wrath of the Winters family.

Giving up after all that felt like a waste.

So, I kept moving. I lived on the streets of Danger for a few weeks, unable to quite bring myself to abandon the city that had always been my home. Living on the streets had been…sobering. More so than the war had been. You truly cannot know how cruel life can be until you have no family, no money, and no purpose.

I was saved when I got hit by a car, of all things. I know that doesn't sound like it could save a person. But being hit by that car saved me. Or, more accurately, the two people inside that car saved me.

Penny and Natalie Starr, a mother and daughter, were on their way home when they collided with me.

It was nine o'clock at night during mid-winter and I was wearing all black. Do the maths on that one.

They only caught the edge of my hip with their bumper, so it wasn't like I was going to die. I just flipped over and smacked my head on the pavement. No broken bones or internal bleeding. Just a potentially massive headache and possible concussion.

I remember the first time I saw her. Natalie, I mean. She was the daughter. Natalie Starr was twenty years old, short, with a mess of wild black hair, hazel eyes, a button nose, and lips that always seemed to be smiling even when she was unhappy. That hair of hers threw me off at first. It reminded me too much of someone else. I thought for a second I was having a nightmare. Only a handful of my nightmares ever included Sam Winters, but the few that did were always the most vivid. It was like even an imaginary version of Sam had to be something bloody special. I'm still a bit irrationally annoyed about that, to be honest.

Sometimes I imagine telling Sam about it. About how I would wake up from nightmares about him and be pissed off that he dared feel more real than anyone else in my subconscious. I wonder what Sam's response would be. Probably nothing polite or dignified. I'm not sure Sam knows how to be either. I would tell him about my nightmares, and he would say something very tactless and Sam-ish. For some reason, it amuses me to think of that scenario.

After a bit of blinking like a twit, I realised quite suddenly that the girl was nothing like Sam. She didn't look like a giant prat for a start. Natalie Starr didn't look like a prat at all. She looked kind. I found out later on that she was kind. And so was her mother.

Penny and Natalie Starr took me home with them. They lived above a café. Their café. The Starr Café. It was a business Penny had built herself, with the help of her daughter.

I was the first man in their lives since Natalie's father left.

Penny let me sleep in their spare room, and when I tried to leave in the morning, she forced me to sit at her table and eat breakfast. I was almost sick after a few bites of scrambled egg. It'd been a while since I'd eaten anything of real substance. Or eaten at all, in truth.

I didn't talk that morning. I thought it better not to. I was bound to say something rude or insensitive eventually. But Penny and Natalie made it hard to stay quiet. They talked to each other like two halves of a whole. I'd never seen two people more in sync. I hadn't even known it was possible to have such an open relationship with your parents.

I quickly learned, however, that Penny and Natalie were special. They treated me like a person. It had been a long time since anyone had done that. To them, I wasn't a criminal, the son of a crime boss, or a traitor. To them, I was just a nineteen-year-old boy without a home.

Penny told me, over toast, that I could stay in their guest bedroom and earn my keep by working in the café. She gave me the chance to refuse, to walk out, or just say no. It was an offer, not a demand.

I didn't leave. I slept in the guest room. I worked in the café, which was another learning curve all by itself. The barista part. Not the making tea part. I knew how to make tea. Penny may have disagreed, but that was neither here nor there.

Penny taught me how to work the till and bake cakes and use a dishwasher. She taught me how to do a lot of things.

Natalie taught me things too. Different kinds of things. Like how to talk to other humans without insulting them with every other word. She taught me when the right time was to be nice, to smile, to finally kiss someone for goodness' sake. That last one was my favourite.

I remember our first kiss, our second kiss, then all the kisses that came after it. I remember all the times she laughed when I said something stupid, and all the times when she called me out on being a complete prick. I remember the day, four years after we met, when I asked her to marry me. I remember when she pretended to say no and gave me a heart attack, then said she was just joking and of course, she'd marry me. Because Natalie had a cruel streak in her right down to the core. I remember our wedding day when it rained and we got soaked during the vows because it was the middle of summer, for bloody hell's sake, and we refused to leave the roofless gazebo we'd paid an arm and a leg for.

I remember going back to school when Penny told me I needed more in my life than the café. She said I needed something that was just mine, the same way Natalie had her other job as a singer at a very popular bar in town. So, I went back to school to figure out what I wanted. I got my teaching degree and eventually came to work at a primary school. For some reason, I have better social skills when dealing with children than I do with adults.

I remember the day my son was born. Penny cried. I cried. Rory cried. Natalie called us all wimps from her hospital bed. I remember my daughter being born. We named her Caitlyn, after my mother, but from day one she's been "Cat" to us. I remember Rory and Cat's first words, first steps, first days at primary school. I remember reading them bedtime stories, giving them timeouts, or at least trying to, baking them cakes on their birthday, and teaching them how to be people in the world.

I remember all the times Natalie and I fought and bickered and screamed at each other. I remember every time we made up and promised to love each other better. It wasn't easy, it was fucking hard most days, but it was worth it. I never doubted that for a single second.

I remember all the Christmases and birthdays and lazy Sundays with my family. I had a family. A family I'd found and created for myself. A family I would get to keep for the rest of my life. Except that wasn't true at all.

Because I also remember the day when the police knocked on my door and told me my wife had died in a car accident.

We'd come full circle.

One car accident to save my life, another one to destroy it.

But my life wasn't destroyed entirely, because I had Rory and Cat and Penny and The Starr Café and my job at the school. I still had too much to lose. I had to put Rory and Cat first.

So, I did what I always did; whatever it takes to survive.

That was five years ago now.

My wife died five years ago.

Penny worries I'm lonely. I tell her I'm not even though I think maybe I am, that I have no idea what I'm doing, or if I'll ever be able to love someone who isn't Natalie.

Chapter Two

WHEN SAM DROPS Rory off home, Penny is upstairs getting Cat ready for bed and I'm closing up the café.

He knocks on the door and waits for me to go let him in. Our eyes catch through the glass and I'm almost surprised to feel very little animosity coming from him. I was worried having to properly interact with Sam would make it impossible for us to ignore the toxic and volatile nature of our past relationship, but it seems time has done its job in dulling the mutual hatred we once felt for each other.

His eyes aren't any less intense than they were when he was a teenager. They're a very pale grey, although sometimes I could swear Sam's take on a metallic hue, closer to moonlight than the overcast sky colour shared by the rest of his family. He still looks like he's ready to fight off any number of rival gang members trying to make a name for themselves by going after a Winters heir.

I can appreciate the feeling, as even now I'm plagued by my distorted memories of the war, which occasionally still lead to panic attacks and restless nights spent fending off nightmares. If I'm being honest, it's gotten worse in the last five years since Natalie died. Grief compounding on top of grief, I suppose.

When I open the door, Rory runs in past Sam and almost barrels right into me. I catch hold of his arm and pull him into a sideways hug, which he readily accepts. Once we draw back Rory grins up at me and I'm struck for about the millionth time by just how much he looks like me. I know some children don't resemble their biological parents, but mine do.

My son has the same sharp features and dark-red hair as me, his having grown long enough now to be tied back with what he refers to as his "lucky" purple scrunchie, and I think he's going to smash past six feet at some point just like I did. He has his mother's kind hazel eyes though. I find it hard to look at him sometimes, which makes me feel like a monster.

Really, it's Cat who should remind me of Natalie. She's small for her age with beautiful dark hair and bow-shaped lips set in a constant pout. Penny is always going on about how similar Natalie looked at her age. Except Cat inherited my rare, amber-coloured eyes, as if in contrast to her brother.

I've always thought my children were beautiful. They got the best traits of Natalie and me. But I suppose most parents must feel the same way. Penny tells me I spoil them too much, which worries me a bit. I was spoiled as a child, at least in terms of material things, and I don't want to do the same with Rory and Cat. Although sometimes I feel like I've already failed them. Their mother is gone. I can't fill the place she left behind no matter how hard I try.

Rory pulls his arm free of my hand and darts around me, already chattering away at a rate of knots.

"Dad, can I have a cake? A chocolate one? Have you baked any muffins? Can I have one if you did?"

I run a tired hand through my hair and sigh. It's been a long day. But at least I'm off from work for the next few weeks for the Christmas holidays. That's one more good thing about being a teacher.

My hair probably looks a right state by now. I've been running my hands through it all day, getting stressed out by all kinds of rubbish. Not that I care much if my hair looks crap. I haven't cared about shit like that in years. Having children will do that to you.

"Go upstairs and get ready for bed without a fuss and maybe your grandma will let you have one of her muffins." I give my son a stern look. "And hey, no teasing your sister for her new haircut, all right?"

Cat nicked Penny's scissors from the kitchen and tried to give herself what she called "bangs", to match a hairstyle she'd found on Pinterest. It turned out about as terrible as you can imagine. Penny attempted to tidy it up and it looks better than it did, but I know my son. Rory won't hesitate to mock her. Little shit is merciless when he wants to be. Cat too, and in truth she's worse.

Rory makes a face but nods in reluctant agreement. Cat and Rory can be so sweet with each other sometimes, then in other moments, they behave more like arch enemies.

Rory makes to run off, but I stop him by saying, "Oi, Road Runner, say thank you and goodbye to Mr Winters." I stumble on the word "Mr" and I'm almost positive Sam catches it if the small smirk twisting his lips is anything to go by. "And take Balt upstairs with you."

Sam has stepped inside at this point and closed the front door behind him. He's dragged in Rory's backpack and the cage containing Baltazar, our pet budgie, and carefully places both on the floor.

I expected Sam to have brought his son, Elijah, but Sam appears to have come alone. Through Rory's non-stop chatter about his new best friend, I have been informed of Sam's situation.

Sam has three children: Elijah, Aiden, and Isabella. Aiden is the same age as Cat. Isabella is the baby at only three years old. Rory also told me Elijah's mother died shortly after giving birth to her daughter.

When I heard that I felt, for what must have been the first time, true sympathy for Sam. I never did when we were young. I always hated him too much to feel sorry for him. But I understand now, intimately, how it feels to lose your other half. I know how it feels to be left behind, stumbling around in the pitch black and not knowing what the hell to do with yourself.

I almost wanted to contact Sam, to give him my condolences. But that would have been strange. It's not like Sam and I are old mates. Plus, when Natalie died condolences meant shit to me. I hated them. And I hated people who thought they had a right to talk about her death like it was some tragic thing that happened to *me*. As if the majority of the loss was mine rather than hers and our children's.

Sam is watching me with those moonbeam eyes of his. He's sizing me up, which is fair. I'm doing the same to him after all.

Rory sighs like the most put-upon child in the entirety of the universe and turns to offer Sam a polite smile. "Thank you for having me over, Mr Winters."

"It was no trouble, Rory." Sam appears to be aiming that at both me and my son. Reassurance maybe? "You can visit any time."

Oh fuck, imagine that. I try to picture myself picking Rory up at Sam's house. Or even stranger, having one of Sam's children in my home to stay the night. After all this time, the concept of Sam and me being just vaguely polite acquaintances whose children are friends is still baffling to me.

Rory grins that much wider at Sam. He opens Balt's cage and the small blue-and-white budgie climbs slowly out to flap onto Rory's shoulder. Without any further hesitation, Rory bolts upstairs with his avian sidekick, in search of muffins.

He took Balt to school for some kind of animal appreciation day project all the children in his class were asked to do. Rory spent ages working on his presentation, saying the best one would be chosen for an official assembly next month.

I roll my eyes and make a snorting sound, which causes Sam to look at me again. It feels odd to be the focus of Sam's attention without the added anger and resentment that tainted our previous interactions. I realise suddenly that we haven't said a word to each other yet. So really it could all still go downhill from here, especially without my son around as a buffer.

I move towards the counter and away from Sam, in the hopes putting some distance between us will make this easier. Or at least not as weird.

I can feel his eyes on me though. I've always been able to feel him like that. It used to drive me batshit when we were teenagers. This once, I want to tell him to just stop looking at me. But that would sound unnecessarily hostile, and I don't want Sam to think I still hate him. Our sons are friends; I won't risk that for the sake of my comfort or pride.

For Rory's sake, instead of trying to get Sam to leave as soon as possible, I ask him, "Would you like some tea, Mr Winters?"

Sam makes a sound that is a cross between a snort and a laugh. "Come on, Max, you're not *really* gonna keep calling me Mr Winters, are you? I think we're a little past standing on ceremony with each other. You don't have to be polite."

He makes it sound mocking, like being dignified and civil is something embarrassing. Something meant for other types of people. Not our sort.

I turn on him then, drawing up my protective walls, just like I did back then. "Would you prefer if I was openly rude to you instead?" I snap, glaring at him. "Okay then, *Sam*. Would you like a bloody cup of tea, you massive *prat*?"

Sam surprises me by laughing. Not a short chuckle either, but a proper bout of laughter that lights up his whole face like a sparkler.

Those stupid eyes of his almost glow with amusement. It makes me want to kick him in the face, the same way I did years ago.

I remember what it sounded like to crack his cheekbone with my boot, and how I felt zero regret in the action. There's been so much violence tossed back and forth between us. A relationship built on cruel words, on split skin, and congealed blood and broken bones.

"That's more like it," Sam says approvingly. "And yeah, I'd like some tea, thanks."

I already regret asking about the tea at all. But it's too late now, so, heaving a great sigh, I go behind the counter to put the kettle on. I look up at a still-amused Sam. He's walking around a bit, which makes me nervous.

I gesture for him to take a seat on a stool in front of the counter. "Sit down before you hurt yourself. I don't want you tripping over your own feet and marking my nice clean floor."

Sam does as he's told without complaint, which is a bloody miracle within itself. As I go about making both of us a cup of tea, Sam gets himself comfortable on the stool. I watch him discreetly out of the corner of my eye.

He looks different. Older, yeah, but it's more than that. He's taller, for a start, and broader across the chest and shoulders. His face has changed too, like he's fully grown into his features. He has the beginnings of dark stubble, and his jaw is more angular than it used to be, stronger, less easy to break, which I would know since I broke it once.

"You look different," Sam comments when I bring over his cup of tea and place it in front of him. His thoughts mirror mine so accurately it makes me want to take a step away from him.

"I do?" I slip just the right amount of boredom into my tone. "Good to know you've been taking notes, Winters."

Sam gives me a droll look in response to the sarcasm. "Yeah, yeah. I just meant you don't look like the boy I knew."

I eye him thoughtfully. "Yes, well, people tend to change a bit when they stop being children and become adults. I've heard it's quite a regular occurrence among human beings. Your intelligence has clearly improved since our schooldays if you've noticed it as well." I make a show out of seeming very impressed. "Has Effia finally convinced you to learn to read or something?"

Effia is another person I grew up with and hated due to her friendship with Sam. She was annoyingly clever, always managing to make me feel like an idiot whenever we crossed paths.

Sam doesn't disappoint me with his reaction this time. "Oh, piss *off*!" he barks at me in obvious annoyance.

It feels good to still be able to get a rise out of Sam. Back in the day, nothing felt more important than ticking off Sam Winters as much as possible.

"So, how has life treated you since I left? Well, I'd imagine." I think Sam knows I really mean *since the war ended*, because his outraged expression becomes much darker. Harder. Dangerous, even. It's the expression of someone who actually fought in one of the bloodiest gang wars in this city's history.

Sam looks a lot more like the man who murdered three of my father's top lieutenants right now than the boy who I used to get into knuckle-splitting fights with behind the school bike sheds.

"My life is. Uh. Complicated," he mutters after a long, tension-filled pause.

"Thank you for that in-depth evaluation," I drawl with only half the spite I once might have injected into it.

Sam makes another irritated grunting noise, though he doesn't seem angry any more. Resigned, maybe, but not angry. He picks up his drink and takes a sip.

"Good tea." He gestures at me with the little white cup.

"I endeavour to please."

Sam appears amused by this but doesn't comment. He takes another few sips of tea, then asks in what sounds like genuine interest, "How about you? Rory's a good kid. Smart. Funny. Very outgoing. Will just about fainted when he found out Eli's new best friend was your son."

I almost make a scathing remark about Will, yet another bane of my existence when we were growing up. He's Sam's other best friend and brother-in-law. But I refrain, not wanting to get into an actual fight with Sam so early on in our reacquaintance.

"My life is also…well…you know. Complicated," I reply neutrally.

Sam hums in apparent understanding.

Did Rory tell Elijah about his mother? Would Elijah have told his father? I don't know the answer to either of those questions, but I imagine it would be yes and yes.

"I used to dream about you," I admit, unable to stop myself once the words crawl up my throat.

Sam locks eyes with me but he doesn't seem particularly surprised by the admission.

"I had dreams about you too, sometimes," he offers like we're exchanging truths.

I wonder what kind of dreams this man would have about me. Maybe his dreams are similar to mine. Twisted memories and shadowed nightmares, conjuring up the past and using it to unceasingly torment.

There's one nightmare I keep having recently, where we're back in that underground fighting pit one of Sam's many cousins ran. He might still, I don't know.

We were sixteen and flooded with pent-up animosity, knocking ten bells out of each other almost every week, not giving a single shit about the damage we might end up doing to each other in the long term.

Sam and I fought and fought, knuckles bared and bloody,

exchanging blows we were too pissed off to block properly.

Then Sam almost killed me. I goaded him one time too many about his dead parents. He hit me in the wrong place and at the wrong time and way too hard. It caused a brain haemorrhage. I was in the hospital for ages. They told me I was lucky to be alive, which I found absurdly funny at the time. All I could think about was how when we had our next fight I was going to annihilate Sam, no more holding back.

But there wasn't a next fight, because after that Sam and I were banned from getting in the ring together.

I've had countless nightmares about the fighting pit, the same incident playing over and over again. Each time Sam would hit me, and I'd go down like a plastic dummy, my head exploding with sensation as my body descended into a state of paralysis. I'll never forget the pain of it or the sense of helplessness I'd felt while lying on the ground, choking on blood and spit and bile.

I wanted to kill him when I got out of the hospital. When they told me we weren't allowed to fight again I wanted to kill him even more. It was galling, to allow Sam the win, not just that night, but forever, because there would be no rematch, no chance to prove I could beat him.

It was the only time I'd ever seriously supported my father's plot to take over from the Winters family because it would mean I'd have full permission to go after Sam like I wanted to.

There'd been enough hate inside me for Sam to do it, to kill the bastard with my own hands, forget a gun or a knife. Neither would have been personal enough.

Eventually the feeling passed, which I'm grateful for.

Having killed since then, I've learned the hard truth. There are some things you just can't take back.

"You made your choices," I intone, not even entirely sure what I mean by it. Sam seems to, which is just typical of him, to understand my own words better than I do myself.

His mouth presses into a thin line, expression sombre.

"And you made yours," he replies gravely.

Yes. We both had choices to make right from the start. But, after all the things we said and did, somehow the two of us ended up in a very similar situation. Life can be awful and funny like that, sometimes in equal measure.

"I hear you're expanding." I clear my throat pointedly. "Bought that waterfront property, yeah? Trying to move into more legit business?"

The majority of their criminally obtained revenue comes from the distribution of huge amounts of Class A and B drugs as well as the selling of black-market weapons by the ship load.

They own countless clubs, bars, and restaurants all over Danger City, most of which will be legitimate avenues for laundering illegal cash.

From Effia's brief mentions of Sam, I know he's heavily involved in the Winters's property development business. They have quite a few contracts with the city, having built the new Danger City shopping centre quite recently. Considering how much of Danger has to be rebuilt every time a supervillain vs superhero fight destroys the city, I'm sure Sam's pulling in some big-time money for the family.

Sam arches a dark eyebrow at me, maybe surprised I know anything about Winters family business. I like to keep my ear to the ground, for the sake of self-preservation. You never know when old scores will come back to haunt you. Some people went to prison because of me, and not all of them are out yet.

"Yeah. Something like that," he replies noncommittally, revealing nothing. He takes a breath, preparing himself. "I've only recently started work again. I took a step back for a while after my youngest was born." He doesn't mention his wife dying, although it's obvious that's what he really means.

Sam looks at me, a knowing glint in his eyes. So, Rory must have told Elijah about Natalie. Or maybe Rory told Sam himself while he was over at his house. I suppose I can't be annoyed about it. Not like my wife being dead is a secret or anything.

But even so, I tense up.

"You adjusting okay?" I ask Sam, not sure of how else to phrase the question.

Sam links his fingers together on the countertop and leans forward a bit. I force myself not to take a step away and keep my arms crossed on the counter.

"Which part? My job, raising three kids as a single father, or not being a husband any more?" Sam asks.

"Considering all three are linked, take your pick," I say, nonplussed by his directness, willing to meet it with my own.

I don't know why Sam and I are having this conversation. It's not like we owe each other an explanation. But I won't pretend I'm not curious.

Sam splays his hands out on the countertop as if surrendering to a private battle previously having been waged inside him. If that is actually the case, then I completely understand how it feels to lose an argument with yourself. You'd think that would be impossible, but no. Even when the only person you're fighting with is you, somehow you can still lose. Don't ask me how that works. There's probably some kind of deep psychological term for it written down in a book somewhere.

Effia will know. Natalie definitely would have. Natalie knew all kinds of random facts about abstract things. Whenever we went on a long drive, she would spout odd information at me for no discernible reason. I miss that. I miss a million things I'll never have again. I try to tell myself to be glad I had them at all.

But that feels like a lie. I'm still too angry to be grateful yet. And maybe five years is too long to hold on to resentment over my wife's death, but it doesn't *feel* too long. It doesn't feel like nearly long enough.

Sam puffs out a breath and looks me in the eye again. I don't know what his new thing with eye contact is about, but it's getting to be a bit unnerving. The last person I ever want to be seen by is Sam. He knows too much about my life without actually knowing me at all.

Truth is, I don't know Sam either. He's just the boy I once hated. Sam could be an entirely new man these days, and honestly, I wouldn't be able to tell the difference due to how little I knew him when we were young.

"Work is hard. Busy. Painful, sometimes. It's like I never left," Sam says, without inflection. His eyes seem to become brighter when he continues, "I love my children. They're more important to me than anything else. But trying to be everything they need sometimes feels impossible."

"It is impossible," I tell him because it's the one thing I can offer to this conversation that I know for a fact is true. I can't tell him it will get better with time, because grief doesn't give a shit about time. "But you can try. You can try and try and keep on trying until the day you die, and then maybe your children will never know all of the things that were taken from them. You'll know. You'll always know. But our job is to make sure our children don't suffer for it."

I've got Sam's attention again, and he's watching me like he thinks I might know what I'm talking about.

I can't *not* laugh.

Now Sam's looking at me like I've lost it.

"Why are you laughing?" he asks, clearly bewildered.

Through my laughter, I manage to get out, "Your face! God, I never thought there would come a day when we'd agree on anything."

Even if the thing we're agreeing on is the state of our grief, it's still a bit ridiculous.

Sam snorts, half in amusement, half something else. Something more angry and bitter than is probably warranted. "It's not like we ever used to sit around debating things."

True. Sam would have been hard-pressed to agree with me while I was punching him in the mouth or wielding my tongue like a particularly sharp blade.

"I don't suppose we can call what we used to do 'debating'," I muse.

"More like throwing insults and knocking seven bells out of each other every chance we got," Sam says.

I tap two fingers on the countertop. "Ah, yes, well, one does not debate with those of lesser intelligence, lest they degrade themselves by allowing their opinion the pretence of equal value."

For once in all the time we've known each other, Sam manages to pick up on the sarcastic edge to my tone. It's another one of those Christmas miracles. Either that or he really has gained some new brain cells in the last decade.

Sam cracks another smile, his voice holding an air of teasing when he says, "Oh, is that another one of your fake rules for gits and ponces? No debating with the rabble?"

"Sam, are you taking the piss out of the Snobs' code of honour?" I say as pompously as I can while turning my nose up at him in mock derision.

Sam makes one of those half-choked sounds of suppressed laughter. "Max, come on, would I ever do that? You know I have nothing but respect for the Elitist Snob Society."

I let a slow smirk spread across my lips. "I think you'll find it's the Elitist Snobby-Git Society of Pretention and Classism, Winters. And you would know that if you were raised properly."

Something dark passes over Sam's face then, like I've accidentally struck a nerve. It feels a bit strange to have not done it intentionally. Even stranger to feel like I should apologise for it.

"Look, Sam—" I let out a deep sigh, all traces of humour

disappearing as if they'd never been there. "I didn't mean... I wasn't trying to insult you or the way you were raised."

Sam studies me with an almost invasive intensity. His stare is piercing. I want to recoil from the look on his face. With a steady, powerful gaze like that he probably inspires the right amount of fear in his people, as well as his enemies.

I try to imagine it. Being on the opposing side to Sam, now, the man who defeated my father and took Danger City back with frightening ease and ferocity. It's bizarre enough to be comical. Or terrifyingly idiotic. How arrogant would anyone need to be to think they could win out against the man who was born to be the gangland king?

"Did you just sort of pre-emptively apologise to me?" Sam asks.

I can't get a read on his tone. He sounds...I don't know. Curious?

"No." I snort as if the idea is absurd. "Of course not. I just wanted to make sure you wouldn't get the wrong idea and have one of your fury fits."

Sam cocks a dark eyebrow at me. "Fury fits?"

I wave a hand in his direction and explain impatiently, "You know. That thing you do when you get really angry and blow up like the end of an ignited fuse."

"I do not have *fury fits*," Sam objects with a feckless amount of indignation.

"Yes, you ruddy well do. I was on the receiving end of quite a few of them. You have anger problems, Sam. Or at least, you did."

I think he probably still has anger issues. People don't change that much. Even if Sam is calmer now, I bet he still flies off the handle spectacularly if you push him past a certain point. Funnily enough, Sam's temper was the one thing I always liked about him. After all, it's no fun messing with someone who doesn't react in a satisfactory manner.

"Are you trying to start a fight with me?" he growls, already getting that *ready-to-rumble* look in his eyes. His hand even twitches like he wants to hit me and make things interesting.

A large part of me wants to rise to the bait. Sharing digs with Sam is and has always been somewhat exhilarating. Mostly because no matter what, Sam never backs down. He's like a stubborn bull who will not be moved by man nor beast nor common sense.

It must be exhausting to be him. I know it's exhausting to be me. My stubbornness is just as much a problem, if slightly less reckless.

"Good job proving me wrong," I say dryly. "It is clear to me now you have your anger completely under control."

"Do you always have to be such a prick?" Sam grits out with barely concealed hostility.

"Do you always have to make out like I'm the one with the problem?" I fire right back.

"You *are* the one with the problem. You're the one who started this," Sam practically snarls, mood already descending into chaos, his hand curling into a fist on the countertop. I don't think he'd hit me, not these days, but the threat is still there, so I react to it.

"Oh, wow, *you started it*? Fucking bullet-proof argument as always, Winters. Please, have mercy, my feeble mind cannot take the mastery of your sound logic and reasoning skills. Are you going to kick me in the shins, next?"

I'm reminded vividly of students who come running in during breaktime to cry about someone being mean to them. Then I have to go and have a talk with a six-year-old about how it's wrong to hurt or bully a person just because you don't like them. I still haven't quite let go of the irony of it being part of my job to explain things like that.

"If I thought it would get you to shut up for once, I might." Sam barks, which is so ridiculously stupid it surprises a laugh out of me.

Sam seems to realise how ridiculous it is a second after I do, then we're *both* laughing. It's not even funny. Except it is. It's painful too. It's funny and painful, in a way I don't think anyone apart from me and

Sam could understand.

When we've finally calmed down enough to speak, Sam breaks the tension. "Effia mentioned you the other day."

The world slows down around me.

"She did?" I ask tightly, unable to hide the irritation in my voice.

"Don't start." Sam raises a placating hand. "She didn't tell me anything about, well, anything. She just said that she'd been speaking to you. That's all."

Effia became a teacher, and by whatever chance, she ended up with a job at the same primary school as me.

We were awkwardly introduced by the headmaster and pretended we'd never met before, which in some ways is true. Effia and I didn't know each other, not really. We certainly didn't know the adults we'd become.

At the time I thought if Effia was determined to be civil and formal about it all, then I could accommodate her.

I'd convinced myself during the school day that we would be able to be politely distant at work and otherwise never interact. Effia had other ideas, never one to be easily cowed. That very same day she came knocking on my classroom door after school had let out. She looked only slightly less uncomfortable than I felt. I invited her in, reluctantly.

It was very awkward at first, but over time we built what could pass for a work friendship. Still somewhat formal, but no longer unbearably strained.

That changed again when Effia and I stayed late at school for a key stage one teacher meeting. I asked her to come over for dinner afterwards and she agreed with surprising ease.

She met my family and watched in what could only be described as rapt fascination as we interacted with one another. I imagine it must have been quite a shock to see me in such a domestic setting. She didn't comment on it, although I could tell she was dying to ask questions.

No, the real inquisition didn't come about until the second time she visited me. Although to be fair, that second time was more casually social, so I suppose that made the difference.

Sometimes I can't believe I've befriended Effia. Mostly, I can't believe she wants to be mates with *me*, after everything.

She gets along very well with Cat, the two of them sharing similar dispositions, and it's nice for my daughter to have another adult woman in her life other than Penny who she can turn to. I'm extremely grateful for it. For Effia's friendship in general, really.

As sad as it probably sounds, Effia is the first real friend I've made since my wife died. After Natalie's death, I couldn't find it in myself to want to be social with anyone.

Not that I was much of a social butterfly before, but still. There's introverted and then there's isolated. It's not the same.

Effia and I don't talk about Sam. We very purposefully skirt the topic whenever possible. She would tell me things about her life, and of course, she would mention Sam because he's still her very close friend, but we never openly discuss him.

I imagine Effia affords me the same respect the other way around. Even though I believe that, it still feels a bit odd to think of Effia mentioning me to him at all.

"All right," I concede, letting it go for now. "How is she?"

"I think you'd know better than me to be honest." Sam sighs. "She's been spending more time with you than me lately. Since I started back at work. We've both been busy."

"Isn't Will staying with you?" I ask, remembering a conversation Effia and I had only last week.

Sam grimaces a bit, then flashes me a wan smile that doesn't reach his eyes. "And there's also that."

I only know what Effia has told me, so it's not like I have the full picture. But from Effia's perspective, she and Will got married in their early twenties and everything was going well between them until they started trying to have children. After a few years of no success, they realised there might be a medical problem.

Effia and Will went to get themselves checked out. The doctors informed Effia there was a very low chance she would ever be able to conceive. Effia told me how devastated she was. But not, apparently, as devastated as Will. They looked into adoption and other such methods, but she said her marriage slowly fell apart and unravelled anyway.

Sometimes that happens. Marriage isn't the be-all and end-all of a relationship. There were plenty of times when I worried that Natalie and I would one day decide we had more problems than happiness in our marriage. I had hope though, and I'd been willing to fight for what we had, no matter what else happened. If she'd lived, I would have kept on fighting for Natalie until the day I died.

Effia and Will divorced three years ago. About a year after their divorce Will got his girlfriend—another woman I knew growing up called Charlotte—pregnant. They have twins.

Will and Charlotte are getting married on Christmas Eve and Will is staying with Sam in the week before the wedding.

I now know far more about Will's life than I ever wanted to. But Effia is my friend, and she's listened to me moan on and on about plenty of my own crap, so fair's fair.

"Do you support one above the other?" I ask Sam, finding myself genuinely interested.

Sam frowns in contemplation for a handful of seconds. "I never took sides, if that's what you mean," he replies steadily. "They're my oldest friends, but what happened between them was—*is*—their business."

True enough.

"Well, I'm biased—" I start, but Sam interrupts with a wry scoff.

"What? You? Max Summers. Biased? I don't believe it." Sarcasm practically drips from his mouth.

"Don't try and be clever," I admonish him scornfully. "It doesn't suit you. Stick with what you know."

Sam gives me an arch look. "And what do I know?"

"Blundering in headfirst without any sense of self-preservation at all," I reply without pause.

I expect Sam to get on his pissy bus again, but it seems he really has calmed down some. Either that or he's finally lost it. His laugh is self-deprecating. "Yeah, that sounds about right."

I huff out a breath. "Stop agreeing with me. It's creepy and wrong."

"Your face is creepy and wrong," Sam quips, still appearing far too amused for his own good.

"Oh, and here he is, Sam Winters"—I gesture at him with both hands—"master of insults. I bow down in the face of your rapier wit."

Sam, the prat, just smirks at me, pleased with himself. He opens his mouth to speak, probably to say something that will make me want to poke him in the eye, but just then Penny comes crashing through the back door which leads to our flat. She's already shouting at me before she even clocks Sam.

"Rory, I swear, if that bloody budgie poos on another one of my cushions, I will strip him of his feathers and use them for stuffing a new one!"

Penny comes striding over to me, dish towel in hand, and whacks me over the head with her weapon of choice. She turns her attention to Sam then and narrows her eyes suspiciously at him.

"Oo-er, who's this then? He's not another one of your old friends, is he?"

I feel a pin drop of satisfaction when Sam's eyes widen comically in reaction to Penny. She is quite a force of nature, very fierce. I was afraid of her a bit when I first moved in here. Well, to be honest, I'm still a bit afraid of her now. It's just common sense. Not that Sam would know anything about that.

Sam holds out his hand, presumably to shake Penny's. "I'm Sam, Elijah's dad. I was just dropping off Rory."

Penny eyes Sam like he's a potential miscreant, which is fun for me. She looks pointedly at the half-drunk cups of tea in front of us then up at me. I see a question on her face that I'm not sure how to answer.

"Yeah, I knew him when we were kids. We grew up together."

That's true, but to call us "old friends" would be entirely inaccurate. Fucking laughable.

Penny waves a hand in a broad, dismissive gesture and returns her gaze to Sam. She regards him with mild interest. I'm immediately concerned. I do not want Penny to take any kind of interest in Sam. He's already invaded enough of my life as it is. It's bad enough that one of his best mates declared herself my new BFF. For *reasons*.

Although I suppose it's not fair to tar Effia with the same brush as I do Sam. She's not his sidekick anymore. If anything, by all rights, Sam should have been Effia's sidekick for all those years. God knows he wouldn't have survived to adulthood without her.

"Isn't this the one who said he'd never be friends with a posh ginger twat when you first met?" Penny asks me without looking away from Sam.

Sam darts an incredulous scowl at me. "Bloody hell, Max, are you seriously still telling people about that?"

I sniff at him and cross my arms over my chest defensively, unable to help myself from snapping back, "Yes. I use it as an example to my children and my students about blatant and uncalled-for rudeness."

"All those years of experience and that's the example of rudeness you go for?" Sam asks sardonically.

"No. Not always. Sometimes I tell them about the time when you tried to kill me." This is a lie, but that's not the point.

Sam becomes immediately irate, much to my secret delight. "That wasn't me being rude, you tosser, that was me defending myself."

"It was you being a giant prat, as per usual."

"Only because you were being weird."

"You were the one *stalking* me!"

"Yeah." Sam is not apologetic in the slightest. "To find out what you were up to."

"Your detective skills were clearly top-notch. Only took you a whole bloody year to figure out that I was up to something and that you should just off me for the sake of it." I also know this is complete bollocks. Whatever else I might think about him, I don't believe Sam would kill someone just because he felt like it.

Sam gives me one of his ten intimidating glares. I'd be afraid of that look on his face if I wasn't so used to seeing it directed at me from our teenage years. I glare back at him with equal vehemence. I also add a bit of disdain to my expression. For old times' sake.

Mostly.

Penny clears her throat at a comical volume.

I force myself to look away from Sam. He shows no such restraint. I can still feel those twin pits of molten silver boring into me.

"Speaking of rudeness," Penny says, directing a stern glower at me, "are you planning on introducing me properly any time soon?"

"Sam," I say, gesturing between them, "this is Penny, my mother-in-law and current light of my life."

Penny whacks me again with her dishtowel of doom. I don't bother flinching away from her. A dishtowel blow to the head isn't so bad, all things considered.

Sam looks both surprised and pleased at the sight of me getting hit with a dishtowel. Penny, of course, notices this and reaches over the counter to whack him over the head. Sam sucks in a sharp breath and ducks.

Penny pokes me on the arm. *Viciously.* "Right, you, stop pouting."

Then she whips around and points at Sam. "And you, stop antagonising him." She huffs at both of us, "You're thirty-five years old, the pair of you. Act like it."

"Sorry," Sam mumbles like he really is a naughty schoolboy. He looks abashed and his cheeks are pink with embarrassment. Good.

I pretend to nod apologetically, but as soon as Penny looks the other way, I shoot a triumphant look at Sam. In return, Sam discreetly flips me off. Bloody tosser. So fucking immature.

I flip him off with both hands.

"I saw that, boys," Penny admonishes us as she takes our now cold cups of tea away from us. She ambles over to the sink to wash them up.

"Sorry, Penny," Sam and I say in unison.

Sam's eyes lock on to mine again, and we engage in yet another bizarre staring contest. It's those eyes of his. So intense and alive, speaking to the wildness that lies behind the refined veneer he presents to the wider world. Sam has always been so *alive*. Impossibly so, given all the things he's been through. No one should have the right to be as naturally magnetic as Sam is. He draws people simultaneously like a light in the dark and a siren song calling out across the waves. A promise of both hope and danger.

Penny clears her throat even louder this time and the connection breaks between me and Sam. He looks away, up at the clock on our wall. It's a blue clock in the shape of a star. Natalie and I bought it together not long after I arrived here.

I accidentally broke their old clock when I was painting the back wall. I panicked at first, thinking that surely Penny and Natalie would ask me to leave after I was so stupidly clumsy. What use could they possibly have for a boy who couldn't even paint a wall without fucking it up?

But Penny had just laughed and said she never liked that clock anyway. She said it was about time they got a new one.

Natalie took me into town to buy a clock. She let me pick it out. We went to get lunch together afterwards. Then we went to the park and sat by the pond. We fed the ducks, and Natalie told me the clock I'd broken was the only thing they had left that had belonged to her father. I'd been horrified when she said that and started apologising all over again. Natalie just smiled at me and asked if I believed in omens because she was pretty sure my breaking that particular clock meant something.

When I asked her what she thought it meant, Natalie said, "That the end of one thing can mean the beginning of another. Maybe even something you never expected or knew you wanted before."

"It's getting late," Sam says, bringing me slamming back into the present. He offers a tight smile. "I better get back. Will's watching the kids."

"All three of them?" I ask, grimacing in sympathy.

Sam doesn't seem fazed that I know he has three children. "Yeah. Elijah can mostly handle himself, and Aiden is the quiet sort. But Isy can be a handful, especially when she gets tired. Plus, if Aiden and Elijah decide to get into one of their rare but epic fights, then I might go home to find my house on fire."

My lips twitch at that. "I understand. Rory and Cat both have a penchant for explosive arguments when left to their own devices for too long."

I can't decide if it's ironic or not that both my children appear to be exceptionally strong-minded individuals, even at their young age. I was so much weaker as a child and as a teenager. I cowed to my father's wishes and my mother's harsh standards.

My children are outspoken and far more emotionally competent than I was. Possibly more than I am now. I'm very proud of them. For a lot of reasons. Mostly I'm proud because they are my children, and I love them more than I knew it was possible for me to love another human being. I was in love with Natalie, with all my heart and soul. But the love I have for my children is unique and unlike anything else I've ever felt in my life. I can't compare it to anything. It just is, unbending and absolute.

Sam and I share a look of commiseration. The path of parenthood is not, and will never be, for the faint of heart.

"Right, I'll…uh…I'll just be off then." Sam's voice holds a note of hesitation. I find myself equally as hesitant to say goodbye. I have no idea why either of us would feel that way. Maybe it's just because neither of us could ever resist a good fight. And no one has ever fought me like Sam used to.

I'm not sure what else to do, so I simply nod at him.

Sam doesn't leave. He just keeps looking at me. Searching my face. For what, I don't know. He seems to find it though, whatever it is, because he says, "Elijah asked me if he could see Rory again during the Christmas holidays. I told him I'd speak to you about it. I completely understand if you've already got plans, but just in case you don't." He shrugs. "One day we could take the kids somewhere? I promised Elijah and Aiden that I'd take them to the Aquarium next week. If you wanted to…" Sam leaves me to fill in the obvious blanks.

Go to an aquarium with Sam. With Sam and his children. Go to an aquarium with Sam, his children, *and* my children.

Sounds like a disaster waiting to happen.

"No, I don't have plans for next week. What day were you thinking?" I ask, against my *will*, I tell you.

Sam barely manages to hide his surprise at my easy acceptance. I take some satisfaction in that, although internally I'm calling myself an idiot for even entertaining this madness.

He recovers quickly. "Uh, Wednesday maybe?"

"Wednesday would be good."

I can feel Penny watching me discreetly. I'm not sure what she must be thinking right now. I don't even really know what I'm thinking, to be honest.

"Okay, so… Um. Can we meet you there?" Sam asks, still sounding tentative and unsure of himself.

I kind of want to smack him for it, even though I'm feeling just as confused.

"Yes. About ten o'clock?" I offer with more confidence than I actually have.

"Sounds good to me," he says with another one of his genuine smiles. Now I definitely want to smack him. He starts walking towards the door. "I'll meet you here at ten o'clock on Wednesday." He waves a hand at Penny. "Thank you for the tea, Penny, and the dishtowel smack."

"Anytime, Sam." Penny wiggles her chosen weapon at him. "For both the tea and the smack."

Sam laughs, loud and deep, as he walks out of the door.

I avoid looking at Penny at first. But Penny is a patient woman. Like a vulture waiting out a dying buffalo. Eventually, I can't take it any longer and I turn to look at her.

"What?" I ask, exasperated.

Penny arches an eyebrow at me and snorts, giving her head a small shake.

"I think you missed something out when you were telling me and Natalie about that boy, Max."

I play ignorant, mostly because I really don't know what I'm pretending not to understand.

"What would I have missed out? I told you all the things we did to each other."

Penny eyes me for another long moment, suspicion written across her face in a scrawl. I try not to react, afraid of what my subconscious behaviour might be telling her.

Eventually, she shrugs. "If you don't know, then I'm not gonna tell you. You can work it out for yourself, son."

I scrunch my nose up at her. "Work out what?"

Before Penny can respond, with something appropriately scathing I'm sure, a small voice intervenes and saves me.

"Daddy, can you tuck me in now?"

I turn around to see my hero, Cat, standing there in her green flannel pyjamas, holding one of her fantasy adventure books and hugging a teddy shaped like a kitten. She's had it since she was a baby. It was the first toy I ever bought her.

"Yeah, sweetheart, let's go."

I take the escape Cat has offered and rush to pick her up. Without looking back at Penny, I carry my daughter upstairs so I can tuck her into bed.

I try to push all thoughts of Sam from my head. It's the only way I'll hold on to the remaining strands of my sanity.

Besides, there are more important things. Like reading Cat a bedtime story and trying to make sure Rory doesn't stay up all night playing games on his computer. And washing the bird poo off Penny's favourite cushion before she notices and commits budgie murder.

Yeah, far more important things than Sam. Right.

Chapter Three

"YOU AND SAM are going on a playdate?" Effia asks for about the billionth time since I made the colossal mistake of telling her all about my conversation with Sam. To be fair, I thought Sam would probably mention it the next time they met up, so there seemed no point in keeping it a secret. I am regretting that assumption tenfold right now.

Effia has the same expression on her face that she's had since I first brought up the Wednesday aquarium visit, otherwise known as the next inevitable disaster of my adult life. I think if she were a little less dignified a person she'd be gaping at me like a guppy fish.

"It is not a *playdate*," I tell her with disdain. "Sam was simply asking on his son's behalf if Elijah and Rory could spend more time together. Since they were already planning on going to the aquarium, it made sense for us to meet there. On neutral ground."

Effia completely disregards my correction, shaking her head in bemusement as she murmurs, "I can't believe *Sam* asked *you* out on a playdate?"

Jesus Christ. Why did I think it was a good idea to talk to Effia about this while trapped at someone else's house on Christmas Eve and therefore unable to run away?

I should have said no when she cajoled me into coming with her to stay with our friend Jade for Christmas, but she seemed so excited by the idea of us all being together that I couldn't find it in myself to turn her down.

Christmas is a bit of a sensitive thing for Effia. After she divorced her childhood sweetheart Will Flint, Sam's *other* best friend, she found Christmas to be a rather awkward time of year. Previously she'd spent almost every holiday with the large Flint family, plus Sam and his lot. After the divorce, she was forced to come up with alternate plans.

For the first year, Effia tried spending Christmas with her parents, but that proved to be a very awkward affair due to her recent divorce and the fact she isn't as close with her parents as she once was. She has confided in me they never quite forgave her for remaining friends with Sam and Will after what happened to her brother, Nik. He fought in the war on the side of the Winters family and was killed by my father's people.

Her parents wanted Effia to cut ties with Sam, as well as Will, whose family has always been close allies of the Winters. But Effia refused and things have been strained between them ever since.

Effia's second Christmas after the divorce was spent with Sam, who managed to escape the clutches of his extended family for at least one day. Say what you like about Sam, and I've said plenty, but he seems to be a loyal friend. Sam took on both Will's wrath and his own family's so he could have one Christmas Day alone with just his children and his other best friend.

Effia almost resigned herself to having a very lonely Christmas last year, but luckily, or very weirdly depending on how you look at it, a newly arrived teacher at our school named Jade came to the rescue.

When she found out Effia would be alone for Christmas, she practically strong-armed her into coming to her seaside cottage for the holidays.

This year Jade invited my family to stay as well. I mostly agreed to it for two reasons, one because her oldest son, Kassian, is another one of Rory's friends from school, which means Rory gave me his best puppy eyes until I said yes. And two, because Penny thought it would be a good idea to celebrate Christmas somewhere other than our flat. I think she worries that holidays are depressing for me because they remind me painfully of Natalie. I wish I could explain to her that I don't need a holiday to make missing Natalie painful. It's always painful.

But sometimes the pain dulls to an ongoing ache that I can pretend I don't notice. I can act like I've gotten used to it. If growing up inside a mafia family taught me anything, it was how to hide emotions I'd rather not show. I can scream on the inside all I like, and still hold a polite conversation with someone. Surviving grief is a never-ending trick of misdirection, as well as a lesson in self-control.

"Sam did not ask me out on a date of any kind. Don't be ridiculous," I snap irritably at Effia.

Effia tilts her head to the side and regards me with discomforting thoughtfulness. One should always be wary when a clever person takes an interest in them. They might end up seeing more than you want them to.

"I hoped the two of you would be able to have a civilised conversation," she says reasonably, "as I believe you are both capable of such a feat—"

"Your confidence in our ability to behave like rational adults is very much appreciated, *friend*," I interrupt in a sarcastic drawl.

Effia goes on as if I hadn't spoken. She does that a lot. It's both very annoying and admittedly effective.

"—but I had no idea you'd end up attempting to become friends. I really didn't see that coming."

It takes me a second to absorb what she just accused me of. I sputter, "Sam and I are not trying to become friends, you lunatic! As I've already explained—"

Effia makes a dismissive hand gesture.

"Yeah, yeah, you're doing it for the children," she says in a decidedly amused tone of voice. "I heard you the first time. I know you and Sam aren't about to go out buying each other friendship bracelets any time soon."

Effia looks far too pleased with herself for working me up into such a flustered state. I narrow my eyes at her.

"Are you mocking me right now?"

"I'm always mocking you," she replies with a jocular tilt of her mouth. "That's why we're friends."

I can't even argue with that because it's true. Well. I suppose I could, and if it were Sam sitting next to me I might. But I've found arguing with Effia to be quite a fruitless endeavour in the past. She's so bloody clever and opinionated, which isn't necessarily a bad thing, of course. But it does make trying to win a debate with her rather difficult.

I sigh in exasperation and lean back on Jade's cool blue sofa. It's very comfortable. Jade's entire cottage is oddly comforting to look at. It's decorated in shades of blue and white, making me think of the ocean waiting just outside, the wash of sea water and foam on a cresting wave. There's a freshness to Jade's home I find soothing.

It's almost as if Jade's home is a clean slate representing the friendship I've built with both her and Effia. I find myself grateful for the reminder of how far we've come since Effia and I knew each other as teens.

Perhaps Penny was correct that I'd allowed myself to become isolated and lonely without even realising it. I could not drown in my grief over Natalie because my children needed me, but just keeping your head above water isn't really living.

It was Natalie who taught me what living felt like in the first place. I know, deep down in my bones, that Natalie would hate to see me alone and sad. She had so much life inside her. She emanated it from every point of her being. When Natalie was alive, I could absorb that aura of life into myself and pretend it belonged to me.

But now all that life is gone. It was taken away in an instant. And all I have left is what has always burned through my body and soul. My own life. Shredded and twisted and worn. I've forgotten how to use it.

Jade comes dancing, and I mean that literally, into the room like a very ungraceful ballerina. I used to find her personality quite jarring. She's the quirky sort, loud in her uniqueness, and completely unwilling to conform. I've come to respect her bolshy attitude and bizarre dress sense, even if I still don't understand it.

Sometimes I think I'll spend my whole life trying to unlearn the lessons my childhood built into me. The invisible rules and limitations of societal expectation are among them.

It takes a lot to be yourself even when people tell you they're insulted by it, like they think you're being different on purpose, just so you don't have to be whatever they are.

Jade gives us one of her patented faraway smiles and lowers herself down between me and Effia. She puts a bottle of wine and three glasses down in front of us on her white-wood coffee table.

All four children, mine and Jade's two boys, are already in bed. Penny is upstairs in her own room too, although she's probably taking the chance to read in peace and quiet. A rare enough opportunity.

Christmas Eve is the only time of year I've ever been able to get Cat and Rory to go to sleep early. They do this under the logic that the sooner they go to sleep, the faster it will be Christmas morning. Even if that doesn't work, threatening to call Santa usually does the trick. Well, not so much now they're older. The last time I tried it with Rory, the little shit laughed in my face. Then he patted my hand and said, "Sure,

Dad, whatever you say."

My son was humouring me about the existence of Santa Claus. I was more than a little bit tempted to buy a bag of coal just to see the look on Rory's face come Christmas morning. Penny reprimanded me for being petty with a ten-year-old child.

I was disappointed but took her point and removed the coal from our supermarket trolley.

Natalie probably would have done it. Her practical jokes were always on the extreme side.

I wonder what Sam would have thought. Considering what he used to get up to when he was a boy, I can't imagine he'd reject such an idea. Sam himself is a study in extremes. He could never do anything by half. Every fight, every game, every task given to him by his grandfather he committed to with unnerving dedication.

"There are fireflies dancing around your head, Max," Jade tells me in that airy way she has of saying bizarre things.

"I upset him by talking about his special outing with Sam this Wednesday," Effia offers, a teasing smile on her face.

I glare at her with the power of a thousand bastard suns. Effia doesn't seem at all affected.

A fire burns hot within Jade's white-brick fireplace. All the other lights in the house are off. Jade's living room opens out directly onto the beach. I can see the stars and the moon reflected in the ocean from here through the glass bay doors.

"Sam is the hurricane to your tornado," Jade informs me as if laying down a long-foretold prophecy. "Together you can create the perfect storm."

Oh yes, as if I need any more reason to think Wednesday will be nothing but chaos right from the start.

"You need a drink," Effia says, obviously clocking the look of panic on my face. She leans forward and fills our three glasses with Jade's wine. I take my glass from Effia when she holds it out to me.

"Sam is not my anything," I tell Jade, even though I know it will do no good. If arguing with Effia is difficult, then arguing with Jade is next to impossible. Mostly because halfway through she'll go off on a random tangent about fairies borrowing her mittens and hiding them, or something equally nonsensical.

"Summers, just drink your wine and calm down," Effia orders before taking a sip of her drink.

I shoot another narrow-eyed look at her. "This is the second time you've tried to get me drunk. I'm starting to suspect you may have an ulterior motive."

Effia rolls her eyes so hard I'm afraid she may have hurt herself.

"Yes, Max," she replies drolly, "you've seen through my master plan to get you drunk and have my way with you. I have in fact lured you here tonight in the hopes of tricking you and Jade into having the most awkward threesome ever in the history of the world."

I choke on a mouthful of wine and sputter helplessly, much to Effia's apparent satisfaction.

"Jade," I plead when I finally have control over my mouth and throat again, "protect me from Effia. She's clearly lost her mind." I wrinkle my nose in distaste and scoff, "*Threesome.*"

I don't object to threesomes in general. As a concept, I mean. But the idea of being part of one involving Effia and Jade is beyond ludicrous.

Jade doesn't appear at all bothered by any of this, which is typical. She's rarely shocked by anything, which is no small thing to say about a primary school teacher. Because yeah. We see some shit.

"That would certainly be uncomfortable, especially considering my disinterest in having sex with any man." Jade gives me an apologetic look, patting my leg as if in consolation. "Even one as handsome as our Max, here."

"Thanks, Jade," I reply, my tone lightly sardonic. "How about Effia though? She's the real stunner of our group."

It's true. In possession of a killer smile and long legs that seem to go on forever, as well as thick black curls and flawless dark-brown skin, Effia is a beautiful woman.

Jade lightly bumps her arms against Effia's and gives her a purposeful once-over. She nods approvingly. "A truly captivating individual, for sure."

Effia snorts out a laugh and gives Jade a more dazzling smile. Jade locks gazes with her and something unmistakable sparks between them. I have to hide a smile of my own, pressing my lips together so they won't catch me out and get all embarrassed.

I'm almost certain Effia and Jade are attracted to each other. As far as I know, they haven't done anything about it yet, but I'm anticipating that changing sometime soon. I hope so. They'd probably make each other happy, and Effia certainly deserves that. Jade too, after everything she went through a few years ago when her long-term girlfriend left her for someone else.

I was confused at first when I realised Effia was into Jade. As far as I knew Effia was straight. But to be fair, that was an assumption on my part.

When I was younger, I didn't give as much thought to my sexuality as I probably should have. Growing up, I knew I would one day get married to a woman and have a child. It was what my parents expected of me. After the war, when my life was turned upside down, I didn't care to think about love or sex in any capacity. Those thoughts felt too hopeful, and at the time I was a hopeless man.

Then I met Natalie and all of those hopes and half-formed dreams fell into place. She was my first in almost every way. There was never anyone else. Why would there be? Natalie was mine, and I was hers. We belonged to each other. It made *sense*, you know?

After Natalie died, my need for both romantic intimacy and sex died with her. I didn't think about anyone else. I didn't ever want to, at first.

Even now, I don't really know what I am. If I was asked to put a label on it, I'd struggle to do so with any real self-assurance.

I've heard Jade and Effia talk about all kinds of different ways to be attracted to someone either physically or emotionally. There are so many things you can be and a lot of them have names. It's sometimes intimidating to think about. I've done a lot of introspection over the years, but this is a topic I've actively avoided.

It didn't feel important enough to warrant too much time and attention. I was with Natalie, so it didn't matter, then I wasn't with her, and it still didn't matter for an entirely different reason. I admitted that to Effia once and she got angry with me for the first time since we reconnected. She became defensive about it, telling me sexuality is a personal thing and it doesn't only apply to whatever relationship you're in.

I understood what she meant, that you wouldn't suddenly stop or start being something just because you're dating someone of a particular gender. Being married to Will didn't make Effia straight, and if she started seeing Jade, she wouldn't suddenly become a lesbian. One experience doesn't invalidate the other.

But just because I know all that intellectually doesn't mean it helps me feel comfortable stapling on a label.

On the surface, it seems simple. I was attracted to Natalie, she was a woman, and I haven't ever been attracted to a man, therefore I'm straight. But the thing is, I've never been attracted to any other woman than Natalie either. So, what does that mean?

Maybe one day I'll meet another woman and boom, everything will make sense again like it did with Natalie. But maybe not. It could be a man. I don't see the future, I'm not a fucking psychic.

All I can say with certainty is the idea of being attracted to anyone else makes me feel untethered and afraid. Whether it's a man or a woman or someone of any other gender identity. It's the *another person* part which scares me.

I wonder for a moment how Sam feels about it. He married his first serious girlfriend almost as soon as they both left school. Has he tried dating since his wife died? Has he wanted to?

Jade and Effia must have been chatting along without me paying attention because I jump when Effia reaches over to smack my arm.

"Hey, earth to Max, did you hear what I just asked?"

I rub at my abused arm and grumble, "Did you ask if I wanted to be violently assaulted? Because my answer would have been *no*."

Effia scoffs at me. "I barely even touched you, you big baby."

"We'll see about that when I wake up tomorrow and there's a bruise on my arm," I mutter. "I'll have to tell the children I was viciously attacked by Santa for eating one of his biscuits."

In truth, I scoffed the entire plate of Santa's biscuits. Come at me, I guess, elf police.

Effia rolls her eyes again. She does that quite a lot around me.

"I asked if Sam mentioned he'd be stopping by tomorrow so I can give the children their Christmas presents."

Now that does get my attention.

"What?" I demand, my stupid voice going all high and shrill like it does when I'm thrown off balance by something.

Effia arches an eyebrow at me. "Yeah, he called me this morning before Will's, uh, wedding." She makes a face at the last word.

Even after three years, it's still a bit weird for Effia to talk about Will moving on with someone else. Personally, I think she's lucky to have escaped the tosser, but I never liked Will to begin with. The fact that he let Effia go is just further proof to me of how much of an idiot he is. I may not have thought that in the past, but after getting to know Effia on a personal level, I believe it wholeheartedly.

"Sam is coming here," I say, wanting confirmation. "Tomorrow. On Christmas Day."

Effia must note my distress because she tries to reassure me. "Yeah. He won't stay long though."

That is not comforting at all. Any time spent with Sam is too much time in my book. I never should have agreed to see him on Wednesday.

Jade places a comforting hand on my arm. Or at least I think it's supposed to be comforting. It can be hard to tell with Jade sometimes. She looks at me with surprising seriousness. "You and Sam share kindred energies. I'm sure they'll become cohesive if you both allow it."

I don't even know what that means, and it still dismays me.

Interlude

Sam

MY GRANDFATHER'S MANSION, the family stronghold, stands as tall and imposing as the man himself. It's one of the largest and finest buildings in England and sits on the outskirts of Danger City. For some in my family it represents a safe haven, a base of operations. For others, it is the perfect exemplifier of the Winters's wealth and station in this world.

It is neither of those things to me. To me, the family mansion is a symbol of the hellscape to which I will one day be damned.

I drive through the ornate metal gates onto the circular gravel drive and park up near the front entrance. I am one of the few with permission to park directly outside the mansion. Others of a lower standing within the family would need to park on the road and walk in.

There are ten cars in total parked up in the driveway, indicating a family meeting is about to take place involving all the most prominent members of the Winters family. I'm running late, a fact my grandfather is sure to berate me for, with one of his scathing looks if not a verbal lecture. He has been very clear in all the years since I was named his heir that he expects me to behave in a certain way. Men like us are not supposed to be capable of fallacy. We cannot afford to look weak to anyone, including our own people.

I take a moment before getting out of the car to check my appearance in the fold-down mirror, half unsure what I'll find. It was a manic rush to get out of the house today. Isabella had one of her bad mornings where she threw strop after strop about every single little thing from breakfast to brushing her teeth to what outfit she wanted to be negotiated into wearing.

My boys weren't much better, arguing over their cereal when it became evident there was only enough milk left for one bowl. In the end, I had to quell the fight by drinking the last of the milk myself and making them both eat their cereal dry. I do try my best to be a fair parent, but one thing I won't do is coddle them. I've seen what happens when you spoil children. They become entitled little brats, and I won't have that. My children have more privileges than most and they will be grateful for them, even it means they hate me for my hard-line tactics.

Upon seeing my reflection, I have to contain a wince. My dark hair is a right mess, the strands sticking up over the place like a particularly haphazard bird's nest. Grandfather will certainly not approve of that any more than my lateness.

I do my best to flatten out the mess, running my fingers through it and wishing for the hair gel Ashley used to insist on. I was never a fan of the slicked-back style. I thought it made me look like a shitty vampire, but Ashley was probably right that it looked more intimidating than my natural state of chaotic bedhead.

Once I'm sure my hair is as tamed as it's going to get without chemical aid, I get out of my car and head up to the main entrance of the mansion, brushing down my suit as I go. There's a chance it might have creases or stains from Isabella's breakfast antics, but I can't do anything about that now. It's bad enough having to wear a suit at all. I know I have to, for the sake of professionalism with my associates in the property development business if nothing else. You can't go to board meetings in jeans. I mean, you can, but people get judgy and start asking if you're okay, like jeans are a symptom of some kind of illness.

Not bothering to ring the ridiculously loud and audacious doorbell, I push my way inside. The hallway alone could probably house at least three families comfortably. Although I'm not sure anyone would be truly comfortable living in such a cold, dark space. Everything is either stone or hardwood. On the inside, the mansion looks more like a castle, which I'm certain is the point. It has incredibly high ceilings and painted glass windows as you'd see in a cathedral. Every window is framed by thick, royal-blue curtains and there are rugs of the same shade perfectly laid out across each partition of oak flooring.

As I move through the house, knowing the way by heart after all the years I spent traipsing these halls, my eyes run along familiar pictures and ornaments. No expense was spared on the art or any other decoration. Everything in this house speaks of wealth and high standing. It's oppressive and intimidating. I've thought so ever since I was a child.

My parents tried to put distance between themselves and this life. Until their deaths, I lived with them in a flat in the heart of Danger City. It was still a nice home, but it contained a warmth and effortless comfort that a mansion like my grandfather's could never hope to match.

The mansion is such a maze, like one of those houses in horror films with an endless number of doors, it takes me a handful of minutes to reach the room where my grandfather always holds meetings with the top brass of our family.

I take a couple of dozen heartbeats to breathe and compose myself before opening the door and going inside. Upon entering the superfluously grand chamber, it becomes clear my family has been waiting on me to arrive. A small collection of my aunts, uncles, and cousins sits at a long dark-wood table. Every single one of them turns their head to look at me in expectant silence.

Most of them know better than to react outwardly to my lateness. They respect the fact it isn't their place. My grandfather is the only one who can berate me for something like this.

The only exception is my uncle Paul. He has no concept of respect for anything, not hierarchy, not boundaries, not decency either. The man is a twisted bastard. The only reason he gets to be in these meetings is the fact he owns our most lucrative nightclub, Black Ice. It's where all our dealers go to meet and receive product for the street. If I could, I'd take that club away from Paul, take away his access to young men and the drugs he gets them hooked on to control them. Paul's brand of deviancy is one of the oldest. There have been men like him since time immemorial. If my grandfather would allow it, I'd skin the man alive and shunt his useless carcass into the nearest incinerator.

I wince inwardly at the expected scowl of disappointment from my grandfather, who sits at the head of the table in a large chair, the thing almost throne-like. A king presiding over his council.

"Good morning, Samuel," my grandfather intones, his use of my full name another indicator that he is displeased with me. "Glad you could make it. We were beginning to wonder if you'd been swallowed up by a black hole on your way here. I am so very glad to see such an event has not taken place."

I bite back any retort, knowing better than to spark off a real argument with my grandfather. You don't win arguments against Jacob Winters. If he can tell he's about to lose, he just stops having the argument without warning and you're left hanging and confused. It's an exceptional talent I've been unable to replicate.

My mind drifts to Max. It was beyond strange to see him after so many years, to speak with him like all that had passed between us was ancient history rather than events that took place less than two decades ago, events that irrevocably changed Max's life. Everything he was meant to be was wiped away by the war. He was forced to become something, some*one*, very different.

At least, different on the outside. From what I could tell, the old Max is still in there somewhere. As spiteful and maddening a man as he was a boy. It was oddly invigorating, perhaps even exciting, to be face to face with the ex-rival I once felt so much vitriol for.

In all honesty, there has not been a single person I've met in my life who has made me lose my shit as quickly or as disastrously as Max Summers did when we were teenagers. He was cruel back then. Cruel and unmistakably brilliant. He shone with a furious flame that threatened to burn and destroy all which surrounded him. He still does now, although the experiences of his life have forced him to temper that raging inferno to something more controllable. I can't help but imagine what it would be like to stoke that fire again, to watch it grow and eventually explode. I used to find great joy in watching Max Summers go off like a car bomb, reduced to a smoky heap of gnarled and molten metal.

Perhaps that's why I asked to see him again, because I want to witness all that glorious destruction once more.

My grandfather continues to stare me down from across the table, but I don't apologise for being late. Winters don't apologise. We make our choices, and we stick by them, no excuses, no apologies, no regrets. That was something my grandfather and I always agreed on, if nothing much else.

Without waiting for permission, or a release of tension, I go and take my place next to my grandfather, sitting at his right hand as I've done ever since I was twenty-one years old. Some in the family did not agree that I should shoot so high up in the Winters family hierarchy given my young age and lack of experience, but my grandfather insisted, and what my grandfather wants he gets, no exceptions.

"Well, now you've decided to grace us with your presence," he begins with no small amount of condemnation, "we can move on to our main point of discussion. There are going to be some big changes when the deal goes through, and we need to chart our way forward."

I beat back a scowl at this, unaware of any big moves or plans other than the usual. I take a quick look around the table. Some faces are blank, revealing nothing, while others appear eager or uncomfortable. Discourse is clearly present. Whatever it is has divided us already, which is rarely a good sign.

"What deal is that?" I ask, looking to my grandfather with low-level curiosity. It would be unwise to give any further opinion than that until I know all the facts.

There's a dramatic pause where my grandfather's gaze locks on to mine, the grey of his eyes like gunmetal, opaque and somehow vaguely hostile. He has a strange amount of intensity about him today. This plan of his seems to have relit a fire under him that had previously been dimming the closer he got to retirement. Hopefully, this means he isn't planning to abdicate the throne any time soon.

"We have been contacted," my grandfather begins, "by a woman named Lucille, half-sister of Titanus Bullet. She has taken over as the representative for his business ever since a faction of British intelligence took her brother into custody."

Titanus Bullet is an infamous arms dealer, probably one of the richest and most dangerous men in the world. He sells thousands of weapons all over the world, with seemingly no compunction on who he deals with, from rebels to terrorists to government sanctioned militias.

"And?" I ask lightly, careful to remain placid even as a pit forms inside my stomach at the thought of where this might be heading.

"Lucille has shown interest in establishing an arrangement with us to expand our own weapons trade from Europe to worldwide distribution," my grandfather explains with a truly discomforting amount of satisfaction, "including Africa and Asia."

It takes great effort to hide my immediate reaction. But then, before I can formulate an appropriate response, my grandfather goes on, pinning me with an expectant stare as he does so.

"I have told Lucille we would interested in discussing such an opportunity. You and I will be meeting with her after Christmas to discuss how we should proceed."

That feeling of dread in my stomach curdles into something closer to resignation.

Since a very young age I have known my destiny was to take over from my grandfather and become head of the family, to rule Danger City as its unofficial patriarch. The criminal underworld was to become my land to preside over, to protect and nurture as many of my bloodline have done before me.

It wasn't until the war between my family and the Summers I realised what that position would truly entail. I watched my grandfather make one horrifying decision after another. I watched him give out kill orders like sweets to children. Our people obeyed dutifully, as was expected. No one refused or spoke up in defence of the lives, innocent or not, wasted during the war. No. The Summers loyalists were slaughtered, along with anyone who got in the way. It was a bloodbath.

I was no stranger to violence. I'd experienced many different forms of it in my short life. The cruel hands of my Uncle Paul. The mad, flying fists of my rival, Max Summers. The crack of a crowbar slamming into the kneecaps of men my grandfather sent me after to teach them what it means when you betray the Winters family.

Violence did not scare me, nor did it make me feel squeamish. But the extent of blood spilled during our war with the Summers gave me pause. It forced me to reconsider my own thoughts and feelings surrounding such things.

I can't pinpoint the exact moment I realised a truth I had not allowed myself to consider before, that I did not want to become king. I did not want to be the heir everyone seemed determined I be. I began to crave the brand of freedom, probably the only one, forbidden to members of the Winters family. To have the choice to become whoever and whatever I wanted. It's a choice I'm determined to give my own children.

Of course, I did not share these thoughts with anyone barring Will Flint, my oldest friend and brother-in-law. Will grew up in the same circles, his family having been tied to mine for decades. I thought if anyone was going to understand my predicament, it was Will, who is an heir in his own right. His father was an enforcer for the Winters, much like his son is now.

My friend won't turn on me, I'm certain of that. But Will doesn't quite get what my problem is either. Unlike me, he is proud of his position, proud to be head of the Flint family now his father has passed him the torch. He was born and bred into this life and feels no hesitation over it.

In some ways, it was my connection to Will through my marriage to his sister Ashley that stopped me from ever trying to break free of familial ties. Three years after her death, I can tell my grandfather is gearing up to hand over the reins of the business and I have no way of refusing without causing a massive rift between me and the entire family.

That day will come, the day when I will have no choice but to stand my ground and betray everything I've ever known. But until then I will play nice. I will do what is asked of me to better our family. I will conduct my duty with thorough and direct attention, as I have done for over twenty years.

"This is exciting news, grandfather," I lie, putting on a look of sedate intrigue. It wouldn't do to seem overeager, as my grandfather is not an idiot and knows I have a certain distaste for things like this. "Thank you for including me in the negotiations. It will be a big step up if we can come to some agreement with Lucille."

My grandfather seems satisfied with my level response, neither too keen nor too reluctant. He nods at me, reaching out to clap my shoulder and give it a little shake. It's his way of showing affection, a thing he rarely bothers to do with anyone but me.

I know I should feel good about it, as many of my cousins would in my place, but I can't bring myself to feel anything other than trapped by his favouritism.

I think of Max again, of all the things we did to each other over the years, and of all the things that were done to us because of what our last names are.

I'm suddenly envious of my ex-rival in a way that feels all too familiar, although this time it's for completely different reasons.

Max might have lost everything to the war between our families, but he gained the one thing that has eluded me my entire life. The ability to become what nobody thought Max Summers capable of being. His own man.

Chapter Four

THE ENGLISH WEATHER is one long-running joke.

Despite the fact it's December, and Christmas Day to boot, the sun is stubbornly shining in a clear blue sky. Any minute now grey clouds could appear, and it might piss down with rain, hail, or even snow. And the bloody sun would still be there, giving us all the finger, shouting, "Fuck you and your holiday expectations, I'm staying."

On the plus side, it means the children are distracted by playing on the beach, which gives me and the other adults some time to relax.

Despite our warnings, the children woke up almost comically early. I tried to convince Cat and Rory to go back to bed, but they refused.

When they were very young, it was Natalie who always woke up first on Christmas Day. She would make toast and cut the pieces up into Christmas-themed shapes, like snowmen and reindeer. Natalie would cook bacon and eggs too, the smell waking up everyone else in the flat. We would all slowly drift into the kitchen to eat Christmas breakfast together.

It was Penny who always cooked Christmas dinner though. She'd let me and Natalie help, but the kitchen was Penny's domain, and we all respected that. Even today, Penny somehow managed to take over Jade's kitchen and cooked us a massive feast that would have been more suited to feed an entire army. Jade is going to have leftovers in her fridge all the way until next Christmas.

Everyone else is outside on the beach when Sam and his children arrive. I only came in to grab a few cans of cola for the adults currently lounging on the sand, watching four children run around screaming and splashing each other with seawater. It's mid-afternoon now. We've already had dinner and completed the hectic present-opening portion of Christmas Day. Rory and Cat both seem happy with their presents. Rory was especially ecstatic about his new tablet. Figures my son would fall in love with technology even though I hate the ruddy stuff.

Cat was the most exuberant about her new ridiculously expensive football boots and sports bag. I'm certain the bag will get a lot of use, since Cat is in several sports clubs, including football, netball, hockey, swimming, and kickboxing.

She's competitive as hell. When I left the beach, she was challenging Jade's youngest son, Xavier, to another race from one side of the beach to the other. She can be a bit of a bully too, which is something I've been trying to keep an eye on.

Elijah and another boy come charging in through the front door one after the other just as I'm walking out of the kitchen and into the entry-way, putting myself directly in their path.

Elijah manages to dodge me at the last minute, swerving around and carrying on. His companion is less agile in his attempt to divert a collision, knocking right into me with considerable force and almost falling over. Used to dealing with children crashing around, I'm able to catch him in time, keeping the boy upright by grasping his arms. Once I'm certain he's steady on his feet I pull back.

"Sorry," he murmurs to me, his gaze averted to his shoes, forehead hidden by a long swath of fringe.

I'm almost taken aback when I get a proper look at him. For a single terrifying moment, I feel as if I've been thrown back in time twenty-four years because standing in front of me is the replica of a young Sam Winters. There could be absolutely no doubt as to who fathered this boy. With his grey eyes, impossibly messy dark hair, and resolutely sullen expression, Aiden is his father's son through and through.

I flicker a glance over at Elijah. He's bouncing on the spot like an overly excited gerbil. Elijah still looks like Sam, but there are definite signs of his mother's blood. In fact, he looks exactly like a combination of Winters and Flint DNA, which is what he is. Ashley, Sam's wife, was Will's sister.

Blond hair, dimpled cheeks, and soft brown eyes, all of it is pure Flint. But he has Sam's nose, the beginnings of his strong jawline, and that fierceness in his gaze I've never seen in anyone other than Sam.

"Are you both all right?" I ask, concerned they appear to be alone when no one follows them into the house. "Where's your father?" I glance over Aiden's head, outside at the empty front path.

"Dad's still in the car. He had to talk to Uncle Will on the phone about something first, so he sent us over," Elijah tells me, still bouncing like he has too much energy in his body and has to constantly move around to expel it, so he won't explode.

Rory can get like that sometimes, although he usually needs to eat a lot of sweets first. Cat is my more energetic child, and I swear she'll be some kind of sports star one day. She has the determination for it, as well as the natural talent.

I kneel in front of a worryingly quiet Aiden to speak on a level with him.

"Hey, Aiden, isn't it? My name's Max. I'm a friend of your aunt Effia. Are you all right?"

Aiden gives a shy nod, eyes still downcast. He bites his lower lip nervously and darts a discreet glance at his older brother, like he's going to be in trouble if he provides any other response.

After all these years working at a primary school, I've learned to notice what a child is feeling and take note of their reactions to certain things. That knowledge can come in very handy when I'm interacting with them or their parents.

Tell you what I hate. Parents' evening. I hate all other parents. Seriously, if you're a parent, then I hate you and the high horse you rode in on. Parents are a pain in my arse.

"Elijah, you can hit the beach if you want. Rory's out there with Kassian." I turn my head to look at Elijah.

"Thanks, Mr Summers," he says, before dashing off outside in search of his mates.

I'm hoping that with Elijah gone, Aiden will feel less reticent about talking to me.

"Aiden, do you want to go outside too?" I ask him.

Aiden seems to consider this for a matter of seconds before shaking his head. He doesn't speak.

I try my best not to frown, plastering a gentle smile on my face instead. "Okay. How about a Christmas biscuit? We have some in the kitchen." I gesture towards Jade's now Christmas-food-packed kitchen.

This time I get a bit more interest from Aiden. He looks directly at me for a start, instead of at his shoes. I take that as a good sign and stand up, already moving towards the kitchen. After an unsure look back at the front door, Aiden follows.

A small, distressed frown creases his face, causing a bad feeling to twinge inside my chest.

Jade's kitchen is rather large and decorated in a mix of blues and white, much like the rest of the house. It has granite worktops, a fancy oven, and a big island smack dab in the middle of it. The strange thing is, I don't think Jade does much cooking. She says she's too busy to ever get a lot of use out of it. I think Penny would move into Jade's house just to have access to this kitchen.

I get out the tin of pre-made Christmas biscuits from one of the spacious cupboards. We baked them yesterday, with the children icing them once they'd cooled.

I sit up on one of the kitchen stools and pull another one out for Aiden. He eyes the offered stool warily, as if it may bite him. I tell myself not to get impatient and prod him to sit.

Aiden just looks so much like Sam that it's very close to being genuinely disconcerting.

I wait until Aiden finally decides to trust the stool of unbidden doom. He climbs up onto it and sits beside me. I open the tin and we both take out a biscuit each. Mine is in the shape of a Santa hat. Aiden has one shaped like an angel. We sit together in silence and munch on our biscuits. I'd like to say the silence between us is uncomfortable, but for some unknown reason, it isn't really.

To my surprise, it's Aiden who speaks first.

"Dad and my uncle were yelling. I heard them before I left."

Oh, fuck me, no. Bloody hell, no. This is not my business at all. Damn Sam for sending his children on ahead and ruining my perfectly acceptable, calm frame of mind.

Aiden is staring down at his half-eaten biscuit. It looks like he's been gnawing on it. Poor angel has no head and only one wing.

I clear my throat, mostly trying to buy myself more time to come up with an acceptable response. I think about what I would say to my own children.

"Adults yell sometimes, Aiden. It's nothing for you to worry about."

Aiden frowns again at this. His tone is a bit firmer this time when he says, "Dad was upset because Aunt Charlotte and Uncle Will tried to set Dad up with someone at their wedding."

Okay, now this is really, really not my business.

I'm not sure if Aiden is just worried because his dad got upset, or if it's the idea of Sam dating someone else at all.

Ah, fuck it.

"I know your dad well enough to be sure he won't ever do something unless he wants to."

Aiden smiles tentatively up at me, which I count as a small victory.

"You really think so?" He sounds eager to be reassured.

I nod emphatically. "Your dad is the most stubborn man I've ever met." Maybe the strongest too, a belief I will not be sharing with Sam for as long as I live. "I think he can do just about anything," I add more quietly, which is another thing I'll never be admitting to Sam this side of the grave.

Aiden smiles a bit wider at me, showing teeth this time. I even see evidence of a recently lost tooth. I find myself smiling back at him.

Just then I hear the front door closing and heavy feet moving through the house. Sam appears in the kitchen doorway a few seconds later. He's holding a small dark-haired girl in his arms. I presume her to be Isabella, Sam's youngest child.

Sam looks, in two words, thunderously angry. I'd go as far as to say *pissed the fuck off.*

I feel a sudden wave of protectiveness towards Aiden, which makes no sense. Aiden is Sam's son, not mine. Even so, I edge closer to the little boy. Aiden surprises me again by reciprocating my action and moving closer to me as well. He grabs hold of my shirt sleeve in a tight fist.

I offer the biscuit tin to Sam and shake it around a bit. "Biscuit, Mr Grumpy?"

Sam's eyes blaze with abject fury. It makes my chest tighten and my body light up with an unknown heat, especially when he shifts his gaze to settle solely on me. He looks more like his teenage self, reminding me of how twisted up he used to make me feel.

"Biscuit!" little Isabella Winters enthuses. She leans forward in Sam's grasp, arms stretched out in front of her, and makes "gimme-gimme" hand gestures at the biscuit tin.

Sam's anger dampens by a few degrees, some of the fire going out of his expression. He seems to finally take note of his son clinging to me, Aiden's other hand clenched around a soggy half-chewed biscuit angel.

Sam sighs heavily and makes his way towards us. "Go on then, hand over the biscuits."

Chapter Five

IF JADE WAS ever somehow magically transformed into a Christmas tree, then I know exactly what it would look like. Jade's tree is orange. Fucking orange. I didn't even know you could get them in that colour.

The tree ornaments and decorations are somehow even odder. Instead of baubles and tinsel and lights, mini torches are attached to the edge of each branch. Baubles have been replaced by random household items such as toothbrushes, keys, small toys, pens, and pencils, and at the very top, instead of a star or angel, there is a stuffed panda teddy. In place of tinsel, sparkly scarves are wrapped around the tree.

Cat and Xavier loved it. Effia just smiled in bemusement when she saw the weirdest bloody Christmas tree in existence sitting in our friend's living room. I'm guessing she wasn't in the mood to put up a fight about it. I thought about protesting myself, but it was neither my tree nor my house, so I decided to just let it go.

I think about all this as a way of distracting myself from Sam and his annoyingly overwhelming presence. He keeps making things worse by darting glances over at me every few seconds.

Surprisingly, no one from outside has come in yet. I thought Elijah's arrival on the beach would have prompted Effia to come inside to greet Sam, but apparently not. Unless Elijah told Effia his father hadn't arrived yet. In which case Effia could be waiting for all of us to go out onto the beach together.

Aiden is still chewing on his soggy biscuit. He looks more content now his dad is in the room and is no longer visibly upset. That is somewhat mollifying. Sam smiles brightly at his second-born son and reaches over to ruffle his hair, pushing it into further disarray. Aiden smiles back at his dad, previous worries seemingly forgotten.

Isabella has her own biscuit and is jovially nibbling and drooling all over it. I notice that she needs a tissue for her nose and get up to retrieve one.

When I can't find any tissues, I tear off a paper towel to use instead. Sam raises an eyebrow at me when I move towards him with a piece of towel in my hand.

I give him a sardonic look. "Don't panic, this isn't for you. I'm hardly going to smother you with a paper towel, am I? Put those fighting reflexes on the back burner for a minute and let me wipe your daughter's nose." *Before she gets snot on your T-shirt*, I don't add.

Sam isn't dressed in his typical outfit of choice, a perfectly cut suit. Instead, he's wearing more casual clothes. Dark, well-worn jeans, a fitted white T-shirt, a black leather jacket, and hard motorcycle boots.

"I didn't think you were going to smother me with it." Sam's mouth ticks upwards. "I figured you'd ball it up and throw it at my eye if anything."

"Yes, well, not all of my decisions revolve around injuring you, as tempting as that thought may be."

Sam laughs at that and shifts Isabella around so I can reach her properly. Isabella eyes me like I'm some new species of adult who might be about to take away her precious biscuit. She tightens her hold on the half-demolished snowman and watches me with open suspicion. I hold up the makeshift tissue in front of her face.

"Don't look at me like that, little miss. I promise not to steal your treat." Isabella relaxes a bit at that. Although her eyes widen again when I wrap the folded paper towel around her nose. I bite down on a smile and instruct her to, "Blow, please." Just like I did with my children when they were her age.

Isabella gives me a look that is one hundred percent Sam. It clearly states what she thinks of being told what to do. I wonder for a moment if she'll refuse just because, but Sam saves the day by saying in a coaxing voice, "Go on, Isy, blow into the tissue. Like a trumpet." He blows out through his nose and makes what I think is supposed to be a trumpet sound with his mouth.

Isabella giggles at this, which makes it a bit difficult to keep hold of her nose. But she does as she's told and blows hard into the paper towel. I pull it away afterwards and use the non-snotty side to wipe off the rest from her face.

I go to throw the paper towel in the bin.

"She's had a bit of a cold since last week," Sam tells me. "I picked up some medicine for it, but she hates the stuff. I can't say I blame her; it smells foul."

"Most things that are good for you smell and taste horrid," I say, coming back to sit next to Aiden again. Aiden is watching Sam and me with concerningly intelligent eyes. His biscuit is soggier than ever and now three-quarters of the way gone. My own biscuit has been left abandoned on the countertop with only a few bites taken out of it.

"Have you tried Calpol?" I ask. "That can help, and it's quite sweet tasting. When he was younger Rory used to pretend to be ill just so he could have a spoonful of it."

Sam arches an eyebrow at me, looking thoroughly amused again.

His earlier anger seems to have melted away completely. Either that or Sam's gotten better at hiding his emotions.

No, nope, nah, I refuse to believe that. Sam Winters is bad enough without the ability to feel more than one thing at a time. He is a blunt, hot-headed, tactless nightmare, and that's the way he should always be.

"Max Summers, are you actually trying to be nice and give me parenting advice?" Sam teases, a glint of challenge in his eye. I don't think he can talk to me without making it a competition of some sort. I know I can't talk to him without doing the same thing.

I go right for the kill shot, because evidence of my father's training is still sometimes automatic.

My family is a lot of things, but nice isn't one of them.

"You remember what happened the last time a Winters trusted a Summers," I say, looking at Sam meaningfully.

My father betrayed Sam's family countless times before he tried to take them down out in the open. It was my father who caused the death of Sam's parents, a fact that wasn't uncovered until years after it happened.

Even so, when it came time to decide my fate, Sam spoke up in my defence. He tried to help me even though I could tell he didn't want to.

So many people died during the Winters-Summers war, especially near the end. There were only a few people left to punish, and the Winters family wanted blood.

Maybe I hated him in that moment. More than I ever had before. When he stood in front of his family and tried to *defend* me. I don't remember some of what I felt in those days. I spend most of my life trying to pretend those days never existed, that the person I was before I met Natalie never existed.

I like to think meeting Natalie changed me into someone new. Someone better, even. Not that the bar was all that high to begin with.

The Winters family used my harsh punishment to show everyone that even a teenage boy who made a series of mistakes would not be pardoned due to his age or inexperience. They told the world I was judged as a man rather than a boy. But in truth, I was made into a symbol, a figurehead for the death of a failed rebellion.

I found that almost painfully funny at the time. Considering how terrible a killer I had been. My mother could see it, which is why she tried to send me away. My father saw it too, which is why he stopped her, refusing to let me run from my responsibilities as his heir.

But I wasn't Sam. I wasn't a natural-born leader who was destined to take over a major mafia family. I wasn't a brave man strong enough to suffer for his chance at true power. I was Max Summers. A disappointment to myself and everyone else for an endless number of reasons that didn't begin and end with the war.

Sam's gaze goes dark for a second, and I think only the presence of his children stops him from saying what he feels like saying. Or, more likely, *shouting*. He liked a good shouting match when we were young. But rather than giving in to his baser instinct to unleash some of that pent-up aggression, he holds himself in check.

He takes a deep breath and meets my steady gaze, expression tight.

"I remember, Max. I remember all of it." His voice is rough with something I can't name. I don't think I want to. It might make me feel like an arsehole for sniping at him and I don't want to feel bad for hurting Sam.

"I know you do." How could either of us ever forget all that hell we lived through?

Sam looks like he wants to deepen our conversation, to make it more than it already is. But his eyes dart to Aiden and his reluctance is clear. Not in front of his son. Isabella wouldn't understand us talking about the past, but Aiden certainly would, and there are some things I'm sure neither of us would want our children to know.

I think it's for the best if we don't get the chance to talk about what happened when we were teenagers. Nothing good could possibly come of digging up old graves. I've done plenty of self-reflection over the years, parsing out every mistake, analysing my decisions and thought processes to death. We don't need to make it a group activity.

Now, I just have to make sure I'm never alone with Sam again and I won't have to worry about having some sort of horrifically personal discussion.

"So, what did you get for Christmas?" I ask Aiden with forced brightness, keen to focus my attention on someone, and something, else.

Aiden looks up at me with knowing eyes and quirks his eyebrows in a very recognisable way. How does a nine-year-old know how to give someone the *you're full of shit* stare? What has Sam been teaching this child? Or maybe he gets it from Effia. Yeah, I can see that happening. Effia is a master of the *you're full of shit* stare and the *oh really, that's what you're going with?* eyebrow arch.

I just keep smiling, possibly a bit dementedly, until Aiden decides to take pity on me.

"Dad got me a piano and loads of books I asked for." Aiden's voice is quiet, but sure. He watches me with a thoughtful expression.

I'm being examined by a nine-year-old version of Sam. I feel like I had a nightmare about this exact scenario once.

"Have you been playing long?" I ask him, genuinely curious this time.

Aiden shakes his head, a small smile forming on his face. "No. I play bass and the drums really well, but I've only just started my lessons with the piano."

I can't stop myself from grinning. From what I've observed so far, Sam was definitely correct in calling Aiden the quiet one of his three children. But just because he might not be as bold as his brother seems to be, or his dad when he was younger, doesn't mean he's suffering from a lack of confidence in himself.

"My mum taught me how to play the piano when I was around your age," I tell Aiden in a low voice, as if it's a secret. "It took me a long time to get the hang of it though. All my music teachers despaired of me and quit, saying I'd never get it. Eventually my mum stepped in and made a musician out of me."

"How?" Aiden asks, eyes alight with interest. I'm struck all over again by how similar he looks to his dad.

I consider Aiden's question, thinking back on all the times I spent with my mum sitting at the grand piano in the parlour room of our mansion. The Summers' mansion, my family home. A place I haven't stepped foot inside since I was nineteen.

It doesn't belong to my family anymore, which is a good thing really, because I can't imagine the family I have now ever living in that overly grand, dusky house. I can't imagine Natalie having married the man who owned a house like that. Not because she would have held my wealth against me, but because of the man that wealth would have made me into.

"Motherly threats, mostly," I admit to Aiden, offering him a self-deprecating smile. "Alongside forcing me to spend endless hours messing up over and over again until the laws of probability stepped in, and I finally got it right by accident." I lower my voice to a fearful whisper, pretending to shudder. "She was *ruthless*."

Aiden laughs at this. His laugh isn't boisterous in the slightest, more of a subdued chuckle, but it's still something.

I glance over at Sam again and almost jerk backwards when I see his expression. His mouth is only a few inches away from gaping. Sam's eyes flicker dramatically between me and his son. He looks shocked and bewildered. I have no idea why.

I'm prevented from asking by Effia, who finally comes striding into the kitchen. Sam's attention is dragged away from me when Effia exclaims his name delightedly and goes over to hug him. She kisses Aiden on the forehead as well and he smiles tentatively up at her. But he seems to have crept back into his turtle shell.

I would never have thought Sam could raise a shy child. During the brief times when I've thought about Sam and his potential family over the years, I always imagined him with a brood of loud, mischievous children, much like he and his friends were.

Perhaps it's something to do with Ashley's death. Aiden would have been about six when his mum died. Rory was also only six when we lost Natalie. That's a very rough age to lose your mother. Well, every age is a rough age to lose a parent, but especially so when you're too young to fully understand the loss but old enough to feel the impact of it.

Cat was only four when Natalie died. I used to worry that Cat wouldn't remember her mother. I worried that Natalie would just be a vague outlined image for Cat and that she would never know just how special her mother was, or how much Natalie had loved her. When I voiced my concerns to Penny, she suggested I tell Cat stories about Natalie and show her pictures and old videos of her, which I did.

Even though it hurt to remember, I would rather feel the pain of remembering how much I loved my wife than the numbness of forgetting. It seemed to help Cat and Rory, to speak about their mother with me. I don't ever want Rory or Cat to feel like they can't talk to me about things.

"So, what have you lot been up to in here?" Effia asks with curious, raised eyebrows. She looks pointedly at the half-eaten biscuit still being held in a death grip by Isabella, and adds, "Apart from raiding the Christmas biscuits, I mean."

"Nothing," Sam and I say at the same time. I groan internally. Because that didn't sound suspicious at all. Sam looks at me. I studiously avoid his gaze.

Maybe if I pretend he doesn't exist then he will eventually

disappear in a puff of smoke, like an unwanted magician. Which is all magicians. All magicians are unwanted magicians.

I can't believe I was stupid enough to agree to spend an entire day with the prat. I must have been high on tea fumes or something.

Effia appears far too amused by my and Sam's reaction to her question. But instead of being evil and purposely pushing the issue, she changes the subject.

"All right, how about we open some presents?"

Aiden looks up a bit at that with interest. Isabella goes off on Sam's hip and starts chanting the word *"presents"*. Then, as if his ears were burning, Elijah comes running inside, with Kassian and Rory following close behind. A few seconds later, Penny and Jade come in as well, Xavier and Cat trailing them like loyal ducklings.

Cat runs up to me and climbs into my lap. She's wet and sandy, but I hold her close anyway. I kiss the top of her head as she chatters to me about a crab she found and how Xavier screamed when she put it on his shoulder.

Effia takes Isabella from Sam and walks away with her in search of presents. Elijah runs after them, talking a mile a minute, trying to get Effia to tell him what she got him for Christmas.

Aiden climbs off his stool and follows his excitable brother. He looks back at his dad once and Sam gives his son an encouraging smile. Then Aiden looks at me and I offer him a playful salute. Aiden copies my action before wandering off after his siblings.

Penny takes one knowing look at me and Sam before corralling everyone else out of the room, talking about going upstairs so they could shower off the seawater and sand.

With no more distractions to hide behind, I reluctantly catch Sam's gaze again. He's watching me with a thoughtful expression that directly mirrors the one his son utilised against me earlier. Something in my chest tightens. It hurts, and it takes me a moment to realise why.

When Penny Starr hit me with her car, she insisted on taking me to the hospital. I'd tried to resist, but Penny refused to let me go wandering off without getting myself checked out. The woman practically dragged me off the ground and manhandled me into the backseat of her car. She called me a "stubborn little tosser" when I attempted to escape out of the car window.

They waited with me in the hospital until I was seen by a doctor. Dr Pond was gentle but brisk as she gave me my stitches.

God only knows what I'd looked like to her, to all of them. I'd purposefully stayed away from anything that could have shown me my reflection once I'd started living on the streets. I'd already felt half dead; I hadn't needed confirmation I looked it too.

When Dr Pond was finished with me, she'd asked where I'd be staying that night. I'd seen on her face that she already knew I had no home to go back to. I hadn't enough pride left in me to feel embarrassed about it, so I told her the truth. And the truth was I had nowhere to go and likely never would. My father would have hated me for admitting such weakness to them.

But I just…I just didn't care.

There's a certain kind of freedom in that. As Penny always says when things seem impossible, "You can get to a point in your life when you've officially run out of fucks to give, and that's when you start to see things for how they really are, rather than how you need them to be."

Not exactly a great philosopher, our Penny, but I think her point stands.

Natalie hadn't looked at me with pity when I told them I had nowhere to go. She'd reached out and touched my hand. Just a simple touch. But it'd made me feel…good. Better. Calmer. She'd looked at me like she saw someone underneath all the grime and spiteful rudeness and grief. I hadn't been sure exactly who it was she saw underneath all that, but for some absurd reason I'd wanted to find out.

That's how it all started. Me being hit by a car, laughed at, stitched up, then touched and seen.

I think people underestimate the power of being seen, even by strangers.

I know it doesn't exactly sound like the beginning of an epic story. And it wasn't. Epic, I mean. It wasn't soulmate magic or a fairy tale. It wasn't epic. It was far better than that.

Our story, mine and Natalie's, was better than anything, because it wasn't a story. It was real. We were real, and what we built together was real.

It hits me like an arrow to the chest when I realise the way Sam is looking at me is evoking the same feeling Natalie did in that hospital room.

Sam is making me feel *seen*.

"Are we still on for Wednesday?" Sam asks.

No. No, we are not on for Wednesday. No. Not at all.

"Yes," I say, because I'm a constant disappointment to myself.

Chapter Six

WELL, THIS IS going about as badly as I suspected it would. Walking around an aquarium with Sam is not an experience I ever expected to have to endure in my life, especially not with all our children skipping along ahead of us and seemingly getting on like they've known one another forever.

Elijah and Rory aren't a surprise, as they are self-declared best friends. But Cat and Aiden, despite their very different personalities, glommed onto each other almost immediately. I can see them now, whispering and laughing together next to a large tank of baby tiger sharks.

They're bloody holding hands and everything! What the hell? Cat doesn't even *like* people. We've always had that in common.

I'm not sure how horrified I should be if Aiden and Cat decide to become best friends as well. Then I'll have no choice but to associate with Sam for the sake of both my children.

If I were a little less sane and a bit more pessimistic, I would call the universe out on its obvious attempt to drive me round the twist.

Then again, nothing has exploded since we got to the aquarium and Sam has yet to piss me off to the point where I might start to think punching him in front of all our children would be worth it. So…

Isabella is asleep in her buggy, which is unfortunate as she provided most of the entertainment for the last few hours. At least with Isabella awake Sam and I could concentrate on keeping her happy while our other children ran around the aquarium.

Things only started to get weird when Isabella decided to take an early nap. It's uncomfortable between us in a way it wasn't before when I saw Sam at Jade's house or when he dropped Rory off last week. I can't tell if it's because this time we've chosen to socialise with each other outside of a mandated setting. To be honest, I'm still struggling to reconcile why I agreed to do this with Sam in the first place.

Or maybe now Sam and I are alone together, sort of, if you don't count our children and the groups of strangers who are also running around all over the aquarium, we've realised we don't have anything to talk about. Nothing appropriate for this setting anyway.

Chatting about the weather or what a nice Christmas we had, or any other inane topic of conversation, feels wrong. Sam and I have said many awful, unforgivable things to each other, but we've never chit-chatted about nonsense like polite strangers.

I would rather get into a fistfight with Sam than pretend to care about how cloudy it is today compared to yesterday when it was still cloudy but not quite as much. That's why I don't have many friends, because every time I've tried to become closer to the teachers I work with at school or the parents of other children, the only two types of people I have time to meet, I can't stand the tedium of it all.

Effia and Jade are the two shining exceptions, and that's only because Effia practically bullied me into blunting my hedgehog quills and accepting their friendship.

It's not just that I can't tell them about my past, I would have no interest in sharing those details with random people anyway. But after meeting Natalie, I realised my social skills are seriously bad. Like, they are shockingly awful.

So much of who I was and how I acted back in the day came from being a Summers and hating that tosser Sam.

I was Max Summers, always, never just Max.

It wasn't my parents' fault, although I tried to blame them, specifically my father for a long time.

After the war, when there was no more underworld politics to play or a Sam to torment, or even a crime boss father to survive, I was at a loss. I didn't know how to be anyone other than the person my parents and my circumstances had demanded I become.

I couldn't be Max Summers anymore, because Max Summers was the son of a mafia enforcer. *Just Max* is not, and without that, without family and money and power, I thought I was nothing. How could I be anything when all that I was had been so thoroughly removed from my being? Torn away like wallpaper and burned to ash right in front of me.

I spent the whole morning before Sam showed up pacing around the flat muttering about how this whole idea is stupid, and I'd somehow end up on the front page of the *Danger Post* with a picture of me attacking Sam. Then the entire Winters family would demand I be sentenced to a million years in prison, and I'd finally be where I belong, sharing a cell with my father. We could trade notes on how to make awful fucking life choices.

Penny got annoyed with me eventually and smacked the back of my head with a wooden spoon. She demanded I stop being such a capital-D Drama Queen, an admonishment she levels at me often.

Once, when Rory broke his arm after falling out of a tree, I drove to the hospital so fast I had to keep telling Rory not to be scared, I was only driving like a maniac so I could save his life.

Rory was not traumatised by my driving at all. He just kept laughing and shouting *"Wheeeee!"* Later, I realised my son had grasped the use of sarcasm. I know this because on our way home from the hospital he informed me that twenty miles per hour is not what most people would consider "fast". I called him a little shit. He grinned back at me and asked if he could take some pens into school so all his friends could sign the new lime-green cast on his arm.

What I'm trying to say is that Penny is completely right. I am a drama queen. I stress myself out to the point of hysterics, and I can't seem to stop losing my shit until someone knocks me off my downward spiral. Natalie used to do that. She would mock me, or say something funny, or quite literally whack me upside the head, and it would take away the panic. At the very least, Natalie would share in my panic, and we could go bonkers about things together.

But since Natalie died, I haven't had anyone who could distract me from my tendency to overreact. Penny tries, but it's not the same. I miss Natalie for an endless number of reasons, and one of them is her ability to bring me back down to earth with just a few words or a wicked curve of her lips.

Sam interrupts my introspection. "So…uh. You're a teacher?" He grimaces a little, obviously regretting his decision to try to make this any less weird than it already is.

I take pity on him, for reasons I don't care to examine too closely. "Yes. I teach a class full of six-year-olds how to spell and make hand-paint collages and instruct them when it is and when it is not appropriate to pee your knickers in public."

Sam cracks a small smile, the first one he's had on his face all day. "And when is it appropriate to pee your knickers in public, Mr Summers, sir?" he asks in an exaggerated child's voice.

"Never," I say dryly, then reconsider. "Unless you're faced with an evil horse whose clear intent is to murder you via hoof. Only then is it okay to pee yourself."

Sam snorts in amusement, likely remembering the incident I'm referencing.

The Winters family has a side hustle in horse racing, more for leisure than anything else, and I used to get taken to their country club stables all the time when they would have meetings there with all their high-ranking soldiers. As the Winters's oldest ally, the Summers family was always invited to important meetings.

"That was your own fault." Sam shoots me a smirk I recognise from our youth, although it's become sharper and more refined with age. It's a lethal weapon, that thing. "If you're gonna go around showing off by pretending to be *the horse whisperer,* then you'll get what you deserve. A swift kick, for example."

As fourteen-year-old boys, Sam, Will, and I were still too young to be included in the actual business meetings themselves, but old enough to feel resentful over being left out. We distracted ourselves from this by hanging around the horses. Sometimes we'd go riding, all of us having been taught how from a young age.

One horse, a massive black stallion, had yet to be broken in. It was left wandering around a paddock, unsupervised. We dared one another to go near it.

Sam, who really *is* the horse whisperer, got close enough to pet the fucking thing like it was a little pony. When Will goaded me into doing the same, Sam told me not to because it was too dangerous. No, hold on. He *ordered* me not to, like the arrogant bastard he was.

I was more spurred on by Sam's presumed authority over me than by Will's scornful urging.

"Bloody beast was aiming for my face," I mutter darkly.

Sam laughs. He *laughs.*

It isn't a mocking laugh, but a loud, genuine one. Sam seems just as surprised by it as I am. Although his surprise appears to be of the more pleasant sort.

A feeling of helplessness rises inside me from nowhere and for a moment I flounder. I should be used to that by now, but I'm not, and it scares me a bit.

Why Sam laughing would incite such an emotional response, I have no idea. The only thing I can compare the experience to is how I felt when I first met Natalie. I was in such a dark place back then and seeing Natalie smile or hearing her laugh at something I'd said made me feel worse rather than better. At the time, I didn't understand why I felt afraid of making someone else happy.

Natalie and I only spoke about it once, the night we slept together for the first time. I'd been nervous as fuck, my hands shaking as I touched her like she was made of glass. Natalie only put up with that for so long before asking me what was wrong. I couldn't explain it to her at first, but she was very patient with me. She waited until I finally admitted I was afraid of disappointing her.

Natalie, far from getting annoyed, confided she felt exactly the same way. It helped, knowing that. I told her she could never disappoint me. All I wanted was her, in whatever way she'd let me have her.

Hours later that night, Natalie asked me why I always seemed so afraid of letting her down. I couldn't tell her about the war, not yet, so I told her about my parents instead. Not the full details, just about how I couldn't save my mother, and how I wasn't the man my father wanted me to be.

Natalie told me I was the only man she'd ever wanted. And on our wedding day, she told me I was the only man she would ever want.

Hearing those words from Natalie didn't heal the wounds left by my parents' disappointment, but it soothed them. It made those wounds bearable.

Sam has stopped laughing now and his expression has morphed

into something speculative, verging on concerned.

"Max, are you—"

I cut him off with a harsh order. "Don't ask me if I'm all right."

"What?" Sam looks bewildered by my response, those intense eyes of his searching my face for answers.

"I hate it when people ask me if I'm all right." I reach a hand up to pinch my forehead, trying to stave off the migraine. "I know how that sounds, but after Natalie…died." I lower my voice so only Sam will hear me. "People wouldn't stop asking me if I was all right and all I wanted to do was scream at them, *no, no, I'm not fucking all right, I'll never be all right because she's dead, so stop fucking asking*." I release a rough expulsion of air, avoiding Sam's watchful gaze. "But I couldn't do that because of Rory and Cat, so I had to pretend like I wasn't breaking into a thousand useless pieces."

I'll regret that outburst later, but right now I'm too frustrated to keep myself in check.

I look over at Sam reluctantly, expecting shock, or anger, maybe even annoyance at me dragging him into my internal anguish. What I do not expect is the level of gritty understanding on Sam's face.

He allows a very long and weighted pause before responding. "It never gets any easier." He sounds resigned to that fact. "No matter how many people you've lost." He sighs wearily. "It hits you with the same strength every single time."

"Sam—" I try to say something, anything, to stop him from sharing with me what I haven't in any way earned from him, but he keeps going, undaunted. Well, that's very Sam, not to be stopped by the likes of me.

"I thought my days of losing people I love was over. After the war. After…" He swallows hard. "Everything that happened back then." His eyes are fixed on my face, like he wants me to really listen. I do. Even though a large part of me doesn't want to hear it.

"I lost people like most kids lose teeth," Sam says, and it's physically painful how matter of fact he is about it all. "But when Ashley and I got married, and we had Elijah, and I started running my side of the business, I felt like I was exactly who and what everyone expected me to become. I had everything my family's enemies tried to take from me." He tactfully refrains from outright stating the fact his family's enemies were *my* family.

Sam's mouth ticks up sadly on one side. "Then we had Aiden. And Isabella. And I lost someone. Again. Not just someone, but *the* one. My wife, the love of my life. It felt like a cruel joke at the time. It still does, some days."

This is not what I expected when we started talking. It isn't stilted or weird between us any longer, which is just bizarre. How is it possible to be more comfortable baring your grief to someone than it is to talk politely with them about the weather?

I have something terribly wrong with me. Whatever that thing is, Sam has it wrong with him as well. I take comfort in that.

It doesn't make me feel better to know Sam understands my sense of loss. Nothing could ever really make me feel better about any of it. But it does…help? Maybe. Or at least, it means something to me that there's another person in my life who knows what it feels like to fight so hard every day of your life to keep what matters and still lose it anyway.

"Well, that escalated rather quickly," I murmur to Sam after another one of those heavy pauses we seem to like so much.

Sam lets out a somewhat strangled laugh, causing me to smile just a bit. There's nothing inherently funny about any of this, but it feels good to make jokes at our expense.

"Yeah, it really did." Sam shakes his head, having finally torn his gaze away from mine. I sag in both disappointment and relief. Sam frowns slightly to himself as if a perturbing thought has just occurred to him. He waggles a finger between us. "We are not good at the small talk thing."

"No," I agree. "We're absolute rubbish at it, apparently. Especially with each other."

"Ah, well, I think I can live with that," Sam says, a rueful smile pulling at the corners of his mouth again.

"I suppose we don't have much of a choice." I shrug one shoulder uncaringly.

"No*pe*." Sam pops the "p" because he is a menace to society.

I run a hand through my hair and groan, making a face at him.

"Quick, tell me something distractingly emotional so we won't lapse back into unbearably static silence. I can't take another hour of pretending to be happily uncomfortable in your presence."

"What would you being *un*happily uncomfortable in my presence look like?" Sam asks, peering at me with an irritating amount of genuine interest.

I sniff haughtily at him because I know he'll get a kick out of it. "A lot like this really, except I'd be continuously hitting you with something as we walk around. Something heavy. Like a brick. Or a chair."

"Aha, that sounds about right." Sam nods to himself. He arches a speculative eyebrow at me and mutters, "Now look who has the anger problem."

"I wouldn't be hitting you out of anger. I would be hitting you out of boredom," I argue drolly. "And are you really still stuck on that thing I said about your temper? It can't be the first time someone has pointed it out to you. I refuse to believe all of the people in your life are that unobservant."

Or scared shitless of being candid with him, which would be more likely in the case of his underlings. Whether it's legitimate business or organised crime, the rules are remarkably the same. Don't piss off the boss by being honest to their face.

"No, you aren't the only one who's mentioned it," Sam admits be-grudgingly. "Effia's brought it up before. Some members of my family tried to discuss my more…*passionate* behaviour. Even Will has sug-gested reining it in a few times when I've made decisions about what to do with people who need sorting out."

By "people who need sorting out", I assume he means either trai-tors who have betrayed the family in some way or people who get it in their heads to try to take down the organisation. For moral reasons, or some such shit.

As far as I'm concerned, anyone, especially if they have a family of their own to protect, who puts themselves in the crosshairs on purpose, is an idiot. To me, bringing down the Winters family could never be worth putting the people you love in danger. They have no problem coming after a person's loved ones to make a point, to protect them-selves. They've done truly awful things to maintain their seat of power in this city. I saw what they were capable of when I was a boy, what Sam was capable of, and I doubt Sam is any less ruthless now than he was at nineteen. He's almost certainly more lethal as a fully grown man.

He has so much to lose, and unlike some others, he understands how deep that loss can cut. What else it takes from you, even years and years later.

Sam is the last person I would expect mercy from when crossed be-cause he knows the consequences of weakness.

"Ever thought about going to therapy?" I ask him, only half-joking.

Sam turns an almost vicious look on me. "Have *you* ever considered going to therapy?" he demands.

"No, of course not." I scoff. Therapy is for sensible people.

"I'm no worse off than you are in that department," Sam mutters, voice tight.

"Exactly," I say, hiding a smirk. "And I'm barmy. Completely off my rocker. Fucked beyond the point of psychological redemption."

Sam looks confused, which is fun for me. "But you just said —" I can almost hear the click inside Sam's thick head, his eyes narrowing suspiciously. "You're fucking with me, aren't you?"

"Sam, I'm always fucking with you," I reply with an acerbic undertone. "It's the foundation of our entire relationship."

Which is true. I've never had anyone in my life who I wanted to bother more than I wanted to bother Sam. I remember desperately trying to think of ways to get under his skin when we were young. I wanted to piss him off to the point where he'd have no choice but to react. Sam very rarely disappointed me in his reactions. They were often extreme. It was very satisfying for a teenage me.

Of course, now all I want is to get through one conversation with the man without it ending in yelling, barbed comments being traded, or a physical altercation. I don't want to hurt Sam any more. Well, okay, I at least don't want to *want* to hurt him. That's progress, right?

Right?

You ever get that feeling, like you don't know whether you're maturing or regressing with age? You know you've come a long way, but at the same time, you also know you're nowhere near being the person you want to be. It's endlessly frustrating. I just want to be able to say, "Right, done now, this is me, this is the version of myself I'm happy with and I'm sticking with it."

Even when Natalie was alive and we were happy, I still didn't feel like I'd truly accepted myself. And I don't mean just as an ordinary civilian. That was the easiest part for me to embrace. It's somehow less complicated to be okay with something when you've got no real alternative.

It makes me think of myself at around fifteen. When I was a lanky string of pent-up resentment and misplaced arrogance being officially inducted into the criminal organisation I was raised to serve. I don't suppose many fifteen-year-olds have deep-set opinions on who they are, fundamentally, but I did. When I was fifteen, I knew exactly what I wanted and why.

But even so, when I successfully completed my first job, given to me by the head of the Winters family, Sam's grandfather, I felt a twinge of…not quite disappointment. A sense of resignation, maybe? I knew what my life would hold from that moment onwards. There weren't going to be any surprises. And for a single, solitary moment, I regretted that my entire future had been clicked into place before I'd reached the age of sixteen. I dismissed the feeling almost immediately, but still, it had been there all the same.

"You're doing that thing again," Sam comments, bringing me out of my thoughts.

"Doing what?" I retort. "Walking? Breathing? Existing? Narrow it down for me."

Sam doesn't appear put off by my derisive tone this time. "You're doing that thing where you go off into your own head and block everything else out." The hidden suggestion is clear: blocking every*one* else out.

"Yes, well, I can hardly be blamed for seeking better company considering what I have to work with at the moment." I make a subtle, sweeping hand gesture in Sam's direction.

Sam narrows his eyes, that strange intensity creeping back into them if it ever really left. His expression is unreadable for once, which makes me nervous. I can feel Sam's scrutiny right down to my tendons, and it makes me want to smack him.

"You do it whenever we start to have a serious conversation about anything," he says slowly, carefully, as if putting a concentrated effort into not pissing me off.

I can't decide if it should concern me how he noticed my tendency to check out when I get uncomfortable with a topic. Either way, I don't know why he's bringing it up now.

To distract me, and hopefully Sam as well, I cast an extended glance over at our children.

Isabella is still sound asleep in her buggy. Sam told me she'd been up most of the night.

I remember the days of small children waking me up every night. The lack of sleep after Rory was born almost drove me batshit. I was tired and frustrated enough by the end of the first month that I might have been inclined to sell what's left of my soul to anyone who asked, had they promised to give me a few hours of uninterrupted rest.

No one ever tells you how possible it is to hate your own child with a fiery passion, even as you love them unconditionally. Natalie and I went to a few parenting classes at the local clinic when she was pregnant with Rory, and I really wish someone there had said, "When you've been awake for seventy-three hours straight and you have gone partially deaf from the sound of your child's almost constant screams and you have your partner yelling at you because you forgot to rinse out the milk pump again and you are covered in a baby sick-piss-poo combo, it's okay to want to sell your child to fairies, as long as you don't actually do it."

Because all that would have been extremely helpful to know.

I felt like a monster for the first year of Rory's life. I thought I was the only one who wanted to break down and smash my head against a wall until I lost consciousness every time Rory spent an entire night screaming his head off. I thought I was a horrible father, and any day Natalie would figure that out, divorce me, and refuse to let me within ten feet of Rory ever again.

But then one day Penny sat me down and told me I was doing a really good job, and Natalie had been telling her just that morning how she never could have done any of it without me. I guess Penny knew I needed to hear those words. I needed to know I wasn't messing everything up. I needed to feel like I was getting it right with both Natalie and Rory. That's one of the reasons why I love Penny. She fills in the spaces even Natalie couldn't.

I realise I'm drifting off again. Sam is giving me another knowing look, so I force myself to concentrate on our children, in the present.

Aiden and Cat have moved on from the shark tank and are now climbing all over the rather large statue of an octopus, still chattering to each other happily as they do so. Rory and Elijah are over by the open-topped crab and stingray tank where lots of people are reaching their hands in to touch the sea life swimming around. I can't quite tell what they're saying because it's so loud in here, but I can infer from their body language and expressions they are daring each other to touch what is obviously a very big and very angry-looking crab.

I half hope one of them gets nipped by the pissed-off crab. It might teach them something about poking at dangerous things. I worry that our city is a lethal place for a Summers, especially since my son is now the best friend of a Winters. God only knows what kind of trouble those two will find themselves involved in.

"That crab does not look poke-friendly," Sam says to me as he watches our sons with open amusement.

I turn to Sam again with a judgemental stare. "The fact you think any crab could be 'poke-friendly' tells me just about everything I need to know about you."

Sam, to my horror, gives my arm a playful nudge. "What, have you never gotten the urge to poke something you know you shouldn't?"

"No, Sam," I say indignantly. "Some of us are too busy behaving like dignified human beings to go around poking dangerous things for the hell of it."

Sam gets a sudden glint in his eyes then and I know the next words out of his mouth are going to be ridiculous.

He takes hold of my wrist and pulls me over to the crab tank. I go along with it out of surprise more than anything else.

"*Touch the crab*, Max," Sam coaxes. He's pointing at a different, even larger, angrier looking crab than the one the boys are fussing over.

"No," I say, glaring down at the crab in question. I think the word *evil* at it.

"Come on, Summers, don't be a chicken," Sam teases me. I can tell it isn't mean teasing. It's the kind of thing he might say to a friend. Which is odd. Because Sam and I, whatever else we might be, are not friends. Ex-rivals, yes. Civil acquaintances, getting there. But friends? I can't even imagine what that would be like. I don't want to imagine it.

"Sam, I am not a child," I grouse. "I will not be manipulated into touching a ferocious killer crab by you calling me names like we're both still twelve years old."

"Killer crab?" Sam questions, eyebrow firmly raised.

"Yes." I scowl at him. "You can tell from his beady red eyes that evil resides within him."

Sam begins making clucking noises with far too much glee for a thirty-five-year-old man with three children and a multi-billion-pound business under his control.

I hate him. My hatred of Sam Winters is renewed once more, and I will destroy him if it is the last thing I accomplish in this life. I made a similar vow to myself when I was a boy. Here's hoping this time it all works out.

"Shut it, you massive prat!" I hiss, wishing I had something to belt him with.

Sam takes a pause from clucking. "Poke the crab, Max."

"I am not going to piss off the aquarium's resident demonic shellfish," I snap at him. "I didn't survive all these years by throwing myself at evil and just hoping for the best. I'm not Polaris. I'm not *you*."

Polaris is Danger City's resident superhero. He came around after my time, but I know for a fact he's been a consistent thorn in the Winters's side for years. I've taken more than a bit of pleasure in that. I'm not immune to the allure of petty vengeance, even if I no longer hate the Winters family as I once did.

Sam bursts out laughing at me. It's the kind of real laughter that makes you snort unattractively. But Sam's snorting laughter is, somehow, not all that bad.

"Ah, yes," he says, voice mockingly wistful, "that time I fought the evil Crabfather and saved the city from his snippy destruction. What a glorious day that was."

He completely ignores the mention of Polaris. The only sign he heard the name was the sparks of frustration and anger in his eyes, which ignited immediately, then got doused with significant force just as fast. It's been clear for a long time Sam has far greater enemies than me, these days.

"You're an idiot," I mutter to him darkly. "And a prat."

Sam flashes me another blinding smile, all perfect teeth and Peter Pan mischief. "You're a chicken," he counters. "And strange."

"I am not *strange*." I am. I *so* am.

"You are though," Sam says, mirroring my thoughts with what seems like genuine enthusiasm. "Like properly, you are. It's brilliant."

"Not poking an evil crab that will probably break my fingers off is not strange. It's common sense. Maybe if you'd ever had some then you would know that."

"I have common sense," Sam argues, looking offended I'd assume otherwise despite the complete lack of evidence he has ever shown me. "I just choose not to let it hold me back from doing stuff."

"And therein lies the problem," I say as if that settles the matter. It should. But Sam is Sam, and there are some ways in which he has certainly not changed.

"Just poke the crab, Summers."

"Why?" I ask, a bit suspicious now. I'm not sure what I'm suspicious of, other than Sam's general intentions, but I feel it would be a mistake to underestimate his inclination towards ridiculousness.

Sam shrugs, giving away absolutely nothing, like I'm asking for the secrets of the universe or some shit. "Because."

"Because, *why*?"

"No real reason," Sam says with a nonchalance I find highly suspect. He leans in a bit closer to my side, wafting his expensive aftershave and whatever else it is that makes him smell like a scary billionaire crossed with a scarier mobster at me. "Haven't you ever done something just because?"

He's being curious, again. I don't like it.

"No," I answer flatly, "why on earth would anyone do that?"

Sam tilts his head to the left, considering me, judgement practically radiating off him. "Wow, that's quite sad."

"Shut up." I feel compelled to defend myself, suddenly. As if I care what Sam thinks about my ability to—to, uh… *Shit*. I don't actually know what I'm defending myself against, here. That's not good.

"You need to live a little," Sam advises, like the coupon discount equivalent of a life coach.

"I'll live a little by poking a crab?" My doubt is so deep and so strong it cannot be contained by a single iteration. "Poking. A. Crab."

"Yep," Sam says, with the overall air and competency of a feckless hype man.

"That's ridiculous," I tell him, slow and deliberate. "You're ridiculous."

"Yeah, I know," Sam agrees dismissively, smirking up a storm, "but you're definitely going to do it though, aren't you?"

What in the hell?

"*No*, of *course* not."

How dare he. I have my principles. I have my self-respect. I have my dignity, sometimes, maybe.

I poke the stupid crab.

"Right, your turn," I say, after narrowly escaping having my fingers clipped off. He managed to get the edge of my thumb. I'll probably feel that for the rest of the day. Evil bloody crab.

Sam rolls his eyes at me and reaches down without even looking to poke the crab. The Antichrist of all crabs latches on to Sam's finger and clamps down hard. Sam hisses in pain and tries to pull his hand away. The villainous crustacean comes flying out of the tank still clinging to Sam's finger.

"Ah, shit!" Sam shouts. He dislodges the crab by flinging his arm outwards. It goes sailing through the air and hits a man right in the face. The man screams, grabs hold of the crab, and throws it across the room. It lands on a woman's head, and she begins screaming as well.

People all around us start shouting and flapping about in response to the crab crisis. A few parents trip over their own feet to grab their children and make a run for it towards the exit. Unfortunately, this causes the exit to become jammed with people and no one can escape, which just makes people shout and scream and stamp around more.

Someone even gets accidentally pushed into the tank, and that really sets people off. Aquarium workers in blue polo shirts attempt to get into the room, but because everyone is trying to get out at the same time, they can't get in.

After a few minutes of panicked frenzy, one bloke loses it and pulls the fire alarm. Because surely that'll help. The alarm goes off, making a horribly loud sound that drowns out all the people screaming, and the sprinklers on the ceiling spray water over everyone.

Elijah and Rory are laughing their little heads off from the other side of the tank, having seen our display. Cat and Aiden look over at us now from their positions on the octopus statue. They both have exasperated expressions, as if this is all just so typical of their dads. Isabella has been startled awake by the commotion. Like a true child of Sam, she looks enthralled by the drama instead of upset at being woken up.

I glance at Sam, who looks very sheepish, as well he should.

"And that's what happens when you do things 'just because'." I use air quotes with my fingers because I don't give a fuck about coming off like a good person.

"Yeah, somehow it always turns out this way." Sam's cheeks flush with embarrassment.

I find myself grinning. Despite the madness, I haven't had this much fun in a long time.

Through all this, Sam still hasn't let go of my wrist. I look down at where we're touching, then back up at Sam's face. He's clearly noticed the same thing, and the flush on his face gets even more pronounced.

Instead of pulling away, I lean in closer to Sam and speak directly into his ear so he can hear me above the racket of the alarm and the panicking people.

"You, Sam Winters, are a nightmare of a man."

Sam sucks in a sharp breath and turns his head to look directly at me. Our faces are inches apart, and I can finally see the barely restrained devotion to anarchy in his eyes.

He moves further into my space, squeezes my wrist, and bumps his temple lightly against mine. He doesn't sound half as teasing as he should when he says, "It's okay to admit you missed me."

And I don't feel quite as ready to correct him as I should.

Chapter Seven

AFTER THE DISASTROUS episode with the demonic crab of doom, death, and despair, we make a discreet getaway. Luckily, it's about time for lunch, so Sam and I take the children to The White Hare, a local family-friendly pub. It's a nice day by British winter standards and we decide to sit outside at a large bench table.

"You hit that bloke right in the face, Dad. It was epic!" Elijah exclaims, sounding weirdly proud of his father for accidentally attacking someone with an angry crab. Well, he is a Winters. And a Flint. Not all that surprising if he has a violent streak in him. He's also an eleven-year-old boy, which means he likely has a somewhat lax relationship with basic human things like empathy. My own son is no different in that regard.

"Yeah, Mr Winters, it was well worth going to the aquarium just to see that," Rory chips in, although he casts a cautious glance at me as if waiting to be told off for voicing his agreement with his friend's assessment.

I give him the double eyebrow raise of appraisal for a handful of seconds before dropping them and allowing some good humour to seep into my expression. "Yes, well, next time to save ourselves some money we'll just go to the park and *Mr Winters* can attack someone with a badly kicked football instead."

"I did not attack that man," Sam argues, glowering at me. "It was an accident."

"Don't be modest." I barely manage to hide a wicked smile. "I'm sure The Family appreciates your crab-lobbing abilities."

"Strangely enough, crab-lobbing isn't looked upon with any great reverence in our business," Sam replies, sarcasm thick in his voice.

"That really is a shame. You, Sam Winters, so rarely get recognised for your unique brilliance."

Sam's expression is a cross between annoyed and amused. It doesn't help that Isabella is sitting on his lap and trying to push a plastic straw up his nose, with great enthusiasm I might add.

"Maybe you should write a letter to my grandfather expressing your feelings on the matter. You know he likes a good, old-fashioned bit of postal correspondence."

It's true Sam's grandfather is not a fan of modern convenience. He was old school back when I was young, and I'd guess he hasn't changed much.

I shrug. "I might."

Me refusing to rise to the bait will frustrate Sam more than if I snapped at him.

Cat snags my attention away from Sam by tugging on my jacket sleeve. "Daddy," she says far too sweetly for it to be in any way believable, "can Aiden and I get down and play, please?"

She is giving me her big kitten eyes. Very pleading and adorable. I don't buy it for even a second. Natalie always said I was a sucker for those looks from my daughter, but I've become somewhat more immune to them over the years.

"My answer is the same as it was ten minutes ago, Cat," I say firmly. "You can get down once you've eaten all your peas."

Cat groans and throws her head back theatrically. "But *Daaaad*, there are like, a *billion* peas on my plate, and I'm only *little*. I'll *explode* if I eat *all* of them." She gestures disdainfully at the small heap of peas still sitting uneaten in front of her.

Fuck me, the drama on this one.

I smile gently at my daughter and heave a sigh of faked weariness. "I'm afraid that is a risk I am willing to take."

Cat immediately pouts and slumps down in her seat. She's usually quite good at eating her vegetables, much better than Rory ever was, or is. But when she gets into a mood like the one she's in right now, it almost seems as if she and I are at odds about everything.

When Cat was seven, she ran away from home because I wouldn't let us get a dog, specifically a rottweiler. She was obsessed with rottweilers for months and took every available opportunity to sing their praises to me. At first, I'd hoped she would forget about it over time and move on to something else, as children that age often do. But Cat isn't like most other children. She is as stubborn and strong-willed as her mother, and if I'm being honest, she's as arrogant as I was at her age.

When Cat finally asked me point blank to get her a rottweiler, I said no without hesitation. Because there was no way in hell I'd ever want to go near another bloody rottweiler if I could help it.

One of my uncles used to run a dogfighting ring. It was an enterprise even my father found distasteful, but it made a significant amount of money, so he didn't try to put a stop to it.

My father knew how much I didn't like it. I made the mistake of asking him if it was the kind of thing we should really have our name attached to. He read the truth behind my reputation argument and took it as evidence of my weak stomach, and he was right to. I was weak. The dogfighting *did* sicken me.

It was one thing to go after our enemies with violence. That was simply our way of life, the ways of our business. But treating animals or other such innocents with cruelty for no good reason felt intrinsically wrong to me.

As punishment, and a test of sorts, my father ordered me to attend the dog fights with my uncle. My uncle forced me to watch the fights, and when he caught me throwing up in the alley out back after a particularly gruesome one, he got some of his people together and locked me in a room with a few of the fighting rottweilers.

It was terrifying. I was…

Locked in.

Space tight and pitch black.

Overwhelming smell of stale blood and dog shit.

The sound of jeering laughter from the other side of the bolted door.

Trapped in the basement of a derelict building with half-crazed dogs.

Teeth and pain and a fear so great it made me sick all over again.

I got bitten badly enough I had to have surgery. There's a particularly nasty scar on my forearm from where one of the dogs bit right down to the bone and viciously ripped the skin open.

My nightmares were filled with the growls of beasts in the dark for years afterwards.

The thought of having any kind of dog, let alone a rottweiler, in my home, was just short of genuinely nauseating.

Cat did not take my refusal to procure her a dog companion very well at all. She got so upset she threw a teapot into a wall, effectively smashing it to pieces. Thankfully it didn't have any actual tea in it otherwise Penny would have gone spare. She doesn't often lose her cool with the children, but there are times when they would test the patience of a saint.

I held firm against my daughter's rage that day because unfortunately having your children shout how much they hate you is too often the price of doing your job properly.

If I'd ever spoken to my parents the way Cat and Rory sometimes speak to me, then I wouldn't have had to worry about the Winters family, because my parents would have already disowned me. Not that they didn't love me; I know they did in their own slightly obscure way. But my parents had certain expectations, and if I didn't meet those expectations then I sure as hell knew about it. My father would lecture me on what I'd done wrong like I let the side down just by existing, and my mother would reiterate that lecture more than once just to drive it all the way home that I'd failed.

I did fail during my childhood. A lot. More than they, or I, thought was possible.

Once Cat was done with her epic tantrum, she stalked off to her room and packed up her school bag with a few random pieces of clothing, some books, three satsumas, and the dreamcatcher that hangs above her bed. Natalie bought it for her after Cat had a particularly horrid nightmare. I told Natalie such things were nonsense, and my wife teased me for being a faithless grump.

Once Cat's bag was ready and bulging with items, she announced to me she was leaving home. Forever. With that announcement made, she put on her coat, slung her yellow polka dot rucksack over her shoulders, and marched out of the flat, down the stairs, through the café, and out of the front door.

I followed her, making no comment, honestly curious as to how far she'd take it.

Fascinated, I watched Cat march onwards, undaunted and determined, down the street. When I could no longer see her from the café entrance I got into our car and drove after her. I caught up very quickly and resigned myself to driving alongside her for however long she would keep going to prove her point. Luckily it was a Sunday, so there were hardly any other cars on the road.

To give Cat full credit, she walked for two and a half hours without breaking, and for the entire time, she didn't acknowledge me driving beside her even once. I was secretly very impressed with her fortitude.

Finally, however, she sat down on a bench, crossed her arms, and glared at me. I parked the car and went to sit beside her.

We sat there together for a long time, not speaking.

Eventually, Cat turned to me and asked, "But why can't I have a rottweiler, Daddy? I promise I would take care of him. I really, really would."

It was almost funny because I believed her. I believed she would take very good care of a pet if I got her one. But that wasn't the point. I realised in that moment, with my seven-year-old daughter giving me the sincerest look of confusion I'd ever seen, I had to tell her the real reason why. It would have felt too wrong to lie. So, I did tell her. Not all of it; I didn't want to scare her with the whole truth.

I tried to keep my voice as even as possible, but it was hard, and I don't think I entirely succeeded, because Cat reached out her small hands to grasp one of mine and squeezed it. Offering comfort even if she didn't completely understand why I needed it.

When she did that, I looked at her. Really looked at her. My daughter looked back at me unflinchingly, her familiar eyes bright with a spark of bravery that made me proud in ways I wouldn't have been able to accurately describe to anyone else.

"Are you afraid of dogs, Dad?" Cat asked me.

"No," I told her honestly. "I'm more afraid of the memories, really."

Cat made a face that reminded me so much of Natalie it felt like a physical blow to my chest to see it so plainly on my daughter.

"Grandma told me nightmares can't hurt you unless you let them. I think memories can be like nightmares sometimes."

"Except, memories are real," I gently reminded her.

Cat gave me an arch look, her expression morphing into something that was all me, full of harsh reproach. "So are nightmares when you're still asleep."

She said it with all the confidence and conviction of a child who knows with absolute certainty they are right, you are wrong, and nothing will persuade them otherwise.

I asked her what her nightmares were about.

"Dogs. That's why I need to get one. So then my nightmares won't be able to scare me any more."

It healed something in me, hearing her say those words. Some deeply buried, torn piece of my soul knitted back into place because I have a daughter who is braver than I ever was. She gave me something in that moment. Cat showed me a small glimpse of the woman she would one day become, and for the first time since Natalie died, I felt genuine excitement for the future.

Before that, it had been one day at a time. I never looked too far forward because without Natalie, I felt lost at sea, head only barely kept above water, riding the waves without any hope of rescue.

But Cat made me eager to move forward, to watch her grow into herself and take on the world.

So yeah. Okay. I told Cat I would consider getting a dog. But first, she had to prove herself capable of looking after a pet.

I made the mistake of telling Cat she could pick any animal small enough to fit in a tank or cage. In my head, I was imagining a hamster or a tortoise.

Cat chose a snake. Because of course. His name is Frank. I still suspect he will one day escape his tank and eat us all, despite the fact he's a tiny grass snake who sleeps most hours of the day.

I'm just waiting for the day Rory's budgie goes mysteriously missing and Penny does a very good impression of an innocent woman.

I turn away from my daughter now and let her sulk about the unwanted peas. She'll hold on to her discontent and write angrily about how mean I am in the fluffy blue diary she has at home. One of the hardest things you have to learn as a parent is to let your kid be pissed off at you. That isn't always the case; some things need to be talked about. But so much of the time you have to back off, allow them their righteous fury, and wait until they've decided if the argument is worth pursuing. Most of the time it isn't, and that's okay too.

Sam is watching me with a kind of grimly amused understanding. He's likely been through similar things with his children.

"That goes for you too," Sam says to his son, subtly backing me up. "Eat all your carrots and you can get down."

Aiden is also slumped in his seat looking mutinous. Cat and Aiden glance at each other across the wooden table and share their own look of understanding.

Their shared look is a long-suffering one. *Parents, ugh.*

"So unfair," Cat mutters.

"Yeah," Aiden agrees, mirroring his dad's instinct to play the part of loyal ally.

I snort a little bit, hiding laughter.

"We are clearly evil, evil fathers," Sam says solemnly, lips giving a discreet twitch upwards.

"Yes." I press a hand to my chest, laying it on thick. "Whatever did these poor children do to deserve such awful parents who ask them to eat the food they asked for?"

Sam hums in agreement. "Someone better call in social services right quick before we can damage our precious little flowers any further by asking them to eat their vegetables."

I pull a mockingly sad face at him. Sam returns it with one of his own.

We only last a handful of seconds before we're unable to hold it in any longer and burst out laughing.

Cat glares at us. "You aren't funny."

This only causes us to laugh harder.

Four of our children are staring at us like we've both grown an extra head. Isabella is the only one who doesn't seem to find anything strange. She's laughing along with us, even though she has no idea why we're laughing in the first place.

I laugh so hard my side starts to hurt. I know it isn't that funny, but something about the expressions on our children's faces makes it so I can't seem to stop.

"Dad, are you, like, having a mental breakdown right now?" Rory asks me. He looks genuinely confused, and a little worried.

"I think they're sharing an old person joke," Elijah ventures, sounding knowledgeable, like he speaks fluent old person.

Sam lightly cuffs Elijah over the head. "Oi, we are not old."

"We're pretty old compared to them," I point out mournfully.

"Everyone is old compared to them," Sam contests, "they're just babies."

That gets us an outraged chorus of *we aren't babies* from everyone. They start to argue with one another about why they aren't babies and who the most grown-up among them is.

I sigh loudly, having had enough of whinging children for one day. "All right, that's it. Cat, Rory, go away."

My children turn to me, startled by my sudden change of heart.

"What?" Cat asks suspiciously.

"I mean it, both of you get down and go play in the park for a while so I can sit here in peace."

There's a playpark area on the far side of the pub's garden.

Surprisingly, Sam takes his cue from me and offers the same reprieve to his sons.

"You two go on as well and behave yourselves. No throwing wet leaves at each other or shoving your brother off the swings. And take your sister with you so she can have a go on the slide."

Sam lets Isabella slip off his lap. Elijah and Aiden take their sister's hands in theirs, keeping her between them as they amble off towards the playpark. Rory joins them, staying close to Elijah's side.

Cat reaches up to kiss me on the cheek and gives me a dazzling smile. "Thank you, Daddy."

"Yeah, yeah." I wave my hand at the pub's playpark. "Go on, off with you."

Cat doesn't hesitate to run away to catch up with the boys without a backward glance.

Sam smiles wryly at me and gestures towards Cat's plate. "What about the peas?"

I pick up Cat's plate and pour the discarded peas onto mine. I eat all the peas in three forkfuls and give Sam a satisfied smile. "What peas?"

Sam laughs again, the corners of his eyes wrinkling slightly. His age is beginning to show. I think it suits him. He always seemed older than he was when we were teenagers. His family asked a lot of him. They pushed him to give up his childhood. Losing his parents at a young age forced him to give up even more of it.

"I found a grey hair the other day," I tell Sam, voice hushed and conspiratorial.

"Must have been pretty traumatic for you," Sam says with a supreme lack of sympathy, eyes drifting up to my hair.

I brushed it this morning, but since then we've been through a trip to the aquarium and a crab attack, so it probably looks almost as messy as Sam's. He has one particular cowlick near his temple that I really want to smooth down. If he were anyone but Sam, then I might consider climbing over the table and doing it.

Sam's hair has been a constant catastrophe ever since I've known him. He was always a bit different from anyone else in his family in that respect. Most of them, regardless of age, present themselves as refined, well maintained, and slick in appearance. Sam, despite possessing a natural charm, has an air of wildness that marks him out as unique.

"I don't find getting old as scary as I thought I would," I admit to him.

Sam raises his eyebrows in mild disbelief. "Really? Always figured you'd be a right dramatic tosser about it."

"Well, that just goes to show how little you know me."

I check in on the children as they run around the playpark causing havoc. Elijah and Rory are in the middle of an enthusiastic leaf-throwing fight with a couple of other boys. Cat is with Aiden, helping Isabella play on the slide.

Sam leans forward and crosses his arms on the table. He's giving me one of his piercing, Wintery stares, causing me to shift in my seat uncomfortably.

"I know some stuff about you," he says quietly.

I give him a dry look. "Thanks for making that sound as ominous as possible."

"You're welcome," Sam replies, uncaring of my obvious irritation.

I shake my head after a somewhat tense pause, forcing myself to look away from Sam. Jesus, has there ever been a man born more infuriating than this one?

"All right, fine, I'll ask. What do you know about me, oh facetious one?"

Sam's mouth quirks, but he doesn't quite smile. His eyes are still laser-focused on my face like he's waiting for a specific reaction from me.

"I know you're still a mopey git even after sixteen years."

I glower at him, ready to throw so much shade he won't be able to see his own shadow for weeks, but Sam goes on before I can say anything in response.

"I know you enjoy being a teacher. I know you're a great father, because of Rory. I know you hate cars—I just don't know why. I know you loved your wife a lot because it's been five years and you're still wearing your ring. I know you miss *the life*, but at the same time, you really don't. Am I right about any of these? Because I feel like I am."

I'm frozen in my seat, unable to move, speak, or even breathe. I can't decide if I want to leap across the table and strangle Sam or just get as far away from him as I possibly can. I feel like he's inside my head, scraping at the walls of my mind with invisible nails, leaving pieces of himself behind for later examination. His guesses reveal just as much about him as they do me.

That doesn't mean it's okay for him to say those things so carelessly.

Sam looks panicked as if realising he just made a major misstep and led this conversation straight off a cliff. "Shit, Max, I'm sorry. Fuck, I shouldn't have said—"

I take in a much-needed gulp of oxygen, then expel it angrily, cutting him off with a raised hand. "You're a massive prat."

Sam winces, guilt permeating his expression. "Yeah, that hasn't changed much either, apparently."

A very long and strange silence follows. I try to get my head in a less messed-up place, and Sam just sits there looking like he always does. Stubborn and alone. I remember that from when we were young. Sam, with all the socialisation and opportunity for connection he had been given, looked lonelier than he had a right to. It pissed me off back then and it…well. It still does now. But I think the reasons why are different.

"Being you must be terrible," I muse, being deliberately opaque because he's annoyed me and deserves some punishment for that.

Sam tilts his head to one side, eyeing me warily. There are questions waiting to be asked, but he seems afraid to ask them.

"Why do you think that?" he eventually manages.

I give a heavy sigh. "Because despite all the ways you and I are different, there are some things about us which are exactly the same."

Sam dips his head in a slow nod, understanding clear on his face. He crosses his arms and rests them on the table, leaning towards me, as if wanting to create more intimacy between us.

"We both suffered because of our names." I lean in too, willing to bridge the divide just that little bit more. "Because of who our parents are, because of all the crap people expected from us."

"We both lost our wives," Sam adds mildly.

"We both lost our fair share of people," I remind him.

"I had to protect my family," Sam says, a crease forming between his brows. Stubbornness is built into him like cement between bricks. The third house. Solid. Unbreakable.

I'm forced to counter, "And I had to protect mine."

The only real difference is Sam succeeded where I failed.

"My parents were taken from me before the war started by your family," Sam responds coldly.

"We were always at war," I murmur, thinking of all the years my father secretly plotted against the Winters empire. "Your family just didn't know it."

Sam doesn't like that, I can tell. But he doesn't argue with me, because he also knows I'm right.

"We could have been friends."

"No. We couldn't have."

Sam looks increasingly frustrated. Though he keeps his cool and doesn't snap and snarl at me like he once would have.

"But we can be friends now, can't we?" he asks, eyes locked on mine. There's no pleading in his voice, or on his face. A Winters doesn't plead or beg, and only the most civilised of them bother to ask most of the time.

Sam isn't usually one of the civilised ones, which means his asking like this means something.

I scrape my thumb over the hard surface of the wooden table, tearing my gaze away from Sam's, unable to take the scrambled heap of emotions currently tumbling around inside me.

My answer is hard-won, barely coming out victorious after the Great War of Conflicting Thoughts, and barely audible besides.

"Maybe."

Interlude

Sam

LUCILLE IS NOT what I expected. She's attractive but austere. Her features appear to be set in stone like the crags of a cliff face. She looks nothing like her brother, who I have met on numerous occasions at pseudo-business functions. Lucille is short but sturdy, her shoulders on the broader side. She dresses like a soldier in green cargoes and a jacket of the same rough material, her feet clad in thick boots, rather than the high-powered corporate tycoon she's rumoured to have been in the past. Her hair is cut short in a traditional military style.

My grandfather and I look overdressed in comparison, which causes me to feel even more uncomfortable than I usually am wearing the expensive suit and overcoat ensemble most of my family utilises like armour.

Lucille has a solid reputation for being tough as nails, with countless stories having been told of her ruthlessness. If half of what I've heard is true, it isn't difficult for me to imagine why her brother left her in charge, despite the fact the black-market weapons industry is less shy about its systematic misogyny than others.

She agreed to meet with us down at Danger City's docks, inside a nearby warehouse that sits unused beside the dirty bay water. She did not seem bothered to be giving in to our home court advantage. That either speaks of her doubt in our capacity to pose a true threat, or confidence in her people's ability to protect her if things were to go south during our negotiations, which is a distinct possibility. My grandfather isn't one to mince words and Lucille shows herself to be similarly inclined within the first five seconds of our meeting.

"My brother has advised me against working with you. He has told me to dismantle your existing operation and establish ourselves in your place," she tells us, her voice a rough bark, the kind meant for giving orders and dishing out verbal laceration to her subordinates.

Speaking of which, Lucille has brought five intimidatingly large men equipped with even more intimidatingly large guns strapped to them to the meeting to act as her bodyguards. They stand behind her, backs straight and eyes forward, like human drones, making me think she scooped up her protection detail from the ranks of ex-army mercenaries. They're the type who would unload a machine gun's worth of bullets into a man and think nothing of it.

I live under no delusions that my status and wealth would protect me if Lucille gave the command to end my life here and now in this barren warehouse. I'm all too aware what she meant by "dismantle your existing operation". There have been many in the past who have tried to wipe us out. Uprisings and rebellions from allies and enemies. Attempted invasions from outside forces. Every single one of them was put down with the decisive might of our well-garnered power.

Lucille, however, might prove more difficult to fend off. Her own power is likely immense. I've seen evidence of it during the brief brushes of contact I've had with her brother.

Despite his age, my grandfather still cuts a rather imposing figure. He draws himself up to his full and impressive height, fixing Lucille with an expression that borders on contemptuous. His gaze hardens, becoming a more ruthless thing.

"I was under the impression we were coming here to meet with the new leader of your brother's organisation." He makes a faux apologetic gesture with his gloved hand. "Please advise me if I have been misinformed."

His reaction reassures me. Gives me hope. As much as he might want this deal, my grandfather will not bow or scrape to anyone. Part of me prays these two will piss each other off enough they'll call the whole thing quits before anything official can be put in place.

There's a reason I've never tried to make direct contact with Titanus Bullet. It's because I know how he works. His organisation is soaked in enough blood to fill the River Thames. It's doubtful Lucille is any less aggressive in her tactics to retain power and dominance over the black-market weapons trade.

I don't want their kind of business. I certainly don't want their weapons moving through my city. There's enough murder on my family's hands as it is, we don't need to be inviting the angel of death into our house. Danger City is home, and it's supposed to be our responsibility to protect it. It's why we swallow up or disband all the gangs who try to build themselves up and compete.

Competition in a business like ours leads to bloodshed, to war, to the loss of innocent lives. At least if my family has complete control, we can limit the amount of collateral damage. We can keep our city whole.

Lucille takes the hit from my grandfather's suggestion she is not truly the one in control here, that her brother is still the one pulling all the strings, that she is little more than a puppet charged with acting out his whims, with the merest twitch of her left eye. She gives no other reaction to indicate if this is a sore spot for her, let alone if it is the truth.

"My brother has made his views clear." Her tone is easy and congenial, yet another mark of her unshaken nerve. "But," she adds, splaying her hands to us and shrugging lightly, "I have no interest in staking a claim to this city, not for so small a return. It isn't worth the investment."

"Does this mean we've had a wasted journey?" I ask before my grandfather can come up with something a lot more scathing and likely to get us shot in the gut. "If it isn't worth the investment to take over our operation in its entirety, an act I have no doubt you could accomplish with little personal effort, then folding us into your organisation would seem similarly pointless as you'd be sharing your profit unnecessarily."

My grandfather doesn't shoot me a warning look, but I can feel it in the stiffening of his body beside me. He'll be talking to me about this later, I have no doubt. I'm sure he didn't expect me to talk at all. He probably brought me for the sake of transition for when I eventually take over from him.

Lucille, who previously had been saving all her attention for my grandfather, turns her harsh gaze on me. She looks me over, curiosity peeking through the tough façade. It's the first time she's allowed herself to show her hand since we arrived.

"My brother has been trying to break into the European market for quite some time," she explains to me, her eyes slightly narrowed as if seeking some specific form of reaction. "But it has been a struggle, as most of the weapons trade in Europe is controlled by families such as yourself and they do not trust outsiders easily. They do not think we have the sense of *honour* they do. They think once we know their secrets we will inevitably betray them and steal their power." She doesn't need to expand further for me to understand her intent in telling me all this.

"You need a foothold," I say, the pieces slotting into place inside my head. "You need a family like mine who can vouch for your 'honour'." Lucille said the word with no small amount of scorn. If she has behaved similarly with other families like mine, then I can see why she would have problems. It seems likely we were not the first family of my type she approached.

"I want access to your connections," Lucille says, subtly correcting my use of the term "need".

"In exchange for what exactly?" I ask, unwilling to offer anything until I know precisely what's on the table. I'm beginning to think all this could be the cause of more trouble than I previously thought, and I already thought it was going to be a shitshow if we got into bed with her organisation.

Lucille tilts her head to one side, a signal to one of her foot soldiers to step forward.

Behind me and my grandfather, our carefully selected pool of men shifts. Among their number is my friend Will, who I fought my grandfather to include, in need of at least one ally who I know is loyal only to me. They're ready to take out their weapons and open fire if Lucille's man makes any move to do the same.

There's a dusty table standing beside Lucille, upon which a large metal case sits. Her bodyguard flips open the latches on the case and lifts the lid. He steps back to stand vigil over the case and its contents.

Lucile gestures at the box and beckons me forward, her eyes holding a challenge, a request for the trust she has done nothing to earn.

After exchanging a loaded glance with my grandfather, I move to join Lucille in front of the case to examine whatever's inside it.

Lucille turns to look at me, her height meaning she only has to tilt her head up slightly to meet my eyes. "You ask what I can offer in exchange for your help in establishing a foothold in Europe. This is my answer."

Inside the case is a weapon like nothing I've ever seen before. It's shaped vaguely like a gun but resembles something out of a sci-fi film, the body of it a shining silver. There's a faint purple glow on the backend of the weapon. It has no clip for bullets, although a latch on top would be used to fill the weapon with whatever it fires.

"What does it do?" I ask, attempting to keep the dread out of my voice. It would be a tactical mistake to show any weakness or hesitancy in front of Lucille, no matter how much I would prefer to tank this deal right here and now.

Lucille reaches out a hand to lightly touch the weapon. There's a strangely grim quality to her expression as she gazes down at the oddly designed gun. When she looks back up at me, I school my expression to reveal nothing of my growing unease.

"It contains a chemical created by a scientist my brother became quite close with whilst conducting business in Southeast Asia," Lucille tells me, twinges of excitement on her face. The most emotion she's revealed thus far. "The chemical can be used to paralyse a target and trigger certain pain receptors in the brain. You shoot someone with this gun, and it drops them instantly. They'll be incapable of movement while they internally writhe in agony. The effect can last for hours, depending on the size and endurance of the target."

Well. That's some evil shit I want nowhere near my city or its inhabitants.

My grandfather, however, appears to disagree. He comes to stand at my side and peers down at the fucking torture device this woman is trying to sell us, the device she's suggesting we let pass through our port, with no small amount of interest.

I search desperately for a way to shut this whole thing down before it can get out of hand, but my grandfather speaks before I can formulate an exit strategy that won't end in our immediate execution.

"How much cargo would you be looking to transport through

Danger?"

Lucille returns her attention to my grandfather, and they begin a negotiation over how many tons of mindfuck we'd be able to run through Danger's ports and how much we could expect in return for this service. A truly absurd amount, it turns out. Too much for my grandfather to ignore, despite the risks all this could pose if these weapons were linked back to us by the authorities, and more troublingly, the violent reactions from competitors and allies alike once they find out who we've gone into business with.

I turn my head to look back at my men, catching Will's eye almost instantly. We've been in sync since we were children and that bond and ability to read each other has only strengthened with time and maturity. As expected, I see my own sense of horror mirrored on his face. Will gives me a subtle nod, confirming his allegiance and understanding. It offers a mild relief to my thundering nerves. There's at least one person I can trust not to behave in a completely insane way.

I want to remind my grandfather what happened last time we dealt in modified weaponry created by a mad scientist. It ended with one of our first altercations with the young vigilante Polaris and the death of Rajan Mehta, a good man, a father with a young son, who had been nothing but loyal to our family for decades. I would have gone to his funeral if I thought it wouldn't have upset his wife to see any member of the Winters family there.

Listening to my grandfather excitedly accept Lucille's offer, damning me to a future spent dismantling this lunacy once I take his place as head of the family, I have this strange thought pop into my head.

I wish Max was here.

I wish he was here to back me up because I'm sure he would agree there's no way we should be making this deal with Lucille. He'd hate the idea of those weapons in our city just as much as I do.

It strikes an odd chord deep inside me, to imagine another world where the war never happened and Max took his place as my second, the way he was always eventually meant to. I'm strangely certain I would be far less reluctant to step up and become the boss if I knew he was there to help me run things.

He was always so clever as a teen. Strong too. Resilient. He needed to be to survive the ice-cold reptile he had for a father. He could talk circles around people, could cut his enemies off at the knees with a well-placed scathing remark.

I hated him when we were teens with a ferocity that shocked me at times. But to be fair, Max seemed to enjoy driving me to emotional extremes. He was willing to cross every line, obliterate every boundary, break every rule, just to get an explosive reaction from me. He made it so easy to hate him.

Max seems to think he's been neutralised, that he's out of the game and no longer a threat to me. But I'm not so sure, because the moment we met again, it was like all the anger and resentment and pain from years ago came slamming back into focus. It bowled me over like a direct body-shuddering hit, a shock to the system. I realised like a revelation from some godly plane, no one has ever made me feel so much so intensely as Max Summers.

In our business, anyone who can get under your skin like that is beyond dangerous. They're a weakness someone like me could never afford to keep.

So why, then, do I feel the desperate and frighteningly overwhelming need to drag Max back into our world and force him to admit he belongs here with me?

Chapter Eight

"RORY SUMMERS! GET that bloody bird away from the fridge right now, before I decide to bake him into a tiny budgie pie," Penny shouts from the kitchen.

I make what I consider to be the wisest choice and stay in the living room rather than going to investigate what my son has done to distress his grandmother this time.

If it's about what I think it is, I really want to stay out of it. There's no chance of me being able to tell my son off for letting his budgie have free rein in the kitchen, again, with a straight face.

If Penny were to catch me looking in any way amused by the situation, she would thwack me over the head with her dish towel. Or perhaps, the dreaded wooden spoon.

Rory goes running into the kitchen sounding like a herd of angry penguins and pleads his case. "But, gran, Balt likes it on there. The fridge's whirring sound helps him sleep."

I can easily imagine the face Penny has pulled in response to that utter nonsense. Hopefully, she hasn't reached the point where the skin beneath her left eye twitches. That usually means someone is about to get banished to their room. I know this because back when I was a twenty-something snarky little shit, I got sent to my room a lot. So did Natalie.

Neither of us minded very much when we started sharing a room, but Penny didn't need to know that. She probably did know, because Penny always knows, but Natalie and I pretended she didn't.

"Rory," I hear Penny say, a very frustrated edge to her tone. "Birds do not belong anywhere near the fridge. In my opinion, they do not belong inside at all. But your dad insisted, so I allowed Baltazar to live in our flat. However, I draw the line at the place where we keep food. Baltazar stays in his cage or your room. Those are his two options. Feel free to relay the new budgie house rules to that feathered nuisance."

I press my lips together to stop myself from outright laughing. Next to me on the sofa, Cat does not share my restraint. She snorts out a laugh that sounds more mocking than amused. I think for a moment about chastising her. My mother would have scolded me for making such an undignified noise. But I'm not my mother, and I've done and said many things over the years that would have horrified her.

When I'm at my most morose, I find myself thinking maybe part of me is glad my mother didn't live to see the man I've become. My mother was far more tolerant than my father, but she still expected a certain standard of behaviour from me. I was the Summers heir, a boy with a legacy to uphold and a responsibility to prove myself worthy, and I had to act as such.

I remember, once, when I was about eight, my parents and I were at a dinner party during our annual holiday to France. Many important and influential people were in attendance and my mother warned me before we arrived, I was to be seen and not heard unless I was spoken to directly. Even then, I was to keep my replies short and polite.

During the party, I sat with the other children, none of whom I'd met before, and we all remained silent and mostly unmoving throughout dinner.

I complied with my parents' expectations until a boy a few years older than me named Stefan started to pick on Maria, a small girl who was seated between us. He pinched her leg under the table and whispered nasty things to her under his breath. I only heard him because I was sitting so close.

For reasons that made little to no sense to me at the time, I grew angry with Stefan. I didn't understand it then, because he wasn't doing anything to *me*, and I'd been taught by my parents to mind my own business. Unless intervening earned me something in return, obviously, then slightly different rules applied.

That night, however, I decided Stefan being cruel to Maria was my problem, and I reacted in the appropriate fashion. I turned my best scowl on Stefan, hissing at him to stop being a massive tosser and leave Maria alone.

Stefan, because he really was a massive tosser, took offence to this and proceeded to turn his meanness on me for the rest of the party.

I put up with his taunts and pokes and pinches with all the dignity instilled in me by my parents, doing my best to ignore him. My lack of reaction was clearly viewed as another insult by Stefan, and he decided to ramp up the dickhead behaviour. He reached under the table and stabbed me in the thigh with his fork. The fork didn't break my skin, but it bloody hurt enough to force a yelp of pain out of me.

If I was the son my parents wanted me to be, then I would have continued to ignore Stefan and planned revenge for later when I wouldn't get caught. But unfortunately, Sam isn't the only one of us who had something of a temper as a child.

I did nothing to hide my fury when I turned a ferocious glare on Stefan. I grabbed hold of the fork Stefan had used to attack my leg and yanked it out of his hand. By that point, almost everyone sitting at the table had stopped talking to stare disapprovingly at us.

If I was a proper Summers heir, I would have stopped, put the fork on the table, and apologised for causing a scene. But in that moment, I was not thinking of myself as The Summers Heir. I was thinking of myself as The Boy Who Wants to Stab that Pillock Stefan in the Face with His Own Fork.

I didn't stab Stefan in the face. I did something worse, in the eyes of my parents. I shouted. I all but screamed at him. I called that boy some of the worst names I knew as an eight-year-old. I lost my collective shit in the worst possible way for someone like me to do.

I was not a proper heir. I was not the son my parents wanted me to be. I was a little boy who tried to stand up to a bully because, in that moment, it felt like the right thing to do.

After the dinner party, my father shunned me for over a month. My mother still acknowledged me, but she behaved even more coldly towards me than she usually did, which is really saying something. Neither of them ever brought it up. I wasn't punished. I wasn't yelled at. I wasn't locked up in a cellar and starved. I was just...

Nothing.

But they didn't need to say the actual words for me to know how much I'd disappointed them. They never did. I always knew, because when I'd done something to truly upset my parents, I became nothing to them.

If I couldn't be the son and heir they both expected me to be, then they didn't have any other use for me. That is a fact I have known all my life. I wasn't even aware some parents didn't see their children as simply assets to be cultivated and used until I got far older.

My mother loved me, I know she did. But it was the kind of love one can only look at and never touch, like a priceless family heirloom. I knew it was there, but I was not allowed to reach out for it. I don't begrudge her that distance. Love made of glass was all she could understand.

I think my father loved me too, in his own way. A very dangerous way that never did either of us any good. But still. We take what we can from our parents, no matter how damaging it may be.

I loved my parents. I loved them with a desperation that scared me, especially during the war. Everything I did, it was for them. Everything I gave up I gave for them. Everything I now hate myself for, I did to keep them safe.

That night in France was the last time I defended someone else for a very long time.

With those thoughts circling the drain inside my head, I slump down in my seat and sigh heavily. Our large, yellow sofa is soft enough from years of use to let me be swallowed up by it. Natalie used to call our sofa "the ugly duckling", and not just because it truly is the most hideous piece of furniture you will ever have the misfortune to set your eyes on.

Cat brings me out of my thoughts by giving my arm a good, hard poke. "Daddy?"

I turn my head, twisting in my seat to look at her more fully. "Yeah, sweetheart?"

Cat is watching me with critical eyes. "You're doing that not-blinking thing again. Like how Frank does sometimes. It's mega creepy."

I bite back a snort of laughter. "Yes, well, maybe Frank has important things to think about." Like how to break out of his tank and consume us all in our sleep.

Cat looks very unimpressed. "Are you thinking about Mum again?" she asks, apparently willing to change the subject now I've begun teasing.

"Sort of," I tell her, mouth tipping up in a smile.

Cat scowls very seriously at me then, in that way only little girls can pull off.

"Daddy, do you think we can only ever fall in love with one person, like, for *real*?" Her question catches me off guard. Before I can respond, she adds, "It's just, Aiden told me his dad was really in love with his mum, but now everyone keeps trying to get his dad to date other people."

I valiantly attempt to hide how much her question has startled me. I've never heard Cat talk about anything romance or love related before. But I have a feeling this is Cat's roundabout way of asking me if I'm going to be dating anyone else. Maybe I should have expected this conversation to take place at some point. Rory and Cat are getting to an age where they want to understand things, rather than just accept whatever I tell them.

"Well…uh," I start hesitantly, wishing I'd had time to think about what I want to say. I should have considered this scenario and planned what my response would be if either of my children ever brought it up.

Cat is watching me like a hawk. She's pretending not to care, but I can tell she does. Although my daughter may look exactly like Natalie, her expressions are usually all me. I recognise the hidden fear behind her eyes. I'm just not sure what exact thing she's afraid of.

I clear my throat and try again, attempting to sound confident in my response. "No, I don't think there's only one person out there for everyone. I think it's possible to fall in love multiple times in your life."

Cat seems relieved by my answer. She takes her time considering it.

"But they'd have to be someone special to match up with the person you loved before," she remarks after a long pause.

I suppress a smile. Of course, Cat would think of it in those terms.

"It's not a competition." I give her arm a light nudge, to show I'm mostly teasing. "You shouldn't compare people like they're Top Trumps cards."

Cat looks dubious about that. "But you want someone just *as* good, even if they're a *different kind* of good, don't you?"

"Well, there's no proper metric for that, is there?" I say gently in the face of Cat's genuine frustration. "Most of the time you can't control who you fall in love with, anyway. It can just happen, even if you're not looking for it."

Cat *really* doesn't like the sound of that. I truly feel for whoever she might fall in love with one day. She'll probably be very mean to them, at first. Hopefully, they'll have a strong backbone and a foolproof bull-shit detector.

She opens her mouth again to speak, probably to ask me another adult question that all parents dread. Questions like *where do babies come from?* and *how do they make chicken nuggets?* and *why is Mrs Hurley from next door throwing Mr Hurley's clothes out of the window and shouting about him shagging that skinny receptionist from his work?*

Natalie almost strangled Mrs Hurley from next door when she told Rory it was only a matter of time before I had it off with some other woman and left to start a new family. I'd never seen her look so livid in all the time I'd known her.

I don't know exactly what Natalie said that day when she dragged Mrs Hurley into the alley between our buildings, but whatever it was caused Mrs Hurley to never speak to any of us again. She wouldn't even look at us, apart from occasionally sending fearful looks Natalie's way. Every time she did Natalie would flash a fierce, smug smile I thought was the sexiest thing I'd ever seen.

Before Cat can ask whatever difficult question she was about to, Penny comes storming into the living room wielding a kitchen towel and a tub of butter. She stops to loom over us and pierces me with a vicious glare. I instinctively shrink back in my seat and resist the urge to hide behind Cat.

Penny is fuming. Steam is practically coming out of her ears. I sigh inwardly. Rory could try the patience of a saint even on his best day. He and Penny have had plenty of run-ins over the years. They love each other, I've never doubted that, but they don't half get on each other's nerves. Personally, I think it's because they're very alike. I'd have my head bitten off if I ever suggested such a thing out loud to either of them.

"What's going on, Pen?" I ask cautiously.

Penny lets loose an almighty huff. She shoves the tub of butter under my nose and snaps, "What's going on? I'll bloody well tell you what's going on, Maxwell Summers. That sodding rat with wings has pooed in the butter!"

Penny waggles the open tub in my face again and I look down into it. There are indeed budgie droppings in the butter.

Cat peers over to have a look too, and jerks backwards almost immediately.

"Ugh!" she exclaims, screwing up her nose in distaste. "That's nasty."

Penny just keeps on glaring at me.

"I'll go buy some more tomorrow," I say in an effort to make amends.

Penny's glare only intensifies.

"I'll go buy some more right now," I correct myself quickly.

Penny gives a stiff nod of approval, although she continues to glare. I rack my brain, trying to think of what I might have missed.

"I'll make sure Balt stays out of the kitchen," I offer.

Penny still doesn't look pleased, but she appears at least somewhat mollified.

"You'd better, young man," she mutters. "And teach that son of yours to mind his smart mouth."

She doesn't really mean that. Penny loves how Rory is just as snarky as she is.

"I'm sorry, Penny," I call after her as she stalks out of the room like a woman on a mission.

Cat and I share a look of amusement before I get up to go and buy some more bloody butter.

"Can you get me some Coco Pops, please, Daddy?" she asks, batting her long, dark eyelashes at me.

"All right. But you better be in your pyjamas by the time I get back. It's getting late," I respond sternly.

"Deal." Cat stands up on the sofa to wrap her arms around my neck and kiss my cheek.

Rory, having apparently heard the entire exchange from loitering outside the living room, peeks around the doorway.

"Can I have some chocolate for my trip tomorrow?" he asks eagerly.

Rory's class is going on a school trip to London Zoo tomorrow, a fact that concerns me greatly. He and Elijah will probably wind up stealing one of the world's last three panda cubs or something.

I fight back the urge to either laugh or cry once again and turn narrowed eyes on my son. "Right then, my firstborn, you and I are going to have a talk about some budgie poo."

Chapter Nine

"MAX!" EFFIA CALLS to me from across the playground. When I turn my head in her direction, she waves for me to join her and Sam.

Ah, shit.

Rory catches sight of both Kassian and Elijah at the same time and goes running off to meet them, lugging his school bag along with him. The three boys give one another a series of fist bumps and high fives and weird back-slap hugs.

I push my way through the crowd of parents and children to reach Effia and Sam.

Sam looks far more like the billionaire businessman today, wearing one of his expensive suits, all dark and suave. It makes me feel weirdly underdressed in my battered jeans and Converse sneakers.

Penny keeps saying I'm too old to wear Converse, but I don't care. They're the most comfortable shoes I've ever owned, and my father would hate them to the depths of his soul, which are two very good reasons to keep wearing them.

Sam locks eyes with me, his penetrative stare causing my pulse to quicken and a sense of anticipation to roil in my gut. I can't stop myself from thinking about the last time we spoke. Sam asked if we could be friends, and I answered with a vague "maybe". God only knows what I meant by that.

I honestly don't know if Sam and I can be anything other than former enemies and semi-civil acquaintances. It's true that we haven't attacked each other yet, which is a good sign. But the fact we've been able to resist resorting to physical violence, largely due to the presence of our children, isn't exactly a ringing endorsement for a future friendship.

I need more than not choosing to punch each other in the face as our first port of call.

Effia clears her throat very pointedly when neither Sam nor I say anything, despite our epic, and obviously incredibly mature, staring contest.

"Wow," she exclaims, clearly amused about something. "It's like we've travelled back in time sixteen years, except without the teenage boy angst."

That gets a reaction.

Sam switches his attention to Effia. He, by contrast, doesn't look amused at all.

"That isn't funny," he grouses.

Effia looks like she wholeheartedly disagrees on that point. "Stop staring at each other like mutual stalkers, then."

I can't argue with her because we were staring, and it probably did look weird from her perspective. It *felt* weird from mine.

"Where's your other two pests?" I ask Sam before this can get any more awkward.

Sam locks his jaw stubbornly for a moment like he might continue the argument with Effia. But then she gives him a judgmental set of raised eyebrows and he makes the tactical decision to answer me instead.

"Isabella and Aiden are with their grandmother. I have to go to work right after this, so it just made sense to let her take Aiden to school later."

That seems sensible. Cat is getting picked up from the café by Jade and taken to school alongside Xavier.

Effia, after having spent the night at Jade's house, has delivered Kassian here to the playground this morning.

For the trip, we had to get to Rory's school a couple of hours earlier than usual. It will take them a few hours by coach to reach London.

"Ah," I say, nodding solemnly. "So, when the coach leaves, you'll be off to continue your life of crime. Making dodgy deals with drug lords, gunrunners, and government officials."

"These days I mostly do paperwork and not much else," Sam admits, grimacing.

"Your family is probably worried you'll break a nail or something equally horrific and you'll be put out of commission indefinitely. Or maybe they think you'll lose your infamous temper and strangle the mayor of Danger City for the crime of being a right bellend. And then, what if the *Danger Post* gets hold of either story?" I say with enough drollness to ruin a wedding. "I can see the headlines now, *Pillar Of The Community Sam Winters Has Stubbed His Toe Today, We Sit Vigil And Pray For His Swift Recovery*, or *Sexy Billionaire Bachelor Sam Winters Has Assaulted A Politician, Should He Be Put In Prison Or Given A Knighthood?*"

Effia's eyes have widened, and she looks worriedly at Sam like she thinks he might explode in response. But Sam doesn't explode. Or at least, not in anger. He bursts out laughing.

"Jesus Christ, you're such a bloody nightmare." Sam doesn't look very bothered by it.

I shrug one shoulder uncaringly. "I bet it's true though. The family is probably afraid of anything bad happening to you, now you're getting old."

Sam snorts. "I am not getting old. I'm only thirty-five."

"Thirty-five is old when you're chasing down the whippersnapper criminal youths of today," I argue, mostly because it's funny to see Sam get all worked up.

"I have no problem chasing anyone down," he grouses.

"Once you've caught up to a baby drug dealer, how do you subdue them? Do you sit on them?" I ask, concealing a smirk.

Sam narrows his eyes at me. "Oh, so, not only am I old, but now I'm fat as well?" He gets all offended. It looks genuine, which is ridiculous considering how fit he looks in that suit. It's perfectly cut, which helps, but even a badly fitted suit wouldn't be able to hide a body as magazine-cover-ready as Sam's.

"I'm not hearing a denial, Winters. For shame." I shake my head at him in despair. "Sitting on people is rude, you know, even if they are obnoxious youths doused in cheap body spray."

Sam scoffs. "A good crowbar to the knee usually sorts them out."

Yeah, I remember. It was a routine job for the younger members who had recently joined the business in an official capacity to go out and track down rogue dealers who broke the Winters's rules. Back then, it was crowbars, baseball bats, and pocketknives. No guns. You had to work your way up to that.

Sam was ruthless when dealing out punishments and reminders to those who dared betray the family. He had a stronger stomach for it than I did, a fact which did not go unnoticed by my father.

"Sounds lazy." It never stops being fun, making Sam get all twitchy and ragey over something I've done or said. He's so easy. "I'm not very impressed so far, Sam. No wonder the family put you on desk duty."

"I am not on *desk duty*. I was promoted. Being promoted means less action and more paperwork," Sam snaps indignantly.

"Sitting on people got you promoted?" I ask in mock astonishment. "Oh, how the mighty have fallen!"

"I do not *sit* on people!" Sam's voice rises quite significantly in volume.

"Well, no, not anymore, now you've been 'promoted' to sit on a desk chair instead." I press on before Sam can get any more flustered. "Is your desk chair a spinny one?"

"A what?" Sam sputters. His face is a bit red, and his eyes spark with an exasperated kind of anger.

"A spinny chair." I keep my voice level and calm because I know it will annoy him twice as much. "I have a spinny chair in my office. I quite like it."

There's a long pause where Sam just stares at me. He's panting a little bit like he's trying very hard not to throw a punch. I smile beatifically at him. He scowls back.

After an extended stand-off, Sam eventually relents and heaves a great big sigh. He pinches the bridge of his nose. "I've changed my mind. I hate you again."

"I never stopped hating you," I inform him, feeling victorious.

This time Sam smiles in return. "Oh, yeah? Still holding on?"

I shove my hands into the back pockets of my jeans and shrug. "Some of us were raised to hold grudges *properly*."

Sam opens his mouth to offer a retort, but before he can get a word out, Effia makes a loud coughing sound to get our attention. Her gaze flickers between us, and the look on her face is a mixture of entertained and bewildered.

"You're both ridiculous," she proclaims.

Yes, she's probably right about that.

We're saved from any further trouble when one of Rory's teachers, Mr Bennett, calls out for all the children to start lining up to get on the coach.

I scan the crowd for my son, wanting to speak to him before he disappears off with his mates.

When I pick him out, still talking animatedly to Kassian and Elijah about something, I shout his name. Rory turns around and runs over when I make a "come here" hand gesture at him.

I shoot a look at Sam and Effia, silently asking for some space to talk to Rory. They both get the message and amble a fair distance away.

Once I have Rory standing in front of me, I kneel so I'm at face level with my son, wanting him to feel the full power of my potential disappointment in his future actions. He looks back at me, blinking with faux-innocence, like a pick-pocketing bush baby. I am not fooled.

"Stay out of trouble, Rory. I don't want to get a call from your teacher to tell me you've nicked a penguin egg, like the museum trip when you took that scarab amulet thing. No setting fire to anything or using bath bombs to explode toilets, either. And *please*, no more getting into fights with the Lake and McKenzie boys. I mean it. Try to behave yourself on this trip. Or at least try not to get caught quite as much."

Rory makes a face at me, his nose screwing up and his eyes narrowing. It's his stubborn little brat face. I can recognise it easily by now.

"It was an *Egyptian* amulet in a *British* museum, and you can't steal what's already been stolen, Dad," Rory argues. "I haven't set anyone on fire in ages. And I fight with Simon Lake and Derek McKenzie because they're absolute tossers who say mean things to Elijah about his family all the time."

Little shit has an answer for everything. They all do. It's infuriating.

"This isn't a debate." I fix him with the sternest look I can come up with. "No more detention letters or when you come home, you'll find your laptop has mysteriously disappeared and it will stay gone for the foreseeable future, got it?"

Rory grumbles half-heartedly, but he acquiesces.

"Okay. Sorry, Dad."

I ignore his kicked-puppy expression and pull him into one last hug before he has to leave. Despite being a bit angry with me, Rory still hugs me back. We hold on to each other for a few long seconds. I squeeze him extra tight before letting go.

Rory steps away, offering me a big grin that softens my heart as much as I tell myself to retain my hard exterior.

"Be safe. I love you," I say just loud enough for Rory to hear.

He flushes a bit in embarrassment. "Love you too," he mumbles. "I'll text you when we get there."

I feel a pang of something hot and stinging inside my chest. Rory knows how much I worry about him being so far away from me. I don't like the idea I'm pushing my fears onto him, but it does help that he seems to understand.

I stand up and ruffle Rory's hair, which I know he hates. He slaps at my hand and backs away from me.

"Dad!" he huffs. He tries to sort out the hair he spent an obscene amount of time styling this morning. It makes me smile.

"Go on," I urge him, "the coach'll be leaving in a few minutes."

Over my son's head, I can see Elijah and Kassian both waiting for their friend near the coach's entrance. They're waving and shouting animatedly for Rory to hurry up.

Rory gives me a final indignant huff over my mistreatment of his hair before racing off to join his friends. Elijah grabs Rory's arm to pull him into the coach, Kassian following close behind them. They trample inside and find seats at the back.

Sam comes up to stand beside me as we wave off our sons. When the coach has left the playground and disappeared down the road, he turns to me and asks, "Did you give Rory the *stay out of trouble* lecture?"

"No." I scoff derisively. "I gave him the *don't get caught* lecture. Big difference."

"You would say that." Sam shoots me a semi-amused look.

I match his playful tone. "Better than being a reckless idiot like a certain person I could poke with an incredibly short stick."

"Your son is a very honest troublemaker," Sam muses, ignoring my implication about his own daredevilry.

"Yeah," I agree, my tone wistful. "Where did I go wrong?"

"I feel your pain." Sam pulls a comically dismayed face. "I'm pretty sure Aiden is gonna be one of your lot."

"One of my lot?" I ask slowly, raising my eyebrows. "You mean a perfectly reasonable human being with a penchant for self-preservation?"

"A little sneak, yes." Sam's mouth quirks up at the corners.

"Well then, it seems we both failed miserably at this whole parenting lark." I spread my hands out in mock despair.

"Apparently so, yeah." Sam nudges my arm with his elbow. "But, hey, at least we gave it a go."

"Was there ever any doubt you would? Give parenting a go, I mean," I ask, curious. I always figured that Sam was destined to get married to his long-time girlfriend and have loads of Wintery children with her.

Sam shrugs, his face creasing into something unreadable. "Honestly? Before Elijah, I thought I couldn't be a father. Mine died when I was so young. What would I know about being a father to someone else?"

Ah. That makes more sense.

"I don't know," I sigh, frowning. "The only time I've used the experience of my own father's parenting was to recognise what *not* to do with Rory and Cat."

Sam nods in understanding. "I did the same thing with my uncle Paul. Although I don't think it takes a genius to know not to give a kid a black eye or a broken arm just because you're in the mood to hurt someone."

My full attention snaps over to Sam.

"Paul got physical with you?" I ask, wanting to know and not wanting to with equal measure.

There were rumours back in the day. After Sam's parents died, he was cycled around the family. But he spent most of his time with his uncle Paul. He showed up at school and family events with unexplained injuries enough times to get people speculating. I didn't know what to believe then. But now, after all these years and all the time I've had to reflect on those days, I wonder how anyone could have missed the obvious signs of Sam's abuse.

I don't know any details, of course, and I'm not sure I want to know either. The thought of someone hurting a small and basically defence-less child-Sam with those big ash-grey eyes of his, full of sadness and pain, makes me irrationally angry. Sam and I may have never been friends, but he was still a big part of my life. He was still important. He is, even now, one of the few people in the world who I trust.

I know that sounds mad. How can you trust an enemy? Even an ex-enemy. But Sam is the exception to the rule and always has been. I trust him to be exactly who he is and never anything less.

"Yeah," Sam murmurs dismissively, like the memory of his abuse means nothing to him now, like he moved past it a long time ago.

But I know from experience that just because something is buried deep, doesn't mean it can't dig itself back up again. Memories like those have claws meant for scratching through dirt, no matter how thick, desperate to find the surface. You give fresh oxygen to nightmares born from truth and they'll resurrect themselves again and again.

Scars don't fade and trauma is fucking immortal.

"Right," I say with equal neutrality. It's not my place to feel indignant or enraged on Sam's behalf. The fact I do anyway should tell me how important it is to keep my distance from him. He's the kind of person who can get under your skin without even trying. He got under mine when we were only children, and I've lost hope of ever scraping him out. But just because I can't hide doesn't mean I can't run far enough away that it won't matter any more.

"You don't sound surprised?" Sam frames it as a question.

"I'm a primary school teacher," I remind him. "In my job, you learn to see how children behave and what that behaviour means about their lives at home. What gives them away isn't anything obvious. But it is always there if you know how to look for it."

"When I was at primary school there was one teacher, Miss Clover, who I think could see it," Sam tells me. "She never said anything. But sometimes she would look at me, just for a second or two, like I made her feel sad."

"She should have said something. Done something. Helped you," I insist, scowling harshly.

"Maybe," Sam concedes, his acquiescence a quiet thing. "What about your parents?" he asks. "Is there anyone who should have helped you?"

"I didn't need help." I'm thrown by how swiftly Sam managed to turn this around on me.

Sam slides over a look like he doesn't quite believe me. He probably shouldn't.

I really don't know how my interactions with Sam keep getting to this place. To a place where I end up feeling exposed in the most intimate ways possible over things that are better left alone.

Besides, a school playground is hardly the ideal location for this kind of discussion.

Luckily for me, the universe agrees the conversation between Sam and me needs to end because Effia suddenly appears out of the ether.

"Hey, Max, you ready to go? We're gonna be late for work if we don't leave soon," she says, her intelligent eyes flickering between me and Sam with far too much understanding.

"Yes. Work. Let's go do that. Now." I internally grimace at the eagerness in my voice.

Sam gives me a look that borders on disappointed, but I don't care. I refuse to care. How dare he try to trick me into having emotions about him that don't begin and end with *I don't like you*.

"You're going to be late for your meeting too, if you don't shift it, Sam," Effia says. I think she might be trying to help me, which is embarrassing.

"Shit," Sam curses, turning his wrist and glancing down at his expensive-looking watch with a scowl. "Grandad will kick my arse if I'm late again."

Effia nods and makes a sound of agreement. "If you go now then you might just make it. I'll see you on Saturday, yeah?"

Sam jerks his head distractedly. "Yeah, see you."

Rather than immediately dashing off, he pauses, turning to me again with a complicated look on his face.

"What, Sam?" I ask when he doesn't spit out whatever it is he wants to say.

"Are you around tonight?" His gaze pins me to the spot like a butterfly in a display case.

"Around?" I'm confused.

"Yeah. If I come by the café after work, will you be there?" Sam asks a bit more slowly like I'm an idiot for not naturally assuming that's what he meant.

I'm so knocked off kilter by the question I forget to lie.

"I'll be there," I say, because why the bloody hell wouldn't I be there, I live there, not quite grasping the consequences of my answer yet.

"Okay, good. I'll see you later, then." Sam sounds far too pleased with himself. Prat.

Before I can make any form of protest, Sam is gone, marching off to his meeting like he's going to war. It's entirely possible he is.

I find myself left standing there on the playground, gaping at Sam's retreating back.

Effia laughs, having clearly understood exactly what just happened. Sam wasn't going to let me escape from him that easily.

I should have known. Neither of us likes to concede defeat if we can help it.

Yeah, well, bring it on, Sam. Maybe this time I'll finally beat you at something.

Chapter Ten

EFFIA CHOOSES TO launch her investigative attack later that day when we're eating lunch together at a small table in the teachers' lounge.

She waits until Jade has gotten up to go make us all cups of tea at the lounge's kitchenette before crossing her arms and resting them on the table, leaning forward to stare at me with raised eyebrows. "Are you all right with what's going on between you and Sam?"

She looks genuinely concerned, which is somewhat of a surprise. I didn't expect concern. I expected mockery. Or a non-stop stream of nosy as fuck questions, knowing her.

"No," I answer flatly. "Your best friend keeps tricking me into having intense conversations with him."

I wait for her to ask me what Sam and I have been talking about that I consider *intense conversation*, but she doesn't.

"Tricking you?" Effia asks instead, squinting at me with obvious scepticism. "How?"

"He. Well, he… You know how he…" I'm frustrated with myself for not being able to give an adequate answer. I eventually settle on a very pathetic, "He asks me questions."

"He asks you questions," Effia parrots back at a sarcastic speed. "Have you considered just not answering them?"

No. No, I have not. What is wrong with me?

I try not to pout and fail terribly. "That's where the tricking bit comes in."

"You sound ridiculous, you know that, right?" Effia says, tone dirt dry.

My answering sigh is cataclysmic. "Yeah, I know."

"Good. Self-awareness is good."

"Oh, shove off," I grouse at her teasing. It's admittedly not my best comeback.

"Nope." Effia smiles at me like she thinks I'm full of shit.

"You are not being very helpful here," I tell her, in case she doesn't know.

"You haven't told me what I'm supposed to be helping with," Effia rebukes me. "If you don't want to talk to Sam, then don't."

"What if I do?" I ask, just to be contrary. "Want to talk to him, I mean."

"Then talk to him." Effia leans over a bit more on the table and pins me with a hard stare. "Look, you and Sam have a lot of history between you, I know that. When we were young, I hated you. For obvious reasons. But you aren't the same person anymore. Hence the reason why we're now friends. The thing you need to understand is that none of us are the same people we were back then. We fought in a war. We did a lot of things that most kids our age would never have to do. But we were still just kids. It's been over a decade since everything went down between the Winters and the Summers."

I narrow my eyes at her, not quite getting what she's trying to tell me.

Effia recognises the confusion and huffs out an exasperated breath. "What I'm saying is you aren't the boy who called me names and taunted Will and went out of your way to fight with Sam. And Sam isn't the boy who saw everything in shades of black and white, who was oblivious to the harmful impact his actions could have on other people unless they were his friends, and who went out of his way to fight with you. You've both changed in some really important ways. All the things that stopped you two from getting on back then are no longer relevant."

She reaches across the table and lightly touches my wrist. She meets my eyes steadily. "So, if you and Sam want to be friends, or…whatever, then…do it. Because this time around the only opinions that matter are yours and his."

I sit back in my seat and swallow hard. There's nothing but complete sincerity on Effia's face.

Jade comes back to the table then, carrying a plastic tray. On the tray are three cups of tea, along with a few sugar packets, a small jug of milk, and three spoons. She sets the tray down on our table and retakes her seat between me and Effia.

"What are we talking about?" Jade asks into the slightly awkward silence.

Effia slides me a questioning glance. There's a reason she waited until Jade was gone to talk to me about the Sam situation. She knows that although I've gotten used to Jade, and have found myself liking her quite a bit, I still don't feel comfortable discussing certain things around her. Effia respects that, because there are some things she doesn't like talking to anyone other than me about either.

"I was just mentioning that thing we talked about last night," Effia says, a smirk forming on her face, making me feel instantly alert and afraid. "About what would be good for Max to try."

"Oh, the blind dating thing?" Jade says delightedly, sharing a conspiratorial look with Effia.

A painful spike of tension ripples to life inside me. "*No.*"

"Seriously, Max." Effia nudges my arm, the amused expression now gone and replaced with something a lot more concerning. "I know quite a few people I could set you up with. There's this one woman, her name's Zara Arai. She's a nurse and she has a son named Stephen. He's in the same secondary school as Rory. Her husband was a right bastard and ran off a couple of years ago with some other woman. No idea why, because she's genuinely funny and smart and drop-dead gorgeous. I think you'd like her."

I push down the panic threatening to choke me. It isn't Effia's fault, I know she's just trying to help, but the thought of going out with some-one other than Natalie scares me in a way I don't know how to handle.

"You don't have to do anything you don't want to," Jade is quick to put in. "No one is going to force you. But it might be nice for you to meet more people you can spend time with other than me and Effia."

Blimey, she sounds just like Penny. How terrifying for me.

"Just think about it." Effia's voice is non-combative and deceptively casual. "Let me know if you ever want to set something up. It doesn't have to be a proper date. It could just be a group outing kind of thing."

For fuck's sake. First Sam wanting to be friends, now Effia and Jade conspiring to get me a girlfriend. The universe has officially gone off the deep end. Would it be too dramatic to say I'm doomed?

Interlude

Sam

Eight years ago

WHEN I FIRST dig the knife into his skin, Mikael lets out a sharp scream around the dirty rag he has stuffed in his mouth. Dark-red blood seeps from the wound I've created on his chest.

I can feel the oppressive stares of my grandfather's most trusted bagmen on my neck, the fine hairs there sticking up like the fur of a pissed-off alley cat. It's bad enough cutting someone up without having an audience of people who desperately want to see you flinch.

They'll be watching for any show of weakness from me to report back to my grandfather. That's why they're here instead of Will and the others of my generation who I would trust to be loyal to me first and foremost.

My grandfather said he wanted me to deal with this problem personally because I'm the only one he trusts to get it done right. But in reality, it's yet another test of my mettle, to see if I'll crumble under pressure. He's been testing me all my life, and I've become used to swallowing my displeasure and playing along with his games.

For the last few years, my family has been waiting for the moment when the young vigilante Polaris would deign to involve himself in our business. It was a surprise when we first heard about him, a child with superpowers running around fighting crime, and most members of my family laughed it off as ridiculous. They refused to give any validity to the idea a little boy could cause any real problems for us, a crime family who have been around for decades, who own the police and local government, who rule over this city with ultimate power. What could a child possibly do against all that?

My grandfather did not laugh or shunt aside the potential threat. He hunkered down and prepared for the day Polaris would give us a reason to strike out at him from the shadows.

A couple of weeks ago, Polaris finally showed his hand by coming directly to my grandfather and telling him to back off one of our drug runners, Ben, who was working off his little brother's debt to us. Polaris openly threatened my grandfather and in doing so gave him the excuse for a statement of reproach, and sealed Mikael's death warrant in the process.

It's been a while since I picked up a weapon other than a gun. I haven't knifed anyone since I was twenty-one. It was never my preferred weapon. As a teen, before I was allowed access to guns, I used a baseball bat on people who had earned a beating for one reason or another. Often it was drug dealers stealing product, or people who owed us money in various avenues of the business.

Back when I was just starting out and got sent off on the regular to retrieve outstanding debts, it was often Max Summers I was paired with. He was meant to watch my six and act as backup. Although Max behaved more like my partner. He couldn't get away with treating me like a subordinate, but he'd push to be on equal footing with me. Max was infuriatingly cold towards me when we were forced to work together and wielded his tongue like an acid whip against me at every available opportunity. It drove me up the wall with how much I wanted to punch the sarcasm out of his mouth.

If Max were here now, he wouldn't stand back like the others are, waiting for me to fail. He'd plant himself right in front of me, his eyebrows raised in expectation, making it crystal clear he thought I was already a failure, already so disappointing to him, no matter what I did with the knife.

That was the thing with Max. It was impossible to make up ground with him because he seemed to enjoy hating me. No matter how hard I tried to build a professional bond between us, Max refused to be anything less than my direct rival. His every barbed dig and hard-thrown punch an outright challenge to my authority.

Mikael lets out another few whimpers around the rag and I have to dampen the swell of sympathy I feel in my gut. If it were up to me, Mikael would already be dead. I'd have put a bullet in his skull straight off, then cut him up afterwards. But that's not how my grandfather likes us to do things, and I can't break rank in front of his men.

Strapped to a table, Mikael looks far younger than he is, and he was already quite young to start off with, barely in his twenties. I've met him a few times before, only in passing, but enough to know he never should have gotten involved with my family. He doesn't have the stomach for our kind of work. So much so that when he owed us money, it was his older brother who had to step in and pay back his debt by working for us in whatever capacity we deemed fit.

Ben, in contrast, was everything we look for in a young recruit. Smart, diligent, loyal, with plenty to lose. He was doing good work for us.

If only Mikael hadn't gone to Polaris and asked the vigilante for his help getting the Winters family to leave him and his big brother alone. Ben could have worked off the debt and moved on without any fuss or broken skin.

But Mikael did go to Polaris and the young super got too big for his boots, as my grandfather predicted, and made the mistake of thinking he was ready to take my family on. That was a massive miscalculation on his part, which he'll come to realise soon enough.

When he finds Mikael's dead body hanging from a warehouse ceiling with a snowflake carved into his chest, he'll know exactly whose fault it is. He'll understand, finally, what it means to start a war with the most powerful family in Danger City.

Hopefully, it's a lesson we'll only have to teach him once.

*

"HOW QUICKLY CAN we get this done?" Paul asks sardonically, looking far too smug for his own good. He keeps looking at me like his face is going to catch my fist and the only reason he hasn't caught it before is that I don't think I'd be able to stop myself once I got started.

After leaving the school playground I rushed to a family meeting, although I needn't have bothered as I wind up being late once again and earning the stink-eye from my grandfather.

Not five minutes into the meeting, Paul demanded we discuss sorting out one of his issues. According to Paul, one of his heroin-addict exes who owes us money for the drugs Paul got him hooked on in the first place has been talking to the supers about his problems with the Winters family. That's a big, fat warning bell for us. There are rules and Danger City's resident superhero, Polaris, knows this all too well.

Paul's intelligence suggests it's another super, the new one called Wrath, who has taken an interest in helping his ex get out from under us. Polaris is just along for the ride.

He should know better. We taught him better than that. Must be some kind of vigilante hazing thing, to let the new super fuck up and see the consequences, which they will. We'll have no choice now they've gotten involved to put a very decisive and permanent end to the situation.

Honestly, the whole thing disgusts me. Not the poor, stupid kid who got himself wrapped up in Paul's bullshit, but Paul and his deplorable behaviour towards said poor, stupid kid. Even now, he speaks about killing him with such callousness, when it was his fault all this is happening. He shouldn't have dragged the kid back in when he was already out. He certainly shouldn't have sent thugs around to beat the boy up, which I'm certain is what got the attention of Danger's supers. We don't go after druggies with hired muscle without good reason, especially not for an amount so comparatively small as what the kid owed.

Ever since Paul began talking, I've had to stop myself from glaring at my uncle in open contempt. I'm holding back due to the attention and presence of my other family members. My grandfather's clear distaste for the necessary result of Paul's disastrous missteps in handling the problem thus far is also assuaging me somewhat.

For all his dodgy weapons deals, and the fact we sell heroin in the first place, my grandfather still believes the same thing we were all taught: we own this city, and as such it is our responsibility. Danger needs the Winters family. It needs us because we hold it together. We have no interest in destroying it from the inside out. That includes offing a random university student over drug debts he wouldn't have in the first place if he hadn't been chosen as my uncle's fuck-toy when he first came to the city at the tender age of eighteen.

"Have the boy dealt with by Mick and his boys." My grandfather issues the order like the weary patriarch he is.

Mick is one of my grandfather's most trusted men, perfect for this kind of job. He's loyal and dedicated to his work. That boy doesn't stand a chance of surviving him.

"What about the girl, his roommate?" Paul presses, never having known when to realise how thin the ice he's walking on is and shut up. He glowers at my grandfather, his lip curling. "Word is she's the one who asked that new vigilante cunt to kill me. The little bitch," he spits.

Unfortunately, every member of my family sitting around the table make noises of agreement. They might not agree with what Paul did, but like hell will they accept a direct threat like that against one of our own.

My grandfather looks to me, a conflicted expression flickering on his face. It's rare my grandfather shows any doubt over what decision to make, and he only ever shares that kind of thing with me. All anyone else sees is the diamond-hewn façade.

I want to shake my head and tell him we should leave the girl alone. She was probably just afraid for her friend. No attempt on Paul's life was ever made, so Polaris likely managed to rein in his new super ally.

But I know my grandfather won't be able to let this go without making everyone think he's going soft. He rubs at his face and heaves a soft sigh, giving me an apologetic look. He also knows if it were me, I wouldn't give a single shit about appearing weak, not if it meant sparing a young girl's life.

"Tell Mick to deal with her too."

Paul looks so self-satisfied it makes my hand twitch. One of these days, I'll wipe that look off his fucking face. It's written on my bucket list in blood.

I hope all this makes my grandfather finally see we need to remove Paul as the owner of Black Ice. He quite clearly cannot be trusted with the responsibility. He brought the supers down on us for bloody hell's sake. There's no telling when Polaris will decide he's had enough and start breaking his own rules just to get rid of us. As far as I'm concerned, it's only a matter of time before one of that lot turns into an avenging angel rather than one of mercy. This new super, Wrath, seems to have a particularly violent streak in him. He's been reported to have killed a whole gang of people traffickers down at the docks not long ago.

I can't say I'm at all broken up about that. If Wrath hadn't gotten to them first, we would have dealt with them. We don't permit that kind of shit in our city any more than the supers do.

"All right then," my grandfather says, leaning forward in his chair with a more pleased expression. It's like a warning shot. "I think we can safely move on to the *actual* reason I called a meeting today."

I get the odd feeling I'm being watched for a reaction, but instead of checking around the table to confirm my theory, I keep my eyes trained expectantly on my grandfather, waiting for whatever hammer is going drop.

"We have discussed the future of our business, of our family's con-tinued legacy"—he gives me one of those meaningful looks that never means anything good for me—"and it has been unilaterally agreed upon that it is time for you to step into my shoes and replace me as head of the family." His expression hardens into something sterner. "This should have happened years ago, of course. I know it's been difficult. It was agreed you needed time after Ashley's tragic departure."

"Departure", like my wife was a sunken ship or missed train. A low simmer of anger begins to rise inside me at the mention of Ashley. They've always treated her death like it was an unfortunate event, a roadblock I would have to manoeuvre around and leave behind. I've resented them all for that, the push I've felt to let go of the woman I loved more than life, the woman I've loved since I was a teenager, just because it was inconvenient for everyone else that my grief sometimes crippled me. If a man can't show weakness when the love of his life dies, then what possible reason could be grand enough to allow for it?

Answer: there is no reason. Not for a Winters. Certainly not for the Winters's heir.

"When?" I demand, unable to hide my anger as a cacophony of panicked strings erupt to life inside my chest like a freshly woken hive of bees. "When did you all get together and decide something this important about my life without any input from me? I never agreed to anything like this, and you have no right to speak of it as if I did."

I should have seen this coming. All the warning signs were there. I think it was a mixture of wilful ignorance, my distraction over whatever's going on with Max, and the looming disaster that is my grandfather's deal with Lucille.

It wasn't until this very second, the true and equivocal moment of no return, I realised just how much I do not want to take over from my grandfather. How much I would hate the job I've been raised to inherit since early childhood.

"Samuel," my grandfather says, a small frown drawing his eyebrows together. He looks genuinely perplexed by my response. "You've known my intention for years, to pass along everything to you when I felt the time was right. Where is this sudden animosity toward the idea coming from?"

Max. I realise then, with stunning clarity. This is because of Max Summers. I didn't allow myself to think about it before, about how much his reintroduction has meant to me, how much it's impacted my life in such a short amount of time.

Max has shown me what it looks like when you break away from the expectation of family and mould your sense of self. He's shown me it's possible to live a life devoid of decades-old obligation and bad blood and violence dictated by archaic notions of power and control.

If I take this position as head of the family, if I become everything I was always told I'm meant to be, there's no chance I'll be able to carve out a pocket of freedom for myself. I'll be Samuel Winters forever more, not Sam. Who I am and all the things I want will have to be put aside and boxed up and kicked into the shadows to slowly wilt and die there.

If I let my grandfather put his crown on my head, I will never get to be the man *I* want to be.

When I don't respond to my grandfather's confused prodding, he goes blithely on talking like it's all a forgone conclusion and my compliance has been silently promised.

"We'll need to discuss introducing you to certain people, changing names on paperwork to give you more footing within the parts of the business you aren't already involved with. You'll also need to give up some of the responsibilities you have filling your time. All this work you've been doing with the waterfront property, trying to set it up as a legitimate enterprise, this can be looked after by one of your subordinates, yes?"

Bracing myself for extreme blowback, I try to deal with this reasonably, although my logical mind tells me I'm being hopelessly optimistic. There's no possible version of what comes next that won't end in the destruction of what tethers me to these people, to my grandfather. I know better than most there is no middle ground when you're one of us. It's all or nothing, and if it's nothing, you become worse than a traitor, you become a *liability*.

"No," I say, quiet but unmistakably firm.

There's a long pause, the air in the room seeming to still, the oxygen level depleting until it feels like there's barely enough to live on. Everyone around the table is staring at us. At the leader of their past and the believed leader of their future. They're waiting to see how this plays out before giving an outward reaction. It's what we were all taught to do. We're all family here, after all.

"What do you mean, no?" my grandfather asks in a voice so low and cold it sounds threatening, which is because it is. A warning for me to tread lightly, to turn back and fix this mistake before it grows into something bigger and less forgivable. "*No* to *what?*" His voice is like a blade made of indestructible ice.

Fuck sounding firm, I need him to understand. I need to be bold and clear. I need to be *resolute.*

"I mean no." I keep my voice level and controlled, my eyes latched to my grandfather's face with an unapologetic lack of respect I've flirted with before but never indulged in to quite this degree. "I will not be giving up control of my plans for waterfront property. I mean no. I will not be taking on other responsibilities, including this nightmare deal you've made with Lucille. I mean no. I will not be taking over the business. I'd rather get up from this table and walk away from everything than become you, Grandfather, and I'm sorry if that hurts you, but I will not live for anyone's sake than my own and my children's."

And maybe someone else, my mind whispers unhelpfully.

There's another long pause where I refuse to look away from my grandfather even as his face goes through a series of unpleasant emotions. He eventually settles on the expected fury, grey eyes like the sky gearing up for a barrage of hailstones. Every wrinkle on his face seems to have been hacked into him like someone shaping stone for a graveyard gargoyle. His hands have fisted on the tabletop, and he raises them once only to bring them right back down, smashing his large hands onto the flat wooden surface.

He looks at me with a level of contempt and betrayal I never thought I would be capable of inspiring in him. I'd be intimidated by it if I weren't so sure of my convictions. I can't bend now. If I bend now, I'll break later and that's just a fact. This has to be it.

My grandfather points a finger at me, his hand literally shaking with rage.

"I don't know what the hell you think you're going to accomplish with this stunt," he snarls at me with no small amount of venom. "But you won't get it this way, I swear to you."

Of course, he thinks this is a stunt. He thinks this is me trying to manipulate something more out of him than the utter and complete control of our multi-billion-pound business.

The potent unease of my family is palpable around me. But I can't spare them anything, not even a glance, because this isn't about them. This is between me and my grandfather, no one else.

He goes on, voice still heavy with an explosive kind of anger I know I inherited from him. "I don't want anything from you, sir," I say, pulling out the old title, the one he told me to stop using when I was a preteen. I think a return to formal is best for whatever's going to happen next. "Apart from the freedom to run my portion of the business without interference as I've been doing for the last decade. I don't want to leave the family, sir. I don't. I am a Winters, and this life is one I will always belong to. But I can't be what you want me to be, not without losing more of myself to it than I'm willing to give."

My grandfather doesn't react at first. He continues to glare at me with slitted, rage-filled eyes, hunched over the table in my direction, hand still shaking with suppressed emotion. When he does give me a response, it's nothing less than what I expected from him at this point.

"You know better than this." His voice is grave and filled with static hostility. "We don't deal in half measures. There are things that come with being a Winters which are non-negotiable." He lets out a stuttered sigh, still more angry than tired as he sits back in his seat. "I'm going to give you the chance to think about this and come to your senses. Leave now, or I will forget you're the only thing I have left of your father and treat you as I would any other man who tried to give me an ultimatum and failed in their loyalty as you have today."

Translation: get out or I'll have you beaten half to death, if not all the way.

I'm sure my grandfather wouldn't kill me, not yet, not without trying to convince me first to change my mind. But there's a large gap between permanent elimination and a painful doling out of justifiable punishment.

I do as my grandfather bids, for perhaps the last time, and push back from the table. In doing so I get my first proper look at the various other family members still gathered. A myriad of reactions plays out across different faces.

Of them all, my uncle Paul's chills me the most. He wears a grim look of satisfaction, almost as if he'd been waiting with bated breath for this day to come, and for all I know he has. He's always seemed to know the inside of my head, where and when and how to apply pressure to elicit the most pain. People who enjoy hurting others for sport often do.

I risk one last glance back at my grandfather, who is now half slumped on his throne, face drawn and white as a sheet, like a king with a freshly broken heart, his devastation clear for me to see, even if it's still a mystery to him and everyone else.

It wasn't my intention to betray him, but there was no other acceptable choice for me to make if I'm to have any possibility of retaining what I've built, let alone the freedom to chase after the one man he would never approve of.

As I stride out of the room with a purposeful gait and the straightening of my back, walking tall and without regret, a great weight lifts off my shoulders.

No matter what happens from here, the consequences and the opportunities that might come from it, I refuse to run from the rest of my life.

Chapter Eleven

SAM SHOWS UP around seven. I'm nervous as hell and trying really hard not to show it. Penny is upstairs with Cat and Rory watching some animated film about a snarky princess. I managed to escape that fate by going down into the café to mop the floor and clean the tables.

Sam knocks on the front door to get my attention. I look up from wiping down the counter and wave him in as casually as I can manage. Sam comes inside and makes his way over to me while I finish cleaning the countertop. I put a healthy bit of distance between us by going behind it. I'm aware it's stupid but having a blockade of some kind makes me feel better.

"Max." Sam tilts his head forward in greeting.

I return the polite nod. "Sam."

We have a bit of a standoff, then. Neither one of us quite knows how to proceed, which isn't fair. Sam is the one who came to me. He should be the one with a plan of action.

"Do you want some tea?" I ask because the silence is getting to me.

"No," Sam answers unhelpfully.

Well, that's me tapped out for conversation. Great.

"I think I'll make myself some tea then—" I start to say, already half-turning, but Sam interrupts.

"Do I really make you *this* nervous?" he asks, watching me with that perceptive Winters stare he's gotten so good at.

"You don't make me nervous," I say hotly. "You make me annoyed. And irritated. Because you are annoying. And very irritating."

Sam does that weird lopsided smiling thing at me, which only serves to make me want to smack him more.

"Liar." He still looks bizarrely pleased. "I mean, I know you think I'm annoying, but you're also nervous. I just don't understand why."

"You forgot irritating," I grumble. "I find you annoying *and* irritating."

"Those words mean the same thing." Sam manages to make it sound like he's slammed down a winning poker hand.

My response is appropriately acerbic. "Yes, I know, Sam. But someone as consistently infuriating as you deserves to have it called out with a liberal use of both reiteration and emphasis."

"Max," Sam says dryly, and just keeps on looking at me.

"All right, you called it. I'm nervous. Congratulations. You win this round of the *call-out game*." I clap my hands sarcastically.

Sam looks triumphant for about two seconds until he realises we've reached another dead end in the conversation and he has nowhere to go.

"Uh, so…" He struggles to grasp for something we can talk about. "How was your day at work?"

Aha, yes, my work is a safe topic for both of us. Very good, Sam, very good.

"Mostly fine. The only troubling bit was when Effia brought up the topic of blind dating during lunch."

Sam makes a sympathetic face. "Will and Charlotte tried to do the same thing to me at their wedding."

"Well," I say with a supreme *lack* of sympathy. "That was your fault for voluntarily attending a social event, wasn't it?"

"True. It came out of left field though. I realised afterwards Charlotte had been hinting at it for weeks and I'd apparently agreed to meet this woman at some point. She probably asked me when I was distracted by work or the children."

"Women, Sam." I shake my head ruefully. "They're evil geniuses."

"Reckon if your father had been a woman then we'd all be living in a Summers-ruled city right now?" Sam muses.

"If my father had been a woman then she'd have knocked you off early on in the war, like a sensible person."

"Your father gave it his best shot, to be fair," Sam offers diplomatically.

"Good thing he never asked me to assassinate you." I wince seconds after the sentence leaves my mouth. It will likely always be too soon for that sort of joke.

Sam eyes me thoughtfully, but he doesn't seem pissed off, which is a small miracle. "Do you think you would have? If he'd asked you to kill me."

Shit. What kind of question is that?

A valid one, maybe.

I think about when my father gave Sam's kill order to someone else, one of his loyal enforcers, and although I felt slighted at having the responsibility which probably should have been mine given away, a tiny part of me was relieved.

However much I hated Sam, and I really *did* hate him back then, I was also afraid I did not have it in me to end him permanently. Not unless it was in the heat of the moment if it was either me or him and maybe not even then.

In truth, by the time the war was drawing to a close, I didn't see Sam as my enemy in the same way anymore. I just wanted the war to end, and I didn't much care how that happened, so long as I and my family survived the experience.

"I don't know." It's as honest as I can be.

Sam nods as if he expected that response. "You would have been a pretty rubbish assassin." He looks at me with an odd fondness.

"I'm not going to argue with you about my murdering skills," I huff, crossing my arms over my chest and glowering at him.

"Nice to know there's one thing you won't fight me on," Sam mutters.

I rest my crossed arms on the countertop and lean forward, releasing a short sigh. "Yeah, well, I've had enough of arguing with a bull-headed prat for one day as it is," I say pointedly.

Sam copies me by sitting on one of the stools and leaning on the counter. "You've been getting into fights with someone who isn't me?" He looks intrigued.

"Jealous?" I joke, raising my eyebrows at him.

"Very," Sam replies without hesitation.

We both laugh, but there's an edge to Sam's laughter like he doesn't think it's all that funny and maybe the jealousy remark wasn't complete nonsense after all. I don't know what to make of the pleasant feelings that idea inspires.

"Who is it I need to fight to win back your antagonism?" he asks, teasing with the same bizarre edge.

I stare down at the counter, frowning at it for a handful of seconds before looking back up at Sam again. Only then do I realise how close our faces have become. Weird. I think about backing up, but that seems like an even weirder response. Besides, I feel comfortable where I am. If Sam really starts to bother me, I'll just have to shove him off his stool and onto the freshly cleaned floor. Sounds like a solid plan to me.

For God knows what reason, I answer Sam's question honestly. "I got into it with this dickhead teacher Craig Pine during a staff meeting after school."

Pine and I started working at Foxwood Hill Primary at the same time. We were both young and had very little experience apart from the schools we'd worked in during our teacher training. Other than that, we couldn't have been more different in terms of personality and teaching styles.

Pine is what some people would call "old school" in his approach. He's also a bit of a yeller. As in, he yells. A whole fucking lot.

I don't mind *how* a child wants to learn so long as they're interested and excited about doing it. Education shouldn't have to be dull or intimidating, especially not for a six-year-old.

During the meeting, Pine and I got into an argument over Jeremy, a child who is struggling more than most with his reading and written work. Pine thinks Jeremy is just lazy, and the fact he's got a smart mouth on him and seems addicted to trouble probably doesn't help.

But after observing him closely for the last couple of months, I think Jeremy may be dyslexic. His struggles seem to go deeper than a refusal to try or a disruptive attitude.

I want to discuss with his parents the idea of getting Jeremy professionally assessed, but Pine thinks it's not worth the effort. Since we both teach him, it would be better if we agreed on something like this before taking it forward. I don't want to sit in a meeting with Jeremy's parents telling them their son might have dyslexia with Pine right next to me saying he thinks I'm wrong. No parent likes being told their child might face challenges other children won't. If one teacher is saying there's something they might need to be aware of and another is saying there's no problem, then it's not rocket science to figure out who they'll want to listen to.

But I do want to help Jeremy. He's a sweet boy really, despite his rudeness and occasional mean streak. Jeremy reminds me of myself in a lot of ways. He's created a hard exterior to protect himself from being taunted for his academic difficulties. I can understand the need to feel safe behind mental walls of your own creation.

I explain all this to Sam, who listens to me like he cares what my work-related problems are. He seems genuinely interested in what I'm saying and appears to be siding with me in the argument.

"If you feel like Jeremy could benefit from the extra support then I say fuck this Pine bloke," Sam proclaims. "Have you spoken to the headmaster about bringing in Jeremy's parents?"

I shake my head, causing a few locks of my overgrown fringe to fall into my eyes. I run a hand through my hair, pushing it back. Sam's eyes follow the movement with an indecent level of focus.

"Not yet," I admit, answering Sam's question. "Pine just pissed me off so much I knew if I went to our head with the idea then I'd end up saying something stupid. The angry kind of stupid."

"Ah." Sam nods in understanding. "I've done plenty of that, especially when I was first making my way up in the business."

"I'm surprised they forced you to go through the usual bullshit and didn't just hand you the top spot," I say honestly.

Sam's expression hardens into something cold and rigid. "They tried to make me take over a portion of the business straight off, but I told them no. I wanted to earn my place. It wasn't about the position or the money or anything like that. It was about respect. No one can give that to you. In our line of work, you have to show you're worthy of it, or the power you hold might as well be made of tissue paper. It wouldn't withstand fuck all."

I can't help but notice he called it *our* line of work. It seems, in Sam's head, I'm still one of them, despite having been out of the game for sixteen years. I suppose he's right to think so. Growing up as we did was a hardcore cultural experience. Once a gangster, always a gangster, whether you're practicing or not.

"'Course, it's all about the come-up. Gotta ride rough before you can glide," I say, completely deadpan. Mocking him. Always mocking him. "Can't have Sam Winters doing anything the easy way. Goes against the natural order of shit, yeah? Who wants a gangster king without grit in his cuts and dried blood under his fingernails?"

Sam's temper gets the better of him for a handful of seconds. Shoulders tightening, fists clenching. Face twisting, mouth forming a snarl. Eyes burning like two radioactive silver coins.

But he doesn't move back, doesn't back down at all. Can't. Incapable. Never does. Never will. I hope. He wouldn't be him if he did. I'd be disappointed if he ever proved to be less than the unrelenting, dark creature I know him to be deep down inside.

Sam is glaring me into the ground, a threat and a promise and an enticement all wrapped up into one expression.

I'm starkly reminded of all the times we fought in the ring, or out on the street, or behind the gym at school. The sound of a crowd cheering for blood and taking bets. Sweat dripping from my hair and red gushing from my nose, the taste of salt and metal on my lips. The absolute rush of it, my heart battering against my chest, the feel of my fist coming into contact with white-hot, soaking-wet flesh covering a body heaving from violence-induced adrenaline.

Sam's jaw clicks with how hard he's gritting his teeth, clearly fighting a losing battle against the torrent of anger threatening to overtake him.

I brace myself for something interesting to happen.

"Do you *want* me to lay you out?" Sam growls at me. Literally growls, like he's a wolf or some shit.

I can't stop myself from smiling back at him, shark-like, all teeth and no regret. A truly irresponsible amount of smugness on my face. Here we are, two different animals from the same band of the food chain, who grew up in equally dangerous habitats.

"Take a swipe if you think it will calm you down a bit." I narrow my eyes at him in confused antipathy. "Jesus, Sam. Feel like telling me what's gotten you so keyed up you're willing to start an actual fistfight with me over some low-heat banter?"

Sam's entire demeanour seems to shift from one blink to the next, switching from full throttle let's-go-bitch to standby.

He rolls his shoulders back to loosen them up and unclenches his fists, pressing his hands down on the counter in a deliberate show of calm. But he still doesn't put any space between us, keeping our faces far too close for barely civil acquaintances.

I don't move away from him either, which just proves how recklessly we both treat our mental health.

"Meeting went bad earlier," Sam admits, voice gruff and marvellously unapologetic. "Guess I'm more on edge than I realised."

"You think?" I scoff, but when his hackles immediately rise in response, I soften my voice to something less baiting. "Chill out, Cthulhu. I'm attempting to understand your ragey feelings. Tell me what happened that pissed you off so much."

Sam appears ready and willing to take this to a more volatile place, but perhaps the fact we're in my family home stops him. Allows him to utilise some of that ingrained self-control all our sort have scratched into our DNA.

"My grandfather wants to retire," he tells me, voice low and miserable and still kind of furious.

"So, what?" I squint at him, thinking over the implications. "The family wants you to step up?"

That can't be a shock to Sam. He was always meant to take his place as head of the family. His grandfather named him his successor when Sam was a child. That's how it works with the Winters family. Sam's dad was his grandfather's favourite son, so Sam was his favourite grandson in turn. We all knew from the word go Sam would be king one day.

I'm honestly surprised it's taken this long for his grandfather to abdicate his throne to make way for his chosen heir. I'd guess if it wasn't for Ashley's death, Sam would have become the big boss well before now.

Sam gets this grim look on his face that I'm not sure how to interpret. "I turned it down. Told them I didn't want to be in charge. Told them I'd rather walk away and go legit than take over the business."

He could have thrown a grenade at my face, and I would have been less horrified. The fuck did he just say to me?

"Sam, you lunatic, do you *want* to die?" My voice has gone all choked and incredulous. "What the hell would you go and do something monumentally stupid like that for?"

This makes no sense to me. Apart from anything else, what he's done is damn near suicidal. You don't just *turn down* becoming head of the Danger City mafia. You don't get to *walk away* from our business, either. Those aren't the rules. Sam knows that. He knows the consequences, better than most. If he thinks they'll spare him just because he's family by blood, he's off his rocker.

I was shoved out, not as a mercy, but as another form of punishment. Publicly shaming my family in the press and banishing me from the business, from *the life*, was just another way of hurting my father. It would have been less painful to him if I'd been killed. Letting me go told everyone, including anyone still loyal to the Summers, exactly how little a threat the Winters family thought I was.

Sam's betrayal would require a completely different response. If he tried to abandon them, his family would need to make a big and bloody statement to regain control in the wake of it.

"I ain't interested in hashing this all out with you, Max," Sam glowers, stubborn as an old goat and not nearly as cute. He puts on his most obstinate face. I want to punch it. He bites out at me, "I have my reasons and that's all you get to know, all right?"

Oh, he has his *reasons*. Well, that's okay, then, isn't it? *My reasons*, I ask you. For fuck's sake.

"Bulletproof reasons, are they?" I mutter belligerently, still unable to believe I'm standing opposite a walking dead man who is not acting like he knows he's going to be fucking dead soon.

"Max." Sam's voice isn't channelling Cujo energy any more. It's gone cold and quiet, a voice meant to evoke the same feeling you get when you're stumbling through the depth of a forest at night with some monster stalking you. You can't see the terrifying thing, but you know it's there. "Mind your own, yeah?"

There are so many things I could throw at him, so many ways to provoke a violent reaction from this person I know both too well and not really at all. He's like a mystery box covered in cracks. Kick him into the wall enough times and he'll smash right open, unleash all that thick shadow and gnashing teeth writhing and roiling within, and make someone saner than me regret taking their boot to him in the first place.

I can't imagine ever being sorry for tearing into Sam Winters and ripping his bullshit secrets out. The satisfaction of watching them scream and thrash as they burn in direct sunlight would be too great.

"All right then, Winters, we'll go on and pretend you're not a liability in a jacket right now if it means that much to you."

Sam makes rumbly sounds of discontent, but he doesn't argue with me.

"If you'll remember, before you decided to get all dramatic for no good reason" — I arch both eyebrows at him scornfully — "we were discussing *my* problem of the day."

"Sorry, you're right, we were." Sam somehow manages to apologise without sounding in the least contrite. It's a unique skill. "Okay then, what's the worst-case scenario if you talk to Jeremy's parents with or without this tosser Pine?"

I think about that for a minute, considering my answer.

"Worst case scenario is Pine actively undermining my attempt to give Jeremy the support he needs. If we're really going to help him, then the situation needs to be taken seriously."

"And you don't think Pine will change his mind?" Sam asks.

I make a sound of contempt. "Pine has hated me from day one, he'll probably go out of his way to cause problems if I try to push this."

"Hated you from day one." There's humour in Sam's voice now. "Why'd you think that? Did he call you a ginger twat as well?"

"Too soon, Sam," I drawl at him, eyes slightly narrowed in his direction. "Still too soon."

Sam looks annoyingly pleased with himself. "Want me to have your new arch-nemesis's car crushed?" His expression makes it clear the offer is a genuine one.

I consider it for about five seconds, imagining the absolute and complete satisfaction I would feel at fucking with Pine's beloved Ford Fiesta.

"Nah, thanks," I eventually respond, disappointment rising inside me. "Unless you'd be willing to crush him along with it."

Sam makes a low humming sound, pretending to mull it over. Maybe. I wouldn't put it past Sam to seriously offer something like that. Making people disappear is very much within his wheelhouse of expertise.

We bicker back and forth for a while after that. It feels more natural to just hang around with Sam than it logically should. Our conversation stays mostly neutral and there are no more almost-brawls, which is a shame because I haven't been in a good brawl for ages.

Sam's children are staying with their grandmother for the night so neither of us watches the clock too avidly.

At some point, Cat and Rory come downstairs to say goodnight to me. A bit later, Penny does the same. She gives me and Sam a knowing look I decide to ignore. I don't know what she means by it anyway.

When Sam does eventually mention going home, I think we're both shocked to discover how many hours have passed. It's close to one o'clock in the morning.

"Yeah, I better get off to bed. I have school in the morning."

"Right, I'll be dead on my feet tomorrow if I stay up much later." Sam scowls to himself. "I used to be able to stay awake all night and then go to work all day without feeling a bit tired. These days I need seven hours of sleep, minimum."

I smirk at him. "Like I said before, that's because you're old now."

"I'm not old," Sam huffs.

"You keep living in that world of denial, mate."

Sam looks very much like he wants to give me a smack. I mentally dare him to try it.

"So, are you going to take Effia up on her idea to go out on a group date or whatever?" he asks instead, eyeing me intently.

The question catches me off guard.

"I don't know." It's a lie. There's nothing in this world that could convince me to go along with—

"Okay, well, I've given in to the pressure," Sam admits, interrupting my train of thought. "Sort of. I'm going out with the girl, Riley I think her name is, that Charlotte and Will introduced me to at the wedding. I caved so they'd stop bugging me about it. I invited Riley to the cinema this weekend. I was already going with Effia and Jade. So, it's not really a date."

I just stare at Sam, feeling too many things at once to respond straight away.

"You could come. If you want," he offers, sounding. What? Hopeful?

No. That can't be right. I must be reading him wrong.

"I don't know if…uh…" Shit. Shit. Shit. What do I say? What do I *want* to say?

"You don't have to answer right now," Sam reassures me, forcing a casual shrug.

"Okay," I manage to croak out, which is just great, really great, thank you.

"Right. Okay then." Sam nods to himself a bit too vigorously. He smiles at me, but it doesn't reach his eyes. "I'll see you…when I see you, Max." He blinks at me for another few seconds before sliding off his stool and striding out of the front door.

I stare after him, feeling an odd mixture of relief and disappointment at his departure.

What the bloody hell is going on?

Chapter Twelve

Five years earlier

"WE NEED TO get Rory a new school jumper," Natalie says to me from across the table. Her hazel eyes practically glow in the candlelight of the restaurant.

It's Saturday night and we're in the middle of one of our official bimonthly dates. Last year, Natalie and I realised we were arguing a lot more than usual. It didn't take us long to figure out the reason we were sniping at each other so much was because we weren't spending any time together just the two of us.

Life can very easily fall into a pattern, especially when you have a full-time job and two children. Going on actual dates kind of goes out of the window after your first child, and basically becomes a mythical event after your second.

Natalie and I spoke to Penny about our problem, and she insisted on setting up a schedule of sorts. I know it doesn't sound very romantic, but honestly, after about seven years of marriage and two children, you have to plan shit. If you don't plan and schedule time together, it just won't happen. There's always something else to do.

So, after a lot of talking between us and Penny, we came up with the Two Dates Per Month deal. I felt a bit guilty about it at first, leaving Penny at home with two young — and bloody loud — children. But it really did help. Getting to be alone with Natalie is worth pretty much anything.

Natalie stabs her fork through a mini carrot and eats it. The carrot, I mean, not the fork. Although that would have been more impressive.

I say this out loud to Natalie and she raises a dark eyebrow at me.

"If I ever decide to join the circus, then that can be my act." She puts on a much deeper, announcer's voice. "Welcome to the stage, Natalie Summers: The Amazing Fork Swallower."

I snort into my glass of water mid-drink and some of it dribbles out of my mouth. I wipe the water off my chin, my face reddening.

"People would come from far and wide to gaze upon such pure talent," I say, completely deadpan.

Natalie grins at me. "Hmmm, yes, and then I would meet a big, muscular knife swallower named Billy the Blade and run off with him to an exotic island."

"Billy the Blade?" I scoff. "Sounds like a right tosser."

Natalie muses over this for a second before saying, "Hm, I do seem to have a thing for tossers." She smiles slyly at me.

"I'm glad you made an exception for me, then."

"Yep." Natalie bobs her head in a nod. "I settled for a ginger twat instead."

My mind brings up the image of a boy with a dangerous right hook and vivid quicksilver eyes full of passionate rage, the kind that only lives inside those who have known true cruelty. Those who have known loss and pain so great they threaten to eclipse every fissure of light you manage to scratch into that opaque wall of grief.

Then there are screams and gunshots and hot blood and constant pain and a never-ending state of despair. I hear my uncle laughing, blood dripping from the blade in his hand. I see my father's face turn ashen and afraid. I smell the stench of dead bodies rotting in what was once my home. I feel the cold press of my mother's hand as I clutched it against my cheek before they took her body away to be burned.

Natalie touches my wrist gently. "Max, come back."

I blink rapidly at her for a long time before snapping myself out of it, promptly flushing with embarrassment.

Even after so many years, sometimes all it takes is a few words to throw my mind into turmoil again. When I turn a corner or open a long-forgotten door, my demons rip free of their shadows and strike.

The remnants of shame coil in my stomach. I call myself weak, despite knowing intellectually the memories I live with would haunt most people. I hate that my past still has the power to affect my present. I hate that I'm reduced to being the scared teenage boy I once was so easily.

But Natalie has a way of looking at me without any sign of pity. She takes my hand and threads our fingers together on the table. Then she turns my hand over to lay flat, palm up, and grasps hold of my wrist. She presses two fingers against my pulse point.

Copying her, I take hold of Natalie's wrist and count the beats of her pulse. Her hand is warm and rough from years of working in the café. There's a scar on Natalie's left palm from where she cut herself with a cake knife a few years ago. It's about three centimetres long and starkly white. I think I've kissed that scar a million times.

I let the monotonous counting of Natalie's heartbeats relax me until I don't feel like I'm drowning any longer. Once I'm steady again, another form of wariness and embarrassment takes hold of me. I almost dart a quick look around the restaurant to see if anyone is staring at us, but Natalie's gaze locks with mine and I'm unable to focus on anything other than her. She watches me with a kindness that is almost brutal in its sincerity.

Natalie doesn't understand what I've experienced, not really. But she's never judged me for anything I've told her, and she always listens, even when she doesn't get what I'm talking about. It's enough for me that just being with her calms me down.

Maybe if I'd fallen in love with someone from my world it would be easier for me to explain the moments when I lose myself to the past. Natalie isn't easy, and neither is our relationship most of the time. But I would choose her every single time if given the chance.

I try for a moderately not-pathetic smile to reassure Natalie I'm all right.

"Why the bloody hell does Rory need another new school jumper?" I force past my lips. "That's the third one this month he's destroyed."

Natalie laughs in the face of my honest indignation. If there is such a thing as souls, her laughter causes mine to sing.

"He used his last jumper as a football goalpost on a field that was wet and muddy from the rain," she says. "The one before that was flung into the road and run over by a bus. The other jumper was lost out of the window on the M4 after being used as a makeshift flag."

"We need to get child locks for the windows. Do they do those?" I ponder.

"Yeah, they do," Natalie informs me, still smiling like I've amused her in some way. "But we'd have to buy a whole new car."

"Well, I was planning on winning the lottery this week, so…perfect timing," I say drolly.

Natalie laughs again, filling the space between us with light and warmth like only she can.

*

TWO DAYS LATER, Natalie was on her way home from work when she crossed the road and got hit by a car.

Both Natalie and the driver died on impact.

*

A BRISK WIND blows past, making me shiver slightly and pull my pea coat tighter around myself. I run a hand through my hair, pushing it back off my face when the chilling breeze threatens to force the loose strands to poke me in the eye. By the time I leave the cemetery today, my hair will probably look like a bloodied hedgehog.

I'm sitting in front of Natalie's grave with a lap full of blue daisies, the first type of flowers I ever gave her.

It was the day after our first date to the cinema, and I was terrified I'd mucked it up and there was no way Natalie would ever want to go out with me again. I imagined all kinds of nightmare scenarios where she would avoid me or insist that I move out. The thought of leaving the flat, the café, struck me like a physical blow. It was the first place where I'd felt even remotely safe in years.

Intellectually, I knew Natalie would never be so cruel. She was my friend if nothing else. But fear is like a particularly brutal disease. It digs in deep and spreads too fast.

I was out for a run that morning. Running was something I'd started doing only recently. Natalie suggested it, to help me clear some of the cobwebs out of my head before the day officially started. I was sceptical about the idea at first; I didn't see how running around the local park would help me feel less…worn. Tired. Tired of being miserable. Tired of hating myself. Just so fucking tired all the time.

But weirdly, it did help. Running around in the early hours of the morning, not thinking, only concentrating on putting one foot in front of the other. It allowed me to unlock a different level of calm, of genuine peace. For about an hour and a half every day, I felt content in a way I couldn't remember ever feeling before.

The morning after our date, I ran around for close to two hours trying to find that relaxing, centred place inside my head. I failed. Epically. And then I got angry. Because, in case you didn't know, I'm emotionally fucked.

I basically lost my shit in the middle of a park like a lunatic.

I kicked a bench because my instinctive reaction to being upset is apparently to become an absolute idiot for exactly ten seconds then spend the rest of my life regretting those ten seconds.

The bench survived the experience and walked away without injury. My foot, however, was not best pleased with the outcome of my most recent life choice.

I yelped in pain and jumped around for a solid three minutes, cursing. I cursed myself, the bench, my entire life…it was a dramatic moment for me, I'll admit. Luckily, I was out early enough there were no other people around.

Eventually, I sat down on the, in my mind, victorious bench and hunched over with my head in my hands. I felt the crushing weight of defeat. It burned to realise all the progress I thought I'd made since I met Penny and Natalie was worth nothing, meant absolutely nothing. Because when things got hard, I reverted to my old angry, broken self without even thinking about it.

I'd been given my first test, and I'd failed. It hurt to acknowledge that fact. It hurt to realise I would probably always be damaged, that the things I'd lived through in my youth would hold me down, press my face into the dirt, and whisper icy, barbed words into my ear for the rest of my life.

At that moment I felt so goddamn helpless I couldn't fathom ever moving again. It took too much energy just to breathe, let alone do anything else.

I don't know how long I sat on that park bench. It might have been ten minutes, or it might have been over an hour. Time seemed to slip away until all I could concentrate on was each and every inhale and exhale, each and every rise and fall of my chest as I struggled not to panic.

I almost shat myself when a hand touched my shoulder.

*

Eight years earlier

MY HEAD WHIPS up and I turn to stare at whoever thinks it's a good idea to touch a seething young person sitting on a park bench at seven o'clock in the morning.

I bite back the harsh words burning my tongue when I see the hand touching my shoulder is attached to an old woman. The woman is quite clearly homeless, with bedraggled grey hair partially hidden by a thatched, hole-filled hat, and a weathered and wrinkled face softened by warm brown eyes. She's dressed in layers of tattered clothing, most notably a large green overcoat with massive pockets.

"Hello," I say to the old woman, trying not to sound as ripped apart as I feel.

The old woman smiles. "You look like my son," she tells me.

"I'm not your son," I respond slowly, carefully, because my time living on the streets taught me a fair amount of tact.

The old woman thwacks me on the shoulder. "I know that, lad. I haven't lost all my marbles just yet. I meant you look like he did when he came home that last time."

"Came home from where?" I ask because the situation is just strange enough not to feel strange while it's happening.

A swell of sadness fills the old woman's eyes. "War. He came home, but not really. Not all of him. I think he left part of himself over there."

Pinpricks of understanding twist and stab inside my chest. "Maybe what he left behind was too heavy to bring back."

Some of the old woman's wistfulness recedes and she squeezes my shoulder gently. "Is that how it is for you?"

"No." I think about my anger and self-hatred and the fear of rejection I feel deep in my gut. "I kept everything."

The old woman peers at me, bringing her face very close to mine. Her gaze is steady and far too knowing. "Might be time to let some of that old stuff go, lad."

"I don't know how," I whisper, my voice sounding a bit hoarse and scratchy. Too emotional. Too honest. Too everything.

The old woman leans away from me and starts digging around inside the pocket of her large overcoat. I watch her in absent confusion until she finally pulls out a small bag. She settles again and pushes the bag into my hand.

It's a bag of flower seeds.

"You let go of the past by grabbing hold of the present with both hands." She taps the bag with one finger. "Plant a seed and help it grow."

I feel something then, a release of air from inside my chest. It's painfully close to relief.

*

I TOOK THE old woman, whose name I later found out was Sadie, back to the café. I made her a cup of tea. She told me I was terrible at making tea. Penny agreed with her. They laughed. I felt very offended. Natalie kissed me on the cheek and told me she had a great time on our date. I shoved a bagful of seeds at her. Instead of looking at me like I'd lost the plot, Natalie took the seeds and insisted on planting them in one of Penny's flower boxes.

By the time Natalie and I went out on our nineteenth date, the flower box was filled with blue daisies.

"I really need to talk to you," I tell Natalie's headstone. "Which would obviously be a lot easier if you were actually here." I pick off one of the blue petals in my lap and rub it between my thumb and forefinger. "But if you were here, then I wouldn't be going out on this stupid group date thing anyway."

Silence.

Then I hear birds chirping quite angrily behind me. I turn around and see two blackbirds battling it out in mid-air. I watch them fight for a few minutes before turning back to Natalie.

"Yeah, you heard that right." I bark out a laugh. "I don't know how it happened, but I am going on an honest-to-God group date. I blame Sam entirely."

I talked myself in and out of accepting Sam's invitation about a million times before finally agreeing to go.

At first, I thought it wouldn't be so bad. I could just stick to Effia and Jade, two people who I do genuinely enjoy being around. I reasoned it might even be fun to watch Sam try to flirt with his date. I honestly cannot imagine what Sam's version of flirting would involve. I *really* can't imagine what dating Sam must be like. Frustrating, probably. I mean, it's Sam. I'm surprised his wife never offed the prat for the sake of her own sanity.

Just as I'd warmed to the idea of a group outing, however, Effia informed me she'd invited her friend Zara. She told me there was no pressure and she only invited Zara along to balance out the group. I felt like a fist was squeezing my lungs and cutting off my air supply.

I managed to calm myself down in the days leading up to it, but tonight is the night and that same choked, panicked feeling is back in full force.

I went out for a walk to try to clear my head. I didn't mean to end up in the cemetery with an armful of blue daisies. But talking to Natalie can sometimes help me put things into perspective.

"If you can hear me from wherever you are, I know you'll be laughing your arse off right now. In all the years we were married, we never went out on a group date."

Because I don't like people. To be fair, Natalie wasn't all that keen on most people either. That's one of the reasons why we worked so well together. We were equally distrustful, antisocial, and apathetic towards the rest of humanity. Neither of us saw the point in having a big group of friends. We had each other and our family. At the time, that felt like enough.

Although now I'm beginning to wonder if we cut ourselves off a bit too much.

"I'm not sure if I'm ready for this, Nat," I murmur. My chest tightens and I force myself to suck in a laboured breath. "But it's been five years, and I'm starting to realise I need more from my life than the children and missing you." I squeeze my eyes tightly shut, fighting back a stinging sensation that will most likely lead to unwanted tears. "So, I'm gonna try this new thing and see what happens, okay?"

Silence.

One of the pro-fighting blackbirds drops onto Natalie's headstone and chirps up at me. I tear off a few petals and hold my hand out to the bird. His beady little black eyes stare at me for a few seconds before he swoops down to steal a couple of blue petals from my hand. I watch as the blackbird flies off back to the willow tree that stands next to Natalie's grave.

After a few seconds, the blackbird returns with his former enemy. Both blackbirds now sit on Natalie's headstone. They chirp at me before settling down together, cuddling as close to each other as they can.

Birds apparently do not hold grudges. Good to know.

I wait for a few more heartbeats, just watching the two birds together, before placing the blue daisies on Natalie's grave and pushing myself up off the ground. I stare down at the headstone, at the words carved so neatly into it.

Natalie Penelope Summers

Beloved Daughter, Mother, and Wife

"My soul is painted like the wings of butterflies"

– Queen

One breath. Two.

"I love you, Nat. I always will."

Silence.

The blackbirds start to sing.

I walk away then, leaving Natalie behind with her flowers and bird-song.

Chapter Thirteen

MY FIRST THOUGHT when I see Zara Arai for the first time is that she's beautiful. Intimidatingly so. With her pitch-black hair, strikingly attractive face, and curvaceous figure, she steals all the attention in the surrounding area. My second thought is that I'm very glad I have no interest in seriously dating her because just the idea of trying to impress a woman who looks like Zara makes me cringe internally.

I try my best not to grimace when I realise Zara and I have arrived at the agreed meeting spot outside the cinema before anyone else. Some apprehension must show on my face though because the smile she initially graced me with turns sympathetic.

"You got tricked into going on this totally-not-a-date date too, huh?" Zara guesses after we've introduced ourselves properly.

I stuff my hands into the pockets of my jacket and mentally fret over deciding how close I should stand to her. I mean, we're strangers, but we sort of aren't at the same time. I hate this part of socialising with other human beings. There are so many invisible lines and secret rules you're just supposed to somehow know.

I shrug. "Sam wanted some backup."

"Ah, so you were emotionally blackmailed into it. Nice." Zara nods along as if that makes actual sense.

"How did you end up on this non-date then?" I ask, beginning to feel a bit less awkward. Mostly because Zara seems completely non-plussed about the entire situation. It makes me feel better that she isn't expecting anything more out of this than I am.

"I owed Effia a favour, and she said something about me being a buffer between you and her best friend," Zara explains.

I gape at her. "A buffer? What's that supposed to mean?"

Zara seems to realise she's put her foot in it and quickly adds, "Effia also told me I'd get to meet a really sweet bloke with great cheekbones."

I can't decide whether to fall over laughing or call Effia to shout at her down the phone.

"She actually used the word *sweet* to describe me?" I ask, pointing at myself, genuinely bewildered by the prospect.

Zara makes a face of consideration, clearly weighing up how to re-spond. "I'm starting to think she was being sarcastic about that part." But then she gets a frightening twinkle in her eye and leers mockingly at me. "The cheekbones thing is definitely true though."

I fight off the embarrassment threatening to overtake me.

What the bloody hell am I even doing here? Why would I subject myself to this crap? I blame Sam. For everything. Ever. Always.

"This was a terrible idea." I groan, wanting desperately to bury my face in my hands and hide.

"Probably," Zara agrees.

"Should we make a run for it before anyone else shows up?" I sug-gest, more than half serious.

Zara seems to genuinely consider the idea for a full five seconds before giving a helpless shrug. "If we run away, you know we'll never hear the end of it from Effia."

I make a sound of displeasure even as I concede that she's right. Effia can be stubborn as hell. Once she clamps down on something, she doesn't let go come hell or high water. It's better, and safer, just to go along with what she wants. Only a fool would tempt Effia's wrath.

"All right, fine." I sigh heavily, shoulders slumping. "But for the record, I only came here tonight to take the piss out of Sam."

"Sounds like a good time to me," Zara replies wryly, flashing me a mischievous grin.

Okay, I'll give Effia points for her good taste in friends, but that's all. I still mostly want to yell at her.

No more than five minutes later, Effia arrives with Jade and Riley.

Riley is tall and willowy, her hair a curly golden blond. She has a heart-shaped face and cornflower-blue eyes. She's prettier than I expected.

Sam shows up last looking like he's spent a week on the run and sleeping under a bridge. His hair is as unkempt as I've ever seen it and he has the beginnings of scruff on his face. He's got on the same well-worn leather jacket and motorcycle boots I saw him wearing at Christmas.

I had a brief moment of panic trying to decide what to wear tonight, which made me feel like an idiot. I kept telling myself it wasn't a real date, and even if it had been, I was too old to give a shit about clothes.

In the end, I settled on light-grey jeans and a white Henley, paired with my dark-brown leather jacket and boots of a similar shade.

When Penny found me dithering over which socks to wear, she laughed so hard she fell over. Her boyfriend, Vick, had to pick her up off the floor.

I might have worried that my going on a kind-of-but-not-really date would be a problem for Penny, but she and I already had that discussion a long time ago. She was the one to bring it up. I won't lie and say it wasn't awkward. But Penny told me she would always consider me her son no matter what. She told me she just wants me to be happy. I felt immensely grateful to her at that moment, for reaffirming the strength of a relationship I've come to depend on.

Sam sidles up next to me where I'm leaning against the wall with my arms crossed, waiting for the others to be done choosing their sweets and popcorn at the counter on the other side of the room.

"Hey, Summers."

"Winters." I draw out his name, slow and deliberate. "Good of you to finally show your face. I was starting to think you were going to stand us all up."

"No chance." Sam's mouth takes on a wicked curve. "I would never pass up the opportunity to see you use your oh-so-smooth dating moves."

Against my will, the left side of my mouth quirks up slightly. "Likewise. I'm looking forward to seeing what passes for good dating etiquette among the top brass criminal element these days."

"This isn't a real date," he reminds me a little indignantly. "I've been coerced. Doesn't count."

"Oh, but it counts as a real date for me despite the fact you tricked me into coming?" I say with a snort.

Sam raises his eyebrows in a show of mock innocence. "It's called *asking*. I *asked* you to come. Your standards for trickery have seriously lowered if you consider me asking you out a form of manipulation."

I stare at Sam until he appears to realise what he just said. His eyes widen in a humorous kind of horror.

His reaction to my responding smirk is immediate and high voltage.

"Piss off, Max."

Sam looks supremely bothered. Good. That's exactly what I came here for. That and absolutely nothing else.

Right.

*

THE FIRST TIME I went to the cinema, I ended up having to make an excuse to walk out halfway through the film. In hindsight, I really should have argued against watching something about a gang war. It was like poking my fragile psyche with a stick. Baiting myself into having a panic attack.

I guess part of me wanted to prove I was strong enough to handle it, that my past didn't have as much of a hold on me as it seemed to. I didn't want to ruin our first date by telling Natalie we couldn't watch the film she wanted because I was an ex-gangster. I would have had to lie about why I didn't want to watch it and, even in the early days of our relationship, I didn't like lying to Natalie. She was such an open and honest person, to the point of blunt obliviousness at times.

Someone like that didn't deserve to be lied to by a person they cared about. But there were some things I couldn't tell her then, not without looking and sounding like a fucking lunatic.

Truthfully though, it wasn't just that Natalie might have thought I was dangerous if I told her who I used to be. I didn't want to invite even the concept of all that violence and terror back into the new life I'd been attempting to build for myself. Trying to forget what happened to me during my teenage years and pretending to be okay with what I'd lost felt like a life sentence back then. It was my punishment for being born on the wrong side.

Things are different now. My parents would not be proud of the man I've become, I know that with absolute certainty. But I feel more comfortable within myself than I ever would have thought possible when we first lost the war.

When I walked out in the middle of the film Natalie and I were watching, I felt like I was drowning. I could barely move, as if I was swimming against the current. I couldn't breathe no matter how much I gasped for air. It was as though my own body was working against me.

Panic attacks are horrible for a lot of reasons, but what I hated the most was the sense I had no control. I'd spent most of my life being manipulated or forced into things by other people, so to have my mind betray me in such a way was both terrifying and infuriating in equal measure.

It wasn't just the fear that got me, not any more. I'd learned the hard way there are far worse things to feel in this world than fear. It was the anger, the all-consuming rage that somehow made me feel too hot and too cold at the same time and dragged me down into the fathomless ocean of my nightmares.

I felt too much. After years of pretending not to feel anything during the war. Having to watch the Winters family break my mother into jagged pieces that no longer fit where they were supposed to. Having to watch as my fiercely proud father was worn down like a piece of chalk until there was barely anything left of the man who raised me.

I think of him, sometimes, still in prison. I imagine him motionless and weak and too numb to feel afraid. There are even times when I think he might be dead. I've hoped for it. Wished for it. Not because I resent or hate my father, but because I know in my heart the man who raised me would rather die than live that way. He would despair of who he became by the end of the war.

Over the years I've thought about going to visit my father. At first, the shame and guilt stopped me. Shame and guilt over not being able to save my mother. My father wasn't there when she died. He'd already been arrested by then.

I was there. I saw her die at the hand of a Winters, one of Sam's cousins. Adam. He was a cruel bastard. Not cold and hard like his grandfather. Not fierce and merciless like Sam. But outright cruel. Killing my mother wasn't a job for him, or a service to the family, it was a game. It was a game he played well and won easily.

If my father had been the same man he was before the war, he would have found a way to get to Adam. He would have found who Adam cared about most and he would have made them suffer. My father would have destroyed the man who killed his wife and made him regret ever crossing anyone with the surname Summers.

As it was, my father was in no fit state to do what needed to be done. Neither was I. But then, I never was. If I'd been capable of doing what needed to be done, then I would have killed Sam. Or better yet, I would have stood up to my father and refused to let him lead us down the path to ruin because I knew it was going to go to shit right from the beginning.

I didn't do the things I should have done back then because I was a stupid, terrified child who felt trapped. I used to wonder if Sam felt just as trapped as I did, maybe even more so. Now we're semi-civil I might ask him. If I ever feel like dodging a punch to the nose.

Natalie found me curled in on myself, sitting on the cold concrete ground directly outside the cinema. She told me later I had my head tucked down between my knees and was choking like a man who had just swallowed a dangerous amount of water. Natalie sat with me for over an hour. She rubbed my back and just kept saying, "you're okay," like she believed it.

Of course, that wasn't true. I was so very far from being okay that Natalie's assurances should have pissed me off. But because it was Natalie, and because I felt something for her that was unlike anything I'd felt before in my life, her conviction I was indeed okay comforted me. I took that comfort and wrapped it around my damaged psyche like a security blanket.

Once I'd come back to myself, I apologised over and over again, feeling embarrassed and weak for breaking down in front of her. But she didn't seem put off at all. She waved away missing the second half of the film, telling me she thought it was a crap film anyway, and she took me to a local pub where we had something to eat.

Natalie acted as if my losing my shit wasn't some awful date-ruining event. She asked me a few questions about it, but then left the topic alone when I made it clear I didn't want to discuss it. Natalie was good at that, knowing when to back off and let me think. She was also good at making me laugh and forget for a while. She never treated me like I was damaged or broken or fucked up.

Even though I was all those things.

Effia chose a film about superheroes I know Rory would love. I sit there in the screening room with Sam on my right and Zara on my left, trying to pretend I know what the hell is going on. It all just looks like a load of shouting and exploding crap to me with the odd snarky quip thrown in now and again.

I exchange a few looks with Sam, who seems to be thinking along the same lines.

A few times I catch Effia glancing over at me and Zara with an assessing look. I have to seriously resist the urge to slap myself out of sheer exasperation. Or fake a heart attack.

Two and something hours later we all walk out. Effia, Jade, Riley, and Zara are busy chattering and arguing about the film.

I find myself walking alone with Sam while we all make our way to the restaurant where we're supposed to be eating tonight. It's only a ten-minute walk from the cinema to the restaurant and in that time, I try desperately to think of an excuse to escape whatever this night is doomed to turn into.

"You know, you can just leave if you want to," Sam says out of nowhere. He quirks a somewhat amused eyebrow at me. "No one's going to chase you down and tackle you."

"You know, you can actually just shut the hell up if you want to," I snap back at him, more irritated than I probably have any right to be considering Sam is technically right. "No one is going to ask you to keep talking."

"Is it the film that got you in this mood or just going to the cinema in general?" Sam asks with a surprising amount of understanding in his voice. Although what he's supposed to be understanding I don't know.

I decide, against my better judgement and sense of logic, to be honest with Sam. We should all be equally horrified by the notion.

"I went out with Natalie for the first time to the cinema. I walked out in the middle of the film because it made me think too much about…the war. And…everything else I didn't want to ever think about again."

Sam's eyes widen and he curses, immediately looking regretful.

"Jesus, Max. You should have said before. I wouldn't have made such a big thing out of you coming if I'd known it might bring some stuff up for you."

I frown at that, feeling a bit stupid for admitting the truth now. I really do not need pity from Sam, of all people.

Pity shouldn't exist between us. Not now. Too much has happened for that kind of shit.

"Piss off, Sam. I didn't tell you that because I wanted you to get all weirdly apologetic or so that you'd feel sorry for me."

Sam looks at me with an oddly curious expression. "Why did you tell me then?"

I have no fucking clue, mate.

"I figured that's our thing now," I say instead. "Telling each other the things we never say to anyone else." It's a bit of a wild guess on my part. Maybe Sam talks to a lot of his friends about the stuff we talk about. How the bloody hell would I know? But something inside me balks at that thought.

I realise then some part of me, some clinically insane part that *seriously needs to die*, likes the idea of sharing something with Sam which is just between the two of us.

"Yeah." Sam throws me for a loop once again. "Maybe it is our new thing." He smiles slightly. "Better than beating the shit out of each other, I guess."

I snort my dissent. "Speak for yourself. I much preferred our days of senseless animosity built on mutual dislike and anger issues due to out-of-control teenage hormones."

Sam laughs and shoves lightly at my shoulder. "Git."

I shove him back because the idea that you mature with age is a concept adults invented and like to pretend is true.

"Prat." I sniff, throwing a bit of haughtiness into it just so I get to see Sam wrinkle his nose and roll his eyes like he expected nothing less from me.

"I took Ashley out for ice cream on our first proper date," Sam tells me.

"Woah, big spender," I mock. "How horrifically sweet. I bet there was a lot of giggling and hair flicking going on."

Sam scoffs at that. "Ashley was more likely to give you a smack than flick her hair."

I think Sam's probably right about that. From what I remember of Ashley Flint, she was a fiery young woman. Confident and strong-willed. The perfect match for a man like Sam.

I give Sam a look like I think he's an idiot. I do think he's an idiot. A reckless, hard-headed idiot with the self-preservation skills of an angry twig. And I will stand by that description until the day I die.

"I wasn't talking about Ashley. I meant you. You would be the one giggling and flicking your ridiculous hair."

"Oi, don't start in on my hair!" Sam slaps a hand over his hair and tries, in vain, to smooth it down. The ebony bird's nest immediately springs back into disarray.

"Now we know the truth — your hair is your real ultimate enemy. I think I might be jealous. I'll have to step up my game to compete," I say, desperately trying to hide what I think might be a fond smile. I do not want to smile at Sam with anything akin to fondness. I cannot afford to be fond of him. I don't have the time or the money for the therapy I would need to deal with that level of mindfuck.

Sam glares at me. But it isn't a real glare, and his eyes are lit up with amusement. Damn him.

"Yeah, well," he murmurs, watching me intently. "Of all of my numerous enemies, you can rest assured you'll always be my favourite."

"So, you admit that I'm still your enemy." I feel oddly breathless for no real reason. No sensible reason, anyway.

I realise Sam and I have wandered quite far away from the others. It's like we're alone, even though we aren't really. I don't know why the thought of being alone with Sam causes my heart to race in a way that isn't entirely unpleasant.

I am losing my mind. I mean, there isn't much left to lose at this point, but still.

We've stopped walking now and even though the night air is cold, I barely feel it. Sam is looking at me with a strange half-smile. He seems more nervous than anything, which makes absolutely no sense to me. We're just standing here. Staring at each other. Again.

I tell myself to look away. To move. To laugh, or joke, or say something scathing to Sam that will make him huff off in a strop. But I don't. I can't. And I don't understand why.

Suddenly I'm nervous too, and I find myself doing what I always do when I'm nervous. I focus on small things. In this instance, I catalogue the details of Sam's face.

I take note of the strong, hard line of his jaw and the dark stubble covering it.

I count Sam's eyelashes, including the one that has escaped and is stuck at the corner of his left eye.

Sam has thick eyebrows which are surprisingly neat considering the train crash in hair form on top of his head.

There are noticeable scars on his face. One on his right cheek, a few inches in length, and another cutting along his right temple. He has a scar on his neck too. Bigger than the others, from the time I shoved him into a brick wall and held a blade to his throat. I wonder for a moment if he has any more scars I can't see. Knowing Sam, the answer to that one is *probably*.

I think about my own scars and try not to imagine how Sam would react to them.

Sam tilts his head to one side and locks his gaze with mine, his eyes burning with an intensity that scares the ever-loving shit out of me. Then, voice deep and rumbling, the sound waves practically vibrating through the air around us, he answers the question I didn't technically ask.

"I don't know what you are to me anymore."

Before I can even attempt to unpack that statement, a voice pierces the bubble Sam and I have created for ourselves.

"Hey, what are we talking about over here? Is everything okay?" Riley asks, sounding both confused and a bit worried.

Riley. Sam's date. Holy shit. We are supposed to be on a group date and I'm standing here on the corner of a dimly lit street *staring* into Sam's eyes like a moony teen.

I tear my gaze firmly away from Sam and turn a hopefully not-too-demented look on Riley. Riley. Sam's incredibly attractive female date. Right. Okay. I think I'm scowling at her. I hope I'm not scowling at her. Riley is looking at me like I'm scowling at her. Shit.

"We were just having a very important debate about whether Sam should keep on fighting the good fight with his hair or just say fuck it and shave his head," I say, desperately grasping at any form of distraction. My cheeks burn like they're on fire, my heart pounding in my chest so hard it physically hurts.

"What?" Riley asks, astonished, and quite rightly so because *what*?

When Effia and the rest come into view I make my great escape by, basically, running away. Or at least walking very swiftly away. But it's the spirit of the thing that counts. In my head, I'm running. And screaming.

"Effia!" I exclaim. Loudly. Far, far too loudly. "I need to talk to you about…a thing."

Someone kill me, please, just shiv me right here in the middle of the street and let me bleed to death. It's what I deserve.

Effia stares at me like I'm an alien for about two seconds before something clicks inside her brain. Her eyes dart between me and Sam.

Sam makes a grab for my arm. "Hold on, Max, wait, I—"

I do not let him finish that sentence, because I know nothing sane or safe will come from it. I pull my arm out of Sam's reach. Because I'm a coward. Just like I was when we were teenagers.

I make my way over to Effia and ignore everyone else. I'm sure Effia isn't bothered, but the others must be wondering what the fuck is going on. Hell, I'm wondering that myself.

Sam, apparently unwilling to concede defeat, follows after me and tries again. "Max, come on, you can't just—"

"*Sam.*" Effia has enough bite in her voice to let him know she's serious. She pierces him with an unimpressed glare and adds firmly, "Stop."

That's all it takes to get Sam to back off. But he looks decidedly mutinous about it, so I don't hold out much hope for the ceasefire to continue.

I see Effia share a very loaded look with Jade. After a moment Jade nods and, without hesitation, she practically throws herself at Sam.

Jade drags Sam off and distracts him with some inane chatter about the magnetic pull of the stars and the cosmic beauty of the moon and blah blah whatever. I don't care. So long as it keeps him away from me, she could unhinge her jaw like a snake and eat him and I still wouldn't care.

Zara and Riley are standing off to the side watching all this unfold. Riley doesn't look like she has any clue what's going on, whereas Zara appears vaguely amused. She's *smirking*. I have no idea what she finds so funny about catching two blokes standing on a corner staring at each other. We must have looked bloody demented.

Effia raises an eyebrow at me. I don't give her anything in response and she eventually rolls her eyes, turning away from me to address the others.

"Let's get going then, or we'll lose our reservation."

That snaps the rest of them into action and we all start moving again. I stay close to Effia this time and do my absolute best to ignore Sam's *entire existence*.

As has been the case all my life, ignoring Sam Winters is a lot harder than it should be.

Chapter Fourteen

HAVE YOU EVER sat through a meal at a restaurant so awkward that part of you genuinely wishes something awful would happen—like the kitchen catching fire, or a car driving in through the front window, or the waiter having a sudden heart attack and falling down dead on your table—just so you would have an excuse to leave?

I hope other people feel that way because otherwise, I'm just a terrible human being.

Luckily, I have an entire childhood of experience and practice enduring uncomfortable dinner situations, so I'm fine. No, really, I'm fine. Very fine. Extremely fine.

I realise, to my utter mortification, that I was muttering all that to myself when Zara leans in to whisper mockingly, "That's good to know, cheekbones. I'm glad you're fine. Thank you so much for telling me. I was previously very concerned. But now I am not, because you have successfully reassured me you are super extra fine with bells on. As of this moment, you can rest easy, as I am convinced of this fact and require no further evidence."

I've learned throughout the night that not only is Zara Arai beautiful, but she is also clever and unapologetically honest and kind of a bitch. I like her quite a lot. She reminds me of Natalie in a pleasant, heartening way. As much as I didn't want this date, I can't fault Effia for her choice of partner for me.

Apparently, I like them mean.

"You can take your snark and eat it, Arai," I mutter grouchily.

Zara smirks in self-satisfaction. "Don't get stroppy," she chides. "You're the one rocking back and forth in your chair and muttering to yourself in the middle of an Italian restaurant. Which is what all sane people tend to do, just by the way."

Effia booked us a table in one of the few nice restaurants in this part of town the Winters family has no hand in, either via partial ownership or protection detail.

It's one of those hole-in-the-wall type places, dimly lit, shabbily decorated, but capable of producing outstanding food. My mother and father never would have stepped foot in this place. I came here as a teen when I wanted a great meal and a safe spot away from prying eyes. The owner, Gabrielle, used to let me do my homework at a shadowed table in the back sometimes. She'd bring me out free garlic bread and I'd leave her outrageously large tips.

Tonight, our group is seated upstairs in the corner by a large window. I've found myself sitting between Zara and Effia, with Sam sitting as far away from me as possible due to Effia's subtle intervention. I knew becoming friends with Effia would wind up being one of the best decisions I've ever made.

Sam is ruining Effia's good work by blatantly looking over at me every ten seconds, trying to catch my eye, because unlike our mutual friend he's a massive unsubtle prat who needs to choke on pasta and die so he won't ever be able to talk to me again.

"Do you always insult your non-dates this much?" I ask Zara without any real heat behind it.

Zara leans her elbows on the table, links her fingers together, and rests her chin on her hands. She smiles with too many teeth, reminding me of a cartoon shark.

"You should hear how much I insult my real dates."

I can't hold in the snort of laughter that comes out of my mouth. "Are you finding it tough to meet anyone you like, then?" I ask, genuinely curious this time. All I really know about Zara's romantic past is she had a bloke who ran off.

"I'm finding it tough to meet anyone I can even tolerate." Zara's smile turns sad. "I haven't liked a man since Ren, and he turned out to be a right bastard, so I'm not sure I can trust my judgement when it comes to men."

I study her thoughtfully for a moment before gesturing at myself. "Okay, well, what does your judgement tell you about me?"

Zara narrows her eyes slightly at me, gauging the sincerity of my question. When she seems to decide I'm being serious, she takes a few seconds to consider. She eventually throws out a guess.

"Reformed bastard."

I don't know if I should laugh or take offence to that rather blunt description.

"Keep going," I encourage. "Tell me all about myself, Zara Arai."

Zara's mouth quirks upwards into an almost smile. She looks me up and down a few times.

"I think you were a right little shit as a kid because you thought you had everything. But then you lost it all, which forced you to become someone different. You met a woman who helped you be better, to change, and you finally thought you knew who you were. But then you lost her, and even years later you're still trying to work out how much of that change is what she made you and how much of it is just you being who you really are."

Sounds like the answer to a question on an exam. *Describe the life of Max Summers in a hundred words or less.* Great.

My response comes out somewhat strained. "I think your judgement's pretty on point, Arai. You shouldn't doubt yourself so much."

Zara seems to consider that for a handful of seconds before asking another question. "Do you?"

I frown, confused. "Do I what?"

"Doubt yourself," she clarifies.

I grimace, feeling compelled to answer with something honest. "Constantly."

"Because of the choices you made in the past?" Zara asks, shrewd in her deduction.

I make a humourless sound, bitterness overtaking me. "Because of the choices I *didn't* make."

Before she can poke at that old wound, I ask about her son, Stephen. A sure way to distract any parent is to bring up their child. Most people could chat for England about their kids.

Zara is no exception. She tells me her son recently joined a local junior football team as their new goalie and his coach apparently thinks he's a ball-stopping prodigy. She admits she still doesn't understand the rules of football, having never been much of a sports fan, and has been cheering along with the other parents at games despite not knowing why. I'm not much of a sports fan myself, but I try to explain them to her.

I tell Zara about Rory and his penchant for getting himself into trouble. Zara laughs and informs me that Stephen has mentioned my son a few times, despite them being in different year groups. Apparently, Rory and his bestie Elijah are creating quite a reputation for themselves, which is low-level terrifying.

For some reason, I feel comfortable enough with Zara to tell her about my recent conversation about falling in love with Cat. Zara is understandably sympathetic. As fellow single parents, we commiserate over our children questioning us about the complex nature of love, romantic or otherwise.

Our conversation catches the attention of everyone at the table.

"Have you really not dated anyone in the *five years* since your wife died?" Riley asks me, sounding aghast at the very thought. Her pretty face scrunches into a distasteful expression.

I barely resist the urge to snarl at her, not only for the implication in her question but also because I've noticed the way she's been pushing herself into Sam's space all throughout dinner. She keeps lightly slapping his arm when she laughs at something he's said and stroking his hand and playing with his hair. Sam has been polite and friendly, but I can tell that he's uncomfortable with her less than subtle attempts at flirting.

I contemplate making a comment aimed to cut and shred, but when I catch Sam's eye, he shakes his head. He must have read the intent in my eyes. I dip my head in a slight nod of acknowledgement and curtail my angry reaction out of respect for him.

"Dating isn't the be all and end all," Sam says, quite obviously in my defence. "You don't need a romantic relationship to be happy with your life."

I can't decide how to feel about Sam actively defending me to someone, so I pretend not to feel anything at all. An arena in which I, thankfully, excel.

"Yes, but don't you want your daughter to have a woman in her life who she can look up to?" Riley mutters timidly.

I hold back the urge to snap again, smoothing out my tone with no small amount of effort. "She does have a woman in her life, her grandmother. And even if I did get into a relationship with a woman again, they still wouldn't be a direct replacement for Natalie."

As the words come out my mouth, I realise I do genuinely mean them. Pulling some woman into Cat and Rory's life isn't going to *fix* anything. It certainly won't bring back what they lost.

I love my children more than life, but I'm not going to date someone for any other reason than because *I* want to. It's my life and I take relationship commitments seriously. It means something to me to really *be with* another person. I don't think I'd ever be the type to flit from one partner to another. I liked being in a long-term, monogamous relationship with Natalie. I liked the security and knowing we were a team, two parts of a whole.

I'm not slamming other types of relationships, here. That was just what worked for me, and I doubt I would feel differently about someone else if I were to fall in love again.

Riley has the good grace to look embarrassed over her assertions about my love life and she gives me an apologetic look, so maybe she's not completely awful. Still all wrong for Sam though. She's too rigid and submissive, nothing like his late wife. Ashley had the kind of fiercely challenging and passionate personality that a stubborn, hot-headed man like Sam needs in his life.

Some people need to be balanced out by their partners. Others crave to be met head-on, in the middle, horns locked, ready to fight both for and against each other.

That might not be the healthiest relationship to have with someone you love, but Sam isn't exactly what I would call a healthy-minded person. How could he be after everything he's been through and suffered?

The rest of the night goes as smoothly as it was ever going to, and I soon find myself outside again saying goodbye to everyone.

I get a kiss on the cheek and a wink from Zara, and she promises to come by the café sometime soon.

Effia and Jade give me a hug each. Effia's is short and fond, whereas Jade gloms onto me and doesn't let go until I'm gasping from laughter at the absurdity of the hug's length. I also make like an adult and exchange an awkward nod with Riley.

Effia gives me a questioning look before leaving me alone with Sam again, like she's offering her assistance if I want to make my escape. But as tempted as I am to take her up on it, I realise running now would only temporarily put off the inevitable.

Sam and I stand around for a while just looking at each other, neither of us knowing what to say. We're awkward with each other in a way we never were as teenagers. It was so much easier back then. Our roles were well-defined. We knew exactly where we stood. On opposite sides of the table, the fighting ring, and the war.

Eventually, it's Sam who makes the first move.

"Wanna grab a drink?" he asks, eyes bright and intense and set on mine.

I nod without hesitation. "Fuck, yes. A drink. Or a lot of them, maybe."

Sam cracks a smile. "I know a place. It's not far, we can walk from here."

I consider that I might be making a big mistake in agreeing on more alone time with Sam. I have no idea how this night is going to play out. There's a spark of dangerous anticipation being around him inspires in me, the likes of which I haven't felt with anyone else in my life.

But, despite my better judgement, I still say, "Let's go."

Well. I've never been much good at backing down from a challenge issued by Sam, whether he means it as a gauntlet thrown or not.

Chapter Fifteen

I'M AT A bar. With Sam. I'm at a bar with Sam, and I'm sitting next to him on the world's most uncomfortable stool. And we're both drunk.

We started with cider, which was fine, but then the vodka shots came into play, and the tumblers of whiskey and woah. I am far too old for this shit.

The bar we're at is called The Refuge. It's in downtown Danger City, well-hidden down a side alley. The inside reminds me of a high-ceilinged cave. It's incredibly dark and far too hot, with strobe lights, a live band, and a very packed dance floor. And yeah, we are about fourteen years too old to be here.

I'm also pretty sure, based on the amount of same-gender couples dancing and kissing and doing the general touchy-intimacy thing with each other, The Refuge is a bar specifically for queer people.

Sam chose this bar. That should have been the first warning sign.

Okay, so I think we can all agree that this whole thing is a bad idea, yes?

Yes, good. Right. Bad idea. Very bad. Very, very, moronically bad.

But luckily, or stupidly, I am now too pissed to give a single flying fuck. About anything. Possibly ever again.

I feel dizzy and too warm and hungry and full and sick, and I can't stop fidgeting in my seat, which is funny because I spent my entire childhood being taught how to stay still. I had to be still, quiet, and cold. Like a very small sociopath, I saw the world through smashed glass. Nothing looked right, but I didn't know that then. How could I?

That's the thing I think people don't get sometimes about people like me. About children who grew up as I did. We are who we are because no one ever told us how not to be.

The truth of it is that you can't know how fucked up you are until you get to know other people. A child who was raised with violence or indifference might understand they don't like pain or being forgotten about, but they won't get that it's wrong in the first place. How can anyone be expected to understand something they've never even been told is an option?

As much as people like to pretend otherwise, abuse is subjective. Or at least, that's the way it seems to me. I would never consider myself a victim of abuse. But there were times when I told Natalie stories from my childhood and she'd make this face, like just looking at me made her feel sad. It was as if I'd told her something horrible, even though I considered the story to be par for the course.

Conversely, Natalie would tell me stories from her childhood, and I'd feel like I was listening to a tale from a children's storybook.

I'm sure part of it was she and I grew up in almost completely different worlds. *But* I know I can't blame all of it on that fact.

I could also argue my parents and Penny had somewhat contrasting parenting styles. *But* I suppose there has to be a point where bad parenting turns into just…doing bad things to another person. When opinion crosses over into breaking someone down from the inside out. The problem is that it can sometimes be hard to know where the line is.

What seems obvious to one person might be utterly indiscernible to another. There's a cycle to it, I think. Maybe if I'd been allowed to keep my money after the war and my parents stayed both alive and free, I would have had a child with a woman more like myself and raised that child the same way I was raised.

I know for a fact that my mother grew up constantly trying to balance on the edge of a blade. But she was brave, in her own way. Braver than I was. She did everything she could, I believe that; I really do. Even if it might not seem like enough to some people.

My parents, most of the time they were probably just trying to do the best they could. They made their mistakes. They made their choices. All I can do is try to make better ones.

Shit, I'm drunk. My thoughts are starting to feel too honest and soppy.

Sam puts me on edge by abruptly sitting up straight and giving me a shiny-eyed look of frightening resolve. "We should play truth or dare," he announces like that's a thing adults say to each other.

"Sam. No," I say as firmly as I can while half slumped over the bar top.

Sam goes on as if I hadn't spoken. "Yeah, definitely, we should play truth or dare. Ash and I used to…we used to play it when we were pissed off with each other."

He pauses, chewing on the corner of his mouth like he does when he's remembering something both good and painful. Why do I know that? I hate the fact I've come to know Sam even that much.

"It helped. I dunno why." He smiles like he only kind of means it.

There's spit on his bottom lip left over from the biting and I want to lean forward and…shove him off his stool. Right off onto his arse. The prat.

Sam is still gabbing on. "It made talking easier, I think."

Oh, shut *up*, Sam!

I stare in disbelief. "That…is the stupidest thing you've ever said. And trust me, that is quite a feat considering the amount of general rubbish that comes out of your mouth."

Sam makes a face at me. He asks dubiously, "Do you even know what truth or dare is?"

"Yes," I huff in exasperation. "I know what truth or dare is, Sam. I've seen…films. And things. I also know truth or dare is a game for thirteen-year-olds."

"So?"

"We" —I waggle a finger between him and myself—"are not thirteen-year-olds."

Sam appears nonplussed by my perfectly logical reasoning. "Did you play truth or dare when you were thirteen?" He peers at me curiously.

"Of course not." I snort. "Why, did you?" I'm sceptical of the idea considering what I know of Sam's life during those years.

"When I was a teenager, I was a little busy," Sam replies drolly. "I don't know if you remember, but I was being initiated into the family business. No time for stupid teenage shit."

I wave a dismissive hand and smirk at him. "Yeah, but you knew that was coming. You should have expected it and planned your teenage hijinks accordingly."

Sam shakes his head, but his mouth is curved into a smile, and he's got laughter in his eyes. "You're a right wanker sometimes, mate."

"I know," I say ruefully, saluting him with my whiskey glass.

There's a short pause where we just kind of look at each other, not speaking or breathing or blinking or even thinking. That's how it is for me, anyway.

Sam ruins it by slapping the bar top and waggling his eyebrows at me. "Come on, then, you can go first, truth or dare?"

I sigh dramatically. "Sam, I am not—"

He cuts me off. "Go on, stop whinging and pick one."

He seems far too pleased with himself. I may need to hurt him.

"I do not whinge." I shoot him a fierce glare. He just keeps staring at me expectantly with those eyes. That face. His whole...*self*.

Bastard.

I want it noted that I only give in because I can't be arsed to get up and leave right now. "Fine." My shoulders slump. "Truth."

Sam must sense my hesitation because he speaks before I take back my choice. "Have you been with anyone since Natalie died?"

I like how he uses Natalie's actual name instead of just calling her "your wife". It's the only reason I don't tell him to fuck right off and die with his question.

"No," I answer simply because I have no real reason to lie. I'm hardly a teenager pretending to have more sexual experience than I do to fit in with the other boys. "I loved Natalie. I see pieces of her in Rory and Cat and Penny. I miss her every day of my life." I breathe out slowly, a pang of anguish hitting me out of nowhere. "She changed me."

"Ah." Sam tips his head in understanding. "So, Natalie is the one who made you into a somewhat likeable human being, then?

"I hope that wasn't your way of saying *you* like me, Winters."

Sam's mouth twists up into an approximation of a smirk. "Not on your life, Summers." He looks away from me and takes a drink from his tumbler still half full of brown liquid courage.

I down the rest of my latest drink before responding. "Okay then, your turn, Sam. Truth or dare."

Honestly, I expect Sam to go for a dare. He surprises me by choosing, "Truth," instead.

I narrow my eyes suspiciously at him, but Sam's putting on a good show of innocence. I shrug it off and think about all the things I genuinely want to ask him. Since his first question was a heavy hitter, I reason that I'm allowed the same leeway.

"Have you been with anyone since Ashley died?"

Sam's jaw clenches and clicks, the anger more instinctive than anything. He answers without inflection. "Yes."

I'm not exactly surprised. It's been years since Ashley died, and I know most people wouldn't remain celibate for that long even after losing someone they truly loved.

Sam finishes off his drink and takes a deep breath. He puts the glass down on the bar top with more force than necessary. "The first time I slept with someone else was a complete mindfuck. Big mistake. Effia would probably have said it was too soon, that I wasn't ready for the *inevitable emotional backlash.*"

"How long had it been since Ashley—"

"Two months."

Shit.

"Effia would probably have been right about it being too soon," I say, tone careful, hoping he won't take that the wrong way. I'm the last person to judge how anyone should respond to loss. My way of coping wouldn't be considered healthy either.

Sam's expression creases into something painful and full of self-hatred. Enough to drown himself in. To choke on. And yeah, I know that feeling. I've known it intimately for the last five years.

Hold on a minute, I just realised what Sam implied with "Effia *would* have said".

"You didn't tell Effia about it." I'm slightly dumbfounded by the notion. I thought Sam told her everything. Or at least, the things that matter.

"I've never told anyone," Sam admits quietly.

Well, shit. Again.

I try to find the right words to use in response. "Sam, I don't—"

But he wraps his knuckles on the bar and talks over me. "Hey, it's your turn. Truth or dare."

I think about arguing, but Sam's got his stubborn face on. It wouldn't end well if I pushed this right now, and maybe I would have pushed anyway just to see Sam's eyes flash with that passionate darkness he's been sharpening against the whetstone of his psyche since we were children. There's something about Sam when he's worked himself up into a good rage over something I've done or said that satisfies a horribly broken part of my *own* psyche. Maybe it's because, apart from my parents, Sam is the only person whose attention I've craved to this admittedly quite toxic degree.

But as much as I might want to poke at the pissed-off aura surrounding Sam, I resist the urge and choose, "Truth."

Sam turns in his seat to pin me with another one of his penetrating stares. The side of my face feels like I'm pressing it up against ice until it burns.

Due to the intense heat inside the relatively small but busy bar, I've been forced to remove my jacket, undo a few buttons on my shirt, and roll my sleeves up to my elbows. I wouldn't have bothered if I knew Sam was going to insist on *looking* at me like he is. It's like being stared at by a hungry wolf.

When Sam decides on a question, it's mean and invasive and nothing short of what I would expect from him. "Why have you never gone to visit your father in prison?"

How the bloody hell does Sam know I've never visited my father?

I don't ask, as I have a feeling I won't like the answer.

My response to Sam's question is grim but truthful. "He wouldn't want me to."

Sam is still watching me closely. He seems to be looking for something, waiting for a reaction he can interpret. But I don't have anything to give him. I accepted that I would probably never see my father alive again a long time ago.

It may sound awful, but in my mind, my father died during the war. I watched him die. Slowly. The Winters family destroyed him, and the justice system dealt the final blow by imprisoning him. A life sentence in prison is what one might call a fate worse than death for someone like my father.

"He was a proud man," I tell Sam as if he didn't already know that much. "His only son seeing him brought so low would only make him feel worse than he already does."

I can't think of a reason why Sam would care about any of this.

Sam tilts his head to one side, still trying to read me. Good luck with that. I don't even know how I feel about my father most of the time. If Sam can figure that one out for me then I might just reconsider my long-standing belief that he is an oblivious div when it comes to other people's emotions.

"Your father is still alive," Sam says, with a surprising amount of gentleness.

I freeze in my seat, every muscle in my body going stiff.

"I suppose you would have been told if he wasn't," I say with as much neutrality as I can manage.

How insane is it that, of all people, Sam would be given the news my father died first, through his family's prison connections?

Feeling frustratingly vulnerable at such a sensitive topic being thrown around so easily by Sam, I can't stop myself from striking back.

"Is the reason you didn't tell anyone about you fucking someone so soon after Ashley died because you think they'll judge you for being weak? Because we all know the great Sam Winters isn't *allowed* to be *human*. Oh, no. The criminal underworld would surely collapse from a cataclysmic revelation of that magnitude."

Sam sucks in a harsh breath, a pained, furious sound, the unforgettable prerequisite for many of our epic fights in the past.

I'd almost forgotten how it felt to really hurt him. How much I used to revel in it.

He responds with the verbal equivalent of returning a punch.

"Is the other reason you won't visit your father because you think he would be disappointed in the man you've allowed yourself to become?"

I consider, very briefly, spitting in Sam's face for that one. But what I said was just as cruel, so…

"You're a real bastard sometimes," I say, leaning back and away from him.

Sam salutes me with his middle finger. "I know."

"And it's your turn," I say, trying not to smile at how unrepentant Sam sounds. "Truth or dare."

"Truth," he responds instantly.

Of course.

"Why don't you want to take over the Winters family business?" I ask.

Sam huffs out a laugh. "Do you really want to know?"

"Nope." Because definitely, no thank you.

Sam looks both amused and puzzled by my response. "Then why would you ask?"

I shrug. "Wanted to see if you would tell me."

Sam nods, accepting that. "I won't," he confirms, voice hard.

"That bad then." I keep my tone neutral, not wanting to push this time.

"Yeah. That bad." Sam's expression twists into something bitter and haunted. He shakes it off after a moment of brooding and nods at me. "Your turn. Truth or dare."

I think I've had enough truth for one night. One lifetime, even.

"Dare," I say, because, yeah, I'm really *that* drunk.

Sam thinks for a full minute before a wicked smirk splits his lips into a sharp curve. Fuck. I'm in trouble.

His eyes dart towards the dance floor. Oh no. No. Absolutely not.

He slides off his stall with an annoying amount of grace and ease, all things considered. He holds his hand out in my direction.

"Dance with me." It comes out sounding like an order, which makes me want to bite his hand.

"That is…a bloody terrible idea, Sam." I scowl at his hand like I think it could potentially grow fangs and bite me back.

"Yeah," Sam agrees amiably. He waggles his fingers at me. "Don't really care."

"Sam—" I try, but it's no good.

"Dance with me." His voice turns low and rumbly, goading, "I. Dare. You."

Against every voice in my head that is screaming for me to run. The fuck. Away. I take Sam's hand, thin wisps of fire spindling up my arm in reaction to the contact, and let him lead me to the dance floor.

He takes me deep into the throng of dancing people. They're all pressed up against one another, moving with the kind of reckless abandon that was beyond my comprehension when I was their age. Hell, it's beyond me now. I have no idea what I'm supposed to do here.

Sam half fixes my problem by tightening his grip on my arm and yanking me into his space.

Someone bumps into me from behind and I gasp as I lose my balance and fall even further into Sam, eclipsing the gap almost entirely. I grab hold of his shoulders to stop myself from landing flat on my face on the dance floor.

Sam wraps his arm around my waist to help me regain my equilibrium.

His touch, however, has the opposite effect.

He is so close to me now that I can smell him. Sweat and alcohol and something earthy that is very male and very Sam. I resist the urge to bury my nose against his neck. But only just. My control is slipping, and it is scary how easy it is for me to imagine pressing my mouth to the spot just below Sam's jaw, to feel his pulse beat against my tongue.

I wonder what his stubble would feel like if I nuzzled my cheek into his, like an animal seeking affection from another.

It's darker on the dance floor, the strobe lights sliding around the room the only things illuminating it. I imagine them as large, drunk fireflies and the thought almost makes me smile like an idiot. I am so fucking drunk, like wow.

Sam's face is lit up with different colours every few seconds. His eyes appear to glow like they're infused with moonlight, in the dark stretches of time between passing hits from the strobe lights.

When Sam begins to move, to dance, I follow his lead. He's clearly more used to this kind of dancing than I am. We lock eyes, and that makes it both easier to move along with the beat and harder to concentrate on dancing at all.

Sam holds me, grip tight and bizarrely intense. Fervent to a level I don't quite know what to do with.

I move my arms to twine them around his neck, taking the chance to mess around with the hair at the back of his head. It feels soft against the skin of my fingers. I tug on it a little, causing Sam to make a sound that is far too low and gravelly to be anything other than a genuine growl. A shot of excitement burns through my stomach like the expensive whiskey we've been drinking.

I feel hot, impossibly hot, and Sam is so close. Our bodies brush and grind in ways so intimate I can barely stand it. Everything and everyone in the bar, in the entire goddamn world it seems like, disappears until it's only the two of us left.

Here we are. Hearts racing. Breathing in tandem. Moving together. Touching each other.

Insanity. This is what insanity is, in its purest form. This right here.

I am losing my fucking mind. And I can't stop it. I can't.

For one truly terrifying moment, I don't even want to.

Sam's hands are sure and confident on my back, keeping me in place, guiding us as we dance. All I can do is hold on and attempt to follow his lead.

When my shirt rides up from the sweat and the fast grind of our movements, one of his hands slips underneath. He touches the hot, damp skin there. It's an electric shock. It's a singe from a flickering flame.

It's another dare.

I let my head fall forward, bumping my forehead against Sam's, my nose brushing his cheek. I can still see his eyes. Close. Too close. Too hot, flickering silver flames, pits of molten moonlight.

I can taste Sam's breath like smoke when he asks, "Afraid, Summers?"

I know the answer to this one. We've both known since we were teenagers. It's the same as it's always been.

"Stop teasing and give me something to be afraid *of*, Winters."

And that is when Sam kisses me. He crushes his mouth to mine in a bruising punishment of lips and teeth and wet heat.

My brain just about deletes itself.

Do you ever get that thing where what is happening to you is so bizarre, so beyond your comprehension, that it just doesn't feel real?

You keep waiting to jerk awake with a gasp or a scream; to open your eyes and let reality drag you back out into the world. It's fear and excitement mashed together in one tight ball, burning with anger and want and a chaotic kind of desperation.

I'm kissing Sam fucking Winters. It's ridiculous. It's insane. And it's simultaneously the worst and best thing I've done in a long time.

Sam is holding me tight against him, his grip very close to painful. But I like it. I like the edge of pain, to remind me of exactly who I'm dealing with here. Sam is not my friend. He's not my enemy either. He's something though. He's always been something to me.

There's music and lights and the overwhelming crush of strangers' bodies all around us. But all I can feel right now is the hard press of Sam's body, his fingers digging into my skin and his mouth taking possession of mine. All I can feel is Sam, his touch and his taste and his overtly masculine presence taking control of my space. It's dizzying and terrifying and stupid. Really, really stupid.

Sam's tongue is in my mouth. His lips are working mine over. And he tastes…he tastes like a warning. His mouth and his tongue and his spit all taste like whiskey and smoke. Like fire and rage. Our kiss is lust with an unmistakable edge; because everything between us is fuelled, at least in part, by animosity.

I've kissed two people in my life who mattered. First Natalie, and now Sam.

I'm kissing Sam, the boy I hated through all my teenage years. A boy who I wanted to hurt. A boy who helped destroy my family.

I hated him. I hate him.

I *want* him.

My eyes sting, wetness gathering at the corners. Because it's wrong. It's all wrong, and I don't know what to do. God, I don't know what to do and it hurts, and I can't…I can't…I can't.

Because of Natalie. And me. And him.

I can't because he's Sam Winters and I'm Max Summers and we don't do this. This isn't how it's supposed to go for us. This isn't who we're supposed to be.

But I like it. I like the hardness of his body pressed up against mine and the roughness of his stubble and the *hot hot hot* burn of his mouth on my mouth. I like how his dark hair feels as I twist the silky strands of it tight around my fingers, holding him close even though everything in me screams to *let go let go let go*. I like that he isn't being gentle with me, isn't treating me like I'm breakable even though we both know I am.

I need him to *stop stop stop*, but I don't have the strength to say it. I barely have enough sense to think about it.

Sam bites at my lip hard enough to maybe split the delicate skin there. I groan into his mouth and bite him back because this isn't a one-way thing, fucker.

I still want to hurt him sometimes. He would let me. He deserves that, for this. He might want to hurt me too. I would let him, I think. I deserve that. Maybe. For this. For so many things.

Sam drags his mouth off mine. I growl like a fucking animal. Sam makes a sound very much like a choked-off answering snarl. Because we've both officially gone batshit insane. In the middle of a bloody dance floor. While drunk and angry and wanting something stupid.

We are both fully grown adults with jobs and children and lives that require us to actually use our heads. We aren't teenagers anymore. We don't get to pull this kind of crap.

Granted, we weren't kissing back then. That would have been horrifyingly destructive, even for us.

But we were fighting and snarling and breaking each other down in the only ways we knew how. Because we both had so much black fury built up inside us; too much to keep locked down and hidden away forever.

That's the funny thing. If I hadn't had Sam to unleash all my frustration and anger on, I would more than likely have lost myself in the darkness our world invites us to inhabit. He gave me something to hate that wasn't myself. I should probably thank him for that one day. Or just start hating him again. That would definitely be easier.

Sam is panting. I can feel his hot breath on my face. His eyes are locked on mine. They flare bright and blinding, scorching my insides to charcoal, swallowing up all the oxygen of my lust and using it to grow bigger and more ferocious.

Then he talks. He talks. With words. Just a few. But they're enough to snap me out of it.

"Max, baby, come home with me."

Mother*fucker*.

No.

I somehow get my hands between us and violently push him away from me. I shove him so hard that if Sam was any less the brick wall of a man he is, he would have probably tipped right over onto his arse.

But Sam is intimidatingly big. He's rough-hewn and larger than life and strong as hell. Inside and out. Fuck, how did I go all these years without knowing that did it for me?

I've never felt that way about anyone else. Not even close.

Maybe it's just Sam, then.

The thought makes me want to stab myself in the brain with a fork.

As soon as I'm free of Sam's grasp, I make a mad dash for it.

I push through the crowd of dancing people with the determination of a man running from a monster.

Fear. I feel it like acid under my skin, rushing through my blood, hurting me. I can taste it on my tongue, in my throat. It's bitter and painful and overwhelming.

I don't look back. Even when I'm outside. I don't have my jacket. I took it off inside the bar.

I'm on the street. It's cold. But I can't feel it. The adrenaline in my system is keeping me shielded from the winter wind. It's dark too, but there are a few streetlights and the moon is full tonight, so I can see where I'm going. Mostly.

I don't actually know where I'm going though.

Home? Right. Home would be good. Maybe. Hopefully.

But I can't drive. I'm too drunk, and I'm not quite scared or psychotic enough to drive anyway.

I have no idea how I'm going to get home.

It can't be too late.

I check my phone.

It's later than I thought. There won't be any buses. Shit.

I keep walking. Needing to get as far away from the bar as possible. Needing that more than I've maybe ever needed anything for a long time.

I pull up the number for a local taxi company. I don't use taxis that much, but I know the bloke who owns Danger's most popular alternative to Uber. He's the father of one of my students. A little girl named Lacey. She's bright, a bit of a screamer, but sweet. She likes answering maths questions and playing football at break time. Her mum, Emma, has cancer. She's in and out of the hospital a lot. Lacey misses school sometimes to go and be with her mum. Her dad's name is Thomas. He's a nice man. He loves his daughter and his wife very much.

It's a fucking unfair life.

I keep walking and call the number of the taxi company.

I keep walking. The phone rings. I keep walking.

A swirl of wind blows past me. I shiver. I keep walking.

If I just keep on walking, maybe I can walk this entire night off. Maybe I should just hang up the phone and walk all the way home. That might help.

The phone keeps dialling. I keep walking.

"Hello, you're through to Cindy at Taxis4you." A polite female voice comes down the phone.

I take a breath. Then I take another breath, just to show off to myself.

"Hello?" Cindy prompts me when I take too long to speak.

I take yet another breath. *Get it together, Summers, you're being pathetic.*

Another breath, then, "Hi, can I order a taxi to come pick me up at—"

A hand grabs my shoulder, fingers digging in painfully right from the start, causing me to gasp.

Sam turns me around and immediately lets go of my shoulder, possibly in reaction to the sound I made. I drop my phone and it clatters to the ground.

Cindy is still speaking. "Sir. Sir? Hello?"

She sounds very far away.

I don't pick it up. I can't. Not with Sam looking at me—no, glaring at me—like he wants to fight me. Or push me in front of a bus. Or fight me, then push me in front of a bus.

We stand there. On the pavement. Glaring at each other.

I'm ready. I'm so ready. If he wants a fight, I'll give him another fucking *war* instead. I will break him with my hands. I will cut him down with words sharper than knives could ever be. I'm ready if he wants to turn this rage between us into something ugly and raw and permanent.

But I also want to run. I want to run so badly. To run and run and never, ever look back.

There's a child in my class, Mickey. His dad ran off a year ago. When I heard about it, I tried to imagine why someone would do that. How could a father abandon a child? It seemed unfathomable to me. As bad as my father had been at times, at least I knew he would always be there. Or, at least, I believed that he always would be.

Now, I'm looking at Sam and I'm feeling like I don't want to go home. I don't want to face Penny or Vick or my children. I don't want to look them in the eye and pretend that I'm okay. I don't want to pretend I'm not cracking up, splintering apart, breaking like an old china cup that's been dropped one too many times.

It was hard enough pretending when Natalie died. But I had to do that. Not for me, but for Rory and Cat and Penny. I did it for them. For the sake of the people I love, I somehow managed to put myself back together over the last five years, and even though not all the pieces fit quite right any more, enough did that I felt somewhat solid. Steady. Able to function.

One kiss from Sam and I'm a load of jagged pieces scattered across the floor all over again. Five years' worth of work destroyed in seconds. I'd laugh if I knew it wouldn't come out as a sob.

I can't even hate Sam for it because I did this to myself. I willingly spent time with him. I went to the aquarium. I went out on the group date. I agreed to go to the bar. I let him pull me out onto the dance floor.

I didn't break me. But I let it happen, which is worse because that means some part of me wanted it. Part of me *wanted* to shatter.

I thought I'd gotten over this tendency towards self-destructive behaviour. Apparently not.

"I know what you're thinking. And you're wrong," Sam says, voice low and volatile. It makes something in me spark to life, that familiar anger rising to the surface.

I narrow my eyes at him, trying to infuse as much *piss off* into it as I can. "Got mind-reading powers now, do you? Should we be letting Polaris know he's gonna have a new supervillain to kick around soon?"

"Do you always weaponise anger to protect yourself from other feelings that scare you?" Sam counters, merciless and razor-edged. "Thought maybe you'd grown out of that damage."

Oh, low blow, Sam. Nice.

"Not scared," I respond coolly, drawing from all my childhood training. *Stay cold and calm and untouchable.* I repeat it in my head like a mantra.

It reminds me of being five years old and falling down the stairs at one of my parents' fancy parties. One of the servers helped me to get up and checked me for injuries. My father came over to tell me not to embarrass him by crying or making a scene. It was the first time I remember biting back tears. Felt like swallowing down a mouthful of glass, sharp and agonising. My spit tasted like blood, metallic and thick. I never really got used to it.

"Then why are you running?" Sam asks, frustration replacing the anger for a moment.

He's probably right to ask. No matter what else has happened between us, we don't run. We don't do that. We don't run from each other. We do battle. Because anything else feels like a lie. Like giving up or giving in or losing something we don't even have a name for.

"I don't want to do this with you, Sam," I snap, backing away from him. "Not now." Not ever.

Sam follows me, closing the space between us. "Too bad," he says through gritted teeth.

I meet his eyes and glare. He glares right back, equally stubborn and unwilling to back down. I don't even think Sam knows *how* to back down from a fight he believes is worth fighting.

"Sam," I say harshly. "What do you want me to say, here?"

He looks unsure for a second, and it's then I realise he doesn't have any more idea what's going on than I do. That makes me feel both better and worse. I thought Sam was the one pushing things, but now I'm thinking maybe we're both just stumbling around in the dark not knowing what the hell to do, which makes us even more ridiculous than I thought.

"Why did you run?" Sam asks again, so quiet it's practically a whisper. It's a pissed-off whisper though, which is weirdly endearing to me.

I let out my own frustrated growl. "You called me 'baby'." Like it's an accusation. It bloody well *is*. I mean, *baby*, for fuck's sake.

Now Sam just looks confused.

"You kissed me." He just says it, like it's...I don't even know. I didn't think he would just say it like that. I didn't think we'd ever talk about it at all.

We lost our minds for a few minutes in the bar. We're drunk. We're both kind of strangely intense people. Shit happens. Or at least I've been led to believe shit like random meaningless kissing happens by TV shows and trashy romance novels.

Oh yeah, and—

"*You* kissed *me*," I correct him, because that matters for some reason.

"You kissed me *back*." Sam squares his shoulders and fixes me with a look I don't know if I want to interpret. I have a horrible feeling it's a *we could kiss again* look. I catch myself drifting toward him automatically in response to it.

Sam reaches for me. Or maybe I reach for him. Who the hell knows? Either way, we're kissing again before I can fully digest why or how it happened.

It doesn't feel any less awful and terrifying and amazing the second time. Or the third.

We wrap ourselves around each other like clingy vines, eclipsing every inch of space, mouths locking together like we're trying to perform an elaborate act of dual asphyxiation. We kiss and kiss and kiss until we're both literally gasping from it.

I'm shaking, trembling from wrist to fingertip, my body quaking hard enough my bones feel like they're rattling under my skin.

Sam is holding me too tight, yet somehow it's still not enough. He's got his mouth pressed against my throat. His stubble scratches my skin. His teeth nip and his tongue licks. I squirm in his arms, aching to get closer, to feel entirely overwhelmed by the sheer strength and heat of him.

A sound like muted thunder rumbles inside Sam's chest when I dig my fingernails into him, urging him on without words. I want more. I want so much more from him than anyone should want from another person.

I'm unable to contain a guttural moan when Sam's big hands grab two handfuls of my arse and he yanks me up against him, pressing our lower bodies together, groin to groin. I can feel the hard outline of his prick even through our jeans. My cock is rock solid and pulsing like it has its own heartbeat. I'm so turned on that I can barely think.

Sam takes my mouth again, hot and fierce, possessive in a way he has no right to be, but which only drives my lust higher. He's a demanding son of a bitch, always has been, and it's no surprise to me that extends to his sexual predilections.

I twine my arms around his neck like I did on the dance floor, pushing myself into him as much as physics will allow.

Then it's all *touch taste bite* and *pain pleasure want,* and I can't *breathe*.

I shove at him again, rasping coarsely for him to stop. Sam hears me and lets go because for all his faults he isn't *that* sort of man.

I scramble to put distance between us again, picking up my phone and shoving it in my pocket. I start walking backwards, keeping my eyes on Sam.

Sam makes a stunted attempt to follow. He's still breathing heavily, his broad chest heaving. His eyes blaze so hot and wild and furious and *woah*, there he is, Sam fucking Winters. He's just so *him* all the damn time. It's maddening.

I shake my head at him. No. This has to end. Right now. I need it to…I need it to stop.

I try to convey that to Sam without having to say it out loud.

After a brief hesitation, Sam nods. He doesn't look pleased about it—in fact, he looks downright defiant in the face of it—but he still nods, backing down for once in his life on my say-so, which is another shock to the system all on its own.

I turn around and walk away from Sam.
I don't look back.

Chapter Sixteen

IT TAKES ABOUT an hour for me to walk home. I don't mind. It gave me time to have a panic attack at a bus stop.

I manage to stave off the inevitable for a while, long enough to put a healthy quarter mile between me and Sam. But, as always, I can't stop my lungs from tying themselves into knots and attempting to kill me.

It's usually worse when I try to fight it.

The panic attack comes at me like a freight train, intense pain shooting mercilessly through my chest. I can't breathe. It feels like I'm dying. Really, truly, dying. It hurts so bad. Scares the ever-loving shit out of me every time it happens, thinking this might be it, this is the one that will finish me off for good.

I go light-headed, eventually blanking out for a few minutes. When I come back to myself, I realise I've curled up next to the bus stop with my face pressed against my knees.

It feels like it went on for hours, not minutes. Hours of not being able to breathe. Hours of clawing panic. Hours of feeling, of *knowing* I was going to die. Hours of gasping and crying and making a spectacle of myself. My father would not have approved.

I haven't had a panic attack that bad since the night after Natalie's funeral.

I hate that Sam affects me so powerfully. He hasn't earned the right to fuck me up this much. I mean, it's been years since we were two stupid teenagers fighting in a war that could have killed us. I've moved on with my life. I barely recognise myself from who I was back then. Sam shouldn't be anyone to me now. Just another bloke. The father of my son's best friend.

Nowhere in our non-relationship should kissing be involved or permitted. I'm too old to be making this kind of mistake. Too old and too tired and too broken.

Honestly, of all the people to find myself attracted to, why did it have to be Sam? I'd have rather fancied Effia. At least that would have made sense. She's brilliant, she's beautiful, she actually *likes* me. *I* actually like *her*.

Sam doesn't make sense. Wanting to kiss Sam doesn't make sense. Wanting to touch him…to touch him and let him touch me in a way no one has since Natalie… It's just…it's horrific and wrong and I wish I could hit a reset button and never agree to spend time with Sam in the first place.

I don't even understand why he seems to want it. He could have anyone. I'm sure there are plenty of people who would fall all over themselves to be noticed like that by him. I can only assume he's lost his mind.

I've clearly lost what was left of mine.

When I get home, I try to be quiet so I won't wake anyone. Luckily, I'm stone-cold sober now thanks to, well, everything.

Unfortunately, my hopeful plans of collapsing on my bed and sleeping for a year are dashed when I come in through the front door.

Penny and Vick are sitting together on the ugly duckling in the living room. Vick has his arm draped around Penny's shoulders and Penny is tucked up against his side. The television is on and there's some action film playing. I don't recognise it. To be fair, most of the films I've seen in the last few years have been for children, as I only really watch TV with Rory and Cat.

I try to sneak past, but Penny isn't having it. She turns around on the sofa and pins me with the stare of a mother who has caught her child doing something questionable. I squirm under her knowing gaze and shuffle from side to side uncomfortably for a few seconds.

"Hey," I say lamely. "You didn't have to wait up."

I sound like something is wrong. I can hear it in my voice. Bloody hell, brain, stop sabotaging us!

Penny's eyes narrow. She looks me over from head to toe, taking me in, and for the first time, I realise I probably look like I've been sleeping in a bush. I didn't bother to check my appearance before I came upstairs. It didn't even occur to me. But I've been mauled by Sam, crushed by people on a dance floor, and I spent a good amount of time scrunched up on the dirty pavement. I must look awful at this point. No wonder Penny is watching me suspiciously.

Vick smiles warmly at me in that way he does. He's like a big teddy bear, all soft and comforting. "Good night slash morning, Max."

I smile back at Vick. It feels brittle and fake. Because it is.

Penny untangles herself from Vick and stands up. She walks up to me and grabs hold of my arm, like an owl snatching a mouse from a field. She strides into the kitchen, dragging me behind her without saying a word.

When we reach the kitchen, Penny lets me go. She turns on the light and goes to pull one of the chairs from the kitchen table out into the middle of the room. Penny motions for me to sit in the chair. I do, because I'm tired, and I know Penny well enough to understand that if I try to go to my room then she'll just follow me there.

I sit in the spongy blue chair and watch as Penny opens a kitchen drawer and grabs a pair of scissors. Then she goes to her bag sitting on the counter and takes a comb out of it.

"Penny?" I ask warily. "What are you doing?"

Penny comes back over to me and starts fiddling with my hair.

"I'm giving you a haircut," she says like that's all the explanation I should need.

"It's half past three in the morning," I inform her like I think Penny will give a crap.

"Yes. It is." She starts combing my hair. It hurts a bit because there are a lot of knots from where I've been screwing around with it all night.

I think about asking Penny why we're doing this now. But that would be a stupid question and I've officially reached my quota for doing stupid shit for one night. I know exactly why we're doing this.

Whenever one of us has something to talk about, Penny will cut my hair, and we'll talk. It's a thing we've been doing ever since I was a snarky nineteen-year-old who didn't know how to talk like a real person. Having the pretext of Penny cutting my hair makes it easier for us to say what we need to say.

For a few minutes Penny combs and snips at the ends of my hair while I sit there. I relax a little bit more with every second that passes. Maybe it's because Penny knows me so well. She knows when to push and when to leave something alone.

Penny changed my life. She saved me. She let me love and marry her daughter. She accepted me into her home and gave me the first real choice I'd had in years. Penny Starr is, no shit, my hero, and I love her. I really do.

And I trust her too, which is why I find myself saying, "I think I'm going to visit my father."

Penny's hands don't waver. She keeps combing and cutting without pause.

"Why?" she asks. No judgement. No condemnation or surprise. Just a question.

"Sam said something tonight." I take a breath. In deep. Then out. "He said I was afraid of my father's disappointment in who I've become."

Penny makes a sound. It's very close to an angry huff. But not quite.

"You're allowed to be afraid, Max," she says calmly. "Just so long as you're not ashamed."

I don't know why I suddenly decided I wanted to go and visit my father in prison. Truly, before tonight, I thought I would never be ready to do that. But something about what Sam said hit me wrong. I don't want to be a coward any more. I don't want to be afraid of my father any more either.

"I'm tired of being scared, Penny," I say, clenching my hands into loose fists in my lap. "And I have nothing to be ashamed of. I know that. I do."

"You'd better." Penny touches my hair, softly brushing her fingers through it, a comforting gesture. "Because you're a good man. A great father. My *son*. Natalie gave that to me. She gave me you, made you part of our family. I'll always be grateful to her for that." She puts a hand on my shoulder and gently squeezes.

My eyes start to sting, and I blink rapidly to force back the tears threatening to fall.

I cover Penny's hand with one of my own and gently stroke my thumb over her wrist.

"I kind of like you too, Pen," I whisper, choking on the words slightly.

"Good," Penny murmurs, the quirk of a smile in her voice. "Then you can go see your father and face whatever it is you need to face with him. Then you can come home, and we'll be here. We love you and we'll be *right here*."

"I know." Because I do know. And that's…that's everything.

Penny finishes up with my hair, then shoos me out of the kitchen so she can clean up.

I think about going to my room, ambling down the corridor, but then change course at the last minute to go and sit with Vick instead. He always has a way of making me feel, not *good* exactly, but…maybe "safe" is the right word. The way a kind grandfather might make you feel.

Vick smiles warmly at me again when I walk into the living room and throw myself down next to him.

Since Penny and I have been gone he's pulled a woolly blanket over his lap. When I sit down, Vick shifts the blanket to cover me as well.

I notice Vick has turned off the TV and is now reading a very pink magazine. I peek a little closer at it and realise it's one of Cat's magazines. This one is called *Pop Girl*. I was surprised when she asked for it, as it's not her usual thing. Cat said she only wanted it for the free sparkly lip gloss.

I debated for a while if letting my nine-year-old wear makeup would be a good idea. But in the end, I decided that it was just lip gloss. It wasn't worth arguing over, and it's not like Cat was going to change dramatically over some sparkly gunk in a pot.

Honestly, I think Rory's gotten more use out of it than Cat. I'm inclined to believe Rory asked Cat to get the sparkly lip gloss so he wouldn't have to tell me he was the one who wanted it.

After speaking to Effia and Jade, I've resolved not to make a thing out of it by bringing it up with Rory directly. I want my son to feel comfortable being himself, whoever that is. But Effia said it might come off as too confrontational to have a whole *talk*, especially over something so seemingly insignificant. I mean, it really *is* just lip gloss, regardless of which one of my children wants to wear it.

Jade told me if there was going to be a bigger conversation in the future, it's better to let Rory be the one to indicate as such.

"What are you reading about?" I ask Vick.

Vick is frowning down at the page in front of him. He makes a thoughtful humming sound.

"I'm finding out which pop star diva I am." He slides a glance over at me and adds, "Spiritually, I would assume."

Despite the shittiness and confusion of the night so far, I can't stop myself from snorting out a laugh.

"Well, Vick, that is something a person really should know. Which diva are you?" I ask, scanning the options the editors of *Pop Girl* have given.

Vick makes a face down at the magazine. "I'm caught between Beyoncé and Rhianna."

Rory often plays Rhianna songs loudly from his bedroom and does elaborate dances from social media I'm certain could have only been invented by drunk people. It wasn't until recently I found out my son was *practicing* for something.

I got a call from Rory's school yesterday about him being given detention for breaking into the gym during lunch for a TikTok dance-off against Simon Lake, along with all their mates. I didn't know what breaking into the gym for a TikTok dance off entailed, but according to Rory's headmistress, it is not permitted and carries with it the heavy sentence of two weeks detention.

When I confronted Rory about it, he smugly proclaimed to have "decimated" Simon, and that he "totally out-swagged" him. He described his two weeks of detention as worth it.

I found out tonight Sam got a very similar call regarding his son, who also has two weeks of detention to look forward to. Sam and I shared a moment of fond exasperation over our son's antics, although Sam admitted to being somewhat proud of his son's apparent dance-off win against his nemesis, Derek McKenzie.

Cat likes to play her music even louder from her room, in what I can only assume is some form of sibling challenge. Although Cat seems to have the music taste of a forty-year-old man with a lot of Queen, David Bowie, Black Sabbath, and The Rolling Stones blasting from her room at all hours.

Queen was Natalie's favourite band. She loved to sing along tunelessly to them in the car. Sometimes she would dance around the kitchen and sing while she cooked dinner.

I remember watching her twirl and almost trip over her own feet a thousand times. She always had a massive smile on her face though. Seeing Natalie like that made my heart feel like it was going to burst with how much I loved her.

"I'd say you're more of a Beyoncé," I tell Vick.

He nods solemnly. "I agree." Then he turns to me again, eyebrows arched in mischief. "You want to find out which diva you are?"

I let Vick ask me questions from the quiz and we discover I am a Taylor Swift type of diva. I'm inordinately unhappy about that. Her songs always get inside my head and never go away even though I don't like them.

Vick lets me vent about Taylor Swift and her bubble gum nightmare music until I run out of steam and find myself suddenly exhausted.

There have been way too many feelings tonight. I am officially drained.

I'm half asleep next to Vick when he draws me back into semi-alertness with a question. "Is he nice?" His tone is oddly gentle.

I blink at Vick in lazy confusion and ask mid-yawn, "Wah?"

His next words knock the wind out of me. "The lad you got that beard burn from. And that mark on your neck. Is he nice?" Vick sounds just as calm and serious as before. He's watching me with a fond look on his face.

I make a choking noise and sit up straight on the sofa. I think I'm gaping at him a little bit.

I press a hand against my neck, pointlessly trying to hide the evidence. God, I didn't even think about the physical marks my kissing whateverness with Sam might have left behind.

Vick brings me back to myself by gently touching my arm. I look at him, blinking like an idiot. His answering smile is kind and part of me hurts to see it.

"You don't have to tell me about him if you don't want to," he says, quiet and sincere. "But I would like to know if he's being nice to you, Max." He squeezes my arm. "You deserve someone nice."

My stupid eyes start to sting *yet again*.

I struggle to explain to Vick what Sam is. He's definitely not nice. But…that's part of the reason why I…I feel attracted to him. I don't want Sam to be nice to me. I want to argue with him. I want him to be rough with me, because, as weird as it sounds, I trust Sam to know where the line is. I trust Sam, which is ridiculous. But that doesn't stop it from being the truth.

I try to answer Vick as honestly as I can. "He's…not nice. He's…got bad in him. Like me. We've both got this…darkness in us. But I think that's part of what makes me want…"

"You like him?" Vick asks, peering at me curiously.

"I trust him," I say, which isn't a yes or a no, but it's the best I can do right now.

Vick seems to understand that because he nods and just says, "Sometimes that's enough." He smiles again. "To build from."

Yes, maybe it is. But what in hell's name would Sam and I be trying to build in the first place?

Interlude

Sam

"MATE, YOU LOOK demented, what the hell happened?" Will asks, eyes wide and full of concern. It's a fair reaction since I've spent the last few minutes banging on his door like a lunatic, as I slowly descended further and further into losing my shit.

I push past him into his house and charge into the kitchen only to start pacing around like a madman trapped inside a four-by-four cell. Will's kitchen is large and homey, full of warm colours and soft textures. It reminds me of countless hours spent sitting at his table drinking tea on good days and whiskey on bad ones. Discussing troubles with the business and our wives and our children. Mostly tea. Remembering the past. Almost always whiskey. Contemplating the future. A mix of both depending on the day and the topic at hand.

Will comes after me and stops in the kitchen doorway, watching me with a look of mild alarm. He can't be too shocked by my behaviour. He's seen me in worse states, but admittedly it's been a while since I got this worked up about anything.

It's the middle of the night and Will is wearing pyjamas, grey tracksuit bottoms, and a white T-shirt. His feet are bare. Will is a large man, but in this state, he looks almost vulnerable. I get this weird urge to berate him for it, despite the fact I'm hardly in any state to defend myself if need be.

"You been out drinking tonight?" Will asks, brows drawing together like he's not sure he believes his own suspicion.

I'm tipsy, not drunk. I haven't allowed myself to get drunk in a very long time. Will knows I don't drink unless it's with him. I can't trust anyone else.

"Yes," I answer distractedly, still pacing like a madman. My hands are shaking, from adrenaline or something else I'm not sure.

"Alone?" Will looks oddly disturbed by the idea, as if he thinks I've been sitting in the dark drinking a bottle of expensive scotch like a dramatic TV show mobster.

"Fuck off," I throw at him over my shoulder.

Will seems somewhat reassured by the response, although if it's the confirmation I wasn't drinking in the dark alone or the show of familiar temper that reassures him I can't tell.

"All right." Will shifts away from the doorway and moves to sit down at the kitchen table. He kicks out the chair across from him and nods at it. "Feel like parking your arse and telling me what brought this psychotic episode on?"

I make an indistinguishable snarling sound at him and belligerently continue my half-marathon. There's no other choice. I can't seem to stop moving like my muscles are vibrating and need constant activity to stop from exploding with pent-up energy. It feels like my brain is made up of loose wires that keep accidentally rubbing together to create a bright electric spark between them. I need motion, not reason. I need to go. To…to *do* something.

Will is right, I should stop. None of this is helping. But since I have no clue what could possibly help, stopping doesn't feel like it would be a solution either.

"Okay then." Will sighs, rubbing at his forehead and slumping in his chair, giving in to my temper tantrum just like he always does. "Keep stamping around if you think that will help any, you fucking nightmare."

He's not wrong. My boots clomp against the creaky wooden flooring and a particularly loud wheeze of a loose floorboard reminds me Will has young children in the house. Charlotte would be livid if I woke the twins. Forget my family, I'd be on the end of a kitchen knife grasped by my best friend's wife.

Part of me balks at taking the sensible option because my own stubbornness has been my enemy since birth, but in the name of avoiding any problems with Charlotte or the children, I force myself to sit down opposite my friend. To keep myself grounded I cross my arms and plant them on the table, shifting forward on my seat and looking right at Will.

Will turns in his seat to face me head-on, meeting my gaze with a mixture of the same concern from before and a flicker of exasperation. He puts up with a lot from me and has done since we were children. I always seemed to draw in trouble and Will was often the shield to my sword, the reinforcement I couldn't go into battle without. If there's anyone I can trust to talk to this thing with Max about, it's him.

"Who did you go out drinking with?" he asks, making it easier for me to do what I want like he's been doing ever since we met.

"Max," I answer, the name coming out heated and angry, which seems appropriate given my convoluted feelings for the man in question. "After the whole date thing, we went to a bar downtown, and things got…weird."

Will knows I've been spending some time with Max, and I've already taken a dose of shit from him for it, both in jest and more seriously. Of all the people in my life, Will remembers what it was like between me and Max when we were teenagers. He was there for a lot of it; waiting on the sidelines of the fighting pit when Max and I took the excuse to kick the shit out of each other, at school as we competed in class like every question asked would be the difference between success in life and utter failure, out on the street where we would face off on a daily basis, at family functions meant to test us and our ability to manoeuvre in the political and socialite circles.

I'm not sure what reaction Will might have to an admission I kissed our old enemy, because Max was my rival, but as a Summers he was *our* enemy. I don't expect Will to have held a grudge all this time, because despite his profession, that isn't who Will is. But I don't imagine he'll be ecstatic to find out I've got a thing for a boy who once cracked his ribs with a crowbar.

"Weird?" Will asks dubiously, eyes narrowing and darting over me like he's searching for answers hidden in my pores. "What does that mean? What did you *do*?" He sounds accusing, which I don't know how to take, especially as the ire and blame seem to be aimed at me, not Max.

"I kissed him," I say defiantly, unwilling to hide or pretend I'm ashamed of it, whatever my friend might say.

There's a beat of shocked silence.

"You *what*?" Will looks at me like I've suddenly grown another head.

"He kissed me back!" I retort as if in defence of my actions.

"He *did*?" Will's scepticism is borderline offensive, his nose wrinkling like a piglet. "Are you sure? Maybe he was just trying to headbutt you and because he was drunk, he missed."

"Of course I'm sure." I scoff. "He kissed me back. Twice!" I announce the last part like it's case-winning evidence.

Will goes back to staring at me all dumbfounded and confused, his world turned upside down by the news I've just imparted. It strikes me that Will seems more shook by the idea Max would kiss me than the other way around.

"You're not surprised I kissed Max," I state boldly, frowning at my friend, unsure whether to be offended again.

Will snaps out of his perplexed stupor and makes a rude noise, waving a hand to the side. "'Course not," he says flippantly. "You've had a thing for Max Summers since the first time he gave you a black eye and called you a 'waste of any tree's good work', whatever the hell that means. Don't pretend this is new, brother. I'm not stupid."

I blink at Will in shock, unable to respond for a moment as my own worldview does a swift right turn and flies right off a cliff. What *the fuck* did he just say to me?

"Mate, I did not have a thing for Max Summers when were kids. I beat the crap out of him whenever I got the chance. I said nasty shit to him all the time. I wanted to *hurt* him. I hated him."

Will just looks at me like I'm a particularly thick puppy. He doesn't seem impressed by my adamance that my feelings for Max are brand new from the oven and not the re-emergence of a long-buried crush. I'd know if I fancied Max back in the day. Wanting to kiss your nemesis isn't exactly something you can't know about yourself, is it?

Of course, I've always known Max was objectively attractive and that has only increased tenfold with age, what with him being so tall and sleekly muscled, his dark-red hair and the finely chiselled cut of his features making him stand out in any crowd. But thinking someone is attractive and being attracted to them are two different things.

I say all this to Will and he shakes his head and makes a face at me like it's complete bullshit.

"You were obsessed with him, mate. Fact." Will shrugs, as if it's that simple for him. He doesn't seem upset by it, which I suppose makes sense if he's known about my feelings since we were children. He pulls a face and shoots me a wary look. "My sister knew as well, just for the record. When we were teens, she kept thinking you were going to dump her and run off to have angry sex with Max."

Then, before I can suitably react to that particular bombshell, he goes on in a more empathetic tone, "Look, I get it, you didn't want to admit it to yourself because you knew it was impossible after we went to war and then he was gone and you were in love with my sister, so it stopped mattering."

There are so many reasons why getting involved with Max was a bad idea then, and quite a few of those reasons still hold true now as well as there being a whole load of new ones to consider. How this could affect our children. The fact is we're both men who have never been in a romantic relationship with another man. The family situation I have going on that could become very dangerous for anyone I care about.

"It matters now," I say fiercely, unwilling to back down and away from something I've realised is important to me, despite the possible ramifications. Then, more cautiously, I admit, "I've made a real mess of it with Max though. He practically sprinted away from me tonight." A fist of pain at being rejected so forcefully clenches in my stomach. "What am I supposed to say to him?"

Will seems to chew on the question for a bit before answering. "Well, do you know what you want from him? Do you know what he wants from you?"

"No idea," I start, then falter, correcting myself, "I mean, I have no idea what he wants. I want to…I dunno. See what happens. With us." I scowl, frustrated I don't have any clear plan to put into action. "Make a go of it, maybe. God, it's so bizarre to be saying all this about Max Summers." I throw myself back in my seat and tip my head up to stare up at the ceiling uselessly.

There's another silence where we sit there, Will looking for a way to help, me thinking in circles.

Finally, Will takes mercy on both of us and lets out a long-winded sigh, effectively breaking the tension.

"I think the first step needs to be putting your own shit aside and finding out where Max stands. No point in making any other decisions until you know if it's possible he might be willing to enter into this bloody madness with you," he says with the brutal honesty I've learned to expect from him at all times. He's never been one to sugarcoat a situation. If he thinks we've got no chance and shit will hit the fan, he'll tell me so.

"I need to be honest with him, don't I?" I ask rhetorically, breathing out through my nose in an attempt to stay calm and not start losing it again at the prospect of showing my feelings to Max only for him to shove them back down my throat until I choke to death. "Jesus, that's going to be shit for me." I give Will a forlorn grimace. "He's still such a fucking prick. Knows just where and how hard to hit to cause maximum impact. I feel like every time we talk there's lasting damage, good and bad."

Will makes a loud snorting sound, shooting me an incredulous look like he thinks I'm deranged, and he wishes we'd never met. "On the plus side," he says, brushing off my lunacy as any good friend would, "if Max is anything like he was when we were kids, he might just be insane enough to want this as much as you do."

Fuck, I hope so.

Chapter Seventeen

I KNOW THIS is probably a mistake. I'm fully aware nothing good can come from seeing him. My father.

Julian Summers made his choices, and it isn't in his nature to feel regret.

I'm not expecting much. From him. Or from me. Honestly, I'm trying not to expect anything at all.

Hope can be a fragile, terrible thing. It fortifies and it corrodes, especially in a relationship between a parent and a child.

I've learned over the course of my life to be wary of wishes and lies such as unconditional love and parental expectations.

My own father's love was often like a trained viper. He knew when to hold back and when to strike to get the most beneficial reaction.

My mother's love was different. It was unbreakable, but coldly cut from her own experiences, like a diamond.

I was taught to love in the same way some children are taught not to talk to strangers. My parents showed me that love was to be wary of.

That love was a weakness I should protect myself against.

I loved my parents with a ferocity they would not have approved of if they'd known the extent of it. They would not have understood how I felt about Natalie. My love for her would have seemed foreign to them. It would have been too undignified for them to accept.

I wouldn't have blamed my parents for how they felt. It was how they were raised. No doubt I would have struggled with the same problems. I would have hit the same wall of forced indifference. It's hard to love someone when you've been taught to see every person you meet as a potential enemy.

From a very young age I found myself automatically cataloguing the strengths and weaknesses of people. It didn't matter if they were children or adults. It didn't matter if they were part of my world or not. It didn't matter if they were supposed to be my friends or if they were complete strangers to me. It didn't matter because my father told me I could only ever trust my family.

I can't help but wonder what my parents would think about Sam. I wonder if they would hate me for letting Sam get close enough to touch me. Not just physically, but emotionally. Tangibly. In a way that feels real and far too raw.

I suppose I may find out today exactly what my father would think about my association with Sam. Today, Julian Summers will be able to tell me how he feels about all the choices I've made over the last decade.

Even imagining his reaction makes me want to be sick. After all these years, I'm still right there, standing in front of my father and yearning for approval I will never receive.

How awful it is to feel this ache again. It hurts. During my youth I thought this feeling would break me apart. I thought one day the hammer would come down and I'd splinter and crack like the marble statue my parents demanded I become. I would crumble to dust at my father's feet, and he would step over what remained of me in disgust.

As terrible as it is, I know I cannot walk away from what I'm about to do. I need to face him. I need to tell my father something important. I don't want him to die not knowing me as I am now. And it would be wrong for me to pretend my father has not been changed by his experiences, just as I have.

He deserves my acknowledgement.

But nothing else.

I told myself again and again, over and over, the words going around and around inside my head, that I have to give my father the chance to accept my choices. Just as I have accepted his.

I talked to Effia about the visit with my father. She seemed reluctant at first, but ultimately, after I'd explained my reason for wanting to see him, she agreed it might be a good idea.

In the end, she asked me, "Is this something you really want to do?"

And I replied, "No. It's something I need to do."

That seemed to be enough for Effia to understand.

It was a lot easier than I thought it was going to be to get a visiting order for my father. I figured I'd have to jump through all kinds of hoops, but the prison almost seemed to be expecting my call.

Now here I am, sitting in a room made of stone and concrete. No windows. One door. A single dim light dangles low from the ceiling, causing most of the room to be cast in shadow. A metal table is bolted to the ground in the middle of the room. Two chairs are similarly attached to the floor.

I sit in one of the chairs, waiting for the guards to bring my father into this room and sit him down in the chair opposite me.

I've been here minutes. It feels like hours. Days. Weeks. Months. Years. Decades. Centuries.

Forever.

All of time has passed, and I'm still right here. Waiting.

That familiar coldness seeps into my body as a twisted sharpness begins pounding out a rhythm at my temples.

Memories long buried rear up and force themselves into the forefront of my conscious mind.

I remember it all, as if it happened only last week instead of years ago. I remember the fear that choked me. I remember the sense of hopelessness that never really went away. It lives inside me, still. A memory scarred across my subconscious.

When the door to the visiting room opens with a creak and a wheeze, I almost jump, only just managing to stop myself. It wouldn't do to show any fear in front of these people. It was hard enough just coming here at all. I don't need the concerned or disgusted stares of strangers added to the difficulty of it.

There are only two guards. Both big and stone-faced.

They bring my father in and for a single moment it feels as if the world has stopped turning.

Because he's right there and I'm right here and it's awful. It's a mistake I can't take back.

My father looks, in short, *rough*.

He's wearing grey jogging bottoms and a large grey jumper. In all the years I lived with my father he never wore anything like this. It's bizarre to see him dressed so casually.

His hair has been cut, or perhaps it was all buzzed off at some point, because I can see the grey very clearly. It shocks me a bit.

My father's face is somewhat gaunt, with obvious age lines that look more like scars of time than a natural part of growing older. He appears thin underneath his clothing, but no more than I would expect from living in this place for so many years. Prison doesn't lend to good physical health. Or mental. But that's an entirely different problem all of its own.

Other than the things I imagined, my father's eyes strike me the most deeply.

Those bright-amber eyes, eyes I see in the mirror, eyes I see on my daughter's face every day, are filled with an abyss I cannot comprehend. They speak of unspeakable horror, of loss and pain so complete and overwhelming that it defies any attempt to be described with words.

I see my father, and he is hollow. A shell that breathes.

I wait to feel furious. I wait to feel grief. I wait to feel all the things I know I should be feeling right now.

I wait, and I wait, and I wait.

But. Nothing.

Do you ever just feel sad? Like, you're not depressed or despairing or devastated. Just sad. Muted. Almost numb. It's the kind of pain that doesn't rage or explode or choke you. It's the kind of pain that's scarier than almost anything, because it feels like it might *actually* last forever.

My father looks at me. I think for a moment he really might not recognise me, but then his face changes. It morphs into something less blank, more animated. Not good exactly, but better than nothing.

The two big guards shepherd my father over to his designated chair. They sit him down with surprising gentleness.

One of them introduces himself as Morris and his companion as Baines. Morris tells me I have an hour for my visit. Then they both surprise me again by leaving me alone with my father.

What the bloody hell is going on here?

I have a thought, and it gives me pause.

Sam is pretty high up in the Winters family ranks these days. He would have considerable influence due to his billionaire socialite status and well-honed political connections. There's no doubt in my mind he is politically connected. He's in big time property dealing, for a start. Plus, men of his level always are in a business like ours. *His.* In a business like his.

When people say the Winters run Danger City, that's no exaggeration. There's nothing they don't have their hand in to some degree.

Taking on the behemoth that is the Winters family would be a lifetime commitment for any form of law enforcement.

It's not beyond possibility that Effia told Sam about me wanting to visit my father. It's unlike her to betray a confidence, but if she thought he could help, she might be willing to break her own rules for my sake.

It would explain why I was able to see my father so quickly. It might also explain why all the guards I've interacted with so far have gone out of their way to behave with polite respect towards both myself and, seemingly, my father.

I can't decide how I'm supposed to feel about the fact that, despite our recent argument, Sam seems to have gone to a lot of trouble for me.

It's been over a week since that night in the bar and I haven't spoken to Sam at all. He hasn't stopped by the café or attempted to contact me in any way. I kind of expected him to show up the day after demanding I duel him to decide which one of us we should blame for what happened between us.

I wanted to feel relieved when he didn't do that. But stupidly, I've found myself worrying that I might never get the chance to yell at Sam for attempting to clumsily seduce me, or whatever it was he was trying to do that night.

I'm almost certain Sam took me to that bar with some intention, although I'm not sure if he meant to kiss me. He could just as easily have had no idea what he wanted, and only knew he wanted *something*. He seems the sort to be completely oblivious to his own feelings unless forced to confront them.

I don't want to think about why Sam would help me see my father like this. It hurts my head too much to think of Sam much at all these days.

I turn my mind back to dealing with my father, which isn't exactly pleasant, but it is slightly less likely to drive me insane.

Julian sits in his chair like a tired politician. His hands are folded on the table in front of him. He's watching me with a singular focus that is quite discomfiting.

I return my father's uncomfortably steady stare with what I hope is the appropriate amount of cool distance. A distance he would appreciate, even now. Maybe especially now.

But my father is empty. When he speaks, I can hear the echo inside him of everything that is no longer there. "Maxwell."

"Father." Quiet. Polite. Formal.

I have my mother's words going around and around inside my head.

Be calm. Be restrained. Never show them how you really feel. Never show them you are capable of weakness.

When she said that to me the first time, I was six. She held my left wrist as she said it, and she squeezed hard enough to bruise. The next day, when she saw the bruises she'd caused, my mother brushed her thumb over them gently and told me the pain would help me to remember.

"Why are you here?" he asks. It's a fair question. I haven't visited him in over fifteen years. He's right to wonder what must have changed.

I think about lying. But that isn't the point of why I'm here. If I was going to lie, then there would have been no reason for coming in the first place.

"I wanted to tell you who I am now." Finding the strength to say those words was near impossible.

Julian's eyes sweep over me, taking in my very inexpensive clothing, and his expression darkens.

"I do not think I want to know who you are, Maxwell," he replies coldly.

"No. You probably don't, Father." I take a deep breath and let it out before continuing. "But I want to tell you, because I'm afraid one of us will die without either of us having ever been truly honest with each other, and that would be wrong."

Julian doesn't reply. His face doesn't even twitch. He appears nonplussed, but I know that for the mask it is. A simmering rage lies beneath the surface, which he will not unleash unless he is presented with the opportunity to do so to his satisfaction.

Ten minutes go by without a word passed between us. It's not what I would call a comfortable silence, but it is familiar. I'm reminded of many family dinners and evenings sat by the fire in our home.

We could both sit here for the whole hour, my father and I, looking at each other and not talking. Julian will never be the first to break, it just isn't in him to concede defeat, even in such a small way.

If I want to get anything done, then I will need to press forward alone and hope that my father will at least hear me.

"I met a girl," I tell him. "Her name was Natalie." I try to find the right words to describe Natalie Starr. But she was beyond words, and my father won't care anyway, so I settle for a simple truth. "She was… incredible. I loved her. She loved me too, which was hard to believe sometimes."

"One of ours?" Julian enquires, although I think he already knows the answer. He probably just wants to see if I'll admit to it out loud.

"No. She wasn't anything to do with our world," I say with a boldness that will displease my father. But he's going to be displeased no matter how I speak, so there's a limit to how much I'm willing to conciliate him.

Julian dips his head in a slight nod of acknowledgement.

"Children?" he asks without inflection.

"Two." I answer. "A boy, Rory, and a girl, Caitlyn."

Julian sucks in a sharp breath through his nose. "Caitlyn."

I watch my father carefully for a few seconds. I thought maybe the reminder of my mother would set him off.

"Yes, but we call her Cat. She looks like Natalie. Except her eyes.

She has our eyes. Rory is the opposite."

I reach into my pocket and take out my wallet. I have pictures of Cat and Rory inside it I can show my father. I'm hoping he'll want to keep them.

The guards searched me when I arrived, but they let me keep my things, deeming them safe enough. It felt strange to have people treating me like a threat again, after so many years.

Soon enough I'll have lived more of my life as a civilian than a gangster. I can't decide how I feel about that, or if it makes me want to laugh, cry, or scream. I've done all those things in reaction to different losses.

Loss of my mother. Loss of my father. Loss of my home. Loss of the world I understood my place in.

Loss of my wife.

I can't help but wonder what, or who, I might lose next. I feel sick at the thought of it. I don't know if I could survive it. Part of me would rather lose my own life than have to try.

Julian watches me as I take the photos of Rory and Cat out of my wallet. I put them on the table and slide them across to my father so he can see them properly.

There are three small photographs, edges slightly creased.

On the left is a picture of a six-year-old Rory and a four-year-old Cat, both of them laughing. They're in the park, playing on a yellow roundabout. It was late autumn, so there are big, brown leaves every-where. Rory and Cat collected some that day and took the leaves home so they could paint them.

On the right is a more recent picture of Rory in his school uniform and Cat wearing her netball uniform. They're sitting at the café bar with their arms around each other's shoulders. Rory is grinning and Cat is smirking. Penny and Vick are in the background, standing behind the bar and laughing about something.

In the middle is the oldest picture. I'm on the floor in front of our Christmas tree with Natalie leaning back against my chest. A three-year-old Cat sits in Natalie's lap and I'm holding on to both of them. Five-year-old Rory is hugging me from behind with his arms wrapped around my neck, his face turned towards the camera.

We're all grinning big, like this is happiest we'd ever be.

Julian is looking at the pictures with what could be described as *avid interest*. I steel myself for whatever he might say.

I'm unprepared for the look my father levels at me. It isn't angry or dismissive. I don't really know how to describe his expression. I've never seen him look this way before.

"Father?" I ask, unsure.

Julian gently touches the middle picture with a bewildered sort of…awe?

"Your children look very content." It cuts at something inside my heart to hear such conflicted emotion in his voice.

He sounds both glad and confused at the same time.

Tears sting my eyes, and I try to blink them away. Neither I nor my father would wish to see me break this easily.

"And that's…good?" I ask, leaning forward on the table to peer at my father more closely.

Julian doesn't seem to know how to answer that, and honestly, I'm not sure how I want him to answer.

After a long pause he looks me directly in the eye and says, "Yes, son. That is…good."

It isn't acceptance of my life, or my choices, or even my children as such. But it is more than I allowed myself to hope for when I first decided to come here.

We spend the rest of the hour talking about nothing and every-thing. I tell him a bit more about Natalie and the children. I tell him about my job. I tell him about all the things in my life that matter.

Julian listens. He doesn't talk much. But he listens, and that's enough.

Sometimes enough is all you get, and in this case, sometimes enough is all you need.

Just before Morris and Bains come back in to collect Julian, I agree to try to visit him again next month. He doesn't ask, but I tell him I'll bring more pictures of the children, and he looks momentarily lightened by the promise.

Once Julian is gone, I ask to use the bathroom. Another guard called Lang takes me in the right direction. Lang says he'll wait for me down the hall. I thank him and slip into the bathroom.

It's a dismal place that smells horrid, but I needed time to myself. I needed time to process the visit with my father.

I grasp hold of a sink edge and lean over it, pressing my forehead against a long mirror fixed into the wall above.

I let the tears fall then, hot and salty. They burn a path down over my cheeks and drip from my chin onto the sink below. I taste them when my tongue licks out to moisten my too-dry lips.

My legs are weak, and I turn away from the sink to slip slowly to the floor. It's probably filthy, but I'm too lost inside my own head right now to care.

I sit cross-legged on the tiled ground of a prison bathroom and cry silently. I'd feel horrified or pathetic about it if I could find the energy to give a fuck.

Luckily for me, I'm far too drained.

I'm not sure how long I sit there feeling exhausted and shitty, but at some point, the door to the bathroom opens and closes, admitting another person inside.

At first, I think it's Lang coming to tell me I can't hang around in the bathroom all day and why the hell would I want to?

But when I look up, I end up locking eyes with someone I never would have expected to see here in a million years.

I choke on spit and tears and blurt out, "Flint!"

Will Flint, to his credit, despite being obviously just as surprised as me, reacts with a bit more aplomb. He doesn't sputter or start shouting either.

"Summers." He looks taller than I remember. Just bigger in general really. Broader in the chest, and like Sam, his facial features have matured. He's every bit a grown man, barely a trace of the boy he once was. Will looks me up and down, brows furrowing in mild confusion. "You're sitting on the floor."

Ah, so he still has a bit of a thing for announcing the obvious. Good, I can work with that.

"Yes," I say, with all the dignity I can muster. "Thank you for your observation report, Flint." Then before he can respond I ask, "What are you doing here?"

"What am I doing?" Will huffs incredulously. "What are *you* doing?"

"If you must know, Flint, I was visiting my father," I say primly.

Will rolls his eyes in response to my mocking tone and waves a hand.

"Yeah, Summers, I know that bit. Sam said. I meant what are you doing on the floor, hiding under a sink. You look like a posh tosser who got drunk at a funeral and passed out in a public bathroom afterwards."

I decide to let the last bit go, because I don't have the mental capacity to unpack that much nonsense right now.

"Is that why you're here? Did Sam ask you to check up on me?" I ask, horrified by the very notion.

Will snorts, his nose scrunching up in the process and reminding me more of the boy I knew at school. He moves a bit closer to me and kneels a few feet away from where I'm hunched half under a sink.

He looks at me like I'm a bit soft in the head, which is unnecessary.

"Summers, Sam is my best mate, and I love him. But surprisingly enough," he drawls, "my entire world does not revolve around his big bisexual awakening."

"His bi-*what*?" I shriek, then wince, because this bathroom echoes like a motherfucker.

Will looks bored and a little amused. He seems to have gotten a better handle on his temper than Sam. That figures. Who knew Will would turn out to be the calm one?

Effia tried to tell me Will had matured rather dramatically over the last decade and a half. I refused to believe it. In my mind, Will was supposed to be a brash, hot-headed idiot and nothing much else.

But seeing him now, kneeling in front of me with a distinct aura of steadiness and a neutral expression on his face, I have to concede that maybe she wasn't fibbing.

"Yeah, simmer down, mate." Will tries his best to placate me. "Sam told me how he tried to snog your face off."

"He *did*?" I ask, incredulous, unsure if I should be pissed off or embarrassed or a combination of the two.

Will laughs a little, like the whole thing entertains the hell out of him.

"He did. He actually showed up in the middle of the bloody night, looking like shit and worrying he'd scarred you for life or some melodramatic rubbish like that."

I can't help but wince. "This is a nightmare." I groan, closing my eyes and letting my head fall against the sink with a loud *thunk*.

"I'm surprised you didn't kick his arse," Will muses. He still doesn't sound bothered, which is just adding to the bizarreness of this moment.

How the hell did I end up sitting on the bathroom floor of a prison talking to Will of all people about what happened between me and Sam the other night?

Actually, forget nightmares; some things are just too odd to be anything *but* reality.

"He didn't scar me," I mutter.

"Obviously," Will scoffs, face screwing up like the very idea is ridiculous to him. "You lived through a gang war with the Winters family. If you can survive that, then one stupid gay kiss isn't going to make a dent."

"Eloquent as always, Flint," I drawl, opening my eyes again.

Will flashes me a sarcastic grin. But his expression sobers when he asks, "Seriously though, what's going on, with, you know, the whole hiding under the sink thing?"

"I'm having a floor moment," I say shortly.

Will looks me over once again and shakes his head. He sighs. "I'm gonna go ahead and pretend to know what that means."

I give a slow nod. "Sounds like the sanest choice."

Will and I sit together for a few minutes, then. It's weird and I have no idea what's going on any more, but I've experienced far worse things than this, so I try not to think too hard about it.

Not thinking helps enough that when Will stands up and offers me a hand, I take it. He pulls me to my feet with annoying ease. Both he and Sam are giving me a complex. I am not by any means a small man, but those two could apparently throw me around like a doll if they wanted to.

"Thanks…*Will*," I manage to get out. Just.

"No problem," Will replies courteously. He gestures towards the bathroom door. "I'm actually supposed to be meeting with one of our people. Do you want me to find someone who can get you out of here first?"

By "one of our people", I'm assuming he means a prisoner who works for the Winters family. It could be an informant or a gang member serving time. I make the executive decision not to ask Will about it.

"No." I say, shaking my head quickly. "I've got a nice guard named Lang waiting for me." Hopefully. I still don't know how long I've been in this stupid bathroom.

Will nods once and turns to leave. I follow him out, hoping no one sees us together like this and forms some very unfortunate conclusions.

"Fair warning," Will says once we're in the hallway. He shoots me a speculative look. "Sam is probably gonna be showing up at your place tonight. He's also probably gonna act like a pushy arsehole. He does that when he cares about something. So…just keep that in mind."

I'm both elated and immediately nervous at the thought of seeing Sam again. God, I am a mess when it comes to that man.

"Why are you telling me all this?" I ask Will suspiciously. "Why are you even being this…nice to me?"

Will rolls his shoulders back and lets out another sigh. "I'm telling you because I know what Sam can be like when he's got an idea in his head. He's like a dog with a bone sometimes." He says this with no small amount of affection. He becomes more serious when he goes on, "And I'm being 'nice' or whatever, because since my sister died, Sam's been sad and bitter and lost, and even though I really don't get it at all, since he's been talking to you, he's started to act like a real person again. So, yeah, just, like, keep talking to him if you can, okay?"

This whole conversation is insane. Will appears completely sincere though, which is somehow worse.

"Okay," I say, because how the fuck else am I supposed to respond?

"Right. Good." Will nods again. "See you around then, *Max*." He shoots me a look I'm almost impressed by the drollness of.

I watch Will walk away for a few seconds before turning to go and find my wayward guard. I need to get the hell out of this place before I really do lose it.

Then again, that seems to be the theme of my entire fucking life.

Chapter Eighteen

AS MUCH AS I hate to put much stock in anything Will has to say, I can't help but be wary. Sam could show up at any time and I don't feel the least bit prepared to deal with him. Every scenario I imagine ends badly between us. I'm almost certain we'll just wind up yelling at each other, no matter how well it starts off.

For all the ways we both seem to have changed, some things will likely always stay the same.

I expect Sam to come crashing in that night as Will predicted, full of rage and indignation. But he throws me for a loop by walking into the café the following morning instead with Isabella and Aiden in tow.

Rory and Elijah are already at the local youth club together. It's only about ten minutes away from the café and I trusted Rory to walk over on his own to meet his friend.

It's a Sunday, so I'm down in the café helping Penny. There aren't many people in at this moment though. Sundays are usually the Starr Café's slow days. I keep telling Penny she should hire someone else so she could take Sundays off altogether. But Penny just gives me a stubborn, disapproving look every time I bring it up. I do understand why. Penny worked so hard to make the Starr Café what it is. The thought of taking a step back, even if it is a small step, must seem quite daunting. Letting go of what you've fought for is never easy.

Right now, Penny is making a black coffee for one of our few customers, and I'm restocking the cake display. Cat sits at the counter with a half-eaten toasted bagel on a plate in front of her and a book clutched in her hands. She's got a small frown on her face. I think the frown is mostly due to the book she's reading. Cat isn't typically interested in fiction books, but her friend Macy insisted that she should read this one. The book is called *A Unicorn's Quest* and when I asked Cat what it was about, she replied with open disdain, "Weird horses and crap."

Suffice to say, my daughter has inherited the Summers' propensity for waspishness and our general lack of tolerance for puerility.

Cat is dressed in her netball uniform. She has a game later this morning. We're supposed to leave for it in about half an hour. I'm sure Macy will get an earful about her latest book recommendation after the game. Cat is unlikely to take having her time wasted lightly.

When Sam comes in, I can't stop myself from meeting his gaze.

He is dressed casually again today in faded jeans and a dark-grey T-shirt, along with that now-familiar leather jacket.

He strides towards me purposefully with an expression that makes my heart quake and the cogs working in my mind grind to a screeching halt.

Sam looks determined, attention focused, eyes bright, and intent on staring me down. There's a question in those eyes I'm not sure how to answer. I'm not even sure if Sam has the right to ask, or if I have the strength to deny him either way. I've certainly struggled to back off from any challenge he has thrown at me before. I think he has to know that; is using the fact maybe.

For the first time, I allow myself to look at him and think about his appearance in more than just the abstract.

I've been avoiding the idea I might be genuinely attracted to Sam, rather than finding him attractive in a general aesthetic sense. It was somehow easier to blame my physical reaction to Sam on anger, a passion that was born more out of frustration than anything else. But I've resolved to try to behave like a rational adult, instead of a confused hormonal teenager. Part of that is being brutally honest with myself about what I feel for Sam.

I realised fairly quickly, despite what happened between us the other night, I'd never taken the chance to look at him as a potential lover before. He has always been just Sam to me. The boy who I once hated. The father of my son's best mate. The man who wants to be my friend, even after everything I've done and said to him.

There was too much other shit between us. It wasn't that I was suppressing my attraction to him, the concept of wanting Sam in a physical way simply never occurred to me.

I resolved the next time I saw Sam I would let my mind wander in the direction of the possibility I could feel more than just frustrated antagonism towards him. I wanted to see if I could want him without being drunk and half-mad from the kissing.

I study Sam now as he comes marching towards me. Instead of just observing he has insane hair, I think about running my fingers through it. Instead of noting he needs a shave, I think about the feel of his stubble scraping against the bare skin of my face. Instead of thinking about Sam's powerful build in detached appreciation, I imagine him holding me securely in his arms. I think about the strength he displayed that night at the bar, the roughness in how he handled me, and come to the conclusion I find almost everything about Sam sexy as hell.

It's somewhat startling to realise I liked how Sam made me feel that night. Both a little bit helpless, and oddly protected. Safe. I know that's mad because the way we kissed was aggressive. Almost violent. But Sam's touch and taste were so overwhelming. I felt, for a few moments, completely consumed by him.

I had no idea that was something I could want sexually. Mine and Natalie's sex life was always warm and passionate and tender. It was never aggressive or violent or angry. I loved having sex with Natalie. She was beautiful and touching her was nothing less than wonderful every time. I considered myself lucky in that respect. I knew other people, other couples, struggled with keeping the spark between them alive. But Natalie and I didn't have any problem with that aspect of our relationship.

What Sam and I have between us isn't a spark. It's a fucking forest fire. I don't necessarily mean that in a good way either. Not when what we have has the potential to burn us both beyond recognition, until we're nothing but scorch marks on a wall.

Even acknowledging my newfound lust for Sam, I still don't know if I want to discuss it with him. I don't know if it's worth the risk to us as individuals, or the lives we've been trying to build for ourselves after the deaths of our wives. I won't even mention the potential damage the failure of our relationship could cause for our children. I don't want Rory and Cat getting attached to someone, then having that person just be gone without warning. They've lost enough already.

I'm distracted from staring, probably quite dementedly, at Sam by Cat, who shouts, "Aiden!" and jumps down from her stool to attack the quiet boy with a hug. Aiden's face is almost comical, his mouth dropped open in shock and his eyes blown wide. But he accepts Cat's hug and even returns it after a few seconds. Probably because he's realised Cat won't let him go until he hugs her back.

When Cat deems the hug over, she drags poor Aiden over to the counter and cajoles him into sitting up next to her. She offers him some of her bagel and he accepts. He nibbles on it shyly and when he notices her abandoned book, he asks about it. Unlike her brief response to me when I asked the same question, Cat launches into an in-depth description, analysing every aspect of the story and explaining to Aiden why she thinks it is the worst thing ever written in the history of published fiction.

"Hello, Aiden," I say once I'm able to get a word in edgewise.

Aiden looks at me with a sweet smile on his face. "Hi, Max."

I lean on the counter and try to think of something to talk to Aiden about. One, because I genuinely like Aiden, he seems like a good kid. Two, so I can avoid talking to Sam for as long as possible.

Yeah, I'm basically using a child as a shield, I'm not hiding it.

"How have you been getting on with your piano lessons?" I ask Aiden.

I already know how he's been getting on because both Sam and Effia have told me.

There have been quite a lot of noise complaints.

Aiden's face lights up at the question.

"It's been great!" Then he deflates slightly. "But I've had some trouble getting the hang of the more difficult stuff I've tried."

"It can be a tough instrument to master," I say with genuine sympathy. "Takes a lot of hard work and practice."

Aiden nods in agreement. "Yeah. It's just frustrating 'cause I learned how to play bass and the drums super-fast."

"It hasn't been very long since you started learning." I remind him. "You shouldn't put too much pressure on yourself, that'll only make it more stressful when you struggle."

Aiden nods again, this time a bit more sheepishly, darting a wary look at his father. I keep my eyes trained on Aiden. Because I'm a grown-up, damn it, and I'll look at or not look at whoever I want.

"You should try listening to piano music as often as you can. Watch some videos of people playing too," I offer. "Emulating other pianists can be a good way of figuring out what techniques work for you."

Aiden bites his lip in thought, considering my suggestion.

Before we can get any further in our conversation, Cat snags Aiden's attention again and he refocuses on her, piano dilemmas abruptly forgotten.

I smile fondly at them, hoping Cat doesn't overwhelm Aiden too much. But Aiden appears to be listening with rapt attention to everything Cat is saying, and my daughter is very pleased to have such a willing audience. I suppose there have been stranger friendships.

I turn back around to face Sam. He's still watching me with that slightly worrying look of determination.

Isabella is sitting on her father's hip. Her long hair has been plaited and tied into two bunches, and she's wearing what is quite clearly a lion onesie costume. Her outfit is completed by a lion-headed hood and little paw mittens. She looks unreasonably adorable, and I half suspect Sam of dressing her this way just to make me more pliable, the sneaky prat.

"Good morning, little miss," I say to her.

Isabella grins and swipes at me with one of her paws. "Rawr!" she growls.

I pretend to cower away from her, shooting a put-on fearful look at Sam. "What kind of dangerous creature have you brought with you today?"

Isabella giggles and announces proudly, "Tiger! Rawr! *Rawr!*"

Sam and I both laugh, and Sam tries to correct her. "No, sweetheart, you're a lion. A little lion cub."

Isabella scowls at her father and shakes her head vigorously. "Tiger," she insists. "I'm a scary tiger. *Rawr!*"

I'm suddenly reminded of Cat and the great Halloween disaster a few years ago. Cat wanted to dress up as a robot and got very upset when other people kept thinking she was a space princess or some other such nonsense. Cat did not want to be a princess. She said that princesses have to wear "stupid dresses and a silly sparkly hat". That was an unacceptable concession.

Rory, on the other hand, was very fond of his plastic tiara. He threw a right fit when I didn't buy him the matching light-up wand to go with it. Penny accused me of spoiling him when I went back and bought it for him later. But it's hard to say no when all your seven-year-old son wants is a big sparkly wand that flashes.

Sam just smiles adoringly at Isabella in response to her stubbornness and concedes, "All right, you're a tiger."

"A very scary tiger," I say in agreement.

Isabella beams at me and swipes her paw out again. I hold my hands up in surrender. "Would the very scary tiger like a cookie?"

Isabella's eyes light up like I just offered to give her the world. She nods enthusiastically. I probably should have asked Sam first, just in case treats have been banned for some reason. But Sam gives Isabella a stern look. "What do you say, Isy?"

Isabella stares at me with pleading eyes and begs emphatically, *"Please."*

I find myself smiling widely at her, reaching down into the cake display to snatch up a freshly made cookie.

Isabella wriggles in her father's arms with so much excitement that Sam sits her down on the counter. I hand over the big cookie. Isabella eagerly takes it from me and begins chomping into it. She immediately dismisses us and focuses her full attention on her treat.

Now that all our children are distracted, I have no choice but to actively engage with Sam.

A fresh set of nerves comes to life inside my stomach, and I feel the instinctual need to escape. But I know that's stupid and childish. Plus, Sam is stubborn enough to follow me, or simply wait me out, if I tried to hide. He's endlessly annoying like that.

"Sam," I say, locking eyes with him once more.

"Max." He matches my slightly confrontational tone.

He's looking at me like he's trying to read me. Like he wants to know how I'm really feeling.

Good luck with that, Sam, *I* barely know how I'm feeling right now.

"I saw Will," I say, mostly to distract us both from whatever it is we need to discuss.

"He mentioned that." Sam's voice goes deeper than usual. He adds, "You went to see your father."

I almost snap at him. But that would be unfair, and it would probably break the unspoken pact of civility we seem to have entered into.

Plus, Sam is the one who helped me to see my father in the first place.

If he is expecting a thank-you from me, then he is going to be disappointed. There is no reality where I would thank Sam for something like that.

"I did."

"How was it?" Sam asks, and I have to give it to him for sounding like he genuinely wants to know.

"Terrible," I admit. "But it could have been even more terrible than it was, so."

Sam absorbs that for a few moments, a flash of something I can't name passing over his face.

"Did you get what you needed from him?" he asks. He's watching me closely, which gives me the odd impression that if I say no, then he'll do whatever it takes to make sure I *do* get what I need.

I imagine Sam storming into the prison, breaking my father out, and bringing him to me. I imagine Sam sitting across from my father in an interrogation room and staring at him until he breaks and agrees to accept who I am completely.

I wonder if this is what it's like to have Sam Winters care about you. It would make sense that his idea of friendship would be as fierce and intense as the rest of him.

I consider my answer to Sam's question and think about my father. Trapped by his bad choices and worn thin by his time in prison. I think about him touching the pictures of my children so gently, like they would disappear if he pressed too hard with his fingers. I think about all the things I'll never be able to fix between us. I think about how some bonds are battered in too many ways to ever be put right.

Some people are already fractured from what came before you knew them, and you don't even realise it.

"I got enough," I answer flatly.

Sam openly appraises me, eyes boring holes into my face. He looks past what I'm showing on the outside, to see the messy and confusing truth hidden beneath.

"Good." He gives me a smile that is far too soft.

I'm more than a little surprised to realise I've given him more than I meant to.

I contemplate telling Sam to fuck right off. I want to. Maybe. But my daughter is sitting only feet away, forcing Sam's son to read the highlighted sections of her unicorn book. Worryingly, Aiden doesn't seem to mind being bossed around, which seems odd for a Winters. But then I remember Effia was one of Sam's best friends, so maybe getting bossed around by an intellectually superior girl *is* a Winters thing.

Sam's daughter is now looking at me with wide eyes as she sucks and gnaws on her cookie.

So, if I can't swear or insult Sam into making him leave, then I suppose I'll just have to put up with his existence. I'm irrationally annoyed about that, and I will find a way to punish him for cornering me like this.

We should stop talking about my father because it's stressing me out.

Isabella provides a good distraction by finishing her cookie. I grab a tissue from under the counter and use it to wipe away the chocolate and crumbs from her face.

She scrunches up her nose and tries to escape my tissue assault. But I'm well versed in wiping the dirty faces of unwilling children, so I make funny faces at her until she's laughing too much to care about me and what I'm doing with my tissue.

Once I've finished cleaning her up, Isabella giggles and tries to stand up on the counter. I pocket the chocolate-smudged tissue and hold my arms out to steady her so she won't fall.

Sam throws me the apologetic look of a parent whose child is misbehaving in public. I roll my eyes at him and let Isabella get to her feet without interruption. My heart jumps a little when Isabella throws herself at me. I manage to catch her, although her weight hits me like a small boulder.

"*Isy!*" Sam admonishes. I look over Isabella's shoulder to see her father scowling.

Isabella turns around in my arms and I shift her onto my hip so I can get a better grip on her.

"Sorry," Isabella murmurs quietly to me.

Something squeezes in my chest. Damn, the sad eyes of children appear to be my ultimate weakness.

"It's all right. You have to be careful though, okay?" I soothe, utilizing what Natalie used to call my "dad voice".

Isabella nods and wraps her arms tightly around my neck.

"Careful," she parrots like it's a promise, holding on to me even harder.

I meet Sam's eyes again, and I'm surprised to see him smiling at me. It's a genuine smile that I'm not sure how to interpret. I kind of want to demand that he explain himself and his bloody confusing smiles. But, again, that possibly isn't a conversation to be had in front of our children and a handful of strangers.

I do, however, consider throwing a teacup at Sam's face. I could explain that away somehow, right? I could say that the teacup… slipped? Yes, I think that sounds plausible.

Penny strides over then and saves me from, I don't know, *myself* I suppose.

"Max, is your *friend* here to buy a drink, or is his plan just to stare at you all day." She turns a disapproving look on Sam that makes me want to hug her.

Sam seems only slightly cowed by Penny's look, which is mildly impressive.

Penny goes on, undaunted by Sam's lack of reaction. "Because if he's just here to bother you, then can I suggest you take him with you to Cat's netball match and let him stare at you somewhere that isn't my café? You're disturbing people. Me. Mostly me. I am the one who is being disturbed."

I take back the saving me thing. Also, Sam is not my friend. Sam is not my anything. Apart from being a complete pain in my arse. Because he is that. Consistently.

Sam gapes at me in shock, and it takes me far too long to realise I just said all that stuff out loud.

Aiden, Cat, and Penny are also staring at me like they think I've lost my mind. Again.

I blame Sam for this. I blame him for everything. Always. Forever. Both of our daughters break the tension. Isabella giggles and joyfully exclaims, "Arse!", making me wince.

Cat shakes her head at me despairingly. "Oh my God, Dad. Just… like… Oh my God." She looks like she would disown me if she could. Well, she can't, she's stuck with her demented, possibly newly discovered bisexual father, who has accidentally found himself fancying the one person in the world who he should not fancy. Because it's Sam, for goodness' sake. What the hell, brain, what are you trying to do to us?

My brilliant plan to make everyone forget what a disaster I am is to shout, "Netball. We have to go to netball!" Because yeah, shouting always makes you sound completely sane, everyone knows that.

Silence.

Now they're all looking at me like I should be professionally examined, possibly by someone with an uncomfortable sofa and a degree in psychology. Someone with the authority to prescribe drugs.

Sam seems to recover first. "Are we allowed to come?"

"No!" I shout, because I am in complete control of my mental faculties, all right.

Unfortunately, my daughter conspires to destroy me by exclaiming, "Yes! Come on, Aiden, I'll teach you how to play. We need a new centre anyway since Laura is off 'sick.'" She makes air quotes with her fingers and everything.

Cat jumps off her stool and grabs hold of Aiden's hand, practically hauling him off his seat.

"Aiden, you don't have to play if you don't want to," I say, giving Cat a pointed frown. "My daughter hasn't quite grasped the idea that other people like to make their own decisions occasionally."

Cat throws me a look over her shoulder that I'm absolutely certain is a foreshadowing of when she becomes a teenager, droll and unimpressed by me.

"Thanks, Max," Aiden says politely, cutting over whatever Cat was about to snark at me. He smiles at her. "I'd like to learn to play netball."

Cat looks far too smug. Oh yes, I genuinely dread her teenage years. She'll probably drive me to an early grave, and I'll have no one to blame but myself.

Natalie used to laugh at me when I would panic over Rory and Cat. When they were little, I used to follow them around the park like I was their bodyguard, and I would have a heart attack when they tried to climb trees or jump off the swings in mid-air like maniacs. I was the very definition of a helicopter parent. I've gotten slightly better over the years, but when Cat starts doing something horrific, like dating, I'll probably revert to constant crisis mode.

"So, we're going now?" Sam prompts.

Cat's already pulling on her coat and dragging Aiden out of the door before I can tell Sam to piss off.

Annoyingly, Sam manages to throw me off balance once again. "If you'd rather I didn't…I can go and pick Aiden up later."

It's an out. Sam is giving me an out. I'm not sure how to feel about that. I should be glad, relieved even, but I'm not. I guess maybe it's easier to deal with Sam when he's being unreasonable. This open and honest side of him is terrifying for all kinds of reasons.

"You might as well come," I say tentatively, gently shifting Isabella in my arms. "We can drop Cat and Aiden off at the netball court and then take Isabella to the park opposite, yeah?"

"Yes!" Isabella crows excitedly. She wriggles in my arms. "Park!" she starts chanting in between bouts of giggling and growling like a tiger-lion.

Sam smiles fondly at his daughter. "That sounds like a solid plan to me."

I find myself caught by Sam's eyes again. Due to the morning light streaming in through the windows, his irises almost seem to glimmer, like diamonds embedded into stone.

Fuck me. I think I'm truly lost on this one.

Chapter Nineteen

"YOU WANT ME to push you too?" Sam asks, a half-smirk curling the left side of his mouth upwards.

"Don't you dare," I snap sharply.

We're in the park, which is surprisingly empty for a weekend. Isabella is in the baby swing and being pushed by Sam.

I made the mistake of settling down onto a swing made for older children. I should have known Sam would threaten me with swing assistance. It's just the kind of outrageous behaviour I would expect from him.

"Have you ever actually used one of these before?" Sam asks me, nodding at the swing I'm currently sitting on.

Oh, here we go with the questions again.

Isabella seems happy just to enjoy her swing time, so I have no excuse not to engage with Sam.

"Yes," I drawl scornfully at him, "in my thirty-five years of life I have, strangely enough, sat on a swing."

Sam makes a face at me like he doesn't quite believe it. "Yeah, but have you ever actually used a swing? You know, for swinging purposes."

"*For swinging purposes*, what are you on about, Sam? Listen to yourself!"

Sam's face lights up with a positively joyful grin. It makes him look younger. A lot younger. And happier. And…yes, more handsome, damn him.

"You've never swung on a swing, have you?"

"Sam." I'm already exasperated, and it's only been about a minute. "The first time I stepped foot in a park, I was twenty-five years old."

"First of all," Sam says, still looking beyond happy about all of this for some reason. "What does your age have to do with swinging on a swing?"

"Swinging on a swing?" I say with an undignified snort. "Swings are for children. Parks are for children."

"But you've never swung on one, even when you were a child?"

I give my head a quick shake. "Not once."

Sam tilts his head. His smile is a little mocking. "Posh boys aren't allowed in parks? Is that a rule? Are parks too common and peasantly?"

I turn my best *you are a prat and I hate you* glare on Sam. I created this glare just for him; he should feel privileged to receive it.

"Only if you're a Summers," I answer darkly.

That seems to cool some of Sam's amusement and for a moment I regret speaking so harshly. I don't want Sam to stop laughing, even if it is at my expense.

I try to explain, despite really not wanting to.

"My parents expected a certain level of behaviour from me. Running around in a park would have encouraged the opposite of what they wanted."

I remember what my mother used to tell me.

Be silent. Be still. Be cold. Be…perfect.

"When I was seven, I was struggling to learn proper dinner table etiquette. My mother caught me trying to sneak outside to play during one of our lessons, and as punishment, she used handkerchiefs to tie me in the correct position. She left me there. For hours and hours. She said that was how her mother taught her to sit properly for long periods."

Of course, as my mother told me, she was only doing what had been done to her. It wasn't that bad. It hurt, of course. But there are far worse things to endure than some aches and bruises.

Sam seems to realise he's accidentally stumbled on something sensitive, and so in true Sam fashion, he compensates for that by showing me a similar vulnerability of his own.

"I used to hide in our local park," he tells me, his expression resolutely sad. "My uncle Paul was…well, he was a cruel man." There's a heavy note of restraint in his voice, the sound of a person holding back bad memories through sheer mental fortitude. "I would hide from him in the park, sometimes all day, waiting for when I knew he wouldn't be at home."

It upsets me to think about Sam being hurt and afraid and having no one really care. I understand all too well the casual cruelty of indifference.

I know there's nothing I can say to Sam about what he's told me. There's nothing I can do. Just like there's nothing Sam can say or do about what I told him. It was a long time ago for both of us, and even though the passing of time doesn't automatically mean the pain or effect of the memory is gone, dwelling on the past won't fix what was torn apart back then.

I take a deep breath and say to Sam with all the resignation my next sentence deserves, "You can push me."

Sam blinks at me in confusion, lost in his bad memories. "What?"

I already regret it, but I'm going to follow through anyway. "You can push me on the swing," I repeat, with a sigh thrown in for good measure. "If you want."

That same bright grin from before comes back to Sam's face and I feel slightly proud I was the one who put it there. It almost makes it worth the sacrifice of having Sam come up behind me and grab hold of my swing seat.

He gets far too close to me for a start, and asks in a voice that I've come to associate with less innocent situations, "You ready?"

I turn my head a little, accidentally brushing my cheek against Sam's. A spark of warmth comes to life inside my stomach in reaction to the contact. I make a high-pitched sound in my throat, like a disgruntled bird. My face flushes with embarrassment.

"I will end you," I hiss at him.

Sam, because he is secretly evil and a right bastard, whispers into my ear, "I never realised it before, but your eyes get all glittery when you're pissed off. I like it."

He finishes that bout of insanity off by brushing his lips against my temple in a barely-there kiss.

And then, before I can…I don't know, annihilate him or something, Sam gives my swing seat a good, hard push.

I will admit that maybe, maybe, it is a slight overreaction to scream when I promptly lose my grip and come flying off the swing in mid-air.

I hit the ground with a wince-worthy thud.

Sam immediately comes rushing to my side to make sure I'm all right. He is also laughing. Because, as I've been saying, he's a prat.

"Are you okay?" he asks in what sounds like genuine concern, despite the laughter.

"I saw my life flash before my eyes," I exclaim with the appropriate dramatic flair.

"You fell off a swing," Sam responds dryly.

"I could have *died*."

Sam raises both eyebrows at me. "You fell from barely four feet in the air, Summers."

I let him help me into a more comfortable seated position on the ground, and we both look over at Isabella to make sure that she's still all right.

Isabella is happy swinging back and forth lazily, not giving a toss about her dad and his weird friend. She isn't even looking at us.

She is, however, singing what sounds like her own made-up song to herself. It's mostly just, "Grr, grr, I'm a tiger. A very scary tiger. Rawr, grrr!"

Sam gives me one of his more annoying smiles. It's very mocking and familiar. "The great Max Summers is crap at swings. How unfortunate."

I channel Penny and cuff the back of Sam's head. "Shut. Up. More like the great Sam Winters is crap at *pushing people* on swings."

"I pushed the swing a whole *once!*" Sam sounds defensive.

"You pushed too hard," I huff, crossing my arms over my chest.

"Oh, I did not," Sam scoffs.

"You did. And you said the thing…the thing that made me lose my grip."

Sam's mouth slowly twists up into a vastly amused smirk. "What thing did I say?" he asks in the fakest attempt at innocence I've ever heard.

I narrow my eyes at him. "You know perfectly well what you said, you giant prat."

Sam shuffles closer to me on the ground and leans into my space. "What, that I like your eyes, you mean?"

A breath gets caught in my throat and I almost choke. "You said they were *glittery*."

Sam reaches out a hand and brushes his thumb against the corner of my left eye, his fingers spreading out to cup my cheek. I can't stop myself from shivering at the feather-light touch. It's intimate. Too intimate. Too intimate for a park, or us. For what we are. Have been. Might be. All of it.

I wrap my fingers around Sam's wrist, holding him in place, or maybe willing myself to pull his hand away from my face. I don't know. I don't know what I want anymore.

I lock eyes with Sam, drawn to him by a feeling that rages like a storm and tugs viciously on my insides.

I can't stand the intensity of it, so I close my eyes and try to fit my breathing to match Sam's.

I let my head fall forward a bit, pressing my forehead to Sam's temple. This causes Sam's hand to slip from my face. He moves it around to the back of my neck and his fingers slide into my hair.

Sam's breath hitches. I open my eyes again. A lot of Sam's confidence seems to have slipped away. Suddenly, he's that same unsure man I saw outside the bar the other night. This is the man who doesn't know any more about what we're doing than I do. This is the man who wants something he is half-afraid to ask for. This is the version of him I'm most afraid of. Because it's the version of him who makes me feel more than I ever thought I would feel again. Not just after Natalie, but after everything. All the pain and loss that chipped away at me again and again.

I realise then, if I take away the fact this is Sam, and our beyond-troubled past, and all of the many reasons why we *can't* do this, I'm still left with one undeniable fact; I just really *like* this person.

I like him, and that may sound as if it should be a simple thing, but it isn't. Not for me. As a general rule, I don't like people. And of all the people in the world, Sam is the one person who I have the right not to like.

But I do. Against all odds, and despite all the things we've done and said to each other, I like Sam.

I know that means I'm mad. Completely off my rocker. How can I like the person who held a knife to my ribs with every intention of following through on his threat, who beat the shit out of me in and outside the ring every chance he got? More to the point, how can Sam like me, the person who tormented him and actively tried to destroy him and his family for years?

It doesn't make sense. Not at all. The only good explanation I can come up with is that it doesn't need to make sense. Because we're people. We're just stupid, messy, fucked-up people, who feel stupid, messy, fucked-up things about each other.

That rationalisation probably shouldn't be as comforting as it is.

I curl my fingers around the lapel of Sam's jacket and tug on him a little. Sam's fingers tighten in my hair, and he rasps against my cheek, "This is… I *want* this. I want…you."

Just when I'm about to press my mouth against Sam's, in a show of willingness to descend into this madness with him, Isabella starts shouting at the top of her lungs to be let down from the swing.

"Daddy! Down! Down now, please."

Sam and I spring apart like we've been doused with a bucket of cold water.

I scramble to my feet faster than I would have believed possible, and Sam follows suit.

Isabella is making grabby hands at us, struggling in vain to escape her rubbery prison. I can't help but laugh. She reminds me so much of Cat when she was Isabella's age.

I move towards her and catch the swing, pull it to a stop, and make quick work of lifting Isabella to freedom.

I set Isabella down on the ground. She grabs hold of my hand. When Sam comes closer, she takes his hand as well and starts pulling both of us toward the large castle-styled climbing frame in the middle of the park.

I meet Sam's eyes. He's watching me thoughtfully, wonder in his gaze, and I do my best to smile at him. I don't want him to think I'm glad we were interrupted. I would have been before today. I should still be now. But I'm determined to be brave. I'm determined to show Sam he doesn't always have to be the one making the first move.

Sam helps Isabella get up onto the climbing frame and we both watch her like hawks as she stubbornly climbs as high as she possibly can.

I nudge Sam. "Yeah, there she goes, another insane Winters adrenaline junkie."

Sam replies sardonically, "It's a climbing frame, Max. Not Mount Everest."

There's a long pause then, where we just watch Isabella climb, and avoid looking at each other like the couple of mature grownups we absolutely are.

"Sam." I give myself a mental shove. *Come on. Don't bottle it, don't be a coward.* "I want to ask you a question."

He tenses, his entire body going taut. He seems to freeze in place, unsure of what to say or what to do in response. He eventually decides on, "Okay."

Which, fair enough, that's probably what I would have gone with too.

I take a deep breath and attempt to sound like I'm not bricking it.

"Would you like to come back tonight? To have dinner…with me — um — us. With the children. Yours. And mine." I say it without looking at him. If I don't look at him, it'll be easier if he says no. Or if he says yes. I'm still not sure what the better option would be at this point.

There's nothing but stunned silence from Sam. That is not encouraging at all.

"I just mean…I wouldn't mind," I continue, somewhat awkwardly. "I…you…you're not the worst company in the world. And I'm making stew. And our children seem to get along quite well. So…there's that."

I risk a glance over at Sam. He's half keeping an eye on Isabella and half staring incredulously at me.

I grit my teeth, feeling embarrassed and stupid, and angry because of those two things.

"Look," I rush to say defensively, "Sam, I was just…I was…it's not…you don't have to—"

"Yes." Sam interrupts my flustered babbling. "Yes," he says again, this time flashing me a smile. "I would like to have dinner with you and our children tonight."

Oh. Oh. Well…that's…good?

"All right then," I say, a bit dazed.

Sam bumps his arm against mine, and says, "All right then."

Chapter Twenty

"SAM, WHAT IS your problem? Have you never seen someone cut vegetables before?" I ask, chopping up some carrots to go in the stew I'm making.

For once, Penny has let me into the kitchen to cook dinner. I think the only reason I'm getting away with it is because she's busy in the living room with Vick, the two of them entertaining Isabella with some of Rory and Cat's old toys. When I left them, Isabella seemed happy enough sitting on the floor, playing with a plastic cash register, a Barbie car, and some Transformers.

Penny also looked happy on the floor, letting Isabella direct her on how to play properly with the assortment of toys she'd been offered. I think Penny likes having a young child in the house again.

Sometimes it feels like Rory and Cat are growing up far too fast.

Rory and Elijah came home around an hour ago, only to hole up in Rory's room for a very loud and boisterous gaming marathon.

Aiden and Cat are in my daughter's room, blasting Led Zepplin and laughing at clips of nonsense they've found on YouTube. I only watched them long enough to ascertain they weren't getting up to anything nefarious, before shuffling off to the kitchen with Sam.

I've been preparing dinner for about twenty minutes now and Sam hasn't stopped watching me like I'm his new favourite TV programme. I tried to ignore it, to ignore him, but that proved impossible. Sam is a hurricane. A volcano constantly on the verge of erupting. A fucking natural disaster waiting to happen every single second of every single day. He's not something anyone could ever forget or pretend isn't there. He's something that turns your life inside out and upside down without even meaning to do it. He's the kind of thing you feel lucky to survive.

I can feel his eyes on me. Those pits of roiling mercury, just burning and burning and burning. I think maybe I should shove him out of the kitchen window. Solve some problems. That way I wouldn't have to deal with him, or the stupid emotions he evokes in me. It was easier when I hated him. I still do, a little. That shit doesn't just go away. It's a small part though. A very small part. The rest of me is a mixture of confusion, lust, awkwardness, and curiosity.

I know I like him. But I don't know how deep that goes, or if it's even a thread I want to pursue. Or maybe that's a lie. Maybe I'm afraid to let myself want whatever this is, or could be, between us. Maybe I'm incapable of trusting my own emotions. I thought for so long that Natalie was my only chance to ever be happy with another person. I thought I was done with all of this. The wanting and the fear and the insanely intense urge to be close to someone.

I didn't expect any of this. I didn't even consider the possibility that I could feel like this. To care for a man who already means so much to me, and not in a good way.

I'm out of my fucking mind. But. I want him here. I really do. That has to be enough, at least for now.

Sam is leaning against the sink, arms crossed over his chest, his expression pensive and his attention laser focused. He looks tall, standing there. Bigger than I remember, although that could just be my mind playing tricks. Either way, Sam strikes an imposing figure.

The mighty heir to the Winters throne. The mafia prince with the moonstone eyes and a killer left hook.

The angry storm of a man still brewing on my horizon.

Every time I look away from him, I think about all the many reasons why this is a terrible idea.

Every time I look *at* him, all those reasons turn to ash in my head. I'm seriously losing it here.

Sam's expression flickers with both humour and annoyance. "Yes, Max, I've observed the cutting of vegetables before. I've even given it a go once or twice myself."

"Someone trusted you with sharp knives?" I say in mock disbelief. "What kind of world is this? You're a dangerous individual. I wouldn't trust you with a spork."

Sam steals a piece of raw carrot and eats it, throwing me a smug look.

I point my knife threateningly in his direction. Sam just grins at me and steals another piece. I roll my eyes and mutter vaguely offensive things under my breath.

"This may be hard for you to believe," Sam says, "but a lot of people trust me to protect them from dangerous individuals. It's a big part of my job. The city relies on us maintaining power and keeping its crime streamlined."

"Well, Danger City isn't known for its good sense and high moral standards," I say, scraping the pieces of carrot into a big pot full of meat and other vegetables. I turn the heat up on the cooker a bit and add some onions I cut up previously.

I raise my eyebrow at Sam as I stir the stew with a wooden spoon. "The city also apparently relies on *literal child superheroes* as well as distinguished individuals such as Mayor Cross, the most corrupt politician alive, which is really saying something, and your biggest fan, the *Danger Post*'s infamous journalist and superhero-hater, Diane Foxley."

"Please." Sam has a look of pure horror on his face. "Please, never compare me to Diane Foxley again."

"Fair enough," I apologise. "That was uncalled for."

"It was mean," Sam corrects, frowning at me. "You're a mean person."

"Yes," I say, flashing him a smirk. "Thank you for noticing. I'm also cruel and maniacal. But never on the same day."

Sam snorts out a laugh. "Max Summers, an evildoer till the end."

"Literally," I say, not looking at him, focusing on the stew as it bubbles away.

I can hear the scowl in his voice when Sam says, "You know that's not what I meant. I wasn't making a dig about the war."

"I know. But that doesn't make it not true," I say calmly. Or as calm as I can manage with Sam standing so close. I flick my eyes over to meet his. He stares right back at me, unyielding as ever.

"I was never on the good side of anything, Sam. I did bad things to protect the people I love. And I'm not sorry for a lot of it." I take a breath and repeat myself, so he knows it's not a joke. "I'm not sorry."

Sam doesn't say anything for a while. He just keeps on looking into my eyes, like they'll tell him something my mouth won't. Maybe they will. Maybe he'll be able to see all the things I can't ever say out loud. That would certainly make things easier.

"I am," he says like it's a secret. He swallows hard. It looks painful. "I'm sorry. I'm sorry that you had to do bad things just to stay alive."

"Yeah, well." My voice is thick with barely restrained emotion. How do we keep getting to this place? What is it about Sam that makes me incapable of hiding from him? "I'm sorry my dad tried to kill your entire family," I tell him, because it's true, and I wish I could have said it back when it mattered. Back when Sam was a teenager fighting in a war, always one move away from being brutally murdered by my father's people.

"I dunno." Sam tilts his head to the side in consideration. He fixes me with a look I recognise. It's steeped in sadness, guilt, and relief. "Even with everything that's happened. I've still had more good days than bad."

I let go of the wooden spoon, abandoning the stew in favour of leaning against the kitchen counter next to Sam. I cross my arms, both of us facing outward, not turned towards each other. "Some of the bad days have been pretty bloody terrible though."

"Some of the good days have been pretty bloody amazing too," Sam argues. He shifts closer to me, brushing our shoulders together. I let it happen, leaning into the touch a little.

Sam can be arrogant. I think it's even part of the reason why I find him attractive. Or maybe I should just call it confidence. I'm not the best at telling the difference between the two. But Sam can also be modest to a fault about some things. He's a humble man in the strangest ways.

"I'm not ungrateful for what I have," he says, distracting me from my train of thought. I blink stupidly at him, having lost my place in the conversation. Our shoulders are still pressed together. I find that a bit distracting. Sam goes on. "My children. My friends. They're worth more than all the bad shit ten times over."

I process that for a moment before nodding. "Yes. I wouldn't change where I am now for anything. Natalie was my world. I can't imagine a life where I never met her. A life without my children or Penny. Or…I can imagine that life." I blow out a breath. "It would have been so much less."

Sam's smile turns into something brittle. "I miss Ashley every single day of my life." His voice is low, and charged with something I can't name. "There are so many people I miss. I lost my parents. Cousins.

Aunts and uncles. Friends. I lost so many people. But Ashley. She was different. She was the one person who was supposed to stay. The war ended. I wasn't supposed to lose anyone else." He takes a shuddering breath. "I know that sounds stupid. People die all the time for all kinds of reasons. It's my fault for thinking the universe owed me something. I should have expected it. People I love have been dying around me since I was a child."

I move away from the counter and plant myself in front of Sam. I stand close to him, moving between his legs and invading his space. He watches me warily as I raise my hands to cup his face. I run my left thumb gently over his stubbled jaw. He shivers a little at the touch, and that sends an answering shiver right down my spine.

I lock eyes with him, making sure that his attention is on me and only me. I'm not usually one for reassuring words, but Sam is standing right here, blaming himself for something he has no business blaming himself for.

"Sam," I say, my voice barely above a whisper. "You are many things. A giant prat, for one. An absolute nightmare of a person. Honestly, I don't know how you get through the day in one piece without destroying the world around you."

Sam huffs out a laugh. He tries to pull away from me, but I don't let him. I tighten my hold on his face and bring us even closer together. Our noses brush. Then our lips. A shock of heat blazes through me like a fast-catching forest fire.

I speak my next words against his mouth. "Sam, listen to me. When I lost my mother. When I lost my entire life… I thought…I thought I was cursed. I thought I was being punished for choosing the wrong side. For not fighting harder. For being a coward."

"You're not a—" Sam growls, vehement and frightening in his attempted defence of me.

I cut him off, talking over him like he hadn't interrupted. "I thought those things. And even when I met Natalie, I didn't just stop thinking them. It took me a long time to accept the truth. Then Natalie died, and I thought I wouldn't survive it. But I did. I did because I had to. I survived because of Rory and Cat and Penny. They reminded me of everything I still had to lose. If there's one thing I've realised after everything, it's that loving someone is always a risk. Because you could always lose them. And that's true for everybody, not just me, and not just you. It's no one's fault. It's a horrible truth we have to accept. It's the price we pay for all the things that make life worth living in the first place."

Once I'm finished, Sam and I just stand there looking at each other. I lose myself in staring at him, consumed entirely by his undivided attention. Sam is examining my face, searching for something. Sincerity? Mocking? I don't know. I don't much care either. As long as he keeps looking at me like I'm something worth taking a risk for.

Without warning, Sam surges forward the last couple of inches and presses his lips to mine. His mouth is warm, chapped, and achingly wonderful. I kiss him back as he wraps his arms around me, pulling my body closer to his in one sharp, desperate tug. Our chests are crushed together, lips locked, our kiss turning messy and wet and dangerous within the first few seconds.

A fire that burns too hot sparks to life inside me, flames licking out along my nerves. Excitement and fear go to war, twisting me up until I don't know what I'm feeling any more, only that it's better than anything I've felt in a long time.

Sam's tongue is in my mouth, slick, hot, and moan-inducing. I make a low, gasping sound into his mouth, and Sam responds by tightening one arm around me and bringing the other up to grasp a handful of my hair between his fingers. He takes control of the kiss, and I let him do it, too out of my mind to put up much of a fight right now.

I bite him when he tries to pull away. I chase his lips with mine, nipping at his bottom lip. I do it hard, to make a point. Sam's eyes flash like lightning, a whipcrack, electric heat traveling from him to me. A warning. I give him a challenging push, kissing him once before taking a step back.

Sam makes a hoarse sound of protest and grabs hold of me before I can escape. He turns us around and lifts me onto the kitchen counter. I huff out a surprised breath, but before I can get my bearings, Sam moves between my legs and yanks my head down into another kiss. Thankfully the door to the kitchen is closed and Cat's music is loud enough to drown out anything else.

I slide my fingers into his hair, fucking with the jet-black strands. Not that anyone will notice. Sam's hair always looks like he's just gotten out of bed.

Our kitchen counter isn't very high, so I can wrap my legs around Sam's waist and still fit comfortably against him. Sam's hand pushes underneath my T-shirt, his roughened fingers touching the smoother skin of my back. He trails those fingers over my spine, eliciting another breathy moan from my throat.

Sam presses his hand flat against my back, nails digging in slightly. There's an edge of pain to his touch that I like more than I ever thought I would.

I tear my lips away from his, my need for oxygen becoming apparent in the dizziness I'm starting to feel. Sam licks at my lips, chasing the taste of me, of us mingled together. We both pant against each other's mouths for a while, breaths hot, fast, and loud.

Sam recovers first and starts kissing my jaw, then my throat. He nips at it a couple of times, and I have to clamp down on the urge to groan.

"This is mad," I get out, still panting.

"Completely fucking mad." Sam kisses the words into my neck.

We probably would have gone on like that for quite a long time, but then the stew starts to boil over and I have to shove away from Sam to stop our dinner from exploding all over the kitchen.

When I've successfully averted a culinary disaster, I turn back to Sam. He's got both his hands pressed flat on the kitchen counter, shoulders slightly hunched, his eyes closed. He looks like he's still trying to get his breath back from before.

"Sam," I say with unusual gentleness. I reach out to touch his arm.

Sam's eyes snap open, and he turns his head to look at me. "Max." His voice is still laced with something distinctly lustful.

Before either of us can get another word out, Penny comes bursting into the room with Isabella on her hip, Vick following close behind her. I snatch my hand away from Sam's arm and clear my throat pointedly. Sam follows suit and goes back to his original position by the sink.

Penny eyes us both suspiciously, but she doesn't say anything, thank fuck. She comes over to me and pushes Isabella into my arms. I take her and she immediately gloms onto me like a little limpet.

"Okay then, let's see what you've done in my kitchen," Penny says, shooing me away from the stew. I shuffle over to Sam.

Vick sits down at the kitchen table. I nudge Sam, who is busy smiling at his daughter and saying nonsensical things to her. He looks at me and nods at the table, indicating we should both sit down. I drop into a chair with Isabella on my lap, Sam taking a seat next to us.

Penny starts telling me off about overcooking the stew and I let her rant at me, pretending to look properly chastised. Mostly because she's not wrong.

Vick asks Sam about his job in property development, and they start talking about scaffolding plans and the different breeds of brick you can get and the commercial housing market and other such shit. Vick was a builder in his younger years and now works as a site manager.

I sit Isabella up on the table so I can look her in the face while she tells me all about the games she played with Penny and Vick in the living room.

Penny dishes up the dinner soon enough and calls in the other children. They come scampering into the kitchen a few minutes later and we all attempt to sit at the table. It's a bit of a squeeze, but we manage it all right. Cat takes over the dinner conversation at first, occasionally permitting Aiden to pitch in with a sentence or two. I have to tell her off twice for talking over people.

Sam listens raptly to Cat though, and even asks her some questions that make my daughter smile brightly at him like she's finally found someone worth talking to around here.

It goes on like that, all of us talking and shouting and laughing. Or in Isabella's case, singing.

Partway through the meal, I catch Sam's eye. He smiles at me. It's a real one. I can't stop my mouth from twitching up into a smile that's equally as genuine.

For the first time since I started to suspect I was developing feelings for Sam that edge towards the romantic, I allow myself to consider the possibility that maybe this whole thing won't end in flames.

Chapter Twenty-One

"SO, I HEAR you're fucking Sam Winters," Zara says. She smirks at me, the vile bitch, and adds, "What's that like?"

I'm already regretting life, and it's only ten o'clock in the morning. I also regret inviting Zara over to the café and she's only been here for thirty seconds. She just came in, sat down on a stool, and gave me the smuggest look I've seen outside of an old family dinner party. I didn't understand what she had to be so smug about. But now I do, and I wish I'd just stayed in bed. Or hidden under it. Or drowned myself in the shower.

I start to sputter. It is as catastrophic as you would imagine it to be. A man who is sitting on the stool next to Zara has frozen in place, a cup of tea still held three inches away from his lips. Instead of frowning at Zara, he's giving me a dodgy look, as if it's my fault that Zara is a horrifying creature without any sense of shame. I glare back at him. Because fuck that shit. This is my family's café and Zara is my friend and we can talk about having sex with Sam Winters if we want to.

I don't want to. I really, really do not want to. But it's the principle of the thing now.

"It's marvellous," I respond pointedly. "Thank you for asking."

Of course, that's bullshit, because I'm not fucking Sam. Not yet anyway. Possibly not ever.

But it's closer to being a possibility than it is to being an impossibility. So…yeah.

Bleh.

The man throws me a scandalous glare. He hefts himself off his stool and shuffles away to the other side of the room to sit with his back to me. When he turns to look over his shoulder at us a few seconds later, I wave at him and give a little wink. He flushes a bit red and turns back around with some disenchanted grumbling thrown in for effect.

Human beings are so strange.

Zara hasn't taken her eyes off me since she sat down. She still looks annoyingly pleased with herself. I lean on the counter, bringing my face closer to hers.

"You're a horrible little person," I hiss.

That makes Zara smile for some reason. She reaches over and ruffles my hair.

"And you're fucking Danger City's most eligible billionaire bachelor." She pulls a face, screwing up her nose and squinting her eyes. "Didn't pick you out as a gold digger."

I slap a hand down on the counter. "I am not—"

"Clearly, I underestimated you. Managing to seduce your old crime lord nemesis. Impressive." She nods approvingly, still smirking. "Risky too. I mean, that's got to be breaking some kind of ex-gangster code, right?"

"There is no code about fucking your old enemies," I say dryly. "Not any more. We revoked it last year at the annual ex-gangster conference."

Zara nods like that makes perfect sense. "Good thing, otherwise Sam would be forced to find some other pissy redhead to get off with."

"I am not pissy," I say. Pissily. Fuck me.

Zara gives my hand a few indulgent pats. "Of course not, Max. Of course not. You're just a pure-bred meanie."

"I could be a nice person," I say, getting far too indignant about it. "If I tried."

"That is a lie." Zara taps out a rhythm on the counter and changes the topic before I can argue any further. "Where are your children? And Penny. I expected to see her hit you with a tea towel or a spoon. I was promised certain things, cheekbones. It's why I agreed to meet you at this ungodly hour on a Sunday."

"Zara, you're a nurse, no hour should be ungodly to you," I argue. But even so, I turn around to pour her a cup of coffee. I set a steaming mug down in front of her before continuing, "Rory's upstairs singing along to pop songs at full volume and pretending to do his homework. Penny took Cat shopping for some new trainers. Her old ones were involved in a tragic telephone wire incident."

"Sounds legit," Zara says. She's holding her cup of coffee like it's her newborn child. I think she'd probably scratch my eyes right out if I tried to take it from her. Natalie was a bit like that. She stabbed me with a fork once when I suggested three cups of coffee was enough and attempted to stop her from going for a fourth.

"Sounds what?" I ask, aghast. I don't do well with slang. It horrifies the upper-class snob in me.

"Stephen keeps saying it," Zara explains. She takes a sip of the coffee and shudders in delight. Or delirium. She does look quite tired. She's still unfairly attractive though, even with dark bags under her eyes.

"And you threatened to disown him, yes?" I venture. "Because that is the only logical reaction I can think of."

"I've been doing some online dating," Zara says, throwing me off once again. She's doing it on purpose to trick me, I know it. I shan't be fooled by her tricksy nonsense. *Shan't.*

"That sounds terrible," I say bluntly.

Zara heaves a sigh. "It was going all right until the penises started filtering in."

I just… I don't… What the bloody hell does that mean?

Zara notes my confusion and tries to explain. I really don't want her to. But it's too late, she's already talking and short of shoving a muffin into her mouth there's not much I can do to stop her. "The men I was talking to online sent me pictures of penises."

That is…bizarre.

"Their own penises?" I ask, for clarification.

"Not sure." Zara shrugs. "But one would assume so, yeah."

A pause. "Did you…ask them to?"

"Yes, cheekbones," Zara says, her voice heavy with sarcasm. "In the bio section of my internet dating profile, I wrote 'Want Dick', and the poor lads got confused."

I choke on air for a solid minute and a half. Zara watches me without sympathy. She is a cold-hearted woman. I like her very much.

"You. I don't like you. You are not welcome here. Be gone!" I flap a hand at the door.

Zara completely ignores me and asks with the nonchalance of a well-trained charlatan, "So, are you and Sam going to get married and have babies and live happily ever after or what?"

"Be. Gone," I grit out, fuming.

There are so many things wrong with what she just said. Marry Sam? Not on his life. Have babies? Been there, done that. Also, kind of impossible. Biologically speaking, I mean. And live happily ever after? The irony, if that ever happened, would probably kill us both.

"I am not… I do not… Sam is a… You are… I can't. It *isn't* like…."

I make a frustrated sound and slap both my hands down on the countertop, feeling a bit like I'm trapped inside a tumble dryer. I let my head drop forward, bowed in defeat.

"I fancy bloody Sam Winters, and I should be ashamed," I admit in a hushed voice. "He's…he's actually a bit wonderful. Still a complete prat, of course. He'll always be a prat. But. I like his eyes and his odd brand of kindness and his ridiculous temper and all the strength he was forced to build up inside him. I like most things about Sam, even the things I hate."

Zara looks beyond pleased with herself. It is impressive and disturbing in equal measure how easily she's managed to get us to this point.

She hooks a finger under my chin and tilts my head up. We lock gazes. She stares soulfully into my eyes for about five seconds. Finally, she says, "I would like a brownie, please."

I get the evil woman a brownie.

I can't believe I just admitted all that to someone who is a virtual stranger. I can't believe I just admitted all that to myself *out loud*.

"Have you gone out on a real date yet?" Zara asks me between devouring the brownie, triumph shining in her eyes.

"We're doing the proper first date thing tonight, actually," I admit.

Zara eyes me suspiciously. "Where are you going?"

I hesitate before answering, "His house."

She stares at me in disbelief. "*His house*?" She makes it sound like I told her we'd be kicking the shit out of each in the street for our date.

"Yes," I say a bit defensively. "He's going to bite the bullet and attempt to make me dinner. The kids are staying with their grandparents for the night so we can spend some time together just the two of us."

Zara gapes at me like the words just don't compute. "Sam Winters, handsome billionaire bachelor, owner of exclusive clubs and multiple five-star restaurants, is taking you on a date *to his kitchen*."

I understand where she's coming from, but the thought of going out to a restaurant gave us both pause. Sam and I agreed we'd rather have complete privacy for our first date; no distractions or, you know, *other people.*

"I made the mistake of telling him I've never had curry before," I explain. "So now he wants to watch me experience it for the first time."

Plus, Sam's house probably has a bed in it.

"Wait." Zara holds up a hand in front of my face. "You've never eaten curry?"

"Nope. Not takeaway or homemade. But Sam said it's the one meal he's good at, so…" I watch as Zara's eyes widen even further. She's looking at me like I'm from another planet.

"Okay. And Sam wants to make you curry so he can watch you do…what, exactly?"

"He said he wants to watch the horror dawn on my face. He thinks I'll hate it."

"And he wants to make you something you'll hate?" Zara asks in obvious confusion.

"Yes." Because yeah, of course, he does.

Zara doesn't seem to believe me. "And you're a-okay with that plan?"

"I mean, I'd do the same." Because yeah, of course, I would.

"You two," Zara says, pointing a finger at me, "have the weirdest relationship ever."

I dip my head in a nod. "Yep. That's pretty much the consensus."

"I wish I had someone to be in a weird relationship with," Zara laments, her shoulders dropping into a slight hunch.

"I think you could have a weird relationship with someone who sent you a picture of their penis," I point out. "Just depends on how weird you were willing to go for."

Zara bites her tongue between her teeth, making a face at me. "Shove off, cheekbones. I'm a goddamn princess and I deserve a prince.

Or at least a very old and very rich man who I can marry for his money, who will then die a week later under mysterious circumstances."

"Well, of course," I agree. "That's just *the dream*."

"Sam isn't old," Zara reminds me. "He'll live for ages if you marry him."

"Yeah." I give a mock sigh. "Just one of my many complaints about the man."

She laughs, ducking her head as she snorts in amusement. I recognise the sadness on her face though, and I understand why it's there.

I tap Zara's hand, getting her to look up at me. "You'll meet someone great," I tell her.

"And if I don't?" Anger and old hurt flicker in her eyes like the dying embers of a fire.

"Then you'll be absolutely fine," I say, putting as much sincerity into it as I can.

Zara slumps a little in her seat, her shoulders loosening, muscles visibly relaxing. She smiles tiredly at me. "Yeah. I'll be all right. I'll be fucking amazing, actually."

"Hell yes." I nod once, firmly. "The fucking amazing Zara Arai."

"You'll be all right too," Zara says in reciprocal encouragement. "No matter how it goes with Sam. You'll both be all right."

I really hope that's true.

Chapter Twenty-Two

SAM, UNLIKE MANY of his family members, does not live in a mansion or some swanky penthouse. He chose, instead, to buy a plot of land and have his own house built near the oceanfront. It's a nice house, very modern in style, with white stone walls and large glass windows, possessing a brightness to it, thanks to the numerous and strategically placed lights softening the harsh angles of the structure.

His house isn't massive, comparably, but it is beautiful. When he told me he designed it himself, I had a picture in my mind, and this is exactly what I expected.

I arrive at eight, as previously agreed, parking my car in the cleanly paved driveway. After a few moments of mentally psyching myself up, I get out of the car and go to the front door.

Sam must have been looking out of the window for me because he answers the door before I have the chance to ring the bell. Either that, or he has cameras out here, which would not be a surprise. I'd imagine his security system to be state-of-the-art and possibly the most expensive thing about his home. He wouldn't put a price on protecting his children.

Standing in the doorway of his home, I feel a strange sensation of surreality hit me. Here I am, about to be on a date with Sam, a man for whom I have a complex barrage of feelings, none of them strong enough to overwhelm the others into insignificance. Some part of my brain still howls and claws with anger at the sight of him. Some part of me still feels like a traitor to my family name.

But when Sam offers me a warm smile, eyes lit up with almost boyish excitement just to have me here, I can't help but be swept up by an odd giddiness I haven't felt since the early days of my courtship with Natalie. The familiarity of the sensation is reassuring to me. I made the right choice before with Natalie, so hopefully, that means I'm making the right one now.

"You planning on coming in?" Sam hitches his hip against the doorframe, hooking one thumb into his front jean pocket, appraising me with open amusement. "Or are you just gonna stand out there until the sun comes up, presumably so you can give the paperboy what will be simultaneously the warmest and creepiest welcome he's ever received."

"Like fuck a paperboy's going to risk coming to your door." I snort, utterly dismissive of that scenario. "Probably afraid he'd scuff your ostentatiously pristine driveway with his grubby little trainers, and you'd set the dogs on him."

Sam blinks at me a few times, making an exaggerated face of bewilderment. "Okay, what kind of Simpsons villain am I to you?"

I walk forward, as if to go inside the house, but stop in the doorway. Sam turns to face me, shifting away from the doorframe. Neither of us being small men, we fill up the space in the doorway, my chest brushing unavoidably against his. The only other thing separating us is the thin material of our T-shirts. I decided to dress casual for our date at home, and Sam seems to have been in the same mindset.

"The kind who sets dogs on innocent youths just trying to make an honest day's pocket money," I answer, drollness tumbling off my tongue with ease. "Like I said."

"Your opinion of me that low?" Sam raises both eyebrows in scepticism. "Still? What, you think I'm too good a person to deal with things properly, to kill a kid and cube his bike like a goddamn professional?"

"Can't have a bike cubed," I respond quickly, not bothering to hide the note of disappointment at this fact, knowing Sam will get it. "Too small."

Sam squints at me, crunching calculations inside his head. "How would you…" His eyes widen. "Oh, fuck, I knew that was you!"

I let out a low, satisfied laugh, moving out of the doorway and striding into his house as if I'd been here a thousand times before. *Own the room*, my mother's voice whispers into my head. *Confidence is currency no one can steal without your permission.*

The inside of Sam's house is very big and open, the walls mostly painted white, the floor a dark wood. Pieces of expensive art hang on the walls. As I move further into the house it becomes clear it was designed with understated opulence, meant to convey the wealth of the owner without overdoing things and becoming too flashy.

Sam closes the door behind us and follows me with purpose. He bumps his shoulder against mine. Hard. "Stole my fucking bike, you prick." He appears mildly outraged by my low-rent crime even after all these years.

I walk in step with Sam as he leads me to the kitchen where I can smell the telltale scent of heavily spiced food cooking.

Sam's kitchen is similarly large and modern in aesthetic. His counters are all pale marble, the cupboards white with silver handles. The appliances are a mix of white and silver. It looks more like a kitchen from a cookery show than something you'd have in your home.

"Figured we were being honest with each other these days," I offer in response to Sam's accusation, feeling no desire to defend myself.

Sam goes to the stove and turns off one of the heaters. There's a big pot sitting on the stove, steam rising from the top of it. A big spoon lies on the counter nearby and Sam picks it up, dips the spoon into the pot, and stirs its contents, eliciting further wafts of pleasant food smells.

"What did you even do with it?" Sam asks me as I move in next to him, parking my hip against the counter and loosely crossing my arms over my chest.

I try hard not to smirk and show how pleased I am about the answer. "Gave it to a nine-year-old girl in exchange for a pack of bubble gum."

Sam turns a shocked look on me for two seconds before his face settles into exasperated amusement. "Absolute git," he mutters with a twinge of petulance in his voice I haven't heard from him since we were twelve. "I loved that bike!"

"Yeah. Kind of the point of me taking it." I unleash a delighted grin, wielding it with abandon, zero fucks given. "Your suffering fed my soul."

Sam makes a sound of dismay and shakes his head at me. His eyes are dancing though, like he's enjoying the reveal of past injustices committed against him as much as I am. But then he frowns at me as if something just occurred to him. "Hold on, did you negotiate with a nine-year-old girl?"

Bloody right I did, and that little demon had the mind of an experienced poker player and master tactician. I wasn't fooled by her pretty pink dress or her pigtails. She would have eviscerated me given the chance if she thought it would get her what she wanted. I hope she's in charge of something now, like a council office or a small country.

"Hey, there are no free rides in this life. I was imparting a valuable life lesson to an impressionable young mind."

"Yeah," Sam says, tone sandstorm dry, "you're a regular Uncle

Iroh, teaching children to barter gum for stolen goods."

"All right, calm down, didn't mean to injure your delicate sensibilities." I make a show out of pressing my hands together in mock apology. "You want me to make amends? Let me stay over tonight and we'll both accost the paperboy in the morning, give him a hundred quid for his bike."

Sam puts his large spoon down on the counter opposite us. He picks up the lid lying next to me and puts it on top of the pot, covering it, likely to conserve heat. It makes me think we aren't going to be eating right away. If so, I don't mind that. Talking to Sam is always some kind of entertaining.

"Oh, gonna do it on the up and up this time?" he asks, fantastically sardonic. "No stealing from children?"

"Since the original child in question was *you*" — I give him a look of flagrant contempt, immensely enjoying the way Sam's hackles rise in reaction to it — "I do not accept your judgemental tone nor your assertion I did anything morally reprehensible. You deserved to have your bike stolen by me. The paperboy, as far as I'm aware, has done nothing to incur an act of such retribution."

"Oh yeah" — Sam leans to rest his arse against the opposite counter, facing off with me at a slight angle — "and what exactly did I do to piss you off enough to instigate bike theft?"

"You were born," I answer immediately, earning another tight look of annoyance from him. "Then you had the audacity to exist in my presence being all…*you* about it." I flap my hands in his direction, to indicate something beyond words.

"Being all…me." Sam draws his brows together, tilting his head to the side, regarding me thoughtfully. "What does that even mean?"

How can he ask that? How can he pretend not to understand? It's the entire reason we were at constant loggerheads growing up.

"You know what it means, Sam," I say, frustrated he's making me explain something he's fully aware of. "You were everything I was meant to be, everything my father wanted for me to become." I let out a loud sigh, averting my gaze from him, that familiar curl of shame in my gut. "Strong and clever enough to stand in a room full of the bad men and make your voice heard, to force them to acknowledge your opinion mattered. Unafraid of the violence our business requires. Capable of gaining genuine loyalty from allies and loyalty through fear from enemies." I turn my head again, catching Sam's gaze, offering a truth I've known almost since the day we met. "You were born to be who you are now. I was only ever pretending at the role chosen for me."

Sam's expression has cycled through several variations since the beginning of my little speech. By the end of it he's looking at me like I've gone temporarily insane, like what I've said is so beyond the realms of his understanding he doesn't even know how to properly respond. I'm a bit shocked by the depth of it, to be honest.

"That's not true," he argues vehemently. "Maybe it's been so long, you've just forgotten." He lets out a short, bark of laughter, but there's no real humour in it. "You were always my only real competition. Before your father started the war, my grandfather told me I had to make peace with you one day, because you'd be my second, just like your father was his. We were both born into this life" — he gestures between us — "and we both belong here."

"No." I give my head a sharp whip from side to side. "I never liked it the way I should have. Running operations. Making high-stakes deals with arms dealers and drug lords." I hesitate before adding, "Hurting people."

Sam still doesn't seem to understand. He's scowling like I've offended him or something. "What makes you think I like it?"

More hesitation before asking, "Don't you?"

"I'm good at it," he says with a strange sort of resignation as if it's an answer he's had to give himself many times before. "Very good."

I'm careful with my response, not wanting this to turn into an actual argument. "That isn't the same as liking it."

"No." Sam's shoulders hunch as he rests both palms back on the counter. "It isn't."

"Is that why you won't take the job as head of the family? Because if you do, there really is no way out."

Why am I pushing? I just told myself I don't *want* to have an argument with the man.

Thankfully, Sam skirts around the issue rather than locking horns at the smallest provocation, like he once would have.

"Did you mean it when you asked to stay the night?" The question comes out genuine and a little bit reserved like he's afraid of my answer.

In the name of reassuring him of my intention for how this date should end, I push away from the counter and step forward, crossing the boundary into his space. I don't quite touch him, leaving the choice to eclipse the distance in Sam's hands.

"Yes," I tell him, lowering my voice to something huskier, more intimate. "I'd like to stay. That all right?"

"All right?" Sam stares at me, eyes already blazing with a dark lust I've begun to crave from him. "Jesus, Max. I've been coming out of my skin with wanting you since that kiss at the bar." The heat in his voice ratchets up another few notches, moving from hot to scalding, risky to full-blown dangerous. "If I wasn't trying to be soft with you, I'd have dragged you in through the door by your throat and fucked you on the floor of my entryway."

I'm struck by how powerfully those words hit me, a strike right to the abdomen, harsh enough to leave a long-standing bruise.

"Oh, you'd be doing the fucking, would you?" I ask, trying to buy myself time to calm the hell down and reassert some control over myself.

Sam shrugs, his body swaying forward, one hand coming up to

lightly grip the side of my neck. He brushes his thumb over my jaw, fingers flexing like he wants to press them into my skin harder, mark me up with visible reminders.

"If you want to have me first, I don't give a shit," he offers, sending another wave of heat roaring through me. "As long as I get my turn at your arse, we can do it whichever way." To make a point of this, Sam uses his free hand to reach around and cup my arse. He tightens his hold when I don't protest and drags me a couple of inches closer to him, pushing his groin into mine. My cock takes an active interest in this and begins to harden.

Sam lets go of my arse to slide his hand up to hold the other side of my neck, rocking forward to lightly press his forehead to mine, breath coming out in a rush and fanning across my face.

I put my hands on Sam's hips, my fingers curling into his jeans, wishing there was a whole hell of a lot less between us. There's naked skin beneath those jeans I want to see and touch and possibly get my mouth and tongue on. I haven't been with a man before, but sex isn't something I'm shy about overall. I should probably have more hang-ups than I do, having only been with one person my whole life. Thankfully Natalie dragged the sense of propriety out of me and made sex fun rather than something to be feared. Yet another thing I owe to her.

"Flip a coin?" I suggest, both teasing and deadly serious at the same time. Our lips are so close, it would take less than a couple of inches of movement to lock them together.

"Nah, you know I always cheat at coin flips," Sam reminds me, although he doesn't sound in the least bit repentant about it. Of course, he doesn't. He's Sam.

He shifts one hand into my hair, fingers twisting in the strands. He doesn't quite fist it, but an energy surrounding the barely restrained gesture tells me he wants to be rougher. "I'm trying to be good," he says, all gritted and wrought, like it's a promise he has no intention of keeping, a battle already lost.

"Don't tempt me with shit like that," Sam warns, and it sounds genuine like he wants me to be careful because he knows he won't be able to restrain himself once this thing between us takes off, takes shape, takes hold, "because I *will* snatch up any advantage in the name of having you. I'm not a nice man, Max. I'm a Winters. You understand that about me. I'd try to be good to you if you were mine, but…" He leaves me to fill in the blanks.

He's missing one important bit of information. He's forgetting the exact thing he tried to reassure me of only minutes ago. That I'm not a civilian in need of protection. I was born in the same shadowed, icy ocean as he was, risen from the pressurised depths to break the surface of water so dark it looks pitch black from above and below.

"Sam, I don't want you to be good. Or gentle," I tell him. "I liked how you handled me the other night. I've got no idea what I'm doing here, but I know I want you, and I know I want you rough and mean, like how we've always been with each other."

I don't want less than that. I demand he treats me with the same respect, even though things between us have shifted into a grey area neither of us had to traverse in our previous relationships. I was his rival before, I should be his partner now we've broken peace. Equal footing. Fury or lust, opponent or ally, enemies or, I don't know, lovers, boyfriends. Whatever. It doesn't matter. The choice is simple. Either we stand side by side, or I knock him the fuck down.

Sam lets out a throaty chuckle that reverberates through his rib cage, his mouth accidentally brushing mine, causing small electric shocks to ripple along the soft skin of my lips.

"Not gonna mention the thing about being mine?" he asks, his pretence at flippancy nothing close to believable. He cares, which is good because I care too. Not going through all this crap on my own.

"Like you said, we were born into this life," I rumble out against him. "To be criminals. To be not-nice men. And people like us, when we want something to be ours? We *take* it." I nip a quick, sharp bite at Sam's full bottom lip. "So be a Winters and stop fucking *asking* me."

Sam surges forward with a snarl of something a little bit like a promise and a little bit like a threat. He catches my mouth in a kiss I feel all the way down to my bones, that fire I've come to expect from our encounters raging to the forefront once again. His hot tongue swipes at my lips and I open for him automatically, letting him in and groaning at the casual possessiveness of it, especially when he manhandles me into turning, switching our positions so my back is to the counter and he's all up in my space.

My skin burns under his fingers as he moves them down to push up under my T-shirt, hands roaming over my torso, pressing in hard and punishing, like he wants me so much he can't control it and needs me to know who he blames for that. His thick erection presses into me through his jeans, ratcheting up the powerful feeling of being wanted so wantonly. My desire to see and touch and possess is so strong it's like a physical pain, a pulsing ache, driving me forward in my need to satisfy it.

I'm rougher than I mean to be when I take hold of Sam's face, thumbs digging into his jaw hard enough to leave bruises, as I kiss him more ferociously than before. I take my turn, sweeping my tongue inside his mouth and tangling it with his, hot and wet, pushing and dominating the kiss like I'm trying to win a battle.

Sam rips himself away suddenly and lets his forehead rest against mine again as he pants like he's just come off a long run. I chase after him, attempting to close the distance once more, desperate not to lose the connection we've forged. He bites at my bottom lip as if in retribution for earlier but refuses to let me draw him back into another bout of violent kissing, instead knocking my hands away from his face and catching my wrists, tugging me forward in one sharp movement so he can restrain them behind my back. He holds them together with one hand, his grip strong enough to grind bone and bruise skin.

Sam's free hand goes back under my T-shirt, fingers blazing a path up over my sternum, nails scraping across my pec muscles before coming back to slide down my taut stomach. He stops at the waistband of my jeans, fingers hesitating over the button, twitching like he wants to pop it. He glances back up at me, his expression unsure.

"Come on, don't be soft, Winters," I goad him, knowing it's the best way to trigger more action from the man who keeps looking at and touching my body like he's one moment away from breaking me and doesn't know how not to. I appraise him with the lazy kind of arrogance I haven't utilised in years. It seems to spark something in Sam just like I hope it would.

"You can't hurt me," I tell him, and it's perhaps a lie because although I'm not afraid of Sam physically, the emotional toll all this could take on me is very much up in the air.

Sam narrows his eyes slightly, contemplating my response with heavy scepticism like he can tell the bullshit for what it is.

Deciding I'll need to go in hard and cruel if I want Sam to snap out of whatever notion of tenderness has taken hold of him, I punch one of his buttons with a verbal fist.

"Sam, I've only been with one person in my life before. I want you to be the second. I want you to be the *only* person who's ever had their cock inside me. Don't make me have to be weird and go find someone who looks like you so I can play a game of pretend." I look him dead in the eye so he'll know I mean it. "Because, no joke, I will. I'll fuck someone else. Send you pictures." I pitch my voice low and tinged with disdain, just to really drive it home. "Then maybe let you be second best twice over."

That does it.

Sam makes a harsh growling sound, a flashbang of anger and

jealousy lighting up his eyes. Hostility radiates from him as he pushes forward, crowding me again, letting go of my wrists and trapping them between my back and the counter. Both hands free, Sam uses one to rip open the button of my jeans and drag down the zipper. His other hand goes back up to grasp a handful of my hair. He gives a sudden, vicious yank on it, baring my throat and attaching his mouth to the exposed skin.

Sam bites along my neck, undoubtedly leaving marks, his tongue scraping out over the patches of skin he used his teeth on. He tugs my jeans down far enough so he's able to thrust his hand into my boxer-briefs and take my rock-hard cock in his large hand. He squeezes the shaft before stroking up and swiping his thumb over the head, pre-cum already leaking from it.

I make a guttural sound at the feel of his fingers wrapped around me. My cock pulses in his grip like a raw nerve when he strokes it a couple more times, testing and teasing in a way that makes me want to thump him over the head.

Sam hums against my neck, like something he's found has satisfied him. He nips at my jaw, moving his mouth closer to my ear. "Already wet for me, baby?"

"Bedroom?" I gasp in response.

As much as I'd be willing to let this go down in his kitchen, if I'm going to follow through on letting Sam take me, I'd rather it be on a bed for my first time.

Sam picks up on the underlying meaning behind the request and lets out another throaty groan. The sound cracks and crunches like clay under extreme heat.

"You gonna hit me if I pick you up?" he asks.

I give myself less than two seconds to think about it, not wanting to get caught up in stuff I only think I should care about, but don't really.

"Go on, then, Prince Winters." I attempt to drawl through my quick, laboured breaths. "Away me to your den of iniquity."

"Den of iniquity?" Sam raises his eyebrows, some of his lust replaced by amusement.

I nod with faux enthusiasm. "There better be black silk sheets and mirrors on the ceiling or this whole thing is off. I have certain expectations for this fuck-a-thon we're about to engage in and if you can't meet them, I'll be supremely disappointed. There *will* be written complaints filed."

Sam lets out a bark of laughter, shaking his head at me like he thinks I'm mad. He still has his hand on my cock and the laughter vibrates right through both of us. It's not unpleasant.

"How about," he offers diplomatically, "I suck your cock before I fuck you instead?"

"If that's your idea of a good deal, well made, then I'm surprised the entire Winters enterprise hasn't fallen to dust."

"You only think that because you haven't had your cock down my throat and mine up your arse yet." Sam doesn't wait for my response, instead doing as he said he would by swiping me up into a bridal carry. I flail a little, despite what I told him, before grabbing on to his broad shoulders to keep my balance.

Sam presses one last hard kiss to my lips, surprising me, then strides towards the large, winding staircase leading to the second floor and hopefully a bedroom with a giant bed in it. He carries me with ease, which is impressive considering the fact I'm only a little slimmer than he is and practically the same height.

Sam takes us to a bedroom nearest the top of the stairs. The door is ajar, so he is able to kick it all the way open, allowing him to walk inside with me.

The bedroom is spacious, decorated in a green and cream colour palette. There's a set of bay windows on the far left of the room, looking out over the back garden. The centrepiece of the room is a king-sized bed. I don't pay much attention to any of the other furniture, pretty focused on the bed and what's going to happen on it.

Sam drops me down onto the bed with a soft bounce. I shuffle backwards to the middle. He comes after me, climbing across the covers to loom over me.

I kick off my boots and Sam helps me to shuck my jeans and underwear, as well as my T-shirt and socks. He pulls them off me and discards the items somewhere on the floor.

When I tug at Sam's T-shirt, he lets me drag it up and off, throwing it away like he did my clothes. He makes quick work of the rest of his clothes, stripping off until we're both left naked and hard in the middle of his bed.

Sam is kneeling between my legs, his hands on my thighs. His gaze travels over me with rapt interest, want, and heat and that same dark possessiveness on his face, in his eyes, making the barbed desire in my stomach curl and grind against my insides.

My own lust writhes and pleads like a creature coming to life within me and taking over my body, demanding I arch my back and spread my legs, the heart of it beating out a painfully fast rhythm, begging to be sated by the man towering above me.

I take a moment to appreciate the glorious sight of a naked Sam Winters. He looks every bit as thick and muscular as I imagined, although nothing can compare to the reality. Dark hair trails down from his chest to the nest of curls at his groin. His erection is well proportioned, dauntingly big, long, and thick as the rest of him. His balls hang heavy, cock leaking just like mine, everything about him seeming hot and hard and ready for me.

My eyes catch for a moment on the black snowflake tattoo inked over his heart. Its position perfectly matches the black sun I have inked on my body. Every member of the family gets the tattoo, as well as a select few of the most trusted loyalists.

Sam leans over me, planting his arms beside my head, hands sinking into the covers. He swoops down to take my mouth in another brain-melting kiss, tongue pushing in again and skating along the back of my teeth. His lower body comes down to lock in with mine, his cock sliding alongside my own erection, eliciting another wave of pleasure, my gut clenching with how much needing him seems to ache.

I'm not sure if wanting someone should hurt like this. It's new, unique only to Sam. He's the only person who's ever made me feel so much conflicting emotion, the good and the bad getting all mixed up together and painting over my world in swirling shades of grey.

I wrap my arms around him, digging my fingers into his back and dragging them down, nails scraping the flush skin. Scars bump under my hands, the skin risen but smooth. Old scars, not new ones. The scars slash like the blade of a knife was taken to his back. Maybe it was. Street fighting can get ugly when you allow weapons and discard all rules. Or it's possible he got taken by someone. A powerful enemy. Got tortured. If that's the case, Sam would have had to fight his way out on his own. The Winters family is well known for not paying ransoms or answering to blackmail for that matter.

It's a good strategy, designed to protect them in the long term. Sam's grandfather always used to say, you give in to that shit once and the rest of the world thinks it can ravage you for your familial sentiment.

I roll my hips with purpose, dragging my cock against Sam's in a harsh thrust. Sam pulls his mouth away with a loud groan, back arching slightly from the zing of pleasure. I keep my hold on him, unwilling to let go of any leverage I have.

Sam meets my next thrust, our straining erections sliding together in the middle of a rough grind. The friction is too loose and not nearly enough, but when Sam keeps rolling his hips, I'm unable to do anything but mirror his actions as we both become equally desperate for the feel of each other. Sam keeps his mouth near mine, our lips brushing with each thrust, neither of us attempting to turn the light and hot touches into a kiss.

"Thought you said something about having my cock down your throat," I manage to get out, causing Sam to release a low sound in the back of his throat that could be another groan, or could be a strained laugh.

Either way, he takes the hint and shifts on the bed, sliding down my body to settle more comfortably between my legs with his face at dick level.

"Keep your hands pressed to the bed, Max," Sam orders, voice a sweet whipcrack in the darkness of the room. "House rules, baby, no matter whose cock is in who, it's always gonna be my show."

My cock gives a jerk at the command in his voice. He isn't joking, not even a bit, his face set and expression deadly serious.

I rise up onto my elbows, still keeping my hands pinned like he told me, just enough to be able to get the full view of Sam as he puts his wet mouth on my even wetter cock. He takes me in and looks up at me at the same time. Our eyes lock, his blazing away, mischief and desire flickering behind them like flames in a hearth.

He goes to work on my cock, sucking on the head, tongue curling around it, and licking at my slit. Eventually, he takes me in deep, keeping to his end of the deal by swallowing me down his throat. It's so good I cry out every time he does it, pleasure fizzing at the base of my spine, stomach roiling with heat and want, and that same intense hurt I can't understand but seem to need just as desperately as the euphoria.

"You own the show," I rasp out at him, unsure what I mean by it.

Something in Sam reacts to my words, his hips jerking against the bed. His gaze seems to darken and there's a flash of furious intensity behind his eyes.

He takes me into his throat again, managing, somehow, not to choke. His lips stretch beautifully around me. After holding the position for a decent amount of time, he drags his lips back up the thick length of me and pulls off with an obscene pop. I let out a mournful moan at the loss, protesting the absence of his tight, wet heat around my cock.

Sam leans down to nip at the skin of my groin, then bites into my thigh before laving his tongue over the same spot. He looks up at me again and gives me a cool reminder. "You're *part* of the show."

Understanding crests and explodes in my chest like a firework. My hands clench the duvet, wanting so badly to reach out and grab hold of Sam, to drag him back up and kiss him until we're both gasping again.

I know I'm tempting the devil by saying this, but I do it anyway. "Yeah, I know."

Sam makes another one of those rumbling growly sounds like he has thunder trapped in his throat. His grip on me tightens, threatening the skin of my hip and thigh with bruises only the two of us will know are there.

"Don't say that shit to me, Max," Sam warns, voice low and harsh and despairing. "It makes me want to *prove it*. Makes me want *inside you,* baby. Wanna take you so much it's like a fucking prophecy I've got to fulfil to save humanity." His mouth takes on a wicked curve. "Or damn it."

Of course. We have never been the heroes of anyone's story.

My eyelids flutter closed at how twisted up and vulnerable his declarations make me feel. I've never had someone want me like that, to want inside my body. There's an inherent intimacy in having someone push their way into your body and carve out a space for themselves, a natural state of possession even the most casual encounters can't possibly disregard.

Sam wants that with me. He *wants* me. I can see it written in every coiled muscle in his body, in how he looks at me like he needs to overwhelm and consume what he sees or he'll burst at the seams, like he won't survive without the thing only I can give him.

That hurt in my stomach seems to grow. Like blown glass it expands, the painful ache spreading through my body until it's taken over, every nerve pulsing with it, every patch of skin buzzing from it.

I spread my legs a little further. Sam clamps down on my lower body like he's afraid I'm going to run out of him or something. Idiot. Even after all this, he's still just a reactive nightmare with no boundaries or sense. Why do I like him so much? It's insane. *I'm* insane.

"Don't be grabby," I admonish him. "I'm not going anywhere, you demanding prat."

Sam looks only a tiny bit relieved and not at all repentant for his behaviour. I suppose I did ask him to act like the Winters bastard he is. Not gonna start complaining about it now I've got it. I will, however, continue to give him shit. Probably until the day I die.

"Come on, then," I encourage him, amused by his look of excited trepidation. "Part two of the deal has yet to be enacted."

Sam doesn't need any more permission than that to come at me. He gets up on his knees and leans over to give me another hard kiss. It drives me wild to taste myself on his tongue, making the need to drive this whole thing forward even more pressing, which I didn't think was actually possible at this point.

He waits until I'm on the right side of light-headed from the kissing before he pulls back and reaches out to his bedside table. He opens the drawer and takes out a white tube and a condom. He opens the tube and squeezes out a liberal amount of clear liquid onto his fingers.

I suck in a sharp breath when Sam lowers himself back down to take my cock into his mouth again as his lubed fingers press at the ring of my arsehole. He sucks hard on my cock as he pushes one finger in, twisting and testing my reaction. He looks at me, keeping his eyes trained on my face, waiting for any sign of discontent.

I look back at Sam steadily, offering sounds of encouragement and spreading my legs wider to accommodate him. Sam takes this in stride and continues to open me up with practiced ease, working my cock with his mouth to keep me from tensing up too much.

After a little while Sam adds a second finger, stretching my hole further, increasing the burn and pressure. It doesn't hurt yet, there's only the soft gnaw of discomfort.

This isn't the first time I've had fingers in my arse. Natalie and I experimented with anal sex, both of us taking turns in the metaphorical hot seat. I've also fingered myself plenty of times when trying to get off, so the sensation of being penetrated and filled isn't a scary one.

Sam waits until I'm breathing heavily and near to coming and threatening him with bodily harm if he doesn't hurry the hell up before twisting his fingers at just the right angle to get at my prostate. When his fingers brush the sensitive skin inside me a wave of intense pleasure rockets through my body with the speed of a lightning strike.

My cock pulses in Sam's mouth and he doubles down, sucking me in hard and pushing his fingers to my prostate again, driving home his unspoken desire for me to come. I break the habit of a lifetime and concede to his wishes without putting up a fight, allowing my rising orgasm to breach the surface and overflow.

With Sam's mouth on my aching erection and his thick fingers stuck up my hole, I come so hard it's almost painful. It makes me feel like I'm coming apart, splitting right down the middle and exposing the vulnerable flesh encased within the hard shell I've spent years layering with thicker and thicker material. Ice on metal on stone, all cracking like the surface of a volcano, hot liquid spilling out of me.

Sam pulls off when I start coming, letting the spurts of white jet from my cock up over my abdomen. He wraps his hand around my shaft and jacks me through my orgasm until I'm wrung completely dry. He stops when I give a dramatic shudder, my cock having become oversensitive. My head feels a bit fuzzy too, body flush with endorphins.

Sam leans back over me to press another kiss to my mouth as he adds a third finger to my arsehole. He works me open with these fingers, taking my lips in hard kisses I'm barely able to respond to because I feel so blissed out.

"Tell me you're ready to take me, baby," he says against my lips, his voice a husky drawl. "I need so bad to fill you up with my cock and make you feel me, make you take everything I have to give you, make you understand how insane you drive me, fuck you so hard you'll *still* feel me for weeks afterwards, feel me like I'm the part of yourself you've always been missing." I've never heard him sound this darkly intimate and covetous about anything and it has my head spinning and my gut clenching in anticipation.

I think I'd carve my heart right out and hand it to him in payment if he would just get on and fuck me.

"Go on," I tell him, impatient and needy and rasping, "stop being nice. Give me the roughest ride of my life, Sam, come on, I wanna feel fucking *raw*, wanna *wince* when I sit down, wanna feel like I'm really *yours*."

Sam makes another one of those low guttural noises that turns into a groan, and he rears back, his expression set in a snarl of want. He takes hold of my body and flips me over onto my stomach, manhandling me onto my hands and knees, getting himself lined up, cockhead nudging against my hole, with breath-stealing speed.

Before I have the chance to get over my heady blast of shock, Sam breaches the first ring of muscle and pushes his thick cock inside me. His cock is large and so hot it feels like it's scalding the walls of my hole. The intense pressure of being filled is a mix of painful and incredible and I bear back on Sam to take more of him at a faster speed.

He makes a low sound of warning and gives my side a harsh smack. "My show, Summers," he reminds me.

I can't help the tiny smirk that appears on my lips. Sam can't see it, but I wish he could. He'd go mental.

Sam takes back control of the slide of his cock into my arse, his hands gripping my hips in a borderline painful hold. Once he's fully seated inside me, he leans over my back to mouth at my neck, teeth scraping my electrified skin. Everything feels sharper, more visceral, after my orgasm and I let another loud moan at the dual sensation of his cock in my arse and his lips latched onto my neck.

"*Sam*," I gasp when he slides a hand around to hold my throat and tilt my head back uncomfortably, forcing me to arch my spine and accept a fierce kiss.

He keeps his hand on my throat as he pulls his cock slowly out of me. It's tortuous, makes me feel every hard, hot inch of him as he leaves my body. When the head of his cock is the only thing breaching my hole, he hangs there for a few seconds, enjoying the twitch and quake of my desperation.

"*Sam*," I whimper again, fisting my hands in the duvet in an attempt to hold on and not lose it entirely.

Sam answers my plea by snapping his hips abruptly forward, filling my hole with his cock once again in a single harsh thrust. He squeezes my throat and growls out against the space between my shoulder blades, "That's right, Max, baby, keep saying my name. Want to hear you scream it before we're done."

I groan at his words and Sam pulls back again. His next thrust punches the air right out of me. After that he starts up a rough, pounding rhythm, slamming into me again and again. His cock brushes my prostate a decent number of times, sending spindles of pleasure directly through my gut and shooting up and down my spine.

My cock stays limp between my legs since I'm not a bloody teenager anymore. But it doesn't matter; the feel of Sam railing me from behind, his thick cock pulsing inside me, and the bitten-off noises slick with wet heat and violent possessiveness pouring from his mouth are more than enough compensation.

Sam doesn't give up on his unrelenting pace, splitting me open and taking hold of my shoulders with both hands to get more purchase. My head hangs forward, sweat beading across my skin, the room heating up to almost intolerable levels.

He only slows down to shift his position and angle himself so he can more effectively hit my prostate, punching more high gasps and body-vibrating moans from me.

As Sam gets closer to what is sure to be an explosive orgasm, his increasingly erratic thrusts indicating as such, I start talking with the hopes of drop-kicking him over another edge.

"Feel so full of you I can't feel anything else. Don't want to. Want you in deep enough to make me ache for your cock when you leave me hot and empty and used."

Sam lets out a noise from his throat so primal it sets off an alert somewhere in my brain to freeze in place and brace for impact. He takes hold of the back of my neck and pushes me down hard into the bed, smashing my face into the duvet. He gives his hips a series of snaps so hard they jerk me forward on the bed.

"*Max*," Sam grits out right before he freezes behind and starts coming. He groans in what sounds like pain as his cum fills the condom in a burning flood. My only regret is not being able to feel it fill me up, coating the walls of my hole in yet another form of claiming.

Fucked out and spent, both of us collapse to the bed. Sam is careful only to crush me beneath him for a few precious seconds before he pulls out of me and rolls over to lie beside me instead. I stay on my stomach, arms folded above me, and turn my head to look at Sam. He's turned onto his back, chest rising and falling rapidly, sweat visible on his skin.

Sam takes off his condom, ties it off, and throws it into a bin near the bed. Then he lies down again and looks over at me. His eyes latch onto mine and I see the hazy satisfaction he's unable to hide on his face. I look back at him from beneath my damp hair, the red locks curled and stuck to my forehead.

Sam folds one muscled arm behind his head and uses his free hand to make a grab for me, looping an arm over my back and tugging insistently. I let him half-drag me towards him until I'm plastered against his side, our slick overheated bodies coming together and locking in place, my leg thrown over him, his arm curled around my back, his hand dropping down to lazily grope at my arse.

I catch his mouth in a lingering kiss, my hand cupping his jaw and turning him into me more fully. Sam allows me to control the length and depth of the kiss, feeling uniquely pliable beneath me. I pull away after a few very immense seconds, propping myself up enough to be able to look at him properly.

When I brush his dark hair back with a tenderness I did not ever expect to feel towards him, warmth pooling in my stomach, that hurt in my gut from before having dulled to a light pang, Sam releases a low hum of happiness and leans into my touch. It's a bizarrely sweet noise for such a big, powerful man to make.

I can't fucking believe I just thought anything about Sam was *sweet*. I'll be saying he's *adorable* next, then I'll be forced to punch myself for thinking such nonsense, Jesus *Christ*.

Sam encourages me to lie down, and I comply, shuffling down his body enough that I'm able to tuck my face into the crook of his neck. He moves his hand to my back, drifting his fingers up and down my spine, making lazy patterns across my flushed skin. He makes another sound of contentment into my hair, and I settle in for a post-sex doze.

For a very long while Sam and I cuddle together, a gentle silence permeating the air. I feel more comfortable lying with him than I would have thought possible. Secure and warm and like this is where I'm supposed to be. How is it the one place in the world I never could have imagined myself wanting to be is the first place I've felt truly right in since I was a teenage boy? It feels almost like a betrayal to realise how much I've been pretending to fit in all these years.

It's not like anything I felt or wanted with Natalie was a lie. My heart still craves her touch and the sound of her voice, my grief still chokes me whenever I think too much about what I've lost, what my children won't get to have.

But it cannot be denied that Sam understands things about me no one else, not even Natalie, ever could. He knows what it was like to grow up as we did, with the families we had and the expectations they heaped on top of us. He also gets what it's like to lose your partner and be left behind to raise children without them.

It might be mad to say it, but Sam and I fit together in almost every way that matters.

"Max." Sam interrupts my reverie, a strikingly serious timbre to his voice. "I think we need to talk about a few things."

Sam's body hasn't quite tensed up, but there's a coiling and contracting of his muscles that wasn't there a few seconds ago.

"Yeah." He's right. There are some things we should get straight. It could probably wait until later, but I'm okay with doing it now.

Sam takes my acquiescence as permission to wrap his arms around me and roll us over, pinning my body beneath him. He crushes me to the bed, making it a little harder to breathe. I don't mind. It feels good to have him on top of me like this, his considerable weight a welcome one, his bulk blocking out the world around us in a way that satisfies my desire to be completely overwhelmed by him.

"I expect certain things from you," Sam tells me without any preamble, straight to the point and unapologetically arrogant in his delivery. He meets my eyes, letting me know this is important to him without words. "If you can't handle it or don't want it, I need you to tell me now."

I consider him for a moment, rolling those words around inside my head before asking, "What things?"

Sam hesitates, sucking in a long breath and expelling it like he's preparing himself to take a big risk. Depending on what he says, maybe he is.

"I can take a lot from you," he tells me, making an attempt at diplomacy that does not suit him in this scenario. I don't interrupt, allowing him to keep going and explain what he means. "You being nasty. Telling me off. Hating me, getting all mouthy. I can even take you hiding some parts of yourself away to start with. But one thing I won't take is you running from me." His voice deepens to a low growl, an unmistakable threat in his voice. "Don't run from me, Max. Don't you ever do that to me again."

It's not exactly an unreasonable request from someone, especially a man like Sam, who was taught all his life to give his trust to no one. If he's going to take the chance on offering me what very few people have gotten from him, his reservations and threats make sense to me. I'm not afraid of him, especially not now. All his rumble of menace tells me is how vulnerable I've made him feel.

"What else?" I ask then, keeping my reaction to a minimum. Better to get everything out of him before I give my full response.

"Exclusivity," Sam comes back with immediately, the word smashing down on me like a hammer. He falters for a second, having probably heard the brutal demand in his voice. "I know I've got no right to ask for—"

"Sam." I do interrupt him this time, because I'd rather this didn't spiral any further. I regard him pointedly. "Be a Winters, yeah?"

That seems to flip the correct switch in Sam's head. His expression darkens, showing a more familiar side of him. It's a relief. There's only so much softness I can take from him in one go. I manage to fight free one of my arms and bring my hand up to stroke his back in a caress meant to offset my harshness.

"Right, real truth, then?" Sam asks, the question genuine and holding a sharp edge that thrills rather than scares me. "No masking it with civility or respect?"

"Go on, try to scare me off. Show me your teeth, babe." Show me the fangs I know you have buried somewhere inside that wicked mouth.

Sam's features seem to twist and contort with frustration, with the battle to hold on to his baser instincts.

"I don't want you with anyone else." He gives an impatient snarl. "No Zara. No more dates, group or otherwise."

"Sam," I huff, annoyed he's still playing nice and holding back his true self. "*Show me.*"

That seems to pull the right trigger. Quick as a bullet released from its chamber, Sam wraps a hand around my throat and squeezes as his expression becomes hard and menacing, reminding me of the would-be-king persona I remember from years ago. He tilts my head to the side, leaning in to speak into my ear with a quiet fury that rolls through us both like thunder in the atmosphere. "Jealousy isn't pretty on me, Max. Got no problem removing the competition, real permanent-like, yeah? I don't give a shit about the who or why. If you're with me, then that's fucking it." He puts more pressure on my throat like it's a warning he'll only give once. "I don't share my things." The last part comes out ice cold and cruel, frightening in its twisted sincerity.

I'd be pissed about being called an object, but I don't actually care. In truth, it stirs something inside me. Something I can't name because I haven't felt it before. Never thought about belonging to someone like this.

Sure, I was Natalie's husband, her partner, her best friend, even. But it wasn't anything murkier than that.

This thing with Sam feels different. Darker. More perilous. Harder to predict or control. I should have expected that.

You don't just *date* Sam Winters, the black-hearted prince, heir to the criminal empire of Danger City.

But as long as we're acknowledging that, there's something I need to get straight with him too. Because I'm no civilian either. I'm a Summers, banished knight of the round table. I know the code and all rules. I know how to play the game and wield the sword.

"Long as you know, the same goes for me," I tell him viciously, with no shortage of malice twisting off my tongue like venom. "Swinging a crowbar is like riding a bike. You never forget how. Plus, I think I have more to worry about. I'm the one who's been celibate for five years, and you're the one who slept with someone five minutes after your wife died."

Sam sucks in a sharp breath, eyes suddenly alight with an anger I've come to associate with the excited rumble in my stomach. It's like getting a hit from a needle straight to the heart.

"That *mouth*," he growls at me, freshly bared fangs gnashing in compliance with my demands. "Fuck. Want to knock your teeth in for that." He sounds like he means it, which is fun. Makes me wonder how far I can push before I lose a hand to those jaws, or possibly a jugular.

"Better to suck you off with?" I tease. "Promise to show you we don't need to resort to such extreme measures."

Sam shakes his head, amusement and despair warring on his face. "*Mouth. On. You.* Christ. I'm in so much trouble."

"If I'm trouble, what does that make you?" I grin wickedly at him. "Mayhem incarnate?"

Sam laughs long and loud until I shut him up by taking his mouth in yet another fierce kiss. At this point, our kisses should probably be languid and tender, but it seems Sam and I don't know any other speed than supersonic, no other state of connection than high voltage and top volume, no other way of communicating than snarl and bite, teeth cutting bone deep.

"So, is this for real, then?" Sam asks when we call a truce and draw back. He palms my face, gripping my chin and holding it just a little too hard. "You and me, we're giving it a go? Properly?"

A dull buzz of panic starts up inside my head, the thought of all the things that could go wrong and all the reasons why this is a terrible idea flashing through my mind like a video reel.

"If you think your family won't try to have me killed for breaking the conditions of my probation."

Sam's lip curls, aggression tightening his shoulders. "Being my boyfriend wouldn't break shit."

"I was told never to get involved with Winters business," I remind him. "You are Winters business. You're their future, you know that's how they see it, no matter what suicidal crap you've told them lately."

"They can get fucked," Sam bites out, a familiar defiance sparking in the depths of his eyes. "No one else decides who I let into my life. I want you; you tell me I can have you, end of. No other voices get heard."

"How about our kids?" I prod. Apart from the obvious, they should be our main concern when it comes to something this big.

Sam doesn't seem as worried about it as I am. "Elijah and Rory will probably demand bunk beds as soon as we tell them, and Cat seems to have semi-adopted Aiden. Isy thinks you're the man with the biscuits. I think we'll be fine."

"Pretty sure my daughter has recruited your son as her minion if anything," I correct him, frowning to myself. "We'll need to keep an eye on that. I don't want her running roughshod over him."

Sam peers at me with a strangely awed look on his face. "You really like Aiden, don't you?"

It's an odd question, but possibly valid. In any case, my answer comes with surprising ease. "Yeah, I think I do."

Sam makes a face I'm not sure how to interpret because it's gentler than anything I've seen on him before. "Don't know why," he tells me, quiet and intense like it's a secret, "but that makes me want to squeeze you really hard and, like, kiss you all soft and shit."

I scowl at him, squinting like I'm staring into the sun. "Is that your weird way of saying you think it's cute?"

"I said what I said," he drawls, shooting me a warning glower. "Don't push your luck."

I almost roll my eyes just to see what he'll do in response, but the tightness of his jaw and the twitch of the muscle there tells me we're getting close to his personal limit, and as much fun as it would be to see him tip right over into hellfire he was born to embrace, I think I'll save that for another day.

"All right, enough real talk, I'm bored. Now we've got the fucking and the relationship discussion out of the way, I demand to be fed and watered."

Sam takes the out for what it is and nods, a slight note of exasperation in his voice. "Yeah, yeah, all right, keep your hair on, we can go eat."

He pulls away from me, rolling his shoulders back like he's working out a kink. After I've stretched out my back to do the same, we both move to get up from the bed and track down our wayward clothes.

Once we're dressed again, I make to leave the bedroom and head back downstairs, but Sam catches me at the door and stops me.

I give him a questioning eyebrow raise.

Sam wraps his hand around my left wrist and gives it a little tug, drawing me closer to him until he's able to cup my face with his other hand and gently bump his forehead against mine. "Prepare yourself, Summers," he warns, "because I'm gonna say one last nice thing to you."

"Oh fuck, please don't." I close my eyes and try to turn my head away, but Sam's hold on me is iron tight. He waits until I'm forced to open my eyes again and meet his.

"Shut up, it's happening." Sam smirks, giving new understanding to the phrase "devilishly sexy". His expression almost immediately clears and becomes more serious as he tells me, "I'm glad we met again, Max. That's all I wanted to tell you. It's a weird thing to feel, but I think I've spent the last sixteen years missing you." He looks abashed by the admission.

As he should.

"Yeah," I agree, unable to keep myself from sounding sardonic, "that is weird." To soften the blow, I offer my own truth. "But you know what, it's the same for me. You were the best arch-nemesis a teenage boy could have asked for, and I've missed upsetting you and pissing you off all the time."

Sam lets out a sarcastically wistful sigh. "I think you were my first and only hate crush."

Possessing no wherewithal to answer that genuinely, I press another kiss to his mouth instead, trying to express how I feel with action rather than words. Sam seems to understand if his intense response is anything to go by. He kisses me back, not missing a beat.

If this is what I can expect from our relationship going forward, this sense of connection, of understanding and fitting together, then I think we might have the slightest chance in hell of not fucking this entire thing up in the first five minutes.

Maybe.

Nah, it's going to be a shitshow. But for some reason that doesn't put me off.

Turns out I've been craving some mayhem to come into my life, and now it has, I'm not giving it up without one hell of a fight.

Acknowledgements

I want to say a massive thank you once again to the entire NineStar team, this book truly wouldn't be what it is without you all, and I appreciate it so much. I also want to thank my friends Beth and Callum for encouraging me to write each chapter of this book just so they could find out what happened. I love you both more than words could express.

About the Author

BL Jones is a twentysomething British author who spends all her free time reading and writing and taming her three much younger brothers. She lives in Bristol and lives with a temperamental bunny named Pepsi. She's been writing stories since she was five, rarely sharing them with anyone except her numerous stuffed animals. BL has had a difficult journey into discovering and accepting her own queerness, and therefore believes that positive, honest, and authentic stories about queer people are very important. She hopes to contribute her own stories for people to have fun with and enjoy.

Email
bljonesbooks@yahoo.com

Facebook
www.facebook.com/bl.jones.33

Twitter
@BLJONES18

Website
www.bljonesbooks.wixsite.com/website-2

Other NineStar books by this author

Liquid Onyx series
Novas Got Nerve
Make Like Mountains
Drowning in Danger

Coming Soon from BL Jones

Sound Can Shatter

Liquid Onyx, Book Four

Barricade and I can't keep this up for much longer.

We've been fighting Mages in a factory parking lot for what feels like hours, although I know it can't have been. It's just my exhausted brain playing with my perception of time.

I'm weaker than I should be, thanks to the Mages' ritual, or whatever the hell it was that made me feel like all my strength was being sucked out of my body by some unseen force, to the point where I almost lost consciousness.

A tall, blond-haired Mage throws a green fire ball in my direction. The flickering emerald ball careens through the air in a terrifying show of magical power, triggering a fear response that clicks and fires off like a gun without a safety. No matter how many times it happens, I'll never get used magical fire being lobbed at my face.

Barricade throws up a shield to absorb the fire ball before the thing can get anywhere near me. In another battle, on another night, Barricade would have kept his shield up constantly, not letting it drop, to make sure I'm protected and able to get close enough to take the Mages down. They're no match for me when it comes to a one-on-one fight, or even a group. These Mages have no formal combat training at all. That was clear right from their first attack at the Anti-hero concert.

Just getting near enough to land a couple of good hits is the challenging part.

Barricade, who stands at my left, close enough for me to reach out and grab his shoulder if I wanted to, turns his head to meet my eyes. He exchanges a look with me that I can easily interpret. He's feeling it too. The only reason he dropped his shield is because he's running out of energy, which means keeping his shield up is going to become increasingly difficult. Barricade is strong, far stronger than me, but we all have a limit, and Barricade is close to his.

We need to shut this down soon, or the Mages are going to end up winning by default.

I try to console myself with the fact that our odds have been worse than this before, during other battles against powered-up armies. Robots. Giant acid dogs. Bizarre, alien-looking creatures with too many teeth and dripping slime that escaped a supervillain's lab. Just. Wow. There have been so many of those, you don't even know.

I dip my head in a quick nod at Barricade, wordlessly communicating *"we've got this, right?"* Barricade is scarily good at reading people. Far better than me, which is funny, and occasionally frustrating. He nods back at me, agreeing with the lie, his mouth twisting up into a somewhat maniacal grin that means *"fucking right we do"*.

A new flush of adrenaline hits my veins like a class A drug, and I grin back at him just as broadly.

At least I know we're on the same page, even if everything else is going to hell. Barricade doesn't revel in the thrill and danger inherent in the life of a super as much as I do. But he gets it more than Frost does. More than Wrath. Definitely more than Polaris. For them, it's about duty, a way of using their abilities to make the terrible atrocity of what was done to us *mean* something. Make it worth everything we lost.

In another world, where there are no superheroes or supervillains, I think I would still crave the fight. I think that I would have always been something dangerous, Liquid Onyx or no Liquid Onyx. Not a FISA agent though. That wouldn't be my first choice if I didn't have powers.

I'm a legacy at FISA, a descendant of many agents before me. But if I was normal, I'd probably choose to serve my country via the military. My family has a long history of becoming soldiers too.

I'm not my brother. Someone able to play a part, to trick and manipulate. That's not the kind of warfare I would ever have been suited for.

But I can see myself in camo, buried somewhere in the desert. Blinded by the sun. Surrounded by enemies I can only get glimpses of. Covered in paint, dirt and blood. Red, not black. Maybe even with Tate Bishop, large and laughing and probably still the best of us, at my side. We'd have each other's back in that world, just like we do in this one.

CONNECT WITH NINESTAR PRESS

WEBSITE: NineStarPress.com

FACEBOOK: NineStarPress

X: @ninestarpress

INSTAGRAM: NineStarPress

BLUESKY: NineStarPress

THREADS: @ninestarpress

www.ingramcontent.com/pod-product-compliance
Lightning Source LLC
Chambersburg PA
CBHW060228100726
47907CB00003B/551